The ELUSIVE MISS ELLISON

REGENCY BRIDES
A LEGACY *of* GRACE

CAROLYN MILLER

Kregel
Publications

The Elusive Miss Ellison
© 2017 by Carolyn Miller

Published by Kregel Publications, a division of Kregel, Inc., 2450 Oak Industrial Dr. NE, Grand Rapids, MI 49505.

Scripture quotations are from the King James Version.

The persons and events portrayed in this work are the creations of the author, and any resemblance to persons living or dead is purely coincidental.

ISBN 978-0-8254-4450-0

Printed in the United States of America
17 18 19 20 21 22 23 24 25 26 / 5 4 3 2 1

To the Giver of the
Ultimate Gift.

And to Joshua.
I love you.

CHAPTER ONE

St. Hampton Heath
Gloucestershire, England
June 1843

"WHY, LIVVIE! WHATEVER are you doing?"

Lavinia Ellison placed down her gardening trowel, swiped perspiration from her brow, and smiled up at her friend. "Good morning, Sophy."

"Oh, er, yes, good morning." Sophia Milton's nose wrinkled as she peered at Lavinia's handiwork: a tall pile of weeds. "But where is Albert? Surely tending the garden is his responsibility. I know Mama would never permit me to do so, let alone without a hat—"

"Albert is tending our old Jersey. She has been rather ill lately." She avoided the question of permission. After all, neither the preparations for Papa's sermon nor Aunt Patience's Sunday school lesson deserved interruption for such a minor matter.

"Oh. That's unfortunate for you all."

Lavinia nodded as she dusted off her skirts. Sally's sad decline was unfortunate not just for their household, but for the poor families in the village blessed by her superior milk production. Still, God would provide. And if He didn't, Lavinia would find a way. She pushed the twinge of worry to one side and led the way indoors, cleaning up quickly before directing her guest to a seat in the morning room. She picked up her embroidery. "So, what brings you here on this glorious sunny day?"

"Oh, Livvie! You'll never guess who is coming tomorrow night!"

She swallowed a smile at her friend's wide cobalt eyes. Sophia Milton was notorious for her passions. "Alas, you are correct. Do tell."

"Father said the new earl has accepted the invitation to our musicale!"

The new earl. Lavinia's chest tightened.

Sophia sighed. "I saw him from the window when he called on Papa yesterday. He's *ever* so handsome. So tall and dark . . ."

Yes, but a handsome appearance counted for naught unless matched by good character and actions. She quashed her uncharitable thought, offered a polite nod, and cast her attention back to her ever-frustrating needlepoint as her visitor continued listing his charms. Why Aunt Patience insisted that Lavinia embroider was beyond comprehension. The list of accomplishments for young ladies was ridiculously long, especially when young *men* did not have nearly so many requirements.

After Sophia finally stopped for breath Lavinia murmured, "Your mother must be very happy."

"Oh, yes! And Papa, too."

But of course the squire would be pleased. The second-largest landowner in the district had a wife whose social aspirations far surpassed their sizeable income. To receive such a distinction would prove most gratifying. She frowned at the miniscule mistake she'd just made in her stitching. Why couldn't sewing be simple and enjoyable, like music? She swallowed a sigh and glanced up.

Sophia's smile had dimmed. "But Mother has heard he is something of a flirt, so we should be on our guard."

"I hardly think *I* need be on my guard. I would think the prettiest girl in Gloucestershire should be more concerned about attracting attention." Lavinia gazed without envy at her visitor's artfully styled blond tresses, crimson cheeks, and fresh new muslin, overlaid with embroidered blue flowers. Lady Milton might have her shortcomings, but dressing her daughter to disadvantage was not one of them.

"Livvie, you do not seem terribly thrilled."

"You should know by now that I am quite unwilling to be excited about someone I have never met. But after I meet him, if indeed he *does* condescend to appear, I shall endeavor to seem excited for you. Will that suffice?"

Sophia laughed. "Must you always talk such nonsense?"

"I'm afraid I must, if only to balance some of the prosiness of ordinary conversation."

The younger girl's brows knit together. "Oh no!"

"What is it?"

"Now we know the earl shall attend, whatever shall I wear?"

SOPHIA SOON SWEPT from the house in a flutter of muslin and ecstasy, leaving Lavinia to open the window, drink in the delightful scent of the late flowering lilacs, and then exchange her embroidery for her sketchbook. As she sketched the glorious rainbow of pansies cascading down the garden's rock wall, she thought on the Earl of Hawkesbury she had once known.

Lord Robert had been as kind as her father: generous, interested in his neighbors, seeking the well-being of his tenants and the local village of St. Hampton Heath. A truly good man. But his death two years ago had precipitated a series of family tragedies. George, his younger brother, had died of influenza within six months of inheriting the title. Less than a year later, while his younger son had been engaged in heavy fighting on the Peninsular, George's elder son, James, had been killed in a hunting accident. Her fingers clenched. *His* death she could not even pretend to mourn.

A blur of tan-and-white fur leapt through the open window. Mickey barked and jumped onto her lap, as if sensing her disquietude. She hugged him close as her art pencils spilled to the floor. Perhaps Sophia and her parents *were* right to be excited about the district's new addition. Lately, Hampton Hall had taken on a slightly neglected look, thanks to the bailiff's less than stellar efforts. And the family's prolonged absence meant the little things Lord Robert formerly noted, such as cottage roof repairs and sending baskets at Christmastime to the poor—services that made a great difference in the lives of the less fortunate—these things had been missed.

"If the new earl fulfills his obligations, he *might* prove a blessing, Mickey."

He barked his agreement, wriggled away, and dashed through the open window to the tangled underbrush of the rose garden beyond. Tangled underbrush she would resume clearing this afternoon, when Papa and Aunt Patience were sure to be absent and unable to object.

She returned her attention to her sketchbook, working to capture the purple heart of a pansy, until the swish of skirts announced her aunt's arrival. "So, little Sophia hopes to snag herself a Hawkesbury, does she?"

"I don't believe Sophy has any such idea, although Lady Milton may."

An appreciative twinkle lit her aunt's deep blue eyes. Over the past fourteen years, Lavinia had learned many things from this independent, intelligent woman, yet sometimes she still found it difficult to believe that Patience West was Mama's sister. Mama had lived up to her name. *Grace* had filled everything from her musical voice to her pretty mannerisms and her compassion for others. Patience's forthright, practical ways contrasted as strongly as her dark hair differed from Mama's—and Lavinia's own—fairness.

"That woman would be far better off teaching her daughters useful accomplishments and knowledge rather than filling their heads with frippery and empty dreams." Aunt Patience smoothed her severe gray dress, which matched Lavinia's.

Lavinia gestured to the discarded needlepoint. "Useful accomplishments?"

A thin smile escaped her aunt's lips. "One of these days, my dear girl, you will realize that not every worthwhile endeavor can be as enjoyable as writing letters to *The Times*."

Memories arose of the past week's efforts to bring solace to two poor tenant families, endeavors of far greater worth than needlepoint, and far from pleasant: The sour stench of sickness, only slightly alleviated by the aroma of the hearty beef stew she'd brought. Dark, dank cottages filled with a dense chill no fire could chase away. The sad-eyed desperation of wee children who seemed to suspect their mother might die soon. The old ache rippled across Lavinia's soul. Tears pricked. She blinked them away. The earl simply *must* help.

Her aunt patted her arm. "Worthy endeavors are most often rather less than enjoyable."

Lavinia nodded. Good deeds were not about personal pleasure but pleasing God: visiting the sick, biting one's tongue, rooting out envy, forgiving enemies.

And allowing the past to remain buried in the churchyard.

❧

The seventh Earl of Hawkesbury leaned back in his saddle. Fields of sun-ripened barley waved golden in the June sunshine. The scent of fresh-dug earth filled his nostrils as a light breeze ruffled nearby hedgerows. In the distance, the village of St. Hampton Heath reposed peacefully, watched over by the gray-stoned church. Such an idyllic pastoral scene, yet its peace did little to ease the tension edging his heart.

Fourteen years since that disastrous day. Fourteen years filled with study, travel, and then war. Fourteen years spent avoiding this upcoming inter-view. Sweat beaded his brow as it had the first time he faced cannon fire. He swiped at the moisture, disciplined his limbs to remain still and not turn his horse for home.

Midnight snorted and stamped his hoof, impatience pulling at the bit.

He patted his horse's neck. "There, there, boy. This surely cannot be as bad as Burgos."

The great horse nickered, as if remembering the chaotic withdrawal of allied troops from that Spanish fortress amidst rain and cold.

Nicholas's jaw tightened. Too many good men had died or been cap-tured in that campaign, back when he'd been plain Captain Stamford. Thank whatever gods may be for his horse whose faithfulness had brought him safely to Ciudad Rodrigo. He stroked the glossy mane with tender affection.

Midnight lowered his head, tugging at young grass.

"At least we have food now, don't we, boy?"

Midnight's ears flickered. No French cavalry had chased them harder than starvation, the pangs of hunger carving deeper than the bullet wound in his thigh.

No, the only thing chasing Nicholas now was his conscience.

He shook off the memories and squared his shoulders. "One can only hope this mission proves as unexceptionable as the first, eh?"

Small hope of that.

After wading through the paperwork his bailiff had prepared, his first port of call had been to visit the local squire and baronet. Sir Anthony's delight at his impromptu appearance had been cast in the shade by his effusive invitation to some local assembly, which made him wonder how many unmarried daughters the man had. All soldierly assurance had fled,

11

replaced by mealymouthed capitulation. This visit would be equally trying, but for very different reasons.

"Come. We best get on, before someone overhears me talking to you, questions my sanity, and insists I be sent to Bedlam."

He tapped Midnight's flanks and rode down the drive. They soon arrived at a modest, red-brick manor house, surrounded by oaks and fruiting trees. A servant girl was kneeling in the adjoining weed-strewn garden.

"Excuse me," he called. "Is your master at home?"

The girl squinted up. Dirt smeared her face, her hair tucked under a monstrously ugly mobcap. He nudged Midnight closer. Her gray eyes widened and she backed away. Poor simpleton.

"There is nothing to be afraid of. He is a good horse."

She raised a hand to shade her eyes but said nothing. Perhaps she was a mute.

"I am the seventh Earl of Hawkesbury." How strange it felt to say so, like he was defrauding the world, just as his brother had defrauded his creditors. He swallowed bile. "Now, can you tell me if your master is within?"

The pink staining her face as he announced himself gave way to something rather less maidenly as she lifted her chin. "I cannot."

"I beg your pardon?" Who was this chit to refuse a major's command? To refuse an earl's command? He put iron in his voice. "Tell me, is your master home?"

"No."

He jerked a nod, wheeled Midnight around, and then paused. "Wait. Do you mean to say he is not home, or do you merely defy me?"

A trace of a smile flashed across her face before her features settled into coolness. "If you are enquiring about Mr. Ellison, he is at home. As for my master, I cannot be expected to own what I do not have."

He blinked. Perhaps he was the simpleton, after all. The most unusual servant girl picked up her basket of weeds and disappeared around the side of the house. He stared after her, until Midnight's restless nickering recalled him to his mission. He secured his horse, rapped on the heavy wooden door, and waited. Apparently the rude maid had neglected to inform anyone of the visitor. What kind of servant was she? And what did she mean by saying she had no master?

A rattle of locks dragged him from his musings. Another servant greeted him, wide-eyed with the customary awe his rank and fashion usually merited, and ushered him inside. Nicholas was announced and led into a cluttered drawing room, lined with bookcases.

An older gentleman looked up. "Lord Hawkesbury! Welcome back."

"Thank you." He sat at his host's request and studied the reverend. Deep lines creased a face topped with graying brown hair. He would have been somewhat plain save for a pair of shrewd gray eyes that gave cause to wonder just how much the older man saw.

"The village trusts you will enjoy your stay here."

"I hope, Mr. Ellison, those are your sentiments as well."

"Of course, sir."

Nicholas glanced away. A pianoforte stood near the window, stacked with an untidy pile of papers. "I never had the opportunity to say how very sorry I am for the incident of years ago."

Which was a lie. He'd had the opportunity. Uncle Robert had begged, cajoled, even threatened both of his nephews with banishment, but the pride running so deep in his mother had forbidden either of her sons to apologize.

Until now.

He steeled himself to meet his host's justifiable recrimination—but saw compassion instead.

The shame doubled and redoubled, twisting his heart into knots. He forced himself to remain still and not squirm like a child. Many years had passed since anyone had made him feel quite so uncomfortable.

The reverend steepled his fingers and leaned back in his leather armchair. "It was my understanding that it was your brother and his friend who were responsible."

He gave a small shrug, dropping his attention to his highly polished Hessians. "For the actual incident perhaps, but I fear my words goaded them. For that I am truly sorry." His gaze lifted.

"And I am truly sorry that you have carried this weight for so many years." Something like peace and acceptance suffused the reverend's face. "You and your brother were forgiven a long time ago."

Nicholas swallowed. "By yourself?"

"Aye. And my daughter."

Memories flashed of the slight, golden-haired girl keening over a broken, bloodied body. He dragged guilty thoughts away and nodded stiffly. "Thank you, sir."

He glanced up at a lovely watercolor of St. Hampton Heath's old Norman church. The square stone tower and small curved windows had spoken of assurance for countless generations. Peace teased the restlessness within him.

"You will attend services?"

He suppressed a groan. Yet another duty he had no wish to perform. "Perhaps." The wise eyes seemed to search his soul, prompting a more enthusiastic, "I will try."

The reverend nodded. "I believe it will be a great blessing for our little village to have one such as yourself take an interest." He smiled gently. "I trust your time here will also prove a great blessing for you, my lord."

His throat cinched. The undeserved warmth and kindness filling the drawing room seemed to almost choke him. He couldn't take another jot. He rose. "Thank you, Mr. Ellison. Good day, sir."

After exchanging a slight bow with his surprised host, he exited the room and strode down the dim hall to the front entrance, fresh air, and freedom.

He dragged in great cleansing breaths as he untied Midnight, his heart hammering its insistence that he get away. His fingers seemed clumsier than when he was a boy in short pants.

From somewhere inside, a door slammed.

As he mounted his horse, a dark gleam of gold flashed through the apple trees on the manor's southern side. A small beagle appeared, yapping at Midnight's heels, drawing a dismissive snort from the great beast. Nicholas wheeled his horse around, down the dusty drive, back toward the lonely three-storied stone pile that was the countryseat of the Earl of Hawkesbury.

His inheritance. Not a blessing, like the reverend seemed to believe, but both a burden and a curse.

🕊 CHAPTER TWO

LAVINIA CLASPED THE leather hand strap as the carriage wheels rumbled over the uneven drive. She glanced at her aunt, seated opposite, whose jerky movements mimicked Lavinia's own.

"I declare, for a man of Sir Anthony's means, he keeps this road in shocking disrepair."

"We're almost there, Aunt Patience."

"I'm sure the only reason Cornelia Milton insisted we attend tonight was to show off her overdressed house and overdressed daughters."

"And to welcome back the earl," Papa offered mildly.

"The earl." Her aunt sniffed. "No doubt he'll be as high-handed as the rest."

"I did not gain that impression when he visited yesterday." Papa's brow creased. "He seemed surprisingly self-effacing."

No, he had appeared everything rude and presumptuous. Lavinia exchanged a look with Aunt Patience but held her peace. Her aunt's protests were nothing new, her vehemence against the nobility and the different rules for which society held them accountable had resulted in many a spirited rectory debate. The former earl had never seemed to mind her aunt's lack of marked deference, but then Aunt Patience had always held he was the exception to the arrogant aristocratic rule. After yesterday's encounter, Lavinia understood why.

"I do wish I had more time to revise those notes for my sermon."

Lavinia patted his arm. "Your notes can be revised tomorrow, Papa."

"I suppose you're right." He grimaced as another rattle swayed the carriage's occupants. "It was kind of the Miltons to send their coach for us, but I confess I will be glad to get there."

"As will I."

Another bump threatened to unseat her. She braced her kid boots on the carriage floor. While she would be pleased to reach the squire's newly extended manor, she held mixed feelings about the guest of honor. Despite his overbearing manner yesterday, a new face—handsome or not—would be interesting. The newspaper accounts of the Peninsular War in Spain, so avidly followed in the rectory, suggested Major Stamford had been one of Wellington's most courageous men, attaining numerous war honors. He must have interesting tales, indeed.

Lavinia swallowed a sigh. She would try to give him another chance. After all, he *did* hold the keys to helping the poor of St. Hampton Heath.

She glanced out the carriage window as the hedges slipped past. Bright sunlight meant she had little chance to study him yesterday, yet everything she had seen tallied with Sophia's description. The earl was tall, his hair dark, his shoulders broad, but his face was in shadow, so she had been unable to see if his features were handsome. What had intrigued her most was the furious manner in which he rode away after his interview with Papa, as if he feared ghosts or some such Gothic nonsense might be after him. Strange behavior indeed for a man decorated for bravery.

Papa had merely said afterward that the earl had expressed his regret at the events of the past, and asked for his and Lavinia's forgiveness. "Which I offered, of course."

"Of course?" Aunt Patience had snorted. "Because he is an earl?"

"Because he is a man."

"So once again nobility slips from responsibility faster than scones from a buttered pan! Do you really think Grace can be so easily absolved?"

"Unforgiveness holds us slaves, dear Patience."

Yes, but how could Papa offer *Lavinia's* forgiveness? He hadn't been there, hadn't seen—

She bit her lip, breathing past the embers of resentment as the old hurts swelled past her good intentions. The frozen terror in that moment before the horse struck. Her mother's cry that haunted Lavinia's nights for years. The village whispers that the younger Stamford had asked for a doctor—only for his brother! Lord Robert's oft-stated sorrow regarding the refusal of his nephews to own their culpability. The injustice flared anew, heating her chest. How *could* Papa offer her forgiveness? She glanced at Papa, offered him a taut smile, and forced her hands to unclench. Enough!

Tonight, she need not follow the rest of the village in paying homage to the guest of honor. Tonight, she would focus on someone far less self-important.

"My lord! Welcome to our humble abode."

Nicholas inclined his head to the evening's host. "Thank you, Sir Anthony."

He looked around the drawing room, filled with the notables of the district. He nodded to Lord and Lady Winthrop, whose estate bounded his on the south; Mr. Jones, the attorney; and Mr. Ellison before glancing across the sea of interested faces. He dipped his head in acknowledgment and then turned to study the pictures on the wall. How many more of these nights must he endure? How many could he politely decline? His gaze shifted from a rather ugly painting of sunflowers to alight on a group of young ladies seated near the Palladian window.

The group were much as any other: brunettes, blonds, dressed in the pale colors society dictated as acceptable, their simpering glances mere rustic versions of London coquettes.

One young lady, however, drew his attention. Unlike the others, she did not glance his way. She was not the youngest, nor the most stylishly attired, dressed as she was in simple gray. Her copper-blond hair was not this year's fashion, and she wore no adornments apart from a smile that flashed occasionally as she listened to a plain older woman. But her poise, her calm assurance, as if she knew exactly what she was about, would not be out of place in a London ballroom. He frowned. She reminded him of someone—

"The young ladies have been quite anxious to make your acquaintance, my lord."

He dragged his attention back to his host, masking his dismay with a polite smile. For months now he had suffered a great deal of attention from young ladies—and more particularly, from their mothers. He restrained a shudder at the memory of the recent London season Mother had insisted he attend. Conversations with insipid young ladies and vacuous young men, people who seemed to have no purpose but to see and be seen, held little interest for a man of action. It had been a blessed relief to finally be rid of the town and his social obligations, but now he was here in this dreary corner of Gloucestershire, and his status and supposed wealth once again drew attention. His smile grew taut. If only they knew . . .

The squire motioned forward a fussily dressed woman of dark hair and two chins. "May I present my wife, Lady Milton."

Nicholas murmured the usual commonplace nothings, noticing with pain her look of awe. His eager hostess beckoned to a young girl as her husband continued. "And my daughter, Miss Sophia Milton."

The blond simpered, eyes downcast, as she blushed becomingly. "My lord."

Sir Anthony continued the introductions. "May I present Miss West?"

"Good evening, ma'am."

The dark-haired woman gave him a cool-eyed look and sharp nod worthy of a duchess and then moved away.

Nicholas frowned.

"And this is our dear reverend's daughter, Miss Ellison."

The poised girl from before slowly drew near, as if reluctant. "Lord Hawkesbury and I have already met."

He stared at her. That voice, those eyes . . .

No. Surely not.

He swallowed. "Miss Ellison."

"As you can see." She mockingly sketched a curtsey.

"I apologize. I did not realize. I did not expect to find you so, so . . ."

She raised an eyebrow. "Clean?"

His hostess gasped.

"So grown," he muttered. Which was stupid. He was no longer a stripling of fifteen. He should have expected something other than the little girl whose cries had cursed his dreams.

His chest tightened with a thousand regrets as the cool, oddly disconcerting perusal continued. Her clear gray eyes held intelligence just as her father's, but *his* had not been set in such a fair face.

The squire turned. "Lavinia, I trust you will charm us all again with your musical prowess tonight."

Aloofness faded as affection filled her features. "Sir Anthony, your willingness to be charmed speaks more to your good nature than it does to my skill. I'm afraid you attach too much to my ability."

"Nonsense, my dear." Sir Anthony turned to Nicholas. "Miss Ellison is a most accomplished young lady and has delighted the neighborhood for many years."

The usual response to such flattery would have been a blushing denial, but there were no reddened cheeks. Her earlier poise suddenly seemed irritating and smug.

Nicholas flicked away an imaginary piece of fluff from his sleeve and drawled, "Such high praise! I am sure all London would be most eager to hear such prodigious talent."

Her chin rose. The sparkly gray eyes narrowed. "You are correct, sir, in attributing vast generosity and kindness of spirit to Sir Anthony's comments. We simple rustics would no doubt bring the oh-so-elegant *ton* to their knees in appreciative amusement."

Ha. So the chit was upset. His lips curved as she made her excuses and left, and he wondered at the contrast between this overly confident young creature and her faded, gracious father.

Insufferable man! How *dare* he condescend to attend one of these country parties and then turn his nose up at everyone and everything? Aunt Patience was right. The aristocracy was all the same, thinking themselves better than everyone else.

Lavinia glanced across the row of silk-swathed ladies to where the earl watched the performances. He barely masked his boredom as Sophia valiantly attempted a Bach sonata—sadly beyond her ability. Lavinia sighed inwardly. Such offerings were only too likely to reinforce the earl's dismissal of local talent.

She straightened her shoulders. Aunt Patience's insistence that Lavinia hone her creative abilities had not been for naught. And Lord Robert's generosity in acquiring an excellent vocal instructor had proved him the exception to Aunt Patience's objections to those of the aristocracy. Her smile at his memory faded. How sad that his nephew held himself so proud and aloof.

Sophy finished with an air of relief, blushing at the applause.

"Thank you, my dear. That was splendid, simply splendid." Sir Anthony's subsequent invitation to her aunt produced a technically challenging performance, and more genuine-sounding approbation. Then he turned to Lavinia. "Miss Ellison? Would you be so kind?"

Lavinia moved to the pianoforte, smiling at the crowd to cover unaccustomed nerves. Her aunt and father watched with very different faces. Aunt Patience's expression was one of pride, that the musical talent that ran deep in her side of the family would once again be expressed and praised—by all except the earl, no doubt. Papa wore a more wistful expression, something she'd seen many times over the past few years as she matured to look more like her mother. She could not disappoint either of them now.

She centered the music sheets and then struck the first note, completing a run before she began to sing. The music was at once comforting and familiar, a Handel aria she recalled Mama playing many years ago. As she sang, her face relaxed, the very action providing greater range as her voice soared clear and true. A quick glimpse at Lord Hawkesbury revealed he now sat straighter, almost leaning forward, astonishment replacing his perpetual sneer.

She played the final bar with a flourish, and the room swelled with generous applause. She caught the look on Papa's face, a look of such deep tenderness she wondered if he really saw her or dreamed of her mother.

At Sir Anthony's insistence, she played a cheerier melody and then bowed, a smile all the acknowledgment she could offer for their generous encouragement. Lavinia couldn't help but notice the earl's eyes follow as she resumed her seat. She glanced at him. He looked away, his features settling into bland indifference.

Later, during refreshments, her friends shared their impressions of the newcomer.

Catherine Winthrop's dark curls bobbed as she fanned herself. "I thought I might faint when he looked in our direction! He's the most handsome man I have ever seen!"

Handsome, perhaps, but scarcely a flirt. On the contrary, the earl seemed to find attention from young ladies trying, probably because he felt the locals so far beneath his notice.

"Perry would be quite jealous." Sophy said. "My brother has always counted himself the veriest tulip of fashion."

"The earl looks *so* distinguished, Livvie," Catherine murmured.

"Because he has a title?" At their puckered brows, Lavinia hurried on. "Don't you think he looks rather a proud man? He has scarcely spoken to a soul all night."

"Proud? No, not at all." Sophia looked over Lavinia's shoulder, her expression growing lamblike.

"You play quite well, Miss Ellison."

The deep-voiced drawl compelled her to turn. "Thank you."

She studied the earl. It couldn't be denied. Despite possessing one crooked eyebrow, his hazel eyes, coupled with high cheekbones and dark, wavy brown hair, made an appealing picture.

If you liked pictures that sneered. Although from the whispers around the room, it seemed many young ladies present would not mind the sneers.

She, however, was not one of those ladies. "I trust the evening was not completely devoid of amusement for one used to London society?"

His gaze wandered the room before settling back on her. "Tonight has been . . . tolerable."

She almost laughed. What a rude individual. "Lord Robert used to enjoy these evenings very much."

"Yes, but my uncle was not a man known for discriminating tastes."

Heat pounded her chest. How *dare* he disparage his uncle's generous good nature? "I fear you did not know Lord Robert as we did."

"That is most apparent."

He pulled out his quizzing glass and studied her as though she were a moth pinned to exhibit paper. She tilted her chin and glared at him until he finally placed the small glass away.

"I am sorry, sir, to learn your eyesight is not as it could be."

"My eyesight?"

She motioned to the quizzing glass. "I gather you have vision problems. Perhaps you should try whortleberries. Hettie, our maid, swears they have helped her eyesight improve immensely."

His eyes glittered. "I see quite well, thank you."

"That *is* something for which to be thankful. However, also something of a shame."

"I beg your pardon?"

"We rustics did not figure you to be such a dandy."

As the mocking glitter in his eyes disappeared, she excused herself and walked away, burning with determination to never, *never* allow the earl to ruffle her equilibrium again.

✠ CHAPTER THREE

A SHOT RICOCHETED through the night. Nicholas's heart thudded in time with Midnight's hooves as the horse pounded away, careless of dry scrubby brush or slippery rocks. Nicholas shuddered out a breath. His mission demanded he stay and seek out the opposition's movements, but the stallion was unusually nervous tonight. No matter. He turned back to the hills.

Red-gold flashed from up high. Fire ripped through his leg. Midnight reared, whinnying in fright. He cursed, grabbing at his throbbing thigh, reaching for the reins, but in the darkness his gloved hand only found air, and he was falling, falling—

"Sir!"

The fire pierced his eyes.

"My lord!"

Nicholas cracked open an eye.

Edwin peered at him, holding a glowing candlestick. His wrinkled brow smoothed. "Just another bad dream, m'lord."

Nicholas nodded, pushing his sweat-drenched body from the pillows. Edwin might be an excellent valet, but his experiences in war were nonexistent. The bad dreams Nicholas found plaguing his nights were lived nightmares. Too many men had died. Too many pointless battles had been fought and lost—against the fever, not just against the French. Too many widows for whom he had failed to bring a scrap of comfort. Too many tears, which had only strengthened his resolve to never allow any woman to engage his heart, or he hers. That way only led to despair. A marriage of convenience would be his only option, if marry he must. He sighed. And as the newest earl, it seemed one day he must.

Edwin pushed open the curtains. Sunshine streamed into the bedchamber. "Might I suggest a bath before you head for services, m'lord?"

Services. Nicholas groaned, rubbing at his aching thigh as he disentangled himself from the sheets. "You remain as subtle as ever, Edwin."

His valet grinned, and Nicholas stumbled to the freshly prepared bath, his spirits sinking as he lowered himself into the water. It did not matter how long he bathed, his guilty stains could never be washed away.

NICHOLAS HELD HIS head stiffly as he walked down the aisle of the village church, gritting his teeth as heads swiveled to mark his procession. No doubt every inch of his dress was being scrutinized, from the careless arrangement of his necktie to the fit of his superfine dark green coat. Not that anyone *here* would recognize Weston's handiwork. He seated himself down the front in the carved-oak family pew, knowing the speculation would continue behind his back, while he sat beneath the reverend's nose.

He nodded to Mr. Ellison and focused his attention on the rather pretty stained glass behind the wooden altar. Light shimmered gold and blue through the trio of round-topped windows. The central image depicted Jesus on a cross. To the left sat an open-armed Jesus surrounded by small children, while on the right the Good Samaritan cared for the beggar on the road. Pretty images, surrounded by carefully carved ancient stone, of long-ago, long-irrelevant tales. His gaze shifted to meet Mr. Ellison's. His fingers tensed. Was that reproach in the reverend's eyes? Could he see Nicholas's unbelief?

A creaky wheeze was followed by sounds of a pipe organ filtering through the stone building. The piece was loud and forceful, as if the invisible organist demanded people's attention.

He glanced across the aisle. Miss Ellison, wearing another shapeless plain gown and a simple silver cross, sat studying her prayer book as if her life depended on it.

His focus moved to the windows once more as he thought on the evening of two nights ago. Amidst the awful boredom of people nattering on about cattle and local issues he had absolutely no interest in, Miss Ellison *had* proved diverting. Her cool scrutiny of him had been most unnerving, almost like she could see straight through him. Her comments about his dandyism maligned his character thoroughly—although he supposed his manner had been a little overbearing. But when she'd played! She might possess the manners of a hoyden but she had the voice of an angel. Why even his mother, fastidious creature that she was, a self-styled expert of musicianship, would be astounded by this not-so-humble daughter of a country reverend.

The reverend cleared his throat, capturing Nicholas's attention once more.

"Good morning, dear friends." Mr. Ellison's smile, full of warmth and candor, suggested he actually did consider these people his friends. "Let us pray."

Nicholas bowed his head in compliance as the reverend seemed to chat to his god. Not that there was much point. He'd seen plenty of good men pray and still end up dead. What was the use? He paid scant attention, although the mellow voice was mildly soothing.

As the reverend led the congregation through the service, Nicholas's thoughts continued to wander. Perhaps church attendance would be of some benefit. If he must live in such a close-knit community, it probably was important to be seen to do the right thing. He didn't really mind the bowing and scraping that went along with his title. And it was oddly endearing to hear the locals esteem Uncle Robert so highly. Father could never understand why his elder brother did not prefer the glamour of London or his principal estate, Hawkesbury House, rather than this dull pocket of Gloucestershire. Perhaps the locals had something to do with his decision, after all.

After several hymns—to which he mouthed along—he noticed Miss Ellison rise and slip away. He frowned. Surely the reverend's daughter was not permitted to abscond. Was she ill?

The reverend's mellow voice regained his attention as he announced the Bible readings and then preached a sermon, during which Nicholas could barely stifle yawns. A kind of mind-numbing stupor settled upon him. How much longer must he endure?

The reverend finally closed the Bible. "Let us pray."

Nicholas bowed his head just in time.

Organ music woke him. His head jerked, and he glanced up to see Mr. Ellison's gaze shift away, his puckered brow ease into smoothness.

He hoped to God he hadn't snored! If he hadn't, the congregation might merely think their new earl was—extremely—pious.

The intricate organ music continued, softer, gentler than before, contemplative rather than containing that earlier judgmental note. The congregation stood, the reverend closed the service, and the aisle soon thronged with congregants seeking his attention. He nodded, listened to their welcomes, all while his heart itched to leave. Miss Ellison flitted by—where *had* she gone during the service? He moved through the huddled villagers to shake the hand of the reverend, as seemed to be the custom here.

"Lord Hawkesbury, it's good to see you here." Mr. Ellison's eyes twinkled. "I trust you will find next week's sermon a trifle more interesting?"

His cheeks heated. "Forgive me. I must have stayed up too late last night."

"I fear many a person here has needed forgiveness for that particular sin."

His lips twitched. "You are generous." He inclined his head and moved outside, blinking at the watery sunshine after the church's dimness. Perhaps a long, hard ride this afternoon would help clear away this lethargy and help him feel more the thing.

"Excuse me, Lord Hawkesbury?"

He bit back a sigh, and turned as the squire engaged him in the usual trivialities, while Lady Milton and her daughter hovered nearby, their faces dimpling whenever he carelessly looked their way. He refused their offer for luncheon, made his excuses, and strode away to the shy smiles of young ladies of the congregation. With a nod to the blacksmith's boy who held Midnight, he swung up and glanced back. He remained the object of nearly everyone's attention.

Everyone, except Miss Ellison. Her attention remained on a stooped, white-haired woman leaning on a stick. The reverend's daughter leaned closer, patted the elderly woman's arm, and smiled.

His breath caught. With her hair gleaming in the sunshine, her face alight, she held a radiance he'd only ever seen in an Old Master's painting in Venice—and certainly never witnessed in a London ballroom.

He frowned heavily, wheeled Midnight around, tapped the horse's flanks, and cantered away.

"Giles!"

Nicholas scowled at the ledger on his desk as he waited for his butler to appear. What *had* Johnson been doing these past years? The figures suggested his bailiff had maintained the estate appropriately, but anyone could see the stables had not been properly addressed in years. It really required a full renovation, but where would he get the money for that? His brother's careless ways had brought the estate within a whisker of bankruptcy; the rents from his tenant farmers barely covered the wages of his staff. His prize money from the Peninsular was nearly all accounted for, spent trying to ease the suffering of his wounded men, or worse but more importantly, provide for their widows. Prize money? He shook his head. Blood money.

Soft footfalls preceded his butler's silver head. "M'lord?"

"Have you any idea where Johnson is today?"

"I believe he is in town."

"Town? Gloucester or Cheltenham?"

"Cheltenham, m'lord. I believe he said he will be back at nightfall."

Nicholas pushed back in his chair, barely acknowledging his butler's quiet departure. Nightfall was too long a wait. He gazed out the window. Clear skies beckoned. Nothing would be gained by poring over books right now; he'd only grow more frustrated. His ride Sunday afternoon had proved beneficial. Perhaps another ride would clear his head.

"Giles!"

The butler reappeared. "Yes, m'lord?"

"Tell McHendricks to saddle Midnight."

"Very good, m'lord."

Half an hour later, he was in the saddle, surveying the land. The barley seemed plumper now, the past days of sunshine doing much to ripen the harvest. He'd never really noticed the crops or their stewards before. He'd never expected to need to care. But watching clouds wisp through the sky, the ground swell with promise, the rhythms of the countryside, a kind of peace washed over him. Here, at least, men were not treated as cannon fodder, and one could be certain to rise as the sun. Farming may be dull, hard, monotonous work, possessing little of the danger inherent with a soldier's lot, but somehow, it gave one an appreciation for life.

He pressed Midnight over the rise to where two men worked with several horses in a furrowed field. As he pulled up, the men stopped, acknowledging him with a touch of their foreheads.

"G'mornin', me lord."

"Good morning." As they watched him expectantly, he scrambled for something to say. "And what are you doing in this field?"

"We be plowing in for turnips."

He glanced at the long wooden contraption behind the horses. "Where are the plough's wheels?"

"The soil be mostly clay and heavy, and wheels get stuck. The long moldboard and skeith and share be far better to break down heavy soil."

He nodded like he knew of what they spoke. "And your yield?"

"That be dependent on the good Lord above."

"Er, yes. Of course."

"Beggin' yer pardon, me lord, but has Johnson spoken to yer yet?"

"I've scarcely seen Johnson since I arrived."

The men glanced at each other.

"I'm here now. What was it about?"

"We be wondering if the lower field could be extended a mite to make more room for planting."

The broad-faced one nodded and began explaining the benefits of this plan.

"It sounds reasonable. What did Johnson say?"

The pair exchanged glances again. "That be the trouble, me lord. He don't favor us with any answer."

Nicholas flicked the reins impatiently. "Well, I'll speak to him about it soon."

"Thank ye, me lord." The men touched their foreheads once more as he rode away.

He glanced at his dirt-crusted gloves. Despite Edwin's fastidious standards, he at least had sense enough not to make a fuss, unlike his previous valet in London. Nicholas frowned. Amidst the mail this morning had been another missive from his mother. Apparently London missed him. His lip curled in disdain. Missed his money, most likely. Mother also reported that Clara had asked after him, *most* particularly. Mother herself would visit him but was creating a rose garden with a water fountain on Hawkesbury House's south lawn, which must be ready for her guests in two weeks' time, and the gardeners were simply hopeless . . .

His mouth drew to one side. How would Mother cope when he brought back a wife, and she was forced to move to the Dower House? She loved Hawkesbury House, with its score of bedrooms, lavish reception rooms, and extensive grounds—that apparently needed constant remodeling. She would not take to a new countess easily unless she could control her as she did the grounds, hence her preference for Clara DeLancey, the daughter of Viscount Winpoole. His lips set in a thin line. He would be hanged to see *that* occur.

He moved onto the road and cantered toward St. Hampton Heath. Fresh air brought a smile to his lips and further ease to his heart. Something that felt like joy welled within. Here, at least, he could be himself: free of expectations, control, and cursed responsibility.

He rounded the corner. Up ahead, he noticed a slight figure holding a basket, trailed by a yappy beagle. A quick glance over the shoulder and the person moved to the extreme edge of the road. He slowed and drew even. Yes. He'd recognize that contempt anywhere.

"Good day, Miss Ellison."

"My lord." She continued walking, eyes fixed firmly ahead, hands grasping the basket as the dog began to bark.

Midnight whinnied in protest, his hooves dancing across the stones.

Miss Ellison shied further away and scooped up the beagle.

Nicholas shrugged mentally, casting another glance at her before giving Midnight his head and cantering away. Just before he reached the bend in the road he glanced back.

He pulled Midnight to a sharp stop and scanned the countryside.

Miss Ellison had disappeared.

※

Lavinia sank into the oak's shade next to her basket. She forced herself to breathe slowly to calm her racing heartbeat. The horse had not bolted, nor reared, nor any other thing from her nightmares. The earl did appear at least to have his horse under control, which should be expected from one of Wellington's most decorated cavalry officers.

She pulled her pencils and sketchbook from the basket, the action helping calm her nerves. She started to sketch the scene: Mickey sniffing at the base of the untrimmed hawthorns nestled with pink-and-white flowers, the tussocks of coarse grass, the young oak in the corner seeded from the large tree beneath which she sheltered. Her own private hideaway.

This triangular patch of land, shielded on three sides by large hedges, had remained untouched, indeed unvisited—save for herself—for years. She and Mickey had explored every corner, knew every stone, every flower. The gap in the hedge might prove more of a squeeze than ten years ago but she refused to relinquish the peace this haven provided.

The violet-blue flowers of the meadow clary defied her endeavors to capture their curling form, so she abandoned the attempt and moved to study the plant more closely. *Salvia pratensis*. The cemetery held pockets of salvia sown on the graves, hinting of salvation as they had for hundreds of years.

Mickey scampered off to the far corner so she placed her drawing materials away and lay down, looking up at the heavens. No doubt Lady Milton would have another fit if she could see Lavinia now. She smiled. A slight breeze tousled curls across her face as her thoughts ranged wide and free as the clouds above: the delicate beauty of salvia, Eliza Hardy and the plight of other tenant families, their children who needed education. Music. Art. Church. The earl.

She frowned. Like Mickey, she seemed to possess hackles that arose every time she saw the earl, which was somewhat odd. She had never felt anything but affection for his uncle. But then, the fourth earl had been nothing but kindness, whereas this new earl seemed to look down his thin nose at them all.

Papa had pleaded with Patience and herself not to judge, but the old resentment refused to be quenched. The village whispers of fourteen years ago resurfaced: how could he demand a doctor to attend his brother and *that* man, while ignoring her mother? Only a heartless person could do such a thing—or as Aunt Patience believed, a nobleman convinced of his family's self-importance.

The sun slipped behind a cloud. Shivers rippled her body until she shifted into the warmth. The oak's wide, strong branches might offer protection from the sun, but the shadows of her heart were not so easily removed. She sighed. It probably didn't help to continually remember his wrongs. He probably couldn't help possessing a crooked eyebrow that gave him a mocking look. How many times had she implored Sophy to not judge a book from its outward appearance? But here she was, judging a man for the very same. Someone she should at least try to get along with, seeing as he needed to help Eliza's family before another winter set in.

A golden leaf drifted from above, twirling, like music in the air. She picked it from her hair, and stretched out, placing her hands beneath her head. "Lord, please help the earl do good here."

She stared up at the sky as the hush of oak leaves rustled and sang, while doubt and apprehension continued nibbling at the edges of her soul.

Chapter Four

AFTER ANOTHER FITFUL night followed by a long morning discussing estate affairs with Johnson, which left him with a hazy impression that he'd been neatly circumvented, Nicholas set out again to clear his head and realign his thoughts. Nothing induced calmness like riding. Midnight cantered down a rough track along the western end of the lake, then through the woodlands that still sported the odd bluebell.

Perhaps some aspects of country life were not completely abhorrent. The countryside was rather pretty, although good company remained pretty sparse. He slowed Midnight to a trot. He hadn't always been such a recluse. Indeed, London would laugh at the suggestion. But war had hardened him, scarring him inside and out. London might enjoy his company but nobody truly knew his heart, save Thornton. Perhaps he should write his old captain and invite him for a visit. *His* company would be acceptable.

Midnight wheeled out onto the road leading to the village. Nicholas spurred him on, down the hill, past the narrow corner, until he noticed that slight figure coming toward him, basket in hand, dog at her feet. An oddly touching, increasingly familiar scene. He slowed. For some reason the girl's stern aversion only made him desire her approval. Whether motivated by guilt or mere challenge, he didn't know, but one day he would make her smile at him.

"Good day, Miss Ellison."

She glanced up. "Lord Hawkesbury."

The dog began its usual tiresome racket. "Can't that thing stop its infernal barking?"

Her eyes narrowed. She turned and with a low command, the dog quieted. Midnight snorted. She stepped farther away. Surely she didn't dislike him that much.

"Is something wrong?"

"No, sir."

He nudged Midnight closer. Her steps shied away again. "Are you sure?"

"I do not like horses, sir."

"There's nothing to be afraid of."

She shot him a look of disbelief, but behind the mutinous lift to her chin he glimpsed fear. Guilt shot through him as he recalled her well-deserved reason for trepidation, and he mollified his tone. "Have you been to the village?"

She nodded. "Mrs. Foster, one of your tenants, has been unwell."

"I trust she will soon recover."

"She'd recover a great deal sooner if her house were in better repair."

"Then she should repair it."

"Precisely how should a poor widow repair her house?" The gray eyes flashed. "Tenant housing is *your* responsibility, Lord Hawkesbury."

"Johnson is supposed to check—"

"Yes, well, your bailiff is supposed to do many things."

"I will look into it."

"Soon, I hope." Her voice gentled. "Mrs. Foster is a dear lady, but aged. Another winter in such housing might be her last."

Weight settled on his shoulders as she walked away. Wonderful. Yet more responsibility. He wheeled Midnight around and followed her. "I believe, even in these parts, that it's not the usual thing for young ladies to be out walking without any escort."

Her shoulders lifted in a slight shrug. "So Lady Milton tells me."

"What should happen if someone should wish to harm you?"

She glanced up at him sideways. "Like carry me off to ravish me?"

"Miss Ellison!"

"Everyone around here knows me, and I don't think anyone would dare try."

"You should be more prudent with your words. Green girls should not be so vulgar."

"But I am not such a green girl! I *am* three and twenty."

His eyebrows rose. Her fresh looks marked her as younger. "Young ladies of my acquaintance do not speak so vulgarly."

"But I am not such a young lady, and you and I are barely acquainted, so your opinions need not concern me."

"But your safety!"

She shrugged again. "I have Mickey to keep me company. He's as good as any person."

"That thing?" He sneered as the dog bounded across the meadow chasing a butterfly.

Two splotches of red highlighted her cheeks. "That *thing* can bite, so pray do not misjudge what you cannot know anything about." She turned and whistled. "Come, Mickey."

Without a backward glance she set off up the hill again, her marked independence leaving him in a mess of frustration—and reluctant admiration.

Two DAYS LATER—AFTER his now daily stern talk with his bailiff necessitated yet another long ride—an ale at the ivy-covered Pickled Hen had calmed Nicholas sufficiently to walk through the village to reacquaint himself with its lanes and stone buildings. St. Hampton Heath was a rather pretty village, with its Norman square-towered church taking pride of place opposite the village green. The shops were few but seemed adequate for the villagers' needs, comprising the blacksmiths, carpenters, wheelwright, cobbler, apothecary, and the village shop. The cobblestones were smooth and even, geraniums leaned from the windowsills, and the bright leaves of the great oaks lining the village green seemed to shout summer as they had for hundreds of years.

The sharp bark of a dog drew his attention to the church. The heavy wooden doors were open, beckoning. Somehow, despite himself, his feet drew him to the dim interior of the porch. From within came the clank of metal. He frowned. Surely nobody would be stealing the church's few valuable artifacts? That's what came of leaving the door open so just anyone could walk in! Mr. Ellison might hold good intentions but he was far too trusting.

He peered round the corner. Stained glass spilled gold and rose onto the wooden pews, the only light in the nave. A shadowed figure stood at the altar, too far away to identify. The person touched the gold vessels then bent down.

He stepped forward, about to reprimand the intruder when the quiet was broken.

"'When I survey the wondrous cross . . .'"

His skin prickled.

"'On which the Prince of glory died . . .'"

A wild beating filled his heart as the glorious singing echoed off ancient stone.

"'My richest gain I count but loss, and pour contempt on all my pride.'"

He exhaled. How could a cross lead to anything but loss? He shook his head. The idea was preposterous!

A sloshing sound replaced the song. Oh . . .

He stepped back and moved outside, sunshine dogging his steps as he hurried away. Thank goodness she hadn't discovered him. Thank goodness he hadn't called out! How would he explain his objection to *flower arranging*—especially to the reverend's daughter? His lips twitched. He could wager the last foot of Hawkesbury land *that* particular encounter would result in icy smiles from Lady Disdain!

The blacksmith hailed him, and they passed more than a few minutes discussing his horses before Nicholas resumed his walk. He was passing along a path near the stream when a voice from an open window reached his ears.

"Mrs. Foster, how are you today?"

"Tolerably well, Miss Livvie."

He stopped. A Mrs. Foster lived in his tenant housing, so Miss Ellison had said. Perhaps if he stayed here, half hidden from the cottage by a tree draped in sweet-smelling honeysuckle heavy with creamy flowers, he might learn more.

There was a sigh and then the thin crackling voice continued. "The bailiff was around earlier and said his lordship will make the necessary repairs as soon as possible."

"Oh! Well, I am glad he at least *said* so."

A wheezy chuckle. "It is good his lordship is here."

Silence.

"Don't you agree, Miss Livvie? 'Tis good the family's back."

"Mmm, I suppose."

His brow knit.

"I be thinking that since he's here, mayhap he will."

"I'm sorry, Mrs. Foster. Who will do what?"

"Perhaps the earl will get that Johnson to finally fix my leaky roof."

"Perhaps."

He frowned. Miss Ellison's dry tone spoke volumes.

"He's a rascal, that one."

"I wouldn't exactly describe him like that. We don't really know him, after all."

There was another wheezy cackle. "Not know Johnson?"

A beat. "Oh, I beg your pardon. I thought you meant . . ."

Nicholas's frown deepened. Miss Ellison thought *that* little of him?

"He is rather a handsome young man, I be thinking."

"Who do you mean?"

"Why, the earl of course!"

"Mmm? Oh, I suppose so, yes."

His lips curved. Praise from Miss Ellison was hard won, indeed.

"I am sure he is greatly missed in London."

"I'm sure he misses it, too. I rather doubt he will be here for long. Our little village concerns surely cannot hold enough to interest *him*."

He frowned and whipped a nearby yellow flowering shrub with his riding crop as he strode back to the blacksmith's. Yes, he was reaping an eavesdropper's reward, but still . . .

Why did Miss Ellison seem to have a kind word for everybody but him?

AT CHURCH THE following day, he again observed Miss Ellison's mysterious exit during the service. And later, he couldn't help but notice the young man standing with the squire and Sophia, talking animatedly while Miss Ellison listened.

Nicholas's eyes narrowed. The stripling—for really, he couldn't be more than one and twenty—was rather handsome, in a florid, somewhat dandified way. No carelessly knotted neckcloth for *him*. His waistcoat was decorated with ornate gold-and-cream flowers, and his coat fitted perfectly—although he suspected padding might have something to do with it. Handsome, certainly, though the girth of his neck suggested he would emulate the squire's rotundity in a few years.

Sir Anthony shifted, his eyes brightening as Nicholas came into view. "Good morning, my lord. Such a lovely day."

Nicholas agreed. Sophia drew closer and smiled up at him, Miss Ellison having moved away to talk with a young mother surrounded by a gaggle of children.

He dragged his attention back as the squire continued.

"May I present my son, Peregrine. He has just returned from university."

Slight bows were exchanged. Young Mr. Milton cast him a less than surreptitious glance. "M'lord."

Nicholas resolved to be polite. "Oxford or Cambridge?"

"Cambridge."

"Ah. I'm an Oxford man, myself."

"My lord, would you do us the honor of dining with us today?" Sir Anthony beamed. "We are having a small celebration to mark Perry's return."

He glanced at the eager faces and was all set to refuse when a thought struck. Refusing too many local invitations would set him up as proud, and he'd never get to the bottom of what was really happening with his estate. "I'd be delighted."

Sophia clapped her hands. "Wonderful! We will make such a merry party. Lavinia is coming, too."

He glanced across at the reverend's daughter. Her cool-eyed gaze shifted away.

He smiled. Suddenly lunch seemed a little more enticing.

TWO HOURS LATER, with the last of the courses cleared away—along with the squire and his wife who had disappeared for a rest—the chatter around the table turned to talk of an outing to the nearby ruins of an abbey. He leaned back in his seat as Sophia and her brother made plans.

"Livvie, what say you to an alfresco luncheon tomorrow? We can ask Catherine, too."

"I'd say it sounds like a wonderful idea. I hope you enjoy yourself."

Sophia's pretty mouth dropped open. "Mean you not to come?"

"I am otherwise engaged. I have promised Eliza Hardy a visit."

"For shame, Livvie! You would pass up a treat for yet another visit to one of your deserving poor?"

"For shame, Sophy." Miss Ellison's tone was gentle. "Would you have me break my word to a poor, motherless girl for the sake of a few hours of amusement?"

Nicholas flicked open his snuffbox with careless grace. "Coming at it rather too brown, Miss Ellison."

Her face tinged a delicate shade of pink but she said nothing.

"Please, Livvie, change your mind." Sophia grasped her friend's arm.

"You will not miss my company."

"But we will!" Perry's face flushed. "I'm sure Eliza won't mind."

"I beg your pardon, but how can you know what she minds?" Miss Ellison's glance sharpened though her voice remained soft.

"But she doesn't need you," Perry complained.

"And how would you know what she needs? When did you last speak with her? You barely acknowledge her when you pass on the street. Do you think because she is poor and defenseless, she is not worthy of attention?"

"I, er . . . no."

"No? Your actions tell a different story."

Sophia rolled her eyes. "Livvie, I do wish you wouldn't get so het up about such things."

Miss Ellison's brow creased slightly. "And I wish that people didn't think that just because someone is poor, they are beneath our respect. They are people, with the same feelings and dreams as anyone so blessed to be born into a more privileged life."

Nicholas snorted. "Hardly the same dreams."

The gray eyes flashed. "While I cannot speak for all, I do believe that most people share similar goals."

"And those would be?"

"To be loved and to love, and to feel one has a purpose in this world."

"This from your years of observation and experience, is it?"

"Not just mine, sir, but from people who have lived longer than I." Her head tilted. "Do you not believe that to be true? Do you not wish to feel accepted and appreciated, to know that your life has purpose and meaning?"

Her words struck his heart like hammer on anvil, forbidding speech. How could she know the driftless state of his heart?

"I would not have Miss Hardy feel that because she is poor she is therefore expendable. She is my friend, and I have given her my word."

Sophia sighed. "You and your words."

Nicholas drawled, "I gather Miss Ellison has high principles that do not allow the slightest modification."

Clear gray eyes lifted to study him. "I gather from *that* remark, sir, that you have no problem altering your principles to suit your whims and desires."

Heat crawled up his neck. "You have a very impertinent tongue, Miss Ellison."

She flushed. "Perhaps. But at least when I say I will do a thing, I actually do it."

Guilt flashed through him at the remembrance of their last conversation. "I said I would inspect the tenant housing, and I shall."

The slight lift of one eyebrow betrayed her doubt. "And I said that I would visit Eliza tomorrow, and I shall." She turned and smiled at Sophia. "Please excuse me. Today has been lovely, but our maid Hettie has been unwell, and I must assist with tonight's dinner preparations."

"I will drive you home." Perry rose, his countenance brightening as it did whenever Miss Ellison glanced his way.

"Thank you, but there's no need." Her cool smile offered little encouragement.

"But I would consider it an honor."

"Thank you, Perry, but I simply must walk off that magnificent meal."

"I'll escort you."

"Thank you, but that won't be necessary."

"But—"

"Do you think Miss Ellison unable to walk home?" Nicholas drained his wine glass, and eyed the tiresome gallant.

"No."

"Worried for her safety?" He placed the glass on the table. "I have it on excellent authority that nobody would dare try to carry off Miss Ellison and ravish her."

Sophia's gasp and her brother's indignant "Sir!" paled into insignificance as a hint of a dimple hovered near Miss Ellison's mouth.

He inclined his head to the siblings. "I humbly beg your pardon."

He caught the amusement in Miss Ellison's eyes before she reiterated her excuses to Sophia, offered a slight curtsey to the guests, and exited the room.

He contrived to remain interested, but the zest had left the room. After another quarter hour of polite nothings, he made his excuses and departed.

He caught up with her, mere steps from the twin cherry trees marking the drive to the Ellison estate. Her hat dangled from the ribbons, her hair spilling from her chignon, as she gazed at the trees, lost in thought.

He pulled Midnight to a halt. "Miss Ellison, I'm pleased to see you're almost home."

"As you can see." She curtsied, mockingly.

"No kidnappers or masked bandits accosted you?"

"Surprisingly enough, no. Nor have they the hundreds of times I've walked this route before." She stooped to pick some pretty yellow flowers from the side of the road.

"Young Milton seems to have an eye on a particular young lady."

She straightened, her cheeks pink. "Perry may have an eye, but his mother has a care to ensure he marries someone with more to offer than some musical ability."

"You do not seem too dismayed."

"No. But then, I have yet to meet a man that has caught *my* eye." With an expression that could only be described as a smirk, she dipped her head and walked purposefully up the drive.

He watched the slight figure walk away. Irritation prickled within his heart, and he tapped Midnight's flanks and rode away.

❦ CHAPTER FIVE

SHE SHIVERED. SOMEONE had left the vestry doors open, admitting a cold draft through the church building. Lavinia pulled the shawl closer as her father continued his address.

"Our Lord said: forgive and it will be forgiven you. Each week we recite the Lord's Prayer, we say to God: 'Forgive us our trespasses as we forgive those who trespass against us.' But I ask you, do we really want God to forgive us the way we forgive others?"

Lavinia swallowed. No, she did not.

"Imagine for a moment, if our heavenly Father really did forgive us the way we think we forgive others. Would He let go of some of those sins we consider minor, like gossip or untruths, and focus on the sins we deem more important, like murder or lust?"

The church drew a collective breath. Had Papa ever spoken of *lust* in services before? His preaching certainly allowed no sleeping today. She refrained from turning around to view the earl's expression. She hadn't seen him this week. Rumor had it he'd traipsed back to London. For a haircut!

"That is how we judge, is it not? How often do we hold sins against others, whether they be petty, imagined slights, or even grave miscarriages of justice, while allowing our own weaknesses to slip through our fingers of blame? Thank God He knows we are but frail flesh. Thank God His forgiveness is complete."

She nodded and subtly stretched her back muscles, stiff from yesterday's hard day of gardening, safe in the knowledge that the curtain screening her position at the pipe organ meant she remained unseen.

"But in thanking God for His forgiveness, let us not pardon ourselves too quickly. Let us be mindful of those times when we need to exercise forgiveness for others and allow no room for offense to set in. Unforgiveness is a slow rot, poisoning our soul, hardening our heart to God and to others. But when we are quick to forgive every offense and wrongdoing, our hearts become softer and more responsive to God's love, until we are like our Savior, who was able to forgive all humanity as He hung upon a cross."

Papa leaned against the pulpit imploringly. "Let us not require people to repent before we offer our pardon. We know we are all sinners, requiring God's forgiveness. 'While we were still sinners, Christ died for us.' So let us do likewise, offering pardon to others, just as God offered His pardon to all mankind, even before mankind asked His forgiveness. In doing so, we represent Christ and His peace. Let us pray."

Lavinia bowed her head as emotions tumbled within. Yes, she wanted to forgive. Yes, she knew not forgiving would bind her soul. But something inside still demanded to hear the earl say, "I'm sorry."

To her, not her father.

She peeked past the curtain, over her shoulder, to see the earl staring straight ahead, his expression one of total boredom.

She closed her eyes, her fingers clenched. How could he not hear Papa's message? How could he sit there unmoved? She fought to refocus her thoughts heavenward as her father's sonorous voice continued. *Heavenly Father, I'm really struggling. I do feel hardness in my heart toward him. I know he didn't cause Mama's death, but part of me still wants him to take responsibility. I am sorry. Please forgive me, and help me forgive others—including him.*

After the recessional hymn, she slipped from her perch and found Aunt Patience, her face lined with exhaustion. "How did the children fare today?"

"I believe they prefer their younger teacher." Aunt Patience lifted a brow. "I think *I'd* prefer they had their younger teacher, too."

"They can be a little wearying, can't they? But it's for a good cause."

"Another good cause for Miss Ellison?"

Lavinia's breath hissed inward. "Lord Hawkesbury." She turned to encounter his sardonic gaze. "*What* a pleasure." Too late she remembered her prayer earlier.

A smile flickered on his lips. "Apparently the pleasure is all mine. Ladies." He inclined his head to her aunt and moved to walk away.

"Lord Hawkesbury."

The earl stilled, closed his eyes briefly, and turned. "Mr. Ellison."

"I trust you found today's sermon topic a little livelier."

"I'm afraid, sir, I cannot answer that question without implicating myself."

Aunt Patience managed a brittle laugh. "You sound as though you're well versed in the art of not implicating yourself."

"Now, now, Patience," Papa said. "Leave our guest be."

"Our guest?" Lavinia frowned at the earl, who offered an inscrutable smile.

"Did I forget to mention it, my dear?" Papa said mildly. "I suppose I did. Last week I asked Lord Hawkesbury to join us for a meal. I'm sure he would enjoy company and our plain fare."

From the look on the earl's face, she was not sure he agreed, but his manners were smooth. "I can think of nothing better."

"I'm sure you can't."

Her aunt's tart reply gave rise to another of those enigmatic smiles, which Sophy would swoon over but Lavinia found smug and annoying. She smoothed down her dress. Perhaps she had forgiven him, but she would *not* let him off the hook concerning his responsibilities to the poor. She exchanged glances with her aunt and smiled inwardly. From the look in Aunt Patience's eye, neither would she.

⁂

Luncheon proved surprisingly enjoyable. The mutinous tilt to the chins of both female family members suggested he would be hard pressed to relax, but Nicholas found himself somewhat comfortable. The dining room was simply furnished and the food—as promised—plain, consisting of ham and egg pie, a roasted fowl accompanied by an assortment of vegetables, and stewed apples with clotted cream. But it was honest food, tasty, perhaps made more so by the reverend's comment that his daughter had plucked the produce from the garden and baked the apples only yesterday. He hid a smile at the thought Lady Disdain should bake a pie for a creature such as *he*.

But a quick glance across the table revealed no pronounced aversion in those stormy silvery eyes. For once the disdain seemed set aside. Instead, she seemed thoughtful, her brow creased, as if she measured him, so he exerted himself to please.

"I must thank you for your kind invitation today. It was a meal fit for a king."

"Coming at it much too strong," Miss West said.

"No, indeed, I have not enjoyed a meal so much in many a month. I have found, after time on the Continent, that the taste for confections and sauces has quite left me. I much prefer honest English fare."

Miss Ellison's eyebrows rose, their little wings dancing.

He met her gaze, saw the questions quiver in her eyes, but she only pressed those rosy lips together. He smiled.

"And where did you serve?"

He turned to Mr. Ellison and sketched a simple description of his time in Spain.

"You led a troop, the Twelfth Light Dragoons, I believe? Were you involved at the charge at Garcia Hernandez?"

"Why, yes." Nicholas shifted in his seat. "I must confess to being surprised, sir. From your words this morning, I thought you would be more interested in peace rather than so conversant with matters of war."

"I believe we all truly prefer peace, don't you agree?" The reverend's eyes twinkled. "Perhaps you would not be so surprised should you know the avid curiosity of my daughter and my sister-in-law. Many a long discussion we held about Wellington's tactics, particularly about the benefits of siege warfare."

The room grew warmer. He sipped his water and studied the rose centerpiece.

"What a waste Burgos was." Miss West offered from her end of the table. "Were you involved in that action?"

He nodded stiffly. One hand clenched the stem of his glass as the memories rose in all their ugliness. The cold, the relentless rain. The cries of men for a morsel of food. Their gasps before they slipped from this world. His men. His men whom he'd failed.

His meal sat uncomfortably heavy on his stomach. He swallowed the bitter taste in his mouth. "Too many good men died for no discernible gain."

He glanced up to encounter Miss Ellison's gaze, her questioning look gone, her eyes now soft with sympathy. Something like a wave of immeasurable kindness, deep, profound, sincere, seemed to flow from her, tugging at him, drawing warmth from his heart to hers, like water surged to shore.

She leaned forward slightly. "I would think, regardless of discernible gain, the deaths of so many would weigh terribly on a man." His throat constricted as she concluded quietly, "I am sorry, sir."

He nodded again.

Silence filled the room for a few moments, until Miss West remarked, "I am sorry, too, for I thought Burgos to be quite beautiful."

This led to a more pleasant exchange about the merits of Spain versus Portugal. They compared travel notes, and the mood lightened as the conversation spun from politics to art to food. Comfortable once again, Nicholas turned to his host. "I was hoping you might clear up a little mystery. I have on occasion wondered where Miss Ellison disappears to during the service."

"Why?" Miss Ellison's direct look held nothing of the coquette. "I fail to understand why you would find my movements the least bit interesting."

"Do you, my dear?" Miss West addressed Miss Ellison; her eyes fixed on him.

Heat flushed his cheeks. "It is only that I cannot suppose the reverend's daughter be permitted to abscond during the service."

Miss Ellison shrugged. "We are attempting to form something of a Sunday school."

His brows rose.

"Many of the villagers cannot afford to send their children to school, as it is either too costly or they are required for work. We are hoping that by teaching letters and basic arithmetic, we might be able to help educate them for life, as well as teach about God."

"Goodness! I'm dining with social reformists."

Mr. Ellison laughed. "It was Lavinia's suggestion."

She colored. "Mr. Robert Raikes of Gloucester first had the idea. Many villages are trying his scheme." She turned to Nicholas. "The world is changing, with manufactories replacing farms. It is important to equip our children with skills necessary for the future."

"I applaud you." He lifted his water glass—no wine here—and watched the cheeks pink prettily again.

"Come now." Miss West leaned forward. "You cannot have us believe you really mean that."

"I beg your pardon?"

"It is only to your advantage that people stay as they always have. Estates such as yours will always require workers for their farms. If they are educated and leave, you will be without."

"But if Miss Ellison is correct and they will leave anyway, why would I object to their being educated? Besides, I would much prefer to deal with someone who has the ability to reason and communicate clearly. Danger lies in relying on people without such ability."

As Mr. Ellison murmured agreement, his daughter exchanged a glance with her aunt. Was it just his imagination, or did he hear the name "Johnson" murmured in an undertone?

Miss Ellison turned to him. "So you approve our school?" A dimple hovered as her lips curved to one side.

"Well . . . yes."

"And would support the establishment of a proper village school?"

"I—"

"Now, now, Livvie. Don't tease the poor man." The reverend smiled. "I'm sure he has many other things to think of."

The conversation rambled easily, the repartee reviving memories of his time in Oxford, as the reverend's family talked of cropping, music, books, and health. If the ladies' bluestocking tendencies appeared occasionally, it only made the conversation more stimulating. Miss Ellison certainly had nothing of the insipid about *her.*

"I didn't see Bess Thatcher in church today," she said with a frown. "I imagine she was kept busy caring for her sick children."

"Very likely, m'dear," Mr. Ellison offered. "Will you visit tomorrow?"

She nodded and eyed Nicholas, "I am certain it is the inadequate housing that makes families such as the Thatchers particularly susceptible to sickness."

He lifted a shoulder. "Surely it is in the nature of some families to be sickly."

"In their nature, perhaps, when the family has lived in the same poor house for generations. But then, you sir, would not be able to imagine that, would you?"

"Now Lavinia . . ."

She ignored her father's gentle protest and lifted her chin. "I am sure it is like what is mentioned in the book of Leviticus, about leprosy in the walls. I have done some reading on the matter, and I believe there are sickness spores that can penetrate the very walls of a house. And if people are forced to live in a dark, damp, little house, what can you expect but that they will get sick often?"

He raised an eyebrow. "They could move, perhaps."

She raised both of hers. "Of course! The perfect solution." Her gaze narrowed. "And to which of their many other houses do you suggest they move?"

"I was of the belief that a good cleanse and a whitewash helped eradicate the infection."

The reverend leaned forward. "Aye, but sickness can be like sin. It doesn't matter how much you try to cover it up, it still has a way of coming out, no matter what we might do."

The Ellisons nodded, as if they'd had this conversation many times before.

"The only way to remove the problem is to demolish the old and make a new. Like our Lord said, you cannot put new wine into old wineskins . . ." The reverend nodded almost absently.

Miss Ellison gave her father an affectionate look. "Papa, we were discussing the state of the Thatchers' house and its urgent need of repair."

"Ah, but no house is in more urgent need of repair than a man's heart."

The words boomed like cannon fire. Repair a man's heart? Did Mr. Ellison refer to him? He stiffened.

"Lord Hawkesbury, please excuse me. I do not want you to feel uncomfortable."

"No, indeed." Miss Ellison's voice was soft. "Heaven forbid you feel discomfited by anything we do or say." The dimple was gone, as was the light in her eyes.

Nicholas swallowed. The meal seemed suddenly tasteless, the conversation flat, his presence obviously unwelcome.

He soon made his excuses and left, as clouds gathered in the darkening sky.

ℛ Chapter Six

Three days later, the weather had cleared sufficiently to permit travel to the village. Lavinia heaved the basket onto her arm and mentally listed the visits she must make: a visit to the apothecary for medicine to help Papa's cough—which the showers of the past two days had done nothing to alleviate—a visit to Mrs. Foster, then Eliza, and finally the Thatchers.

She sighed. If only Lord Hawkesbury would replace Johnson, then perhaps the modifications to the tenants' houses would be accomplished. Should she ask the earl directly for help? Perhaps if he visited firsthand, he would come to understand their plight.

The cherry trees, already ripe with red goodness, drew her to pick several clusters. The Thatchers would enjoy cherries, as would Eliza, although Mrs. Foster would decline, on account she always said they made her insides ache. She popped a succulent morsel into her mouth and walked along the road until the clatter of hooves made her peek over her shoulder. The earl, resplendently attired in starched neckcloth and dark coat, sat up high in his silver-gray phaeton.

She nodded as he pulled the matched pair to one side. She must remember he was forgiven. She hefted the basket higher. "Lord Hawkesbury."

"Miss Ellison." He looked around her and frowned. "No escort today?"

"As you can see."

He opened his mouth to speak but then closed it, as if he'd changed his mind.

She curtsied, and moved to walk on.

"Where are you off to on such a fine day?"

"I have several calls to make in the village."

"Would you permit me to carry your basket?" His lips drew into a half smile. "I would offer you a ride, but I gather you hold my driving to be rather poor."

"No, it is not that, sir."

"Merely you wish to avoid my company?"

"Must you persist in misunderstanding, sir? I am happy to walk."

"It is muddy underfoot. Surely you don't wish to make your visits and track muck inside."

She glanced down. Already the hem of her dress was flecked with brown.

"You may find your visits unwelcome if they necessitate your hosts cleaning up your mess."

He was right. She ignored the stab of recrimination and said, "Once again, I fail to understand why you would concern yourself with my visits."

"Ah, but we cannot have the virtuous Miss Ellison thwarted in her attempts to better the world."

Fiery words rose. She bit them back and walked on. "You are laughing at me."

"I would much prefer to laugh with you."

She glanced up. His hazel eyes watched her carefully, his lips still pulled to one side, one gloved hand holding the reins as he lounged in his seat. His tone was more lighthearted than she had heard before, yet his very attitude displayed all the arrogance she had come to expect. "Have you *no* regard for the plight of others? No desire to help?"

"Most certainly I do. That is why I am here, offering you—or at least your basket—a ride to the village."

"You are *excessively* kind."

He flicked at a speck on his coat. "One doesn't like to announce one's virtues . . ."

"But as it is a distance I am accustomed to walking most days, I must thank you, sir, but I'm—"

"Independent and unaccustomed to taking advice."

She gasped. "How dare you presume to know whether I—"

"Take advice?" He smiled wryly. "I presume only because you consistently ignore mine."

"Perhaps that's because you appear smug and condescending and—"

"Condescending!"

"And so self-important that you never for one moment think that people might have a mind of their own and might actually want to finish their own sentences!"

His eyes widened, then a smile flickered on his lips. "Touché." He laughed, instantly transforming the harsh planes of his face into something far more boyish. "Miss Ellison, please accept my sincere apologies. I had no intention on waking this morning to argue with you."

"Nor I, you."

"Please allow me to offer you—and your basket—a ride to the village."

"Thank you, my lord, but unaccompanied as I am, I'm rather afraid that accepting a ride without an attendant . . ." She paused, her cheeks warming.

"Would be considered somewhat scandalous?" His crooked brow rose. "You surprise me. I did not think you missish, but rather impervious to the opinions of others."

"My lord, I—"

"Miss Ellison, it is muddy. I am simply offering you a ride. If anyone questions that, they are miserly minded indeed." He proffered a hand. "Please, let me be of service."

She drew in a deep breath. He was attempting to be conciliatory; so should she. "Very well."

His eyes gleamed as if with victory before he reached down to assist her—and her basket—past the enormous black-spoked wheels to the top. He placed the basket on the floor as she settled herself into the seat.

"I had no idea it was so high."

He gently snapped the reins, and the bays moved along the road. "Not too high for you?"

Her fingers tightened on the side. "No, sir."

"Bravo."

"Do I detect more condescension?"

"Not at all, Miss Ellison. I would never dream of condescending to such a superior female. I am merely remarking on your courage in accepting so onerous a challenge from one such as myself."

"The challenge would scarcely be less onerous even if presented by another."

"Indeed? I *am* flattered."

She bit back laughter. "Do not consider this a huge victory, my lord."

"Only a very mild one, I assure you."

She did laugh then and glanced across to see a smile on his face.

"See? Laughing with me did not hurt, did it?"

"You, sir, seem rather fond of the ridiculous."

He nodded, his attention back on the road. "I have learned an appreciation for the ridiculous is sometimes necessary in this world."

His wry tone hinted at the pain she'd glimpsed last Sunday. Her heart softened. Perhaps there was more depth to the man than she realized.

She eased back in her seat, holding the side firmly. The hedges bloomed with wildflowers, the green hills singing of summer as they made their way down the hill. Despite the light, springy equipage, he was a smooth driver, although traveling at a much slower pace than she'd noticed him travel on previous jaunts. He carefully negotiated the curve in the road near her tree. From this height, she could almost see her sanctuary, although the bushes were creeping dense and high.

"I must speak with Johnson about the hedges."

His muttered words brought to mind her earlier ponderings. Perhaps this was an opportunity after all. "My lord, I was wishing to speak with you on a matter of importance."

"A matter of importance? I can scarcely wait to hear."

"I was hoping you might condescend to visit Mrs. Foster with me."

"I am all astonishment. For what purpose, may I ask?"

She fought to calm her voice. "You expressed an interest in the conditions of the tenant housing. The Foster house is in dire need of much attention."

"I thought you mentioned the Thatchers the other day."

"Yes, but I would not have you visit them, as they are quite unwell with influenza."

"But Miss Ellison may visit?'

"If I may say so, you, sir, do not seem terribly comfortable with children. The Thatchers have six, and I'm afraid they are not the quiet and well-behaved kind."

"That makes me afraid indeed." He glanced at her. "I only wonder that you do not fear such wild creatures."

"As you have so rightly pointed out, I am a superior female."

"A *most* superior young lady." He smiled.

Her heartbeat quickened. She pressed her lips together firmly and lifted her chin. She was being ridiculous. Lord Hawkesbury might possess a warm smile and hold a certain charm, but she refused to be beguiled. He was a colossal tease; that was all. To believe anything more was to be a vain fool. But she couldn't help notice a certain degree of disappointment mixed with relief when they reached the village's outer buildings. "Thank you, sir. You may drop me here."

"Why? To avoid the gossipmongers?" He frowned, slowing. "This is not Mrs. Foster's house."

"You know where she lives?"

He lifted a shoulder. "I have some idea."

"Mean you to visit her?"

"That is what you requested, is it not?"

"But not now. She would not be expecting you!" She touched his cloaked arm. "Please, sir. Drop me here." Too late she noticed Sophy and Perry traveling in a chaise, Sophy's eyes wide with interest, Perry's face tight with consternation. She sighed.

"I see." The earl's voice was flat. He pulled up in the middle of the village, near the tiny row of shops.

She noticed the glances they were attracting and quickly jumped down before he could move to offer her assistance. "Thank you, my lord. I have errands to run."

"Did you not wish to show me Mrs. Foster's house?"

"You truly wish to see it now?"

He shrugged. "Why not?"

"I thought you knew where she lived."

"Nevertheless, I would appreciate the introduction."

She bit her lip. If she did not assist him now, perhaps he would never find time to visit poor Mrs. Foster. "Very well. I must first attend to Papa's medication; then I will accompany you."

He nodded, and she exhaled, thankful to escape his scrutiny—and the feelings of fluster he seemed to evoke within her heart.

The sun burned hot on his neck. A large bumblebee buzzed past lazily. From his perch on the phaeton, he could see inside the small shop to Miss Ellison's discussion with the apothecary, who was now joined by a plump woman holding a tiny bundle. Miss Ellison's stiff posture—no doubt his doing—relaxed as she smiled tenderly at the tiny babe.

His heart clenched. She had guessed rightly that he did not particularly care for young children, but if he had a wife, he would want her to look exactly like that, right down to the curly golden tendril resting on her cheek.

He blinked, and glanced away, across the green to the square, gray tower of the church. He would *not* allow himself to be distracted by a mere chit of a girl. Especially such an unsuitable girl. The heat must be addling his brain. He continued a steadfast perusal of stone and mortar while the scent emanating from the basket at his feet tickled his nose.

"He's so handsome."

He turned. Miss Ellison stood next to a rosy-cheeked woman holding a bundle of blankets. She glanced up at him, her hand caressing the baby's head. "Isn't he sweet?"

"Very."

The dimple hovered; then she turned and smiled at the woman. "You must be so proud."

"Aye, we are, miss, that's to be sure."

The apothecary handed a small package to Miss Ellison. "There you go, miss." He caught sight of Nicholas and nodded. "Good day, m'lord."

"Good day." He smiled at the new parents. "My felicitations to you both."

"Thank you, m'lord."

He waited as Miss Ellison thanked the apothecary, who promised to see her at services, and offered his hand to help her into the phaeton. "May I look after your father's medication?"

"There's no need. It's not heavy."

The wariness was back. He glanced around. Faces at windows were swiftly replaced by the flutter of curtains. Ah, the joys of village life.

"Very well, Miss Ellison. Take me to meet the famous Mrs. Foster."

He drove behind the blacksmith's shop, gave the horses into the care of a youth who looked awed at the sight of such horseflesh, and followed her—and her basket—to a nearby ramshackle cottage.

An attempt had been made to prettify the outside with daisies and geraniums, but mildew was taking hold, mottling the whitewashed walls with its telltale color and odor.

Miss Ellison knocked on the door then murmured, "Every year it reappears, no matter Mrs. Foster's best efforts."

The door swung open to reveal a stooped, white-haired woman, her soft, lined face wreathed with smiles. "Miss Livvie! 'Tis lovely to see you." Dark eyes glanced over Miss Ellison's shoulder and widened dramatically. "My word! The earl hisself!"

"Mrs. Foster." He bowed.

She stepped back inside before fluttering about. "I wasn't expecting company, my liege."

His mouth twitched.

"But I can offer you some tea."

Miss Ellison frowned at him. "That won't be necessary, dear Mrs. Foster. I don't think—"

"That would be most kind, thank you." Nicholas glanced at Lavinia. "Let's see what things Miss Ellison has been cooking. It certainly smells delicious. She has tantalized me all morning."

She gasped. "You, sir, are the outside of enough!"

He smiled.

She blinked. "I did not cook for you."

"No? A thousand pities."

Mrs. Foster barely noticed the exchange, muttering to herself as she searched for teacups and matching plates.

Lavinia leaned forward as their hostess disappeared from the room. "She can barely afford to give away her tea. You should have refused."

"My dear Miss Ellison, you proposed a visit to an elderly woman's house and did *not* expect her to offer refreshment? I'm surprised."

Her cheeks pinked, but before she could speak, Mrs. Foster was back, murmuring something about a neighbor's silly daughter who had borrowed a plate for her cat.

He restrained a shudder. Still, he had survived worse on the battlefield, and to win the villagers' trust, he could not afford to be fastidious.

But apparently Miss Ellison could. "Mrs. Foster, allow me." She retrieved the offending plate and moved away, carefully wiping it with a handkerchief from her reticule. She offered him a beseeching look and resumed her seat.

As the minutes passed, tea was drunk, the delectable baked goods were consumed, and he listened to their talk of village affairs—which bored him immeasurably—until Miss Ellison noticed his barely constrained yawns and began conversing about the state of the building.

As Mrs. Foster continued her litany of complaints he exchanged glances with Miss Ellison, before offering his hostess a wry smile. "So the problem is in the walls."

"Yes, m'lord. Every spring, sure as sure, the mold reappears. Mortal nastry it be."

He nodded. "I gather Mr. Foster worked on the estate?"

"Yes. He worked the farms for nigh thirty years."

"And you have no children?"

"Only one, but he passed away, when just a wee lad."

"I'm very sorry to hear it."

Miss Ellison glanced at him, as if surprised. Did she think him incapable of feeling? But as her face softened into lines of approval, he found a growing desire to please her.

"Has Johnson been informed?"

"Yes, my liege, numbers of times. He always says he'll get to it."

"And never does," Miss Ellison murmured.

Nicholas glanced at her. "He will now."

She arched a brow. "Really? Because promises are mere words on the wind until something is actually done. And we are growing heartily sick of that man's word."

"And we all know Miss Ellison despises those who don't keep their word."

She eyed him narrowly but held her peace until it was time to take their leave.

Once outside, she frowned. "That was too bad of you, sir!"

"What? I thought I did remarkably well. Especially when she threatened to serve your lovely cake on a cat-dish! I don't believe I looked dreadfully appalled."

"No, merely horrified." She shook her head. "Imagine serving tea to an earl on a cat-dish!"

"I have no desire to imagine it. I have every intention of forgetting it."

Her gurgling laughter was quickly smothered in a sigh. "But it was truly bad of you to use up her tea-leaves. And to eat all my baked goods."

"But they were so delicious! And I found myself prodigiously hungry. It must have been the fresh air and stimulating conversation of before."

She gave him a severe look.

"Ah. How may I make it up to you?"

"I know! You should come and visit Eliza Hardy with me! Her house has rising damp and a roof problem."

"I'm afraid I might have to leave the joys of rising damp for another time. I have an appointment in Stroud this afternoon."

Her face fell.

"But I would be very much obliged if you could introduce me to your Miss Hardy tomorrow. That is, if you don't mind being seen around the village in my company."

Her chin lifted. "*My* reputation is faultless, sir."

"Let us hope it remains so." He smiled at her rising color. "Shall we say tomorrow at eleven?"

She nodded stiffly. "Thank you."

After giving brief directions as to where to meet, she said goodbye and crossed the street, basket held high, her posture unbending until she paused to speak and share smiles with an elderly couple.

His heart skipped a beat.

Quite possibly he was the world's biggest fool, or perhaps it was merely heat-affected boredom, but he couldn't help feel certain of two things. One—that yes, Miss Ellison was a most superior young lady, indeed. And two—his heart sank a little—that despite possessing such superior qualities, Miss Lavinia Ellison could never meet his mother's criteria for suitability.

🎔 Chapter Seven

Lavinia glanced at the faded young woman rocking patiently beside the fire. Eliza Hardy stitched a pair of trousers seemingly more patches than original cloth, while her own poor skills were applied in mending a vest as they both attempted to avoid the obvious.

He wasn't going to come. The church bell had already struck the half hour as both the tea and this morning's fresh baked currant scones cooled. She glanced at Eliza, her face lined with weariness—small wonder as she cared for three brothers.

Heat filled Lavinia's chest. He must have forgotten. Or, more likely, been too busy.

She forced her fingers to unclench. No, she would be gracious. He *had* been surprisingly kind yesterday with Mrs. Foster. When she had visited this morning she had learned he had gone so far as to send Mrs. Foster a large basket of tea and supplies. His generosity had put her own meager offering in the shade, so she'd kept the tea leaves she'd brought to compensate the widow and given them to Eliza instead.

Dust motes floated through the freshly scrubbed room as Lavinia attempted to think of a reason that might reflect well on the man. Perhaps an emergency had arisen. He may have succumbed to illness. Or been thrown from his horse. Surely he could not have forgotten?

She glanced across as the chair continued its rhythmic wheeze. "Eliza? Shall we have some tea?"

The lines of long-suffering grooved deeper. "He's not coming, is he?"

The resignation in Eliza's voice clogged Lavinia's throat. She peered through the dimness at the tiny knots in the mending until her voice was steadier. "Something must have prevented his coming."

Her friend nodded, busying herself with tea preparations as Lavinia finished her stitching and laid the mending aside.

Eliza's lips lifted in a ghost of a smile as she handed Lavinia her cup. "To be sure, Livvie, I thought it but a dream. An earl? Sitting in my parlor?" She waved a hand around the green-furred walls that no amount of scrubbing could ever erase. "I'm sure he had something far more important to attend to."

Indignation filled Lavinia. She took a sip, tried not to grimace at the tepid temperature. How *dare* Lord Hawkesbury forget? Had he been listening to Perry Milton, or worse, his mother? Eliza was too young to be so resigned to being ignored. He might be an earl and Eliza a poor cottager, but she was a human!

"*You* are important, Eliza." She rose and placed her teacup on the table. "And I intend to let him know."

The dark eyes, so often clouded by sorrow, seemed to lighten with amusement. "I'm sure you will."

Lavinia managed a smile and hugged her goodbye. She whistled for Mickey, who came running from playing with Eliza's brothers, and walked up the hill to the Hall.

The sun beat down as she passed the fields. Somehow she managed to nod and wave to the farm workers, but inwardly she seethed. How *dare* he forget?

She crossed the stone bridge. A hot breeze threatened to whip her bonnet from her head. She reached the bend in the road, her heart clenching as it always did until she was safely round the corner. Resentment deepened with every stride, the earl's crimes trudging across her mind.

By the time she and Mickey made it to Hampton Hall's shallow front steps, any desire to be conciliatory had quite gone. Indeed, she felt almost ready to scratch the perpetual smugness from his face.

She rapped on the heavy oak door, which was soon opened by a familiar face.

"Miss Ellison!"

"Good day, Giles. How are you?"

"Quite well, thank you, miss."

"I need to speak with Lord Hawkesbury, if you please."

If he was surprised, he didn't betray it with a single flicker of an eyelash. "I'm afraid he is not within."

"Oh." Well, at least he was not simply at home twiddling his thumbs. Her resentment eased, replaced by concern. Perhaps he had been thrown from his horse after all.

Giles cleared his throat. "I believe he is in the stables."

The *stables*? She drew in her breath, managed a polite sounding *thank you*, and stomped to the nearby stone building as the sense of injustice flared again, hot and heavy across her chest. How dare he?

She entered the large, hay-strewn room, and the vile smell of horses assailed her nose. Mickey barked and bounded up to where Lord Hawkesbury stood with McHendricks and a stranger. McHendricks leaned down to rub the dog's head, while the earl—hale, hearty, and definitely *not* sporting a broken leg—glanced down. His conversation ceased. He turned, saw her, murmured something then strode toward her.

She stepped back from the shadowed doorway into sunlight. Nobody should overhear this.

"Miss Ellison. What a pleasant surprise. To what do I owe this honor?"

His affected drawl only fueled her ire. "Did you forget something today, my lord?"

"Judging from the icy tone, I gather I did, but I confess I'm at a loss."

"You, sir, had an appointment this morning."

His crooked eyebrow lifted. "Yes, with my stable man here. We are improving the stables—"

"Your *stable* man? You ignore poor Eliza Hardy because you wish to beautify your *horse* accommodation?"

The other brow lifted. "It would appear so."

"How could you?" Her fists clenched. "Poor Eliza's cottage is falling down, and you care more about horses than people!"

"Miss Ellison, control yourself, please."

"Oh. Am I not docile enough for you to understand?"

"I understand you perfectly well. And no, you are not docile. At this moment you rather remind me of a bull, all quivering and red."

She gasped. "And you, sir, remind me of a puffed-up peacock, mere pride and showy feathers!"

His eyes grew hard. "Miss Ellison, if you cannot be civil—"

"Civil? Is it civil to ignore a poor girl whom you promised to visit today? She cleaned and cooked for you and was so disappointed when you failed to show—"

"Was she?" His eyes gleamed. "Or were you?"

Anger filled her until she could scarcely speak. "You have an obligation to help the poor!"

"The poor, the poor." He waved a hand. "Even your father says we will always have the poor with us."

She blinked. He listened to her father's sermons? She shook her head, drew herself up to her full height. "The tenant housing is still your responsibility."

"A fact you remind me of almost daily."

"Which I wouldn't have to do, if you or that wretched steward of yours actually did something—anything—to alleviate the situation!"

Her breath came unevenly. Mickey circled her, barking at her upset.

"Have you quite finished, Miss Ellison?" He flicked a speck of dust from his sleeve and glanced at her. His look was cool, bored even.

She blinked away angry tears. "You are not a man of your word!"

His eyes flickered then he bowed. "Thank you for reminding me of my sins."

She gasped, whirled around, and stamped across the gravel, almost tripping over the still barking Mickey in her haste to flee.

Useless, flippant, arrogant, *stupid* man!

She hurried down the drive, desperate to run, except her skirts would only cause her to stumble, and there was only so much humiliation she could endure today.

Uncaring, selfish, horse-mad man! She was *glad* to remind him of his sins!

She exited the iron gates and crossed the road, down to where the cherry trees marked the drive. Condescending, *insufferable* man.

His words rippled across her mind, and her pace slowed.

He might be condescending, but . . . she was supposed to remind people of God's love, not their sins.

Her steps grew slower still. How would someone like the earl ever know about God's love if all they heard was badgering and nagging?

She stilled. Was the earl correct in identifying her pride as being more piqued than Eliza herself had been? Her shoulders slumped, and she crossed the parsonage threshold dragging her feet.

Nicholas stared at the flames flickering in the drawing room fireplace. He sunk in his seat, one hand grasping a brandy glass, as the episode of three days ago continued to trek across his mind.

The look of shock on her face. The almost childish temper she displayed. The tears.

Tears that signaled her disappointment in him—*that* was the rub. He could stand almost anything but her disappointment. And this only a day after he had finally felt hopeful of eventually gaining a smile from the elusive Miss Ellison.

For elusive she remained.

She wasn't home when he had called at the parsonage. He'd been forced to endure her father's platitudes and Miss West's hard stare—which made him wonder just how much her niece had shared—and kept his apology in his pocket. He hadn't encountered her traipsing down the hill to the village, hat in hand, basket in the other, although one time he could've sworn he'd heard that wretched dog of hers. He even thought he'd glimpsed her golden head down near the tall oak at the curl in the road, but it must have only been leaves caught in the hedge.

His brow lowered. He hadn't seen her at all today in church. He supposed she was out with her blessed poor children. He shook his head. Why *did* she care so much? She certainly didn't care about him.

He sipped his brandy as the wood crackled and hissed. He hoped she wasn't sick. Her constant ministering to the poor would make her susceptible to all kinds of diseases, although she never seemed unwell: quite the opposite, in fact. Almost in rude health—certainly nothing of the fainting miss about *her*.

Miss Lavinia Ellison: she of the outlandish name and outspoken ways and glorious singing voice. He frowned. Was that voice merely a figment of his imagination, too?

"M'lord? Can I get you anything?"

"Thank you, Giles, but I am quite satisfied."

Another lie.

He barely noticed his butler's faint good-night and exit as the heavy discontent pressed in again. Everything was too hard. Nothing satisfied. Even Mr. Ellison's sermons only tugged at his heart momentarily, lifting his spirits with promises that proved empty. Inside, he felt much the same. Hard. Cold. Disappointed. Purposeless. Guilty. Lost.

He swirled the amber liquid then swallowed the remainder. Pulled a face.

Nothing was working out.

He would fire Johnson if only he had a replacement, but he didn't want to stay to hire a new man. He scrubbed a hand over his face. What difference would a few weeks or months make, anyway? The harvest would be taken in, as it had for hundreds of years. People would continue living, dying, giving birth, just as they had before he had entered the neighborhood.

He would not be missed.

Perhaps it was time he left. He nodded. Retreat sometimes proved to be the better part of valor. Blast these rustics. Blast this place.

He had almost started to . . . care.

CHAPTER EIGHT

LONG DAYS MELDED into long weeks of sunshine. The barley was brought in, a surprisingly good harvest, ensuring the stock would eat well this winter. The new crop was planted. The sun shone, rain fell, grass grew, the apple trees rounded, the lettuces plumped.

Everything was just as it had always been, only slightly . . . different.

Lavinia pulled at the cow parsley polluting her flowerbeds. The slim stems with dainty white flowers looked innocent enough, but they had a nasty way of dropping seeds and infesting the plot. She swiped the moisture on her brow and resumed her reflections.

Johnson continued with his smirks and high-handedness. Perry continued with his flattery and flirtations. Sophia continued confiding about her latest beaus. Aunt Patience continued on the evils of the aristocracy. Her father continued preaching love and forgiveness. And Lavinia continued to ignore the hurt in her heart and the disappointment in her soul.

"Miss Ellison?"

She squinted up at the distraction: Mr. Simon Raymond, the curate up from Bristol to assist her father, who had still not completely recovered from his nasty cough. "Yes?"

"I, er, hesitate to question a lady's good judgment, but I cannot help but wonder whether your aunt and dear father would, er, approve of your industrious actions in the garden."

"Mr. Raymond," she smiled sweetly, "your scruples are commendable, your reluctance to share them most admirable."

He stared at her blankly.

She swallowed a sigh, rose, and dusted off her hands. "Mr. Raymond, do you remain because you wish to assist me?" She gestured at the flowerbed. "Weeds do not remove themselves."

"I, er—" He flushed. "Sadly, I must confess to a lack of appropriate attire for such a venture."

"That *is* sad. Well, let me not keep you from your sermon preparation."

"I, er, thank you, Miss Ellison. Pray do not allow yourself to become too sunburned."

"Thank you, Mr. Raymond, for your concern. I will endeavor to be sunburned just the right amount."

His brows knit in confusion as he reiterated his farewell and made his exit.

She shook her head and resumed digging. No wonder Aunt Patience called him a wet goose. He might be bookish, possess obsequious manners, and love the church, but his wit was sadly lacking, which provided plenty of fuel for her aunt's sense of humor—and her own.

But despite his awkward attempts at gallantry, it was rather nice to be told she was pretty, and her voice was lovely, rather than be the object of sneers, enigmatic smiles, and allusions, and being made to feel she was in the wrong all the time. *Sometimes* in the wrong, she would happily own, but all the time? Never.

She frowned. Her failure to convince the earl of his responsibilities continued to stalk her, striking most poignantly at that time between wake and sleep, when fancy danced and imagination was at its most alluring. What *could* she have said to convince him? What should she have left unsaid? Every time she saw or spoke to Eliza, or Mrs. Foster, or the Thatchers, she felt sick, shivery with the shame of failure. She almost wanted to avoid them, preferring this silent garden to the self-reproach she experienced with others and the underlying fear that if only she'd left well enough alone the earl may have—by God's grace—done the right thing.

She dug savagely at the roots. Perhaps selfishness lived at his core, and he was unable to care beyond his immediate needs and wants—what then?

But—a little voice whispered—look what he did about Mrs. Foster's tea. And to his credit, he *had* spoken to Eliza regarding his nonappearance. When Eliza had mentioned that during Sunday school, surprise had rendered Lavinia speechless for almost a full minute. Eliza had said he'd been most gracious, promising something would be done about removing them to a new cottage as soon as possible.

The heaviness descended again. That indeed was the problem. He had done nothing but offer empty words, because the cottages remained unfixed. He contained nothing of substance, nothing anyone could pin their hopes on. He believed nothing, stood for nothing, and—despite a tickling fancy that he was most definitely *not* a wet goose—he must remain nothing to her.

Which he most definitely would!

A VISIT FROM Sophia two days later provided diversion from the visiting and household chores that constituted Lavinia's daily routines. A proposed dinner at the Miltons to celebrate Sophia's birthday had grown into quite an affair, with the addition of several of Perry Milton's university chums. Sophia was most excited, having been to Cheltenham with her mother to acquire fresh silks for new gowns.

She showed Lavinia her pretty lace gloves and dancing slippers made of Denmark satin. "For Mama insists we have dancing!"

"You will enjoy that."

"Oh, yes, but so must you!"

Lavinia pressed her lips together. Dancing rated only slightly higher than embroidery on the scale of enjoyment.

"Livvie," Sophy's brow puckered. "You have seemed a trifle out of sorts of late."

"Have I?"

"I mean no offense, but are you quite well?"

"Yes, thank you."

"Hmmm. Perhaps it is the effect of all those visits to the poor."

"Sophy, I—"

"Regardless, dancing will be just the thing!" She smiled suggestively. "Mr. Raymond can come, too. And your aunt, of course."

"You know Papa does not really approve of such things."

"Then we must ask him."

And Sophy—for once, decisive—almost dragged her to Papa's study, where her smiles and cajoling won his permission for Lavinia to partake in the dancing.

That night at the dinner table, Lavinia was surprised even by Aunt Patience's ready acquiescence.

"It will do you good. You cannot stay moping around inside here."

"Moping?" Her father's brows knit. "Why would Lavinia be moping?"

"I have *not* been moping, Papa."

Her aunt raised a skeptical brow. "You have not been yourself for weeks. It will do you good to be out among new faces and get some color into those cheeks."

ONE WEEK LATER, wearing her one (freshly made over) gown appropriate for dancing, her aunt's loaned pearl necklace, and dancing slippers, she waved farewell to Papa as Mr. Raymond helped Aunt Patience and Lavinia into his gig and drove them to Sophia's.

"I must confess to being quite taken aback at your beauty tonight, Miss Ellison."

Lavinia smiled at the backhanded compliment. "You are too kind, sir."

"Not at all. To be able to travel with two such lovely ladies is a pleasure indeed."

As Mr. Raymond's compliments continued she was almost inclined to believe he actually meant what he said. But for all of that, something about him just did not sit right.

When they arrived, Lady Milton eyed Lavinia's gown doubtfully, her countenance hardening even more as she offered a stiff nod in the receiving line. "Patience. Mr. Raymond. Lavinia."

"Cornelia."

"Er, good evening, Lady Milton. You must allow me to extend my gratitude at the inclusion of someone so humble as myself to such a, er, wonderful event as this evening." Mr. Raymond bowed over the hand of his hostess.

"Thank you, Mr. Raymond. You are *most* welcome."

Lavinia smiled at both her hosts. "How is Sophia? She must be so excited and no doubt prettier than any picture!"

The harsh gaze softened fractionally. "She looks well enough."

"Well enough?" Sir Anthony's booming laugh echoed around the room. "She's the prettiest girl here." He winked at Lavinia. "Even including yourself, my dear."

"I am very glad to hear it, for then all is as it should be."

As they moved toward the drawing room, Mr. Raymond murmured, "Perhaps he does not see very well. I am convinced there could be no prettier young lady here tonight than *you*, Miss Ellison."

She resisted the urge to wipe her ear. "Do you not think it appropriate for a father to praise his daughter? Or do you think me so poor-spirited that I cannot bear to hear another praised? It is well known that Sophia Milton is the most beautiful girl in these parts."

"Miss Ellison"—he bowed—"I would never disagree with you."

She stared at him. *That* was his problem. He never did disagree, so she never knew what his real intentions or thoughts were on any topic.

Her aunt chuckled. "Well may Sir Anthony praise his daughter's fine looks—she has little else to offer."

"Aunt!"

"There's no need to look scandalized, my dear. Everyone knows it, except her parents, of course."

Lavinia glanced across the drawing room to where Sophia stood under the costly chandelier Lady Milton had recently installed. It cast a golden glow over her daughter who smiled and flirted with several young men. Truly, Sophy was the belle of the ball.

Mr. Raymond murmured something about procuring refreshments and disappeared, leaving them watching the clusters of conversations and gaiety from the room's perimeter.

An unaccustomed loneliness trickled across her sanguine mood. She bit her lip. Is that what men wanted? Someone who merely smiled and looked decorative? Who kept house, and bore children, and never thought an independent thought in her life?

Sophia's tinkling laugh carried across the general hubbub of the room as she gazed up at a handsome young man.

"Sophia's certainly not in want of admirers."

Her aunt's dark blue eyes held shrewdness. "Do you really want admirers, Lavinia?"

She swallowed.

A figure emerged from the crowd, his face wreathed in smiles. "Miss Ellison, you look positively radiant!"

As Perry Milton kissed her gloved hand, Lavinia's gaze connected with her aunt's and she laughed. "No, I don't believe I do."

St. Hampton Heath still lay snug below the quiet hills. The barley was cut now, the fields fresh sown with new crops. Summer would soon draw to a close and the leaves would start to turn.

Two months had passed. Two months in London, at his clubs, at parties and dinners, where the talk bored, the flirtations wearied, and the pretensions disgusted. Time at Hawkesbury House had not been much better. The House had never felt like home, and his mother's airs and graces proved an irritant, her flagrant waste of money an abomination.

He'd tried to curb some of her excesses, insisting she did not need another water feature in the rose lawn, but her wide-eyed offense was too much, so he'd made his excuses and scuttled back to town. *Brave* man that he was—beaten by a woman. In London, he'd met up with Captain Matthew Thornton. The second son of Viscount Astley was a faithful and true friend. His bravery and practical common sense had proved invaluable during the campaigns; his supportive understanding upon the deaths of Nicholas's father and brother, one of the few buoying factors of recent years. During a particularly dull evening at White's, he'd even convinced Nicholas that he'd like nothing better than to visit Gloucestershire, a part of England he had never seen.

Nicholas glanced across at his friend: broad shouldered, lightly tanned, bright eyed with perpetual enthusiasm, he carried himself with a confidence that belied his twenty-seven years. Perhaps Thornton's fresh eyes might even provide some suggestions for how to deal with his problems in St. Hampton Heath. His *estate* problems. Not any other problem—even if the problematic young woman in question had barely left his thoughts these past weeks.

Fool that he was.

The church bells pealed their summons for services. Nicholas glanced across at his friend, wishing he wasn't quite so pious that he needed to make attending church the priority for the first day of his return. But perhaps that piety was what made his actions so very trustworthy. Thornton reminded him of the Ellisons: a concern for others, a solid reliability, and an ability to keep his word.

He frowned. Perhaps in Thornton, Miss Ellison might find a man she could approve.

"I MUST CONFESS I enjoyed that service. The reverend is knowledgeable, yet able to communicate truths so simply. Did you not think so, Stamford?"

"He seems to have improved of late," Nicholas muttered.

"The music was very fine. I'm sure I've not heard better in a country church before."

Nicholas tapped Midnight, and his horse cantered up the road.

"Yes, I find this a very agreeable part of the country."

"I find it so, too." For despite everything, Nicholas was glad to be back. Something akin to ease had settled in his heart the moment he had entered his gates. Ease, mixed with an underlying anticipation.

"And so many charming young girls!"

Nicholas frowned. "Charming young girl" did not fit any of the ladies he was acquainted with here. The squire's daughter was tolerably pretty but rather witless.

"I had a very pleasant chat with Miss Milton. The other pretty one I did not meet, but she knew you." Thornton glanced across. "Come now. You saw her sitting in the front row, with hair the color of a guinea, and such a lovely smile. She nodded to you. I had hopes of an introduction, but she disappeared at the end. Who is she?"

He'd ceased thinking about Miss Ellison as a young girl, memories of her insistence at not being a green girl ringing firmly in his ears. "Miss Ellison, the reverend's daughter."

"Aha. That accounts for it."

Nicholas raised an eyebrow.

Thornton laughed. "Major Stamford has never been able to resist a challenge."

"This is not the Peninsular—"

"Thank God!"

"And I *can* now."

They cantered in silence for a few moments, the thudding of hooves re-iterating the drumming disappointment in his heart.

"She seems very lovely." Thornton eyed him keenly.

"She holds no interest for me." He had none whatsoever in a girl who continually rebuffed him. Lovely and innocent she might be, but apart from that one cool nod she had resolutely fixed her attention elsewhere—although she'd been quick to dimple a smile to welcome his guest. "None whatsoever."

"Yes. I'm sure she doesn't." Thornton's dry tone belied his words.

Nicholas snapped the reins. "She dislikes me."

"Methinks thou doth protest too much."

"Seeing as you have such an interest in the young miss, perhaps we should invite her to dinner," he drawled.

Thornton grinned. "I'd like that very much, indeed!"

And Nicholas plunged his heels into Midnight's flanks, leaving Thornton and his disconcerting amusement behind.

71

🎋 Chapter Nine

FIVE DAYS LATER, Nicholas was playing reluctant host to an innumerable number of awed guests. His elderly cousin Maria Pettigrew was staying from Bath, to play equally awed hostess—her presence necessary, because otherwise he suspected Lady Milton would take it upon herself to assume that role. The Miltons, the Winthrops, the Ellisons, Dr. Hanbury, along with several other gentry and notable families from surrounding districts had somehow all managed to cancel whatever other engagements they might have had in order to attend his first dinner party.

While the room's gilt-edged moldings were not exactly his taste, being a relic from before Uncle Robert's time, the reception rooms were somewhat spectacular, well worthy of the hush of appreciation as his guests stepped inside. His housekeeper, Mrs. Florrick, had completed a remarkable trans-formation, employing a veritable army to remove dustcovers, polish brass and mirrors, and iron a multitude of linen. He and Thornton had dodged so many maids and footmen these past few days, he was thankful no house parties would ever be held here. He grimaced. A house party? Perish the thought.

He moved closer to Mr. Ellison, who was studying the highly decorated ceiling.

The reverend smiled genially. "Ah, our host. I visited your uncle many times in this room. I do not recall seeing it quite so beautiful."

"Uncle Robert preferred this drawing room and the library above all."

"Yes, I remember." The gray eyes studied him. "We are glad you have chosen to return, my lord."

We? His heart lifted. Did he mean—? No. He battled the agitation pro-voked by one word as the reverend continued his steady perusal. How much *did* the man see? He swallowed. "I hope you will avail yourself of the library should you desire. Nothing has changed since my uncle's time."

"Thank you, my lord. That is very kind."

"You are most welcome. Uncle Robert had so many treasures, and I am continually finding more. I don't believe he ever rid himself of anything."

"When we get older, we cling to the memories of our youth."

He fought the curling lip that would reveal too much of his thoughts on that subject. Men clung to memories only when they were good.

The reverend offered another searching look before inclining his head. "I seem to remember he had some rather interesting maps of the Antipodes?"

"I'm afraid I will need to hunt for them. I have not had time—"

"I understand. You have been busy with other matters."

"Excuse me. Lord Hawkesbury?" Lady Winthrop beamed up at him, next to her slightly horsey-faced daughter.

Nicholas bit back a sigh, bowed to an amused Mr. Ellison, and braced himself to engage in light banalities with the other guests.

In between ensuring the good graces of Lady Milton—assuring her that yes, Sophia was as pretty as a daffodil—and Lady Winthrop—from the *Avebury* Winthrops, he'd been made to understand—he'd barely had a moment to appreciate his other, younger guests. Apart from a cool greeting at the door, where Miss Ellison's eyes met his for the briefest moment, she had certainly stayed away, hugging the room's boundary as she talked with Sophia and Catherine, her aunt, Sir Anthony, and Thornton.

Envy spiked his chest. Any doubt about her preference had been shot to smithereens the moment she was introduced to his guest, Thornton, the recipient of the warmest smile he had yet seen her give. Since then, they'd been almost inseparable, laughing and chatting like long-lost friends. Every time Nicholas ventured near she seemed to find reason to move away. Elusive as always.

At the dinner table, he had occasion to study her as Lady Winthrop engaged in a limp battle of wits with Lady Milton. If Sophia Milton was a daffodil, all showy gold in her yellow gown, Miss Ellison was like an apri-cot rose, dew-frosted in the dawn. Her dress was old-fashioned, creamy ruffles encasing glowing skin. She laughed at something Thornton said, that dimple peeping once more as she smiled a brilliant smile she'd never offered him. His heart dipped.

He picked up his wine glass, swallowed the remaining claret, and continued his surreptitious perusal. The single strand of pearls gleamed at her throat as her head tilted once more. She shifted slightly, her smile fading as she caught his gaze. He lifted his glass.

A faint rose stained her cheeks before she dipped her chin and glanced away.

His chest tightened. He remembered her as being too independent, too untidy, too perceptive. But tonight the hair that usually ran rampant was neatly tied, and so far she'd curbed her wild opinions and was playing the part of a proper young lady surprisingly well. If he thought he caught the glimmer of a smile or the flash in her eyes at some particularly prosy conversation from the witless Miltons and Winthrops, it was gone so suddenly he was unsure if it was just his imagination.

The mild behavior continued after dinner when they joined the ladies in the great saloon. After mediocre performances from Miss Milton and Miss Winthrop, Miss Ellison was persuaded to play, and once more he was entranced by her lovely voice.

Casting a sideways glance at Thornton, he was perturbed at his expression. Good God, the man looked like he'd seen an angel! He stifled a groan. He didn't need his best friend besotted with a woman who would only bring trouble.

Thornton leaned over and whispered, "She is astounding!"

"So it would appear."

"Come on, man. You must admit she has prodigious talent!"

He shrugged. "She has talent, I admit, but one need not gape like a fishwife."

The captain snorted and pushed back his chair. "Miss Ellison, may I assist you?"

"Why, thank you, kind sir."

The reverend's daughter smiled prettily at his friend, who grinned in return.

And Nicholas was left with a disquieting sense of loss.

CAROLYN MILLER

The viridian leaves of high summer had faded to a softer hue. Lavinia stretched out beneath the oak tree's branches, studied the cloud wisps above, and smiled.

Now *there* was a man. The captain might be the earl's friend, but he held *true* goodness, whereas the other man held it only in his appearance. Last night had proved it all the more. One man had been open and easy, warm in his interest; the other cool and inscrutable, more interested in talking with the titled guests than those without. Not that she minded, of course.

A wet nose and rough red tongue pushed into her face. "Mickey!"

Her laughter caught as she rubbed the faithful dog's head. He was growing old, nearly fifteen years, and didn't move as he once had. She could not bear to think what life would be like when the dog finally no longer trotted beside her. But the trusting eyes still beseeched, and she pulled him close and hugged him tight.

"I think you'd like Captain Thornton, sweet boy."

His ears pricked.

"*He* wouldn't call you a *thing*." She rubbed his belly, and he slowly wriggled in low ecstatic moans. "He's kind and personable, happy to talk with everyone, not just those who appear socially expedient. And he told *such* interesting stories of life in London and abroad."

She rubbed the top of his head, a circular movement a local midwife had taught her, that induced sleep in babies—and canines. "I think he might be a believer, too."

She'd noticed him that first Sunday. It had been hard not to, when he'd accompanied the earl on his surprise return to St. Hampton Heath. Two tall, lean men, whose erect carriage marked their previous military occupations. And while he might not have the chiseled features of his friend, his open countenance and ready laugh appealed far more. As had his willingness to sing the hymns, a clear baritone she appreciated for its tone as well as for its sure melody. And his rapt attention as her father preached contrasted mightily with the man beside him, whose bored expression had only changed when she'd mistakenly caught his eye and been forced to nod from sheer politeness. No. The captain was *far* more appealing.

75

She pulled out her sketchbook and tried to capture his likeness.

Half an hour later, still unable to remember whether his eyes were Prussian blue or something less bold, she packed away her sketchbook, woke a snoring Mickey, and made her way through the hedge back onto the road. She had only taken a few steps when the pounding of hooves rumbled up the hill.

She pressed against the hedge, basket in one hand, Mickey in the other, as she fought to stifle the old fear. Two horsemen appeared around the corner, and Mickey broke from her grasp, barking.

The horses shied, their whinnies mingling with their riders' mutters—and the earl's soft curse—to create a cacophony of confusion. Mickey continued barking as the horses, now under control, moved nervously.

"Mickey!" Heedless of the horses she moved forward to drag her dog away.

"Miss Ellison."

She glanced up at the drawling voice. "Lord Hawkesbury."

"I trust you will keep that pesky thing under better control next time."

Heat filled her cheeks. "And *I* trust you will get these hedges trimmed, so innocent pedestrians will not be run down!"

His face blanched, and he offered a slight nod and moved his black horse away.

She pushed wisps of hair from her forehead. Did he think she referred to the incident of fourteen years ago? Remorse twisted her insides.

"Good day, Miss Ellison." Captain Thornton dismounted and smiled. "I am very happy to see you."

"And I you." Her heart lifted at the regard in his eyes.

He bent to rub Mickey's head, which put an end to the barking. "I had a beagle when I was a boy. Beautiful dogs, with a lovely nature."

"Mickey has been a very faithful friend these many years."

"Animals can be, can't they? Kinder than us humans."

She resisted glancing at the earl. "We underestimate their loyalty."

"Miss Ellison, you surprise me."

She did look up at him then, still sitting high and mighty on his horse. "Pardon?"

"You once gave the impression you value humans of infinite significance over mere animals."

Her fingers clenched. She battled for moderation in her voice. "I believe humans are of greater significance. After all, the Bible talks of God desiring relationship with people, not animals." She turned from his cold eyes and smiled warmly at the captain. "I *do* hope you will come for a visit soon."

"Nothing would please me more."

He walked her to the drive and then insisted on accompanying her to the house, ensuring she was safe—like a true gentleman ought.

It was only much later—as she recalled every word of his conversation, remembered the timbre of his laughter, and decided his eyes were most definitely Prussian blue—that she realized: she hadn't missed his friend at all.

With the evening reception out of the way, Nicholas's responsibilities concerning the estate once again grew heavy around his neck. Johnson remained as smooth as ever, presenting figures that suggested all was well, but still something did not sit well. Coupled with this was the uncomfortable feeling that he was growing old, hinted at with the cooler nights that caused the bullet wound in his thigh to ache, but perhaps suggested more in the way Thornton and Lavinia spent so much time together.

He fingered his water glass at the Ellisons' dinner table. No doubt his invitation for dinner tonight had been a mere politeness, extended because of his relationship with his far more favored guest. The meal had been tasty, and the lively discussion about books Nicholas had never read but Thornton had was swiftly followed by Thornton's exchange of favorite biblical texts with Lavinia while her aunt and father looked on fondly. As the witticisms had flown across the table, he had started to feel almost as aged as Mr. Ellison, watching mildly from the side, nodding occasionally to seem interested.

Which was preposterous. Thornton was only two years his junior, and Lavinia's aunt must be at least a good five years his senior. But the smiles and laughter and sparkle the others shared made him feel very old indeed.

While Lavinia's words were all that was polite, her refusal to look him in the eyes only seemed to enlarge the hollow spaces of his heart. Too much time had passed since that encounter by his stables. He wished mightily that he had apologized for his high-handedness before he had left for London. Her fixed aversion seemed an insurmountable barrier.

"Nick? What say you?"

He looked up. The entire table faced him enquiringly.

"Lord Hawkesbury, do we bore you?" Miss Ellison's brows arched. "You have been very quiet."

Thornton smiled. "Perhaps he is thinking on his new stables."

"Oh. Of course." The light in her eyes drained away, replaced with something like disappointment before she averted her face. Again.

His cheeks grew hot as Thornton expounded on the plans they'd discussed yesterday.

"You will have to come riding with us! Nick was considered the finest seat in the regiment, and nothing is better than exploring the countryside on horseback. He has a lovely mare that would suit you admirably. What do you say, Miss Ellison?"

Nicholas watched her, sure of her answer.

"Thank you, but I do not care for horses."

"Ah. Then perhaps we could explore the countryside another way."

"There are several good walks and vantage points not too far away."

"Marvelous! We should make a party of it. Invite your friend, Miss Milton, along. And Miss West, of course."

"Of course." Miss West spoke drily, but her eyes were full of approval as she gazed at the two fair heads discussing their picnic plans.

He wondered what Thornton's intentions were. The second son of a viscount who was widely known to have mortgaged his estates up to the hilt, Thornton was expected to have to marry extremely well in order to live in the manner to which he had been accustomed as a child.

But then, material possessions and matters of estates had never mattered terribly significantly to him. Thornton was like Miss Ellison in that regard. People, ideas, and *God* seemed to weigh far more with the pair of them.

The pair of them.

His heart plunged deeper.

🕮 Chapter Ten

The picnic day dawned bright and sunny. Nicholas was tempted to leave Thornton to the fair charms of the young ladies but his friend would hear none of it.

"You are becoming dull, Stamford."

"But the estate—"

"Will still be here tomorrow. Come, man. I must insist you come."

So with great reluctance Nicholas joined the excursion, meeting the others at the lane behind the Miltons'. Peregrine and Sophia Milton stood chatting with Lavinia and Miss West. When they arrived, he couldn't help but notice he received only the most cursory of greetings compared to the fawning welcome Thornton received.

"Captain Thornton! We are *ever* so glad you are here." Sophia glanced his direction. "Oh, and you too, my lord."

"Thank you," he said wryly, catching the glimmer of a smile on Miss Ellison's lips before Perry Milton reclaimed her attention. He returned his focus to Thornton's conversation with Sophia.

"Miss Milton, how lovely you look."

Sophia blushed. "Thank you, sir."

Nicholas raised an eyebrow at Thornton, who after his usual warm greeting had barely given Lavinia a second glance. Strange behavior from their previous meeting—and, judging from the pucker in her brow, Lavinia didn't understand it either.

"Sophy, are you quite finished?" Perry said. "Come on! Let's not waste the entire day."

A short walk up the lane led to a stile through which a tract of birch and elm nestled thickly on the hillside. After refusing assistance from Perry to cross the stile, Lavinia kept an energetic pace that soon left Sophia struggling behind, with Thornton and Miss West.

Nicholas trudged up the hill, trailing Perry Milton, who followed Lavinia like a lost pup.

"I say, Livvie, must you keep up such a cracking pace? The others are far behind."

She shot a scornful glance at Perry. "I cannot help it if the others are slow."

A few minutes later, it was, "Livvie, allow me."

"Perry, I do not require your assistance. I am quite capable of doing it myself."

Nicholas smiled. Apparently the tramp in the woods wasn't living up to everyone's expectations.

He trudged on, careful not to get too close to Miss Ellison's line of fire. His thigh protested the climb as he mounted the roughly hewn stone steps to the rocky peak.

There was another low murmur, then, "Perry, please don't carry on. This is growing extremely tiresome."

"You let Thornton say such things."

"Captain Thornton is a gentleman and treats a lady with the greatest of civility."

"But Livvie—"

"Mr. Milton." Nicholas rounded a tall rock to make his appearance. "Miss Ellison."

"Lord Hawkesbury." Her tone was icy, as was the look in her eyes before she turned to observe the view.

He faced the flushed boy. "I trust you are aware your conversation can be overheard."

"I trust, my lord, that *you* are aware it is impolite to listen to such conversations!"

"If you must insist on paying tiresome compliments to a lady who has no wish to hear them, then may I suggest you do so more privately."

He glanced at Miss Ellison. A dimple lurked near her mouth, but her profile remained steadfast. "Now Miss Ellison has the right idea. The view here is remarkable."

Perry grumbled something and moved away.

Nicholas moved closer to her. "I do not think he fully appreciates such charming pastoral scenes."

"I did not think you would either."

"You might be surprised at what I find charming."

Her lips pressed together.

He laughed. "Bravo, Miss Ellison. I applaud your self-control."

"You, my lord, are insufferable!"

"Livvie"—Perry's plaintive voice reached them—"come and look at the view here!"

He glanced at her clenched hands. "But perhaps not as insufferable as some?"

Her laughter spurted but then concluded with a sigh. "I don't know why he had to come."

"No? I would have thought it obvious."

The color rose in her cheeks.

"Your delightful company aside, I am sure her ladyship sent her son to chaperone her daughter."

"Then he *should* chaperone her. I don't know why she had to wear such silly shoes for walking. She's making everybody late."

"The view will still be here when *everybody* arrives."

She turned away.

"Do not blame your friend for her mother's ambition."

"I do not. Sophia is a sweet girl—"

"With a protective parent who only desires to see her daughter well situated."

"I know." Her shoulders slumped.

"Thornton is the best of fellows, but his prospects are not as promising as some."

"Meaning yourself, I suppose?"

He held his peace as her chin took on a mutinous tilt.

"Money is not everything, my lord!"

"But it tends to be to hopeful mamas."

She paused, lips pursed, before muttering, "Lady Milton does very little that does not suit her."

"Now, now, Miss Ellison. It is not very charitable of you to notice such shortcomings in others."

"And I must always be charitable, mustn't I?"

The edge in her tone caught him by surprise. He stepped closer, but her look quelled further advance.

"I may sound uncharitable, but we hold fewer pretensions in the country, Lord Hawkesbury. Perhaps we are just more honest than those who hide who they truly are. That is yet another benefit of living in a small village; we know each other, often only too well."

"Benefit indeed."

Her gaze narrowed. "Yet despite our faults, we still accept each other with affection."

"Really? Because from where I stand, you seem to see a lot of my faults, without showing much acceptance, much less affection."

"Are you saying you desire my affection?"

His heart skipped a beat. He cleared his throat. "Let us not get carried away, Miss Ellison." She flushed. "I would, however, appreciate at least a cease-fire in the hostilities."

She glanced away, controlling her temper with a visible effort.

He took pity on her. "Perhaps I—"

"Before you say anything, I am well aware of my own faults, sir."

"Like a certain propensity to leap to conclusions?"

"You don't need to enumerate my failings." Her shoulders slumped. "We both know how extensive a list of my faults would be."

Before he could contradict, she moved away, the moaning complaints of the remaining party announced their arrival, and once again the moment for reconciliation was lost.

LADY MILTON WAS not to be underestimated. Not content with picnics or merely promoting her daughter, she had apparently mounted a campaign to rival that of Wellington's, devising an offensive to propel her daughter into the path of eligible men, at the expense of others.

CAROLYN MILLER

Nicholas realized this during a particularly insipid dinner at the Miltons'. Surprised at the few guests, he was made even more so by the absence of Sophia's particular friend.

He glanced across a table groaning with delicacies. "Lady Milton, could you please enlighten me? Are the Ellisons unwell?"

She colored. "I'm sure I do not know."

"Mr. Ellison has a slight cold, my lord," Sophia offered with a pretty smile. "Lavinia says he gets a trifle run down at times. Probably from all those visits they make."

Nicholas watched her from under hooded eyes. For all her soft prettiness, sometimes the squire's daughter reminded him of a gilded gong Uncle Robert had brought back from his travels: although delicately inscribed with oriental decorations, the noise it produced was a harsh clang. He had always much preferred the plainer brass one, which commanded a rich resonance.

Thornton smiled. "You are good friends with the reverend's daughter, Miss Milton?"

"Livvie and I have been friends since we were in leading strings."

"Perhaps you might help clear up a mystery about her. I wondered—"

"A mystery?" Lady Milton interrupted, frowning. "There is no mystery as far as Lavinia is concerned. I have always found her to be remarkably, indeed, almost overly forthright."

Nicholas exchanged glances with Thornton over the top of his wine glass. So Lady Milton had claws . . .

He leaned back in his chair, eying his hostess. "Miss Ellison *is* refreshingly candid."

"Shockingly candid, more like." She sniffed. "I have always found her to be far too independent and unwilling to accept the merest suggestion regarding genteel behavior."

"Indeed." He strove for a nonchalance he did not feel, his heart stinging as Lady Milton's comment echoed his past words to Lavinia.

"She treats people in such a high-handed manner! Unlike my sweet girl, here."

Nicholas lowered his eyelids, covertly studying the woman whose lips were loosened by a potent mix of wine and jealousy.

The squire cleared his throat. "Come, come, Nellie. She has proved to be a good friend to our Sophy."

"And she seems quite a good friend to many in the village," Nicholas murmured.

Lady Milton's gaze sharpened. He met her look blithely.

"That's right," Sir Anthony frowned. "Lavinia is always visiting and helping the poor, taking meals to the sick in her basket."

"So that's what her basket contains." Thornton nodded. "Mystery solved."

"But she's forever disappearing to goodness knows where! The number of times I've called at the parsonage and she's been unavailable."

Nicholas bit back a smile. He understood perfectly why Lavinia would not choose to linger with Lady Milton's barbed kindnesses.

"I have been forced to have tea with that aunt of hers." Lady Milton shuddered visibly. "That woman, with her letters to the newspapers, and her outlandish ideas . . ."

"Well, I'm sure Lavinia's visits to the poor must be very disagreeable, and I for one would not want to undertake them," Sophia smiled, "but for all that, I have never once heard her complain. Livvie always has a smile and a kind word for everyone."

Everyone except him.

Lady Milton sighed. "Well, I suppose I forget that sometimes. Perhaps it's to be expected when a girl grows up motherless." Her face settled back into its usual lines of discontent as she glanced his direction. Her mouth formed a perfect O, her cheeks deepening to scarlet. "I am sorry, my lord. I didn't think."

Nicholas bit back an acidic comment and drained his wine glass.

Thornton shot him a sympathetic glance and swiftly changed the subject. But as the talk turned to village matters, he grew uncomfortably certain of two things. Miss Ellison deserved his support, not his censure, especially as it seemed her family was one of the few who actually *did* anything to help the village. The other conviction held equal challenge: the decidedly lax and complacent nature of his bailiff could go on no more, which meant he would need to spend more time here in St. Hampton Heath.

He gritted his teeth.

᷍

Clearing the undergrowth from the gardens proved a place of solace from the turbulence of Lavinia's emotions. Here nobody flattered or flustered her or, worse, called her motives into question. Here she could just be.

She knelt down, her gloved hands pulling at the ivy. No doubt her back would ache as it did every time she weeded, but that was a small price for the shrubbery being brought into something resembling her memories. She smiled to herself. Papa had been pleasantly surprised by "Albert's" efforts this summer, his pleasure soon drifting into reminiscence as he recalled the afternoons he and Mama had spent on the little timber love seat, chatting, dreaming, so many years ago.

She sighed as she pulled the innumerable, stubborn ivy tendrils. Papa's cough had worsened of late, and Dr. Hanbury seemed unable to offer anything more than the suggestion he rest. Of course, Papa's idea of rest was much like hers: unwilling to cope with the confines of a bedchamber, he preferred to read in his study until late in the night, despite protests from her and Hettie. Her eyes blurred. If the unthinkable occurred, and Papa were no longer here—

"Ahem!"

She gasped and glanced up to see the earl, face shadowed in the afternoon sun. "You startled me!"

"I'm sorry, that was not my intention. My humblest apologies."

She pushed back her bonnet to see him more clearly. He stood tall and lean as always, but the harsh planes of his face seemed softer than before, the expression in his eyes warmer than what she recalled from that ridiculous walk three days ago.

He waved a hand at the shambles she'd made. "Your garden design is not quite that of Capability Brown's."

"So it would seem." She returned her attention to the stubborn roots of the ivy that had plagued this stretch of the garden for years. Every single little stem must be removed and burned, else it would reappear, and this horrible process must begin again.

"May I enquire as to why you do not employ the gardener for this task?"

"You may." She pulled out another weed, then another.

"Miss Ellison"—amusement lined his voice—"why is the gardener not clearing this? Surely it's not something for a genteel young lady to be attempting."

"As always I must beg to disagree—"

"As always," he murmured.

"But I am not merely attempting." She pulled out the last one before smiling up at him. "I am succeeding!"

His lips curved, his gaze meeting hers steadily, thoughtfully, disconcertingly. "I gather this garden is another project for the indomitable Miss Ellison."

She leaned back on her heels and surveyed her handiwork. "One that's needed attention for years."

"And as usual you are not content to sit idly by in the hopes someone else will be inspired to do something."

"Papa enjoyed this garden in his younger days. I want him to enjoy it again, before—" Her voice caught.

"Your filial concern does you much credit, Miss Ellison."

His voice was soft, surprising her into a need to blink away tears. She moved to rise when a fawn-gloved hand appeared. "Allow me."

He helped her stand, but confusion at his nearness and his unlooked-for gentlemanly behavior refused her ability to look at his face. She removed her gardening gloves and saw his pristine glove now held smudges of mud.

"I'm sorry. I didn't mean to dirty your gloves."

"Alas! Whatever will Edwin say?"

She glanced up and saw his eyes were wide with tease.

"Despite my valet's best efforts, Miss Ellison, I am not as dandified as some may think."

Her cheeks heated in remembrance of her long-ago comment. To hide her embarrassment she reached to move some rose cuttings. A thorn bit into her palm. She winced.

"Are you hurt?"

"It's nothing. Only a thorn."

He grasped her hand and examined it closely before raising his gaze to hers. "May I?"

She nodded, surprise rendering an inability to speak.

He stripped off his gloves and with long, slender fingers gently kneaded the flesh. From such close proximity she could see how his hair curled behind his ears, the dark thickness of his eyelashes, smell his scent so clean and masculine and appealing . . .

Her breath hitched.

He paused. "I'm not hurting you, am I?"

"N–no, my lord."

He smiled, continuing his tender ministrations until the thorn was released. "There."

"Thank you, my lord." She contrived to pull her hand away—heaven forbid he think she desired such attention—but his grip firmed, accompanied by a frown.

"You are bleeding." He pressed his thumb to the small red mark, his hand clasping hers gently as his intent study continued. "Such a small hand to hold so many cares."

Heat shivered up her arm. Her breath continued to hold in abeyance, as if one whisper might puncture the earl's fixed concentration.

He glanced up, gold glinting in the green depths of his eyes, his lips pulling to one side in what could only be described as a rueful smile. "It's always best to deal with these things before infection sets in . . . or so my nanny used to say."

She fought for her voice to sound natural and not like she was still gripped by wonder. "Did your mother not attend to you as a child?"

His lips drooped, his jaw tightened. "She did not."

Her heart panged for him as she searched beyond the nobleman's arrogant polish to the lonely little boy she suddenly knew he had been. Was that why he held people so aloof?

As if sensing her sympathy, he released her hand and stepped back.

She swallowed in a desperate attempt to steady her thoughts, her heart. "Thank you, my lord, for your assistance."

"I am glad to be able to render a small service to you, even if"—his lips curved up on one side—"you still refuse to tell me why I find you and not your gardener completing this chore."

"I don't refuse."

"No?" He raised an eyebrow.

She smiled at the return of this characteristic action. "Albert, Hettie's husband, takes care of the outside work, but because there's so much garden, I help him sometimes."

"I see. And do your father and aunt approve?"

"I *like* gardening."

"Yes, but do your father and aunt approve?"

The wretched heat flooded her cheeks once more. "I fail to understand why you concern yourself with this matter."

"Only that you seem to delight in concerning yourself in mine. Surely what is good for the gander is also good for the goose?"

"Are you calling me a goose?"

"Are you calling me a gander?"

"You—you are impossible, my lord!"

"And you are right as always, Miss Ellison."

She laughed. "Now *that* is a sensible answer."

Light filled his eyes as his smile flashed. "I remain your most humble servant."

"Now, may I be so bold as to ask the reason for your visit? I presume it was not to retrieve a thorn?"

"Rest assured, madam, that if I had the slightest indication you required my assistance, I would be here at your service instantaneously."

"You *are* kind. However, I think the ability to appear anywhere in an instant might sadly be beyond even a man of your vast resources. Your visit, my lord?"

He smiled. "I understand from the housekeeper your father and aunt are not available."

"Aunt Patience attends a symposium in Gloucester. Papa is unwell."

"It is he I came to see." He withdrew a small book from his coat pocket. "I found this small volume in my library and immediately thought of him. It is John Foxe's *Sermon of Christ Crucified*," he added almost apologetically.

"Oh! Papa will be *so* pleased. John Foxe's book of martyrs is an inspiration to us."

"I rather thought it might be."

"It is very thoughtful of you to be so kind to Papa. Thank you."

He inclined his head. "And remember, Miss Ellison, if I can assist you in any way, I would be honored."

"Thank you."

As he bowed and strode away to his horse she couldn't help but wonder over the earl's strange transformation—and why he'd sought her out, instead of simply giving the book to Hettie.

🦋 Chapter Eleven

Nicholas rode home in a state of bliss. Finally, he seemed to have made amends with Miss Ellison, his efforts to charm put to better use than in any ballroom. Yet he'd meant every word. Something about his neighbor drew truth from him, fired protectiveness within. And it felt good to see approval in the eyes of an intelligent young lady, someone whose wits matched his own, whose compassion for others led to surprising activities. Life with her would never be dull indeed.

This content lasted until he caught sight of Johnson riding off to goodness knows where. His frown continued as he entered the Hall and found Giles.

"Do you know where Johnson goes?"

"I'm afraid not, m'lord."

Thornton entered the hallway. "What's the matter, Stamford? I looked for you this morning, but you had already gone."

Nicholas ignored the guilt riding through his stomach. Not for nothing had he refrained from telling Thornton where he would go. Petty though it might be, he would never have been able to smooth matters with Lavinia if her captain had been along. "I need your help."

"Ah! I sense adventure. What can I do to assist?"

After withdrawing to his study, Nicholas poured out his concerns about Johnson. "But I just cannot find any real evidence. The books always seem correct, and few of the tenants offer complaint except to say he's a trifle high-handed in his demands for rents. But he says the estate never seems to have enough money to make improvements."

"Such as?"

"Improvements to the tenant housing. Haven't you heard Miss Ellison's diatribes? She is passionate about her poor."

Thornton regarded him steadily before saying slowly, "And *your* poor. You are responsible, whether you like it or not."

"I know, I know. But how can I spend money I don't have? James's recklessness has always carried a high price." Like the death of Lavinia's mother. Sorrow rippled across his heart. How could he ever make amends?

"Your brother's actions are not yours, Stamford," Thornton spoke softly.

But he still paid the consequences. Nicholas grimaced.

"And you are the earl now, so you must do what is best for your estate and your tenants. Now, do you think Johnson is stealing?"

"Perhaps. I don't know. I do not wish to accuse an innocent man."

"That sense of justice is something I've always liked about you." Thornton grinned. "Let's see what we can discover—and if we can get you into Miss Ellison's good graces at last."

Within the hour a plan was formulated. Thornton would use his scouting skills from army days to watch Johnson's movements, while Nicholas would carry on as usual with his steward. "Your many visits these past weeks will provide a nice cover for you." Nicholas raised an eyebrow. "If you're sure the young ladies won't mind missing your company?"

"Miss Ellison is a good sport. She won't miss me."

"Lady Milton may."

Thornton's cheeks took on a reddish hue. "I did not think it would be *quite* so difficult to extract myself from her invitations."

"You may need to tread carefully. That woman desires nothing less than her daughter marry eligibly."

"She does not attempt for you?"

"Lady Milton may attempt but will never succeed. Sophia holds no interest for me."

Thornton stared at him hard.

"Come." Nicholas pushed back his chair as his own cheeks heated. "A few days of covert operations might be just the thing."

NICHOLAS PEERED OVER his letters from the past week. His mother's missive that he return from the wilds of Gloucestershire he ignored, likewise the invitations from the Winthrops and Pavenhams to stay as their guest in upcoming house parties at their flourishing estates. House parties meant young ladies he had no interest in courting. Not when his only desire was to see his own estate prosper.

He leaned back in his chair and gazed out the window. How was Thornton getting on? He'd barely seen him these past two days, save for late at night. His friend's remarkable surveillance skills were taking up considerable time, but whenever he asked, Thornton only laughed and said it was the most fun he'd had since Spain.

A scratch came at the door.

"Yes, Giles?"

"Today's post, m'lord."

Nicholas retrieved the thick cream envelope from the platter, glanced at the red seal and sighed. A quick perusal of the contents only confirmed his fears. The Viscount and Lady Aynsley expressed the desire for the company of the Earl of Hawkesbury for a small house party at their estate in Somerset.

He grimaced. Small house party meant unavoidable contact with unmarried daughters. And the Aynsleys had three!

He scrawled a polite refusal then pushed to his feet. Sitting around waiting for something to happen was making his head ache. He found Giles in the hall.

"Get McHendricks to saddle Midnight."

And he raced up the wide steps to change.

HE CAUGHT UP with Thornton at the Pickled Hen. "Well?"

"The landlord says Johnson is often here, never for long, but meets various strangers along by the river. He is not particularly well liked. Apparently he never buys enough pints."

"Crime indeed."

They ate in silence until Thornton glanced out the window. "He's here. At the stables."

Nicholas followed Thornton to the stables, thankful he'd had the fore-sight to house Midnight at the blacksmith's—stabled here would have been rather too obvious.

Thornton peered through the window and whispered, "He's talking to a young boy—no, he's leaving. I'll follow him. You talk to the lad."

"Don't you think—?"

"No. He's wary of you. The lad might respect an earl, though."

Thornton disappeared, and Nicholas strolled round to the front of the stables. "Hello there."

The young lad's sweeping stilled. He looked up, eyes widening. "Yes, me lord?"

A few minutes of discussion—and an appropriate coin—elicited the in-formation required. The lad had shamefacedly admitted to allowing Johnson to make use of an abandoned barn on the southern outskirts of the property.

"Me uncle told me to clears it out—'e's got no use for it, 'e said. So I didn't think I was doing wrong by letting someone else use it."

"Perhaps in future you'll consider why someone may wish to be so clan-destine."

He followed the directions the boy gave, down to a dilapidated byre sit-uated next to the river, toward which Thornton moved stealthily. Nicholas slipped behind a tree, his actions recalling similar missions in the Peninsular, only this time he doubted lives hung in the balance.

Thornton peered through the door. "I say, Johnson, is it? Whatever are you doing here?"

A murmur came from within. Nicholas stole closer.

"Aren't you the earl's steward? Why are you here and not off stewarding?"

There was a sudden clank and thud and then the pounding of footfalls. Nicholas peered round the door to see Thornton's prone form. He raced to kneel beside him, his stomach twisting at the sight of a bloody gash in his head. Memories flashed: Burgos, battle-scarred men, his failure—

"Go after him," Thornton groaned. "Forget me."

"Never." He hoisted Thornton to his feet and half carried, half dragged him halfway to the public house, where the red-faced landlord appeared, wringing his hands. "Get someone to guard your barn in the southwest cor-ner and send for the doctor. My friend here is hurt."

The portly man hurried away, shouting orders to others unseen.

"I don't need your coddling." Thornton pushed his arm away. "Go, get Johnson. He's already got a lead."

"I won't leave—"

"This isn't Spain, Nick. I've been hurt far worse than this, and so have you. Give me a moment, and I'll be able to stand."

"But—"

"Go!"

Nicholas turned and raced toward the blacksmith's. A minute later he was in the saddle, spurring Midnight to a fast trot, peering round corners in the hopes of discovering Johnson's whereabouts. Finally, he spotted his bailiff's roan, cantering along the lane and up the hill toward the Hall. Of course. Nicholas grimaced. Johnson would want to secure whatever else he'd pilfered.

He pressed Midnight to a faster pace. Thankfully few people were out to speculate at the earl racing after his bailiff—no doubt word would soon filter out about the scandal it was sure to be. His hopes were dashed as he rounded a corner to see old Mrs. Foster's gaping face behind a donkey cart. He nudged Midnight's flanks, and together they soared over the cart to the cheers of two boys nearby.

"Good boy." He patted Midnight's neck as he cantered up the road. Midnight's panting grew more frequent, but the steady surefootedness did not falter. Slowly they gained on Johnson.

They raced along the straight to where the road curved narrowly, at the tall oak. Miss Ellison was right—the hedges were too high here. He slowed, rounding the next corner, when a bark and a whinny were swiftly followed by a yelp and a scream.

He tumbled off, into the dirt, rolling to avoid the clashing hooves, catching a flash of tan and white and gold and green before the world went black.

PAIN SEARED HIS forearm. He cursed. Blinked. Who knew rocks contained so many colors? He always supposed them to be brown. And since when did grass grow sideways?

He swallowed. Thunder filled his senses. Groans, the cries of horses, a whimper, more pounding of hooves, dust. He coughed and pushed himself up, wincing as discomfort sliced his arm.

"Oh, how the mighty have fallen. The great Stamford, indeed!" Thornton wavered before him. "Seems this is a day for disaster."

"I don't know what happened." He grimaced and moved into a sitting position and gingerly tested his other limbs. "What are you doing here anyway?"

"My horse was much more handy than yours. And when I saw you chasing—Oh no."

Nicholas followed Thornton's gaze to where Miss Ellison crouched on the far side of the road. "Miss Ellison! What the devil are you doing here?"

Ignoring his arm's throbbing, he pushed to his feet and moved closer. She cradled something white and tan. Memories flashed of a time long ago, images of a man cradling something infinitely more precious. Guilt burned his chest, froze his steps.

Thornton knelt beside her. "He's still breathing."

Tears stained her cheeks. She shook her head.

"McHendricks is wonderfully insightful with animals. We can take him there." Nicholas moved to pick up the dog.

"Don't touch him!" She pushed him away.

Pain slivered his heart.

"Miss Ellison, please allow me."

She ignored Thornton's plea, cradling the whimpering dog closer to her chest.

"I'll let McHendricks know, then."

Thornton gathered Midnight's reins and galloped ahead while Nicholas accompanied Miss Ellison to the stables. She clutched her dog, her hair loose, her cheek dirt-smeared, blood staining her dress, her steps slow, faltering as she stopped regularly to shift her laden arms. But each attempt to relieve her of her burden met with fierce resistance.

"Miss Ellison, I am so sorry."

She said nothing, the broken look on her face saying it all.

"I did not see him."

She shot him one scornful glance and returned her attention to the animal, whispering affection as a mother might murmur to a sick child.

Remorse grew. Why hadn't he insisted on the hedge trimming? Why had he never at least pretended to like the dog?

They reached the stables, McHendricks's grizzled face softening as he hurried forward.

"Ah, Miss Livvie."

"Mickey. He's—" She gulped.

"You leave him with me." He collected her burden and hastened to the barn.

She moved to follow, but Nicholas placed a restraining hand on her arm. "Come inside. Mrs. Florrick will help you clean up and give you something to eat."

"Clean?" She jerked her arm away. "Do you think I care about being *clean?*"

"Miss Ellison, please. Come have a cup of tea. Mrs. Florrick is convinced it is the answer to all of life's troubles."

"No! Mickey needs me."

Thornton stepped forward. "Miss Ellison, how may I assist you?"

She pushed hair from her eyes, smearing her face further. "Could you tell Papa where I am?"

"At once." Thornton ran to his horse and galloped away.

As if in a trance, she moved inside the stables to where McHendricks ran his fingers over the dog's body. She crouched beside him, heedless of the hay and muck, crooning to her pet, whose whimpers eased.

Her head down, she didn't see McHendricks look up, catch his gaze, and shake his head.

Nicholas's heart panged. He nodded, and after checking that Midnight had suffered nothing more than a fright, removed himself to the house, where he met Giles in the hall.

"M'lord!"

"Tell Edwin I need a bath and some new apparel. Oh, and send for the doctor."

"At once, sir."

Half an hour later, clean and freshly clothed, he made his way downstairs to find Thornton in the dining room, the cut on his head now bandaged. He glanced up. "The doctor's here, not that there's anything he can do."

Nicholas nodded and moved to the window where he could see the corner of the stables.

"What happened?"

"We were racing round the bend and next thing I knew Midnight was rearing and I was falling." Nicholas shook his head. "I didn't see them."

"You're lucky it was the dog."

Thank God. If it hadn't— He shuddered.

"Johnson got away?"

His head swam with yet more recrimination. He groaned and moved to the door. "Giles!"

"Yes, m'lord?"

"Take a footman to Johnson's rooms and check through his possessions for anything you think might not belong to him."

"Very good, m'lord."

At Giles's exit, Thornton ran a hand through his hair. "Johnson won't show his face around here again."

"I should have got rid of him long ago. He's cost me too much." Nicholas moved to the decanter and, using one hand, poured himself a whiskey, swallowing it in one gulp. Fire roared down his throat.

Thornton frowned. "Why are you holding your arm like that?"

"I fell on it."

"And you sent the doctor to examine the dog first? Why, Stamford, I do believe you're getting sentimental in your old age."

Mrs. Florrick, his aged, rotund housekeeper, appeared at the door. "Excuse me, my lord. I thought you should know the doctor's almost finished."

"Miss Ellison?"

"Still refuses to eat. I did try."

"Thank you."

He glanced at Thornton, and they moved to the stables. McHendricks and the doctor met them halfway.

"I'm afraid there's nothing I could do." Dr. Hanbury's eyes held apology.

McHendricks rubbed his grizzled jaw. "Mickey is old. Miss Livvie said he'd been walking stiff and sore for some time now." He jerked his head to the stables. "The lass is in there, saying goodbye."

"She seems quite attached."

"Aye. She was given him as a wee pup, after she lost her mother."

Fresh guilt pulled tight around his heart. He nodded to the doctor. "Thank you for coming."

"I'm sorry I could not be of greater assistance." Dr. Hanbury's faded blue eyes sharpened as he cast Nicholas an appraising look. "You are hurt, my lord."

"Ah, yes. I landed on my arm in the fall.

"May I?"

He nodded, and the doctor felt his arm. "You have a nice bandage."

"I had some training with wounds and illness in the war."

He restrained an oath as a particularly tender spot was pressed.

"I suspect it might be broken."

Nicholas managed a wry smile. "I rather thought that might be the case."

"You should have had it seen to at once!"

As the doctor steered him back to the house, he thought he heard the doctor mutter, "A dog!"

🎋 Chapter Twelve

Weeks passed. Trees turned, apples plumped, pumpkins were picked. After a few days lying quiet in her room—and being scolded by Aunt Patience for caring more about a dog than real relationships—Lavinia had picked up her basket and recommenced her visits to the village. But many visits had to be cut short when well-meaning kindness threatened her composure. Only years of habit enabled her to go through the motions of caring, because her heart hurt.

Mickey might have been merely a dog, but he'd been her best friend, the one who had comforted her all those nights when she cried for Mama, his soft body squished beside her, his heartbeat thumping reassurance. Now he was gone.

As was her independence.

Traipsing across hill and dale was lonely now. Without Mickey's reassuring bark to guide her, fear lurked behind tree and rock. Everyone from the earl to Eliza had offered to find her another dog, but she refused. It was too raw, too soon. Another animal would never be Mickey.

She leaned against the old oak tree, guardian over Mickey's grave. Only McHendricks had been permitted into her sanctuary, to bury him, and she'd caught a tear in his eye before he gruffly turned away. Every time she visited the grave, her heartache eased for an infinitesimal moment. Here they were still together. Beyond the hedge, the loneliness overwhelmed again.

A cool wind sang a desperate song, shivering the leaves above. Her face pressed against the sharp bark of the tree trunk, but she cared not. Nothing hurt like her soul's forlorn emptiness.

Captain Thornton had gone, summoned by his father, as he explained in an apologetic interview. The earl—after a thousand apologies she could not bear to listen to—was in London. Sophia was away also, visiting cousins in Weymouth. Even Perry Milton had gone back to university; that, at least, was a blessing.

There *were* some blessings, she supposed. Johnson's mysterious disappearance had fueled gossip, but had resulted in immediate repairs to several village houses. Work had commenced on new houses for those where the worst of the damp could not be remedied. The earl's broken arm had given rise to speculation, though the captain had soon given her the facts.

She lifted her gaze to the faraway hills, golden-green in the shafts of afternoon sun. Her lips flickered. How strange to think the proud earl would consider her poor dog should receive the doctor's attention before himself. Perhaps there was some hope for him after all.

A russet-colored leaf drifted from above, its fragile descent fitting her mood. Coolness nipped her skin. She shivered. Her sanctuary wasn't the same. It was too quiet. Her eyes blurred as she studied the hedge, now cut so severely it seemed impossible it would ever bear flowers again. Not that it mattered. She had no inclination to draw, or paint, or sing. She didn't visit her sanctuary except to talk to Mickey. She only played at church, but even that was mere facade.

God was so very far away.

⁂

Nicholas perused the books Mr. Banning presented him. "They appear in order."

"I can assure you, my lord, they are in order," the small man said primly.

He swallowed the smile. Thornton had warned him of the pedantic manner of his father's former estate manager, while assuring of his complete trustworthiness, proven over twenty years of service until Banning's wife's ill health had forced early retirement. Nicholas's time in London for tedious legal duties had been alleviated somewhat by Thornton arranging for him to meet the recent widower.

"It seems we have enough to ensure the new houses have slate roofs."

"If I may say, sir, slate is quite expensive."

Nicholas met the keen-eyed face and said softly, "I want what is best for my tenants."

"Of course, my lord."

Was that a spark of approval in the other man's eyes? He stifled a groan. Was he that desperate for praise he sought it from his employees?

As his new steward exited the room, he stared out the window, the momentary lift of spirits sinking to something more somber. He shouldn't feel this way. Remorse had dug new resolve, resulting in a flurry of activity these past weeks. Johnson's swift disappearance had at least allowed the recovery of the missing rents from a small chest in the barn. Giles and Martins had discovered a second set of accounts under Johnson's bed, detailing the length of time he had skimmed the estate's rents—since just after Uncle Robert's death. His fingers clenched. If only he had taken a closer interest in the estate, perhaps this could have been prevented.

Miss Ellison had been right.

He rubbed a hand over his face. His visits to the Ellisons had resulted in his seeing Lavinia only once, his renewal of his regret and promise of a new pup waved away. She had changed, shockingly so. She'd faded, having lost the roses in her cheeks. Instead of sparkly light, her eyes seemed empty, reminiscent of men he had fought alongside who had lost their minds. She'd always seemed slight, but now it appeared as if a veritable breeze could blow her away. She'd sat next to her aunt, unsmiling, abstracted, a second too slow to answer a question. Seated next to Miss West he could almost see the spinster she would become.

And it was his fault.

Regret twisted knots in his stomach. He rose and moved to the window, where the muted purple of the hills forecast further rain. If nothing else, at least he was learning to read the weather signs, like the yeomen who worked his estate. Spending time with his tenant farmers, grasping details of estate business, helped to fill his hours. But inside he still felt the sharp pangs of longing—for what he did not know.

Or dare to admit.

Lavinia wearily made her way out the church doorway. There were fewer people today, the Sunday school held a mere half-dozen children. Unseasonal bleak weather had too many in their beds, trying to fight the ravages of influenza. At least there'd been no sign of the dreaded smallpox.

"Good day, Miss Ellison."

She stifled a sigh and turned to face Mr. Raymond. He had been far too assiduous in his attentions of late.

"I missed you this morning. I had hoped to escort you to church today."

She mustered what she hoped passed for a pleasant expression. "That was kind, but I always get here earlier to prepare for the Sunday school."

"But surely—"

"Mrs. Foster!" She smiled at the approach of the elderly woman. "Excuse me, sir."

He nodded, leaving her to listen to the white-haired woman's familiar litany of aches and ailments. At least she'd avoided further conversation with the curate. Thank God he was only visiting for the day, and not staying like he had previously. Her head ached; she rubbed it absently. She was growing too tired to think of a polite way to let him know she was uninterested.

"Mrs. Foster."

The deep voice intruded. She glanced up to see the earl regarding her seriously.

"Miss Ellison."

"Lord Hawkesbury." She dipped her head as Mrs. Foster fluttered her attentions, thanking the earl for his kindnesses in securing her new accommodations. Lavinia moved to speak with Mrs. Thatcher, who was attending her last service before her confinement.

"Miss Ellison, a word." The earl's gloved hand stayed her, as if he knew his domineering tone would make her want to flee. "Your father is still unwell?"

She eased her arm from his grasp. "Yes."

"I hope we will not be forced to listen to too many lectures from his replacement."

"Mr. Raymond is young and still learning."

"He is sanctimonious and a bore."

"You surprise me, my lord. I did not think you listened to the sermons."

He inclined his head. "Your father's I concede to be a trifle more interesting than some."

"I'm sure he will be most gratified to know that." She glanced past him at the distant hills, awash with lilac and gray. She sighed. More rain on its way. More would be sick. More visits to make. She turned back to where the earl continued to watch her closely. "If that is all?"

"Are *you* quite well, Miss Ellison?"

His concern filled her eyes with unfamiliar tears. She turned aside, blinking them away, only to encounter the piercing stare of Lady Milton. She bit her lip and stepped back, bumping into Mr. Raymond.

"Miss Ellison! Please do me the honor of an introduction."

Somehow, despite her head whirling with confusion, she managed to perform the introductions.

Mr. Raymond puffed up like a bantam rooster before bowing and grasping her arm. "My lord, pray excuse us. I am charged with escorting Miss Ellison home."

The earl's hazel eyes glittered and he inclined his head. "But of course."

Moments later, Lavinia sat on the front seat of Mr. Raymond's antiquated gig, forcing a smile at the faces of the congregation as they waved and called their farewells.

All except one.

Lord Hawkesbury had his arms crossed, his brow lowered, as he studied her thoughtfully.

SHE COUGHED, PLACED the basket of apples on the ground, and rubbed her eyes. She would *not* be sick. It was enough that Papa and Aunt Patience were unwell, but she refused to succumb.

"Miss Livvie?" Albert's broad face loomed above. "There be a small boy at the side door asking for yer."

"Thank you." She dragged herself inside and summoned a smile. "Hello, Frederick."

"Mama says sorry to trouble ya, but could ya please come. She thinks the bub be ready."

She nodded and placed a dozen apples in a sack. "Tell your mother I'll be there directly." She smiled and handed the sack to him. "Take care you only eat *one* on the way."

"Yes, miss."

She waved him goodbye then sank against the closed kitchen door, avoiding Hettie's concerned gaze as she summoned the energy necessary for caring for six youngsters.

TWO DAYS LATER, she turned past the cherry trees, now devoid of leaves, and trudged down the road. A sharp wind cut through her cloak, hurrying her steps. She felt slightly better today, the bone weariness of the past two days slightly alleviated by resting in her own bed last night, instead of the hard wooden chair necessitated by caring for the newborn. She carefully sidestepped mud puddles as the breeze whistled in her ears.

"Good day, Miss Ellison."

She glanced up, stifling the fear and loathing she felt every time she looked at that great, dark horse with wild eyes. "Good day, Lord Hawkesbury."

After a moment, he swung down and walked beside her, his arm no longer strapped awkwardly as it had been for the past four weeks. "May I carry your basket?"

"With your arm? No, thank you. Besides, it is not too heavy."

Midnight nickered behind her. She couldn't stop the tremor.

"He is a good horse. He did not mean to hurt your dog."

She blinked away tears, forced a nod.

"I gather you're off to save the day again?"

"If by that remark you mean am I to visit someone needy, then yes, I'm going to visit the Thatchers. Mrs. Thatcher gave birth two days ago, and several of her children are quite sickly."

"Don't you ever wonder if all this earnestness frightens off eligible suitors?"

"As I'm not plagued with suitors, eligible or otherwise, it is of no consequence to me." She stepped around another puddle. "I must confess to surprise at how my affairs could possibly interest you."

"Let me assure you, Miss Ellison, I have not the least concern about your affairs."

Her chest grew tight. She raised her basket higher and fought to maintain her composure. "I gather your objections to earnestness mean you prefer ladies to be insincere, who seek only for their personal comfort and amusement." She peeked across.

Shadows flickered across his face as his lips tightened.

Remorse for her biting words filled her. "I am s—"

"Enough." He interrupted her apology and waved at the hawthorn. "Do you approve the hedge cutting?"

She glanced at the wreck of gnarled and broken branches. "They are much improved."

"Have I finally done something that meets with your approval?"

"I'm sure I don't know why you require *my* approval, my lord."

"Ah, but the approval of Miss Ellison is so sparing, it becomes all the more worth winning."

Was he teasing? His words could be so cutting, but when uttered in that low tone, he sounded like he actually cared. Which only served to increase this aching confusion in her head.

"How is your father today? I trust he is feeling better?'

"Unfortunately, he is not. Dr. Hanbury thinks it is pneumonia."

"Give him my regards."

"I'm sure he'd prefer a visit to your regards. He always seems to enjoy your company."

"Unlike his daughter."

Another thinly veiled barb. Ignoring him was the better part of prudence. She wiped her brow as she plodded on toward the village. Despite the gray clouds, today seemed unseasonably warm for early September. She was very thirsty, too.

"You will not be of much help to your father if you become ill from these visits to the sick."

"Thank you for your consideration for my father. He, however, is in the blessed position of having faithful servants who take care of him and money for a doctor. Many others are not so blessed, so if I can alleviate some of their burden I believe it is my duty to do so."

His gaze narrowed. "Your Christian duty?"

"It is what our Lord commanded his followers to do." Her foot caught in a deep rut carved in the road. She stumbled.

The earl reached out to steady her. "Careful."

She shook off his hand. If only she could so easily shake this lightheadedness that made the village's small stone bridge swim before her. "I am quite well, thank you." Her breath caught on a cough.

"I believe you're more stubborn than well, Miss Ellison. I do not think it wise to be visiting others when you are vulnerable to succumb to illness yourself."

"Would you rather we ignore the weak and frail? Who will look after them if we don't?" Her chin lifted. "My father is of the same opinion. He urged me to visit the Thatchers."

"I did not think your father so foolish."

A scathing reply was restrained only by the greatest of efforts. "As you profess to holding no concern for my affairs, may I suggest you cease from acting like you do? Now, if you'll excuse me, I have some visits to make."

She walked stiffly on toward the whitewashed house on the edge of the village, aware of his scrutiny, and his lack of faith, and a familiar feeling of disappointment in him.

❧ CHAPTER THIRTEEN

"EXCUSE ME, SIR?"

Nicholas glanced up from excessively dull parliamentary correspondence. "Yes, Giles?"

"There is a servant from the parsonage wondering if anyone has seen Miss Ellison."

"How should I know where she is?"

Giles looked apologetic. "Apparently no one has seen her since this morning, when she went to visit the Thatchers."

"The family with sick children?"

"I believe so."

Nicholas rubbed a hand over his face. Had he not told her it was most imprudent to visit the poor and infirm? Did she ever listen?

Giles murmured something, and a stout man he vaguely recognized appeared at the door.

"Begging your pardon, m'lord, but the reverend is worried. She is normally back by now, and the weather be blowin' in."

Nicholas looked out the study's tall windows and frowned. The darkening clouds and a keen breeze rippling the tree branches foretold of likely rain showers.

"The reverend and Miz West are both still laid up with nasty colds, so they asked if anyone had seen her. But if not, I'll let 'em know, and then begin searching again."

Nicholas furrowed his brow. This morning Lavinia had seemed tired and out of sorts. He'd put it down to the effect his charming personality always

107

seemed to have on her, but perhaps—despite her denials—caring for her own family had taken its toll on her health. The reverend must indeed be concerned if a search was to be made.

"We will search for her, too."

With a grateful murmur, the man disappeared.

"Giles!"

The butler's white head soon appeared. "Yes, m'lord?"

"Miss Ellison has not visited today?"

"No, sir."

"It seems she has disappeared. I'll be heading out to assist with the search. Please inform the footmen their assistance is required."

"At once."

A quarter hour later, he stood issuing orders, dividing the men to search the estate. "I'll ride into the village and see what news there is. Hopefully we'll find her before night falls."

"Or the rain sets in." McHendricks's frown looked etched in stone.

Moments later, Nicholas rode off, his thoughts as grim as the sky.

Foolish girl. This was just how he had hoped to spend his evening, racing around the countryside in search of a mere slip of a girl. He pursed his lips, almost able to hear her exclaim, "I am not a green girl. I *am* three and twenty."

He pushed on across the stone bridge, achieving the village as fingers of fog rose from the river. He shivered. A minute later, he rapped on the Thatchers' door with his riding crop.

The wooden door jerked open with a loud creak. A wizened old woman's eyes grew large. "Your Lordship? Oh, sir, you shouldn't be here!"

"Miss Ellison. Is she still with you?"

"No, m'lord. She left hours ago. Awful good she was, giving me some time to spend wi' my Peter before coming back here to nurse the missus and the wee ones. Said it was no trouble."

He inclined his head. "Thank you."

Where could she be? He rapped on the doors of her more particular friends, but Eliza and Mrs. Foster—both smothered in heavy scarves—denied seeing her that day.

He hurried Midnight on, scanning the laneways through the misty rain, puzzling the answer. He couldn't see her hiking all the way to the Miltons. She wouldn't have accepted a ride from a stranger. And even if she had, the parsonage wasn't so far from the village that the trip should take too long, unless—

No. She wouldn't have been abducted!

His heart twisted as he wished for the hundredth time that her dog's life had been spared. The creature's relentless barking surely would have revealed her whereabouts by now. He shoved regret to one side as he continued his search. Nothing. It was as if she'd vanished into thin air. Only the air wasn't thin now, but heavy, with a foreboding gloom.

He shook his head. Nonsensical. The twilight was playing tricks with his imagination.

Rain beaded on his brow. He swiped a hand to displace it and tapped Midnight. "Come, boy. We must find her."

The darkness grew thicker. He secured his cloak around his neck more closely. If she was not in the village, where was she? He followed the lane over the stream, up the hill.

Midnight's ears pricked as the road curved at the big tree. He glanced back. A few lights glowed from the village below. She wasn't there, he felt certain. He turned, remembering something McHendricks had once implied. He wheeled Midnight to the right, up to the shorn hedge. Standing on his stirrups he peered across the twisted branches.

"Miss Ellison!" He listened carefully. Nothing but the rustle of branches and swoosh of grass met his ears.

"Lavinia!" Rain spat into his mouth and eyes. He coughed.

Midnight nickered.

"Steady, boy."

He strained through the darkness. Rubbed his eyes. Was that a faint smudge of color?

Sliding from his horse, he tied Midnight loosely. "Stay."

He pushed through the hedge, almost tripping over a familiar basket. His heart hammered. "Lavinia?"

The rain was heavier now, icy pellets driven hard by the wind. Twigs pushed through the air, scratching his skin. A branch from the tall oak creaked ominously. He stumbled over a slight depression in the ground.

Leaves, slick with moisture, slapped his face. He wiped them away and trudged on. What had he seen? Where?

He tripped.

The darkness had all but obscured her as she lay huddled on the ground. "Lavinia!"

She was shivering, her dark cloak heavy with water. He pushed back the hood that half hid her face. Through the gloomy dimness, he could see her eyes were closed but her mouth was moving, her usually rosy lips now a pasty white. He leaned closer. "Not . . . spirit of fear . . . Timothy . . ."

He frowned. Who was Timothy? "Lavinia, it's Nicholas Stamford. Can you open your eyes?"

"Nick . . ." The word was a mere breath before the wind whisked it away.

He shoved a hand through his sopping hair as the rain continued to beat down mercilessly. This corner of land was surely closer to the Hall than the parsonage. If he sent Midnight . . .

He knelt in the mud beside her. "I need to get help."

"Don't . . . leave me."

He touched her cheek. "I promise to return."

He raced through the field and pushed through the hedge to the road. Midnight snorted, stamping his hoof as the rain sliced almost horizontally. "Steady, boy." He untied him, attached the basket to his saddle, and slapped his rump. "Head home!"

He watched until Midnight headed the right direction and then shoved through the hedge once more, grimacing as twigs scratched his neck. Water dripped down his collar as he stumbled over the uneven grass to where she lay.

Still.

No! He stripped off his gloves and checked her breathing. The slightest warmth on his palm calmed his racing heartbeat. Lifting her carefully, he removed her saturated cloak and wrapped her in his relatively dry one. He scooped her up, his arm protesting, but he wouldn't let go.

He nudged his burden. "Lavinia, we need to get you home."

She gave no answer.

Nicholas shouldered through a different part of the hedge, taking care to shield her face, calling upon years of army reconnaissance to approximate where the Hall stood. He trudged on. It couldn't be more than half a mile.

Once Midnight arrived, surely his message would be understood. In these conditions, they would be there in ten, possibly fifteen minutes.

His boots squelched. Ankle deep mud clung desperately, treacherously, refusing release. Rain spattered, plastering his shirt to his body. Memories of the flight from Burgos arose in all its awfulness. But this time there were no bullets, no desperate army, only relentless rain and a desperate burden.

He stumbled, but refused to fall, instead pulling her closer, tugging at the folds of the cloak to keep her dry. He climbed over a rise. In the distance stood the Hall ablaze with lights. Relief coursed through him.

The rain intensified as if the heavens defied him. He gritted his teeth and walked on. Thank God Lavinia was so slight—his arm ached as never before. His back protested, but he ignored it. He glanced at the white face, her eyes still closed. Hefting her nearer, he marched on.

Through the darkness, he could vaguely see a skittish Midnight near the stables, loud neighs cutting through the rain patter as the stallion avoided being secured. Second-floor window curtains twitched. Someone was watching. He wished he could signal, but he couldn't let her go.

He trekked on. About a hundred yards from the Hall, he stumbled to one knee. She slipped in his arms, her repose interrupted by long shudders. With a groan of exertion, he forced himself to rise and moved forward.

"M'lord!" Martins ran toward him. "Allow me!"

He tugged her closer. "Get the doctor."

Martins turned and sped away. More wide-eyed servants surrounded him, their dirty, wet clothes testifying to earlier search efforts. "Inform Ellison she's safe." He stumbled to the door.

Mrs. Florrick gasped. "Lord Nicholas!"

She looked at the shivering bundle in his arms, shouted for Lily, and bustled him up the stairs to the best spare room. She pulled back the covers, and he carefully deposited his cargo on the pristine sheets. He drew back, his shoulders slumping, and caught his breath.

"Oh, the poor dear." Mrs. Florrick clucked. She issued soft orders to the maid, and Lily soon had a fire crackling in the hearth.

Lavinia lay ominously still. He fought the fear rushing through him and passed a hand over her cold face. A faint breath brushed his skin. "Thank God."

Edwin appeared at the door. He hissed. "My lord! You look dreadful. We must get you out of those clothes and into a nice warm bath at once!"

Nicholas focused on his housekeeper instead. "What can I do?"

"You *should* have a good hot bath."

He scowled.

Mrs. Florrick shot him a considering look that would have got a lesser mortal fired. "She needs her boots removed. She's ice cold and must be warmed as quickly as possible."

He stripped off his saturated vest, dumped it on the floor, and drew closer to the bed. He scrutinized the boots with a frown.

"If you please, me lord . . ." Lily motioned to a side hook and disappeared.

The muddy boots were quickly divested, Lavinia's stocking-shrouded toes smudged with dirt.

Lily returned with a hot brick to place in the bed, and Nicholas returned to the fire. Warmth slowly filtered through his sodden clothes.

"Lord Nicholas, you'd best be leaving now for your bath." Mrs. Florrick, having removed the cloaks shrouding Lavinia, looked sternly at him.

His cheeks heated. "I'll be back presently."

AN HOUR LATER, after the best bath of his life and a nip of brandy that warmed his insides sufficiently, he returned to find Dr. Hanbury examining the patient.

"How is she?"

"Not good. You don't know how long she was lying there?"

"An hour? Perhaps two? She'd been visiting the Thatchers."

Dr. Hanbury pressed two fingers to Lavinia's limp wrist. "So not only have we got influenza, we also have possible smallpox to deal with."

"Smallpox?" Mrs. Florrick gasped.

"It was only confirmed this afternoon. The Thatchers' run of ill health made it difficult to diagnose. But when Mrs. Thatcher's face broke out in the telltale pox, we knew."

"That poor family!" Mrs. Florrick's hands flew to her mouth.

"Lavinia has always given her time generously, and she wouldn't have known. But it means anyone who has touched Miss Ellison must be quarantined. Smallpox is highly contagious." Dr. Hanbury peered at him. "We won't know if she has it for a week or two, so she will need to remain here for that time. Everyone who has been within six feet of her must be kept away from others. That includes you, my lord. I am sorry."

"We understand." Nicholas glanced over his shoulder to the figure standing at the door. "Hear that, Edwin?"

"I'm afraid so, sir."

He studied the pale form on the bed. Smallpox? How would she survive? How cruel was God to allow this?

"It is good you warmed her up as quickly as you did. She's a very sick young lady." The doctor clasped his bag. "I'll need to get some cowpox vaccine. I think it best she receive a vaccination."

Mrs. Florrick shuddered. "You mean those nasty needles?"

"Experience shows if given within the first three days of exposure, it helps lessen the severity and alleviates the worst of the symptoms. I've been inoculated. If she and also anyone who has come into close proximity of her can be inoculated, that will hopefully stop the disease from getting too advanced."

Nicholas nodded. "I was inoculated during the war. Perhaps I can be of some assistance."

"Your assistance here may certainly be necessary. I must return to the Thatchers now. I fear their young one is not going to make it."

"Before you go, please stay long enough to eat something. Edwin?"

Edwin reappeared at the doorway. "Sir?"

"Arrange food for Dr. Hanbury, and make sure someone has gone to the Ellisons to let them know. If not, send McHendricks."

"Yes, m'lord. You must eat also."

Nicholas waved an impatient hand. "Bring it here. It seems we'll have a long night of it."

THREE HOURS LATER, Nicholas remained seated on the chair near the fire, eyes fixed on the figure in the bed. Mrs. Florrick and Lily were asleep on small cots in the adjoining dressing room, their snores testament to deep slumber. But rest eluded him. His eyes still felt gritty and his arm might ache, but the breathy cry of *"Don't leave me"* continued to resonate, necessitating his seat in the sick room. Giles and Edwin had begged him to rest, to no avail. He couldn't sleep. He would *not* allow any more harm to touch Miss Ellison.

The pale form in the bed stirred. He pushed to his feet and moved closer, but she quickly settled and resumed sleep. If what Hanbury said were true, this sleep would be necessary for her to cope with upcoming days. He resumed his seat by the fire and wished for the first time that he knew how to pray.

❧ CHAPTER FOURTEEN

THE CHATEAU'S GREAT hall was filled with pallets of the desperate and dying. Nicholas looked up from his crouch beside the prone figure as the doctor finished his examination with a shake of his head. "I'm sorry, sir."

No. He stared at the young life before him. The flickering candlelight revealed the yellowish tinge to the skin, the sheen of the forehead, the heavy lids that refused to open. He couldn't die. Not now. Not after all they'd gone through. Hadn't Corporal Lennon just married? How could God permit this?

"Sir, you should rest. You look all done in."

"No. I must—"

"Sir, I insist. You haven't slept in days. You'll be no use if you sicken too."

The faces blurred in the shadows, tumbling through time: James, soldiers, Father, Celia Lennon, Dr. Hanbury, Lavinia. And as always the darkness crept closer, closer, closer . . .

"Good morning, my lord."

Nicholas blinked against the light trickling gray and drab from the windows. He sucked in a deep breath, forced his rapid heartbeat to slow. After being driven to his bed by Mrs. Florrick's assurances, his attempts to rest had been punctured by the severe wind that howled through the trees and whistled under the eaves. "How is the patient?"

Edwin's face remained impassive. "No change."

"Ellison knows?"

"Yes, sir. Miss West sent a message saying she and the reverend remain quite unwell, but she hopes to attend as soon as possible."

Nicholas nodded. It would be hazardous for either to come, given their current states of health. He shifted, testing his aching limbs, and winced as the old bullet wound in his thigh made its presence felt again.

"Sir—" He waved off his valet's concern, but Edwin's brow remained creased. "The reverend said to let you know his prayers are with us."

"They'll need to be," he growled.

Miss Ellison would require a miracle to survive.

THE DAY PASSED gloomily, inside and out, the threat of smallpox casting fear into every soul. Dr. Hanbury appeared with the promised vaccine mid afternoon. Lavinia barely twitched at the injection.

"I don't like administering the vaccine this way, but with her condition such as it is, the sooner the better." He also dosed Mrs. Florrick and Lily, those deemed most at risk. "You may feel slightly feverish and require your beds, but I assure you receiving an inoculation is much better than if you had direct exposure."

Nicholas nodded. "And it will enable us to keep the sickness contained so no more members of the household are affected. We can manage the nursing, can't we, Mrs. Florrick?"

Dr. Hanbury frowned at him. "Sir, I do not think that is prudent."

Nicholas shrugged. "During the war we all had to pitch in. I assisted with the care of not a few ill men. And I suspect you and your nurses will be kept exceedingly busy in the village."

"I'm afraid so. The Thatchers are not well at all." He sighed. "I do not like it, but Lavinia really should not be moved, and if her aunt does not object, I suppose I cannot. Poor Mr. Ellison is hardly in a fit state to even know what he should object to." He sent Nicholas a hard look. "If you're quite sure she'll be safe?"

He nodded, refusing to take offense at the implication.

"We'll look after her," Mrs. Florrick assured. "There's no need to worry."

"Yes, but this form of influenza . . ." He shook his head. "If the fever takes hold and she becomes anxious, try to keep her quiet. Calmness is essential. She'll need as much rest as possible."

"Thank you, Doctor. Your haste and assistance are greatly appreciated."

"I'll endeavor to call in a few days."

Nicholas nodded, and the older man departed.

THE FIRST DAYS passed relatively quietly. Lavinia spent much of the time asleep, and seemed only to suffer from a severe case of influenza, her coughing prolonged, but nothing out of the ordinary. Mrs. Florrick seemed to have the situation well in hand, enabling Nicholas time in his study to focus on Banning's excellent accounts.

On day five, Giles interrupted. "Excuse me, m'lord, Mrs. Florrick is asking for you. She believes Miss Ellison is worsening."

His stomach clenched. He bounded up the stairs to the spare bedroom.

Mrs. Florrick looked up at his entry. "She's got the fever."

Lavinia's face was flushed, her eyes closed, her body shifting in an agitated manner.

He sat by the bed, thankful for last night's dreamless sleep. "Where is Lily?"

"Resting next door. She complained of feeling tired and chilled."

He chewed the inside of his bottom lip. Surely Lily wouldn't succumb.

Lavinia coughed, her head moving from side to side. "Mama." Her fingers plucked at the blankets. "Mama!"

"Poor pet. She's been this way for the past hour, crying for her mother so."

Guilt gnawed his heart, refusing coherent thoughts, let alone speech.

Lavinia groaned again, her hair damp on her forehead. "Mama! Don't leave me!"

Mrs. Florrick retied the handkerchief around her mouth and moved closer. She firmly grasped Lavinia's hands and peered into her face. "There, there, Miss Livvie. You're safe. It's just a bad dream."

Lavinia stiffened then collapsed back onto the pillows.

"The poor, poor dear." Mrs. Florrick wrung out a cold compress and applied it to her forehead. "It shouldn't happen to such a one as she."

"You know her well."

"Oh, yes. A few years back when my poor Arthur died, she was such a comfort. She has this way of listening, like she listens with her eyes, that makes one feel she truly understands."

He nodded. He'd seen that look when he'd shared about Burgos, felt her almost tangible compassion. His chest tightened.

"Listen to me, rattling on. But Miss Livvie's been a part of our lives for so long. And your uncle was so fond of her, treated her almost as a daughter, he did. After the accident the poor reverend was lost for so many weeks— Lord Robert did what he could to distract the child. Why, he even bought that lovely big piano to try to coax Miss Livvie to play again."

So that's why the grand piano sat downstairs. "I did not realize . . ."

"Yes, well, Miss Livvie was always over here, playing her music, visiting the library, chatting with McHendricks, and seeing the puppies he'd concealed from Johnson."

"McHendricks? Puppies?"

"Oh yes, my lord. That beagle she had was one of them. That is why she named it Mickey." She dabbed at her eyes. "Miss Livvie's always been a great favorite of his. Of all of the staff really."

He nodded. He'd wondered at the many anxious enquiries he'd fielded concerning Miss Ellison. The grim countenances and red-rimmed eyes told of their love and concern.

"Lord Robert loved her very much. It's such a sh-shame . . ." She stuttered to a stop, biting her lip as she glanced at him anxiously. "But never mind my tongue, my lord. I'm so glad you found her when you did. I just hope she doesn't end up with scars to mar her pretty face."

He gazed down on the now quiet form, the bright vivacity he'd admired a distant memory. He swallowed. God forbid any permanent reminders.

TWO DAYS LATER, several flat red spots dappled Lavinia's face and, toward evening, Dr. Hanbury was summoned.

The doctor shook his head. "It's the influenza I'm most concerned about. I'm hopeful the inoculation will prevent the worst of the smallpox, but . . ." He sighed. "It's a good thing she's always been a healthy one. All those visits to nurse the sick have no doubt strengthened her ability to withstand ordinary disease. If she'd been one of these delicate ladies, I doubt she'd still be with us."

Nicholas winced, remembering his admonishment against her unladylike striding around the countryside with only a small dog for protection. "Will she live?"

The doctor rubbed a hand over his lined face. "We must pray so. I'm sorry but I need to return to the village."

"What? You can't leave now. What if she worsens? Surely Miss Ellison's life—"

"The Thatcher baby died last night, and now the mother has sickened significantly. The entire family is in dire straits."

Nicholas swallowed further protest. "I'm very sorry. Please send their bill to me."

The doctor looked at him curiously, then shrugged. "Aye, sir, as you wish. Lavinia has a fair chance of survival with you three caring for her. Offer her broth whenever she rouses, and have some faith."

Faith? Nicholas tried not to grimace. Look where Lavinia's faith had got her.

"Now I best be going."

He escorted the doctor to the top of the stairs and bid him a good night.

Refusing the whirl of worries he drew back his shoulders and marched to the sickroom. Illness was only the enemy to be defeated. They would defeat it. *He* would—this time.

Mrs. Florrick sat by the bed, continuing to soothe the flushed brow with cool compresses. Tears rolled down her cheeks.

His gut tightened. No. Lavinia couldn't really die.

"I'll sit with her." He placed a hand on the housekeeper's shoulder. "You need to rest."

She glanced up, purple shadows under her eyes. "She needs me—"

"She will rest better without hearing your tears." He helped her up. "Go. Sleep."

He guided her to the cots in the adjacent chamber where Lily slumbered peacefully. Soon she was fast asleep.

Nicholas tried reading his uncle's prized copy of Homer.

Couldn't.

Struggled through Euclid, but his attention kept slipping from the page to the still form in the bed. He was on guard, almost like his presence kept the danger in abeyance—only no bullet would destroy his defense this time.

"Mama."

The whisper wrenched his gaze from the blurring words, wrenched guilt through his chest as long ago memories surged.

His brother's witless friend. His own stupid pride. An even more stupid boast.

"Did I hear correctly? Nicholas the great cannot manage to drive such a distance?"

"I did not say *I* could not manage."

"Just that others couldn't?" The Honorable Gerald Fitzgibbons flushed. "James, I don't believe your brother is the excellent a horseman you say."

James laughed joylessly. "My brother prefers a safe bet."

"Or none at all?"

Nicholas had refused to rise to the bait, moving from the stables as the two commenced their wagers. He caught the groom's frown. McHendricks didn't like this either, but servants, like younger brothers, had blessed little influence over James. As much as Nicholas enjoyed racing, he refused to put himself or any horse in danger for the sake of a stupid dare. Gravel crunched underfoot as he walked to the Hall.

In the library he found his uncle perusing maps. The fourth Earl of Hawkesbury glanced up. "What is my nephew up to now?"

"I . . . I'm not sure, sir." Tattling on his brother only led to strained relationships.

The earl sighed and motioned to the table. "Come. I rather think you'll enjoy this."

Nicholas peered at the atlas as his uncle shared about a Royal Society lecture he'd recently attended in London. Minutes later the butler entered. "Sir, there's been an accident."

A sense of ominous foreboding filled the room. The earl's beetling gray brows pushed up. "Yes?"

"Mr. Stamford and his friend were racing their carriages and crashed outside the village."

"The fools!" Maps scattered to the floor. "Is anyone injured?"

Emotion clouded the butler's usually expressionless face. "We believe there may be, sir."

He didn't need his uncle's "Nicholas!" to propel him to the stables. Fear churned his insides as he saddled his favorite chestnut and galloped along the landscaped drive, out the iron gates, and down the lane toward the village. At the corner, where the road narrowed and veered sharply on the edge of his uncle's estates, stood a crowd of villagers. He tied the horse to the fence and pushed his way through the chaos and confusion to find his brother lying on the road, grasping his leg in pain, next to an overturned curricle.

"James!"

His brother looked up, wincing. "Dash it, Nick! He's really done it now."

"Where's Gerald?"

But his brother merely moaned and shut his eyes, clutching his knee.

Nicholas straightened, looking over the scene. How stupid to have thought they could take such a bend unscathed! Gerald always was a reckless one, but for James to put Uncle's horses in danger was the outside of enough! Nearby, the horses shied nervously. He spoke softly, stroking them as he released the harness.

He nodded to a local man, a farmer, judging from his smock and wide hat. "Hold them." The man moved forward to hold the reins.

Nicholas hurried to the other carriage. The nauseous feeling intensified. "Someone get a doctor!" He crouched over Gerald's unconscious body, passing a hand over his mouth. But no warm air reassured. He glanced up. "We need a doctor!"

Grim villagers huddled together, a wall of animosity staring accusingly at him.

Beyond the low mutters came the sound of hooves and wheels striking rock as a small cart clattered to a stop. The crowd parted for the reverend he recognized from Sunday's foray to church. "Grace!" A sharp, agonized cry filled the air.

Nicholas frowned, and pushed to his feet, past the broken transports to encounter a scene far more desperate. A woman lay beside the road, blood staining her pink dress, an overturned basket at her heels. Nearby, a young girl's tears fell unchecked as the reverend sank to his knees and clasped the body to his chest, his broken sobs joining the sniffles of the surrounding crowd.

Nicholas stumbled forward as the full horror of his brother's reckless thrill seeking sank in. "Get a doctor!" He shouted at the nearest bystander. "Quickly, man!"

The man shook his head. "She don't be needing no doctor."

Dear God . . . "But the others!"

"Stupid young eejits." Spittle flew onto the dusty road.

"Nick! Where are you? This hurts!"

Muttered oaths drew Nicholas's attention to the nearby stone-faced villagers. Mortification—viscous, scorching—squeezed his heart. Never, in all his fifteen years, had he ever felt so ashamed. He ducked his head as recriminations swirled. If only his parents had checked his brother's willfulness more often. If only Nicholas hadn't boasted so proudly. If only others hadn't happened by at that precise moment. If only, if only, if only . . .

He hastened to James, whose cries of pain only magnified the crowd's disgust. As he tried to shush him, Nicholas glanced back at the golden-haired girl, wet-faced, now clasped in a large woman's arms.

Memories wavered, dissolved, as the deep, hot guilt from fourteen years ago speared his soul anew. He would *not* let Lavinia suffer any more.

A rasping cry drew his attention to the invalid. He tried spooning in water as Mrs. Florrick had done, but succeeded only in spilling yet more on the covers. Not that it mattered. If—no, *when*—she recovered, the bedding would all be burned anyway, lest any remnant of smallpox remain.

A shiver rippled down his back. He rose and threw another small log onto the fire, stirring the embers until sufficient heat warmed the room again. He gnawed his bottom lip as the flames crackled and glowed.

"Mama!"

Nicholas hastened back to the bed. Lavinia moved restlessly, eyes still closed, her breathing increasingly shallow.

He glanced through the dressing room's opened door at the cots. Both women continued their slumbers.

"Mama!"

"Hush, Lavinia."

She made a noise, low in her throat, halfway between a groan and a whimper, and he was instantly transported back to the war, the men, weakened by disease or starvation, lying on pallets, groaning in dark hallways in abandoned French chateaux. Men, *good* men, marked with the red scourge across their palms and faces, before the pox burst into pus and left craters on their faces. Men who'd gasp the names of loved ones before breathing their last. Men he'd been helpless to defend.

"Why? Why did you leave?"

He glanced at her. Her eyes were wide open, staring at him. She was talking to him?

"Why couldn't you stay?" She grimaced, and coughed violently, her breath ending in a wheeze. "Mama? Why won't you answer me?"

He swallowed. This kind of delirium was familiar, too, and had often heralded the end.

The end? Desperation flooded him. "Lily! Mrs. Florrick!"

They ignored him, the past nights of nursing making slumber too deep. He pressed another cold compress to Lavinia's forehead. Regrets swooped in like foul birds upon a carcass. Why had he not shown more kindness? Why hadn't he exhibited more self-control instead of enjoying the constant sparring? Why had he tried to maintain this ridiculous charade of aloofness, when deep within he burned to have her near?

His heart thumped.

Her eyes fluttered and her lips parted in a long rasping breath.

The heaviness in his chest mounted. If only the doctor were still here! Miss West! Anyone! He gritted his teeth, pushed down the fear, and forced his thoughts to the job at hand.

"Mama . . ."

Her breath was whispery thin, coming in hurried bursts, like she was trying to draw in a lifetime supply of air. His skin prickled. She would not die. She *could* not die.

Could she?

He called to the sleeping servants. To no avail. Panic whirled through his brain. What could he do? What could he *do*?

Fragments from a sermon Mr. Ellison had preached months ago flashed through his mind—something to do with prayer? The doctor's advice to have faith jumbled with Mrs. Florrick's words, mixed with the fear. He lowered his head. *Lord, I know I have done nothing to make You proud, but Lavinia is such a good person. Don't let her die.*

But good people died. His men had died. The reverend's wife had died! The swelling in his throat enlarged. *Lord, please . . .*

The gasping sound worsened.

Lord, I'll do anything, whatever You say, please bring Lavinia back to health.

He stared, horrified, as her fingers jerked, as if life itself tried to escape her body.

Lord, please!

Lavinia's recriminations flashed across his mind: he would keep his word. He would! *Lord, I promise. Take my life, my life for hers. Please heal her!*

The thrashing continued until she gave a final cry and slumped back against the pillows. Motionless.

"Lord, no!"

Mrs. Florrick staggered to the bedside. "Is she . . . ?"

He reached a shaky hand to touch the side of her neck. Nothing. He shifted his fingers. Still nothing.

Lord!

He tried once more. A faint rhythmic beat met his fingertips. "There's a pulse!"

Mrs. Florrick placed a hand upon Lavinia's forehead. "The fever has broken." She smiled blearily. "Thank the Lord!"

"Thank You, Lord." He slumped in his chair, placed his head in his hands. "Thank You, Lord, indeed."

🎋 Chapter Fifteen

She sat on a small stool, holding the small rag doll Mama had sewn. Her mother spoke soft, soothing words to Mrs. Hardy, who hunched in a chair in the corner. The room felt sad. The walls had grown new cobwebs since their visit last Monday, and a bitter smell came from the cooking pot. Thin, dark-eyed children huddled around their mother, dressed in rags. She met Eliza's haunted gaze then looked away, her throat growing tight. She clasped her doll more firmly.

"Lavinia?" Her mother rose, offered an encouraging smile. "Would you pass my apron?"

"Yes, Mama." She slipped the doll into her pinafore pocket, retrieved the apron from the basket, and glanced at the black-clothed woman again.

Poor Mrs. Hardy. It *wasn't* her fault little Thomas had drowned in the river, no matter what people like Lady Milton might say. But despite it being weeks since the tragedy, her sorrow never changed. If Mr. Hardy were here, things might be different. But Papa said he was away, working in Bristol, leaving Mrs. Hardy to care for five—no, four—children younger than Lavinia.

Mama reentered the room with a large pail of water. As Lavinia swept the dirt floor, Mama scrubbed the big iron pot, while the children—apart from Eliza, who kindled the feeble fire—watched from near the bed.

"Lavinia, could you please find the buns?"

She placed the broom away and removed the cloth from the basket. Her stomach skipped as the scent of yeast and currants filled the room. She looked up. Eliza's dark eyes met hers.

"Would you like a currant bun, Eliza? Mama made some this morning."

The dark head bobbed, and Lavinia distributed the buns among the children. After Mama filled the pot with fresh broth and prayed for the family one more time, they exited the dim cottage, but the bright sunlight could not chase away the sadness. Lavinia bit her bottom lip. How *terrible* it would be to lose a family member. When she had first heard of the tragedy, she could scarcely believe it. Every night since she had prayed for the Hardy family, most often as tears dripped onto her pillow. She had no siblings, but she could imagine losing a beloved playmate would be *awful*.

Poor Eliza. If only Lavinia could offer her something more than currant buns, but what? She peered over her shoulder at the cottage.

Eliza stood, watching.

Her heart throbbed with compassion. "Mama, may I speak to Eliza a moment?"

"Of course."

She hurried back to the cottage, pulled the doll from her pocket, and thrust it at the younger girl. "Her name is Cecilia."

Eliza's thin face softened as she clutched the doll, wonderingly.

"Look after her." Swallowing regret she turned and ran to her mother's side, away from the temptation to snatch her doll back. Upon recognizing her mother's faintly exasperated expression, she slowed her steps to a more ladylike walk.

"Sorry, Mama. I forgot."

Mama stroked Lavinia's cheek. "That was very kind. I'm proud of you."

Warm sunshine filled her heart at Mama's approval, chasing away the pang of giving away her favorite doll. "Eliza looked so sad. I love Cecy, but I think Eliza needs her more."

"I think you are right, Lavinia."

She slipped her hand into Mama's as they walked across the stone bridge, over the stream where little Thomas had drowned. *Poor* Mrs. Hardy. Mama's comforting words had brought some solace, but words could never replace the loss of a child. Lady Milton wasn't the only one Lavinia had overheard reproaching Mrs. Hardy for not noticing her small son had disappeared. But as Papa often said, blame and recrimination did not change hearts, only God could.

They walked up the hill, the sky a bright bowl of blue. As they approached the bend in the road, hooves thundered in the distance. Her hand tightened its grip, her heartbeat racing as the shouts grew nearer. Her breath caught as she was pushed gently, closer to the road's grassy verge. Dust trembled. A horse shrieked, its eye wild and terrible. It reared, high, high in the sky, like a black behemoth trying to crush her. Hooves swung violently through the air. Swoosh! Swoosh! Then the sickening thud . . .

"Mama! Mama!" Heavy limbs refused movement.

Vague images and impressions swirled around her—of the past or the present, she knew not. Someone holding her close. Whispered assurance. Breath catching. Tears. Cool hands on her face. A solid heartbeat. An indefinable scent.

Light subsided as the darkness claimed her once more.

HER EYES REFUSED to open, weighted as though with rocks. Something heavy sat upon her chest, making breathing difficult. She tried pushing it away but her arms wouldn't lift. "Mickey, get off."

Lavinia coughed, the sound shotgun-loud in the quiet, jarring her brain. Where was she? Her ears strained for clues. Was this even real or just a blurry dream? Confusion pounded her head. She *had* seen Mama, *had* felt the warmth of her smile as she'd turned on the road one last time. She'd tried to catch up to her, but to no avail.

She coughed again. Heat rippled across her chest. At least Mickey was here. She groaned at him to move. He ignored her.

She could hear people's voices now: one close by sounded quite tired and gruff, another was higher, feminine, and the third was cool, low-pitched. Recognition tugged, fluttered away.

"Her breathing seems clearer. Apart from those few lesions on her forehead and arms, she seems to have escaped the worst of the pox."

"Thank the good Lord."

She pried open her eyes. Everything was blurry and dim. She turned her face. Pain streaked through her head. She forced heavy eyelids to remain open, to focus. Pale blue drapes drifted from the corners of a huge four-poster bed. The bed coverings were unfamiliar and heavy. The mattress and pillows were too soft. Her back ached excruciatingly. Where—?

"It appears our invalid is awake."

"The reverend and Miss West will be so relieved."

"Perhaps now I'll finally get some order in my house."

Faces swam before her: Dr. Hanbury, Mrs. Florrick—the earl?

"Welcome back, Lavinia." The doctor placed a cool hand on her forehead.

She could only groan. Her throat felt more parched than her rainless garden last summer.

Mrs. Florrick moved close, offering a small glass of water. "There you go, dearie. Take your time." She clucked. "You gave us all a big fright."

Her head swam. "Why . . . here?"

The earl spoke from his position at the door. "It was nearest."

She frowned, but even that small action caused pain. Nearest? To what? Where were Papa and her aunt? She attempted to sit up but the sheets were too heavy, pinning her down. "Papa?"

"Shhh." The doctor placed a gentle hand on her arm. "Your father and aunt are both well."

She sagged against the pillows. "Then why?"

"You've been extremely ill with influenza, Lavinia, exacerbated by a mild dose of smallpox."

"The pox?"

"The Thatchers."

Her breath hitched. "Are they . . . ?"

"I'm sorry, my dear. Bessie and the babe are in heaven now."

"No. *No.*" Tears clogged her throat, spilled from her eyes. She turned her head to escape intense scrutiny. The poor Thatchers. That poor, poor family . . .

"We almost lost you, too." Dr. Hanbury sighed. "It was a bad case, due to influenza."

She kept her gaze averted, willing the tears away. She would *not* cry.

A floorboard creaked. She turned to see the earl move closer. His neck-cloth was carelessly tied, and his face seemed paler, heightened perhaps, by his shadowed eyes and jaw. Had her presence here disturbed his household *that* much?

"We're all glad you are well, Miss Ellison, but I trust you'll now learn to leave the nursing to others." The hazel eyes flashed while his voice remained silky smooth. "Your illness has affected many. I hope you will take greater regard for your actions in future."

Her bottom lip quivered. "Has anyone else passed away?"

"Not for want of trying." He turned and strode out the door.

Her throat cinched. The doctor and housekeeper blurred.

"Now, now, Miss Livvie, that's a dear. Lord Nicholas has been very worried, that's all."

An errant tear trailed down her nose. "Why am I here if he resents me so much?"

"He saved your life, dearie."

"He found you in the storm after you got lost coming home from the Thatchers." The doctor packed away silver instruments in his bag. "If he hadn't brought you here right away, you could have easily died."

"He helped nurse you through the worst of it, Miss Livvie."

What? The pressure on her chest now moved to her head. She rubbed uselessly at the ache. "He was exposed to smallpox, too?"

"Aye."

She glanced at the housekeeper. "And you?"

Mrs. Florrick offered a smile. "The doctor jabbed us all with one of those nasty needles, so none of us got sick like you."

Lavinia closed her eyes. "I'm sorry for putting you all to so much trouble."

"It was no trouble."

The housekeeper's words floated away on a tide of smothering weariness, chased by the earl's condemnation. The doctor murmured something further, but she could not heed his words. Poor Bess and her tiny Meg. Fresh tears seeped onto her pillow. "I'm so sorry. So, so sorry . . ."

Nicholas unclenched his fists, thrusting away from his desk where he'd sat trying to understand some missive from London in a vain effort to distract himself from his earlier stupidity. He shoved a hand through his hair. Who was he to condemn Lavinia for her reckless behavior, when he couldn't even curb his own tongue?

A shiver curled up his spine. She'd almost died! He pushed to his feet and moved to the window, but the hazy afternoon light over yellowing trees refused to offer solace. And she still seemed to have no clue about how her actions had affected his household—let alone himself.

His resolve to appear unmoved and hide the turbulent feelings she produced had merely resulted in a harshness she did not deserve. But allowing his real feelings to be displayed simply would not do. Tender as those feelings might be, she was not for him. They were too different. Held different social ranks. Nothing could change that.

There was a knock on the door, and he turned to see Martins. "The doctor, m'lord."

"Send him in."

He rubbed a hand over his aching face as the doctor ambled in. "Hanbury, I'm extremely thankful for all you've done."

Dr. Hanbury nodded, the grizzled jaw and shadowed eyes testifying to the long hours he'd put in over the past weeks. "I think your staff will be right as rain in two days."

"And Miss Ellison?"

"She should keep to her bedchamber for at least this week. Then we'll see how she fares." The doctor studied him gravely. "She didn't know the Thatchers were infected, you recall."

Nicholas crossed his arms.

"If she had not assisted when the Thatchers became sick, many others would have died."

"I know. I spoke rashly."

The doctor lifted graying eyebrows. "She was very upset at the thought she might be responsible for making others ill. Your housekeeper and I tried to assure her, but . . ."

"I will make amends."

"I'm glad to hear it." The doctor heaved out a sigh. "I do not want her worrying, not when she needs to concentrate on getting better."

He nodded, proffered a hand. "Again, I thank you. Please send all the bills to me."

"I'll be sure to do that." The doctor's eyes twinkled.

After he exited, Nicholas moved again to the windows, the tranquil scene doing little to restore his equilibrium. Hanbury was right. Apportioning blame to Lavinia for any of this farrago was most unfair—she'd been innocent throughout. In fact, if anything, he was to be held responsible for putting his household staff at risk. Guilt tore through him, and he leaned his forehead against the cool glass. "God, forgive me." He groaned. "Again."

HE MADE HIS way upstairs circumspectly, relieved no servants were around to carry gossip downstairs. He entered the room. The curtains were drawn, the lamps low. He moved closer to the bed. Lavinia was asleep, her hair tumbling round her shoulders, the sheets pulled up, revealing nothing save for her creamy throat with its beautiful lines. He studied her features, looking past the sores marking her forehead to see if he could find a trace of the confidence that had long ago fascinated him. How had she stolen past his defenses?

One red-marred hand rested above the coverlet. A sudden, senseless longing rose to hold her hand again. His fingers twitched, craving the touch. Desire begged to slip the reins of self-control.

He dropped his hand. Drew back. Exhaled. Shook his head. Fool. He was such a fool.

A slight creak came from the door. He turned.

Lily held a bundle of clothing. "She's sleeping, me lord."

He nodded, and resumed his focus on Lavinia. When Lily disappeared into the chamber next door, he leaned closer to the figure on the bed. "I'm sorry, Lavinia."

Her lashes fluttered slightly.

"Me lord?"

He rose, schooling his features to ambivalence. "Take good care of her, Lily."

She bobbed a quick curtsey and resumed her ministrations as he exited the room.

He drew in a breath and exhaled slowly. And shook his head at himself. Again.

THE ARRIVAL OF Miss West brought a sense of relief to the Hall. Although somewhat gaunt after her illness, she declared herself fit for the challenge of nursing her niece. Lavinia's face and forearms still held a number of marks, but only a couple of scabs near her hairline bore witness of the pus-filled lesions Dr. Hanbury had feared. She took one look at Lavinia, another at Mrs. Florrick and Lily, and immediately banished them to rest and recuperate. Their remonstrations proved to no avail as she quickly assumed control, scaring the staff into such levels of efficiency Nicholas wondered if he'd ever have his household back to normalcy again.

After a week in which she cared for Lavinia—and refused him admittance to the room—she cornered him in his study. "Hawkesbury?"

He lowered his London solicitor's latest report. "Yes, Miss West? How is the patient?"

"She's spent most of the time asleep. Her cough has improved, it must be said."

"I'm glad to hear it."

"I'm hopeful we need not trespass on your hospitality for too much longer."

"She must stay until better. I hope you will treat this as your home."

She eyed him, the relentless blue stare penetrating as if she attempted to read his heart.

"Was there something else, ma'am?"

She frowned. "My niece has always been too kindhearted for her own good."

"A matter on which we both agree."

A smile flitted across her face. "Lavinia is too unworldly at times and doesn't see things as perhaps we both do, which brings me to a matter of some delicacy."

His skin prickled. "Yes?"

"Whilst Mr. Ellison and I, and indeed most of the villagers and your staff here, are generously minded, there are some who will query the propriety of a young woman staying in the home of a young, single man."

He frowned. "I did not believe Miss Ellison to be so missish about the opinions of others."

"And that is the problem. Because she is not, she will not see this as others may. Now I know you can have no interest in my niece"—the hard gaze sharpened—"but there will be some who may ask questions. So in order to allay some of those concerns I propose to employ Lily as a kind of lady's maid for Lavinia, at least for the next few weeks, until she is safely at home and free from speculation."

"Lily is but a parlor maid."

"No matter. She appears a good, pliable girl. With a little training, she will suffice."

He studied her thoughtfully. "Thus alleviating the lack of chaperone in those first few days. Yes, it has some merit."

"A great deal of merit I would say."

Her Lavinia-like remark made him smile.

She appeared nonplussed for a moment before recollecting herself. "It is not just my niece whose reputation is on the line. Yours will be, too, unless something is done."

"By all means, something must be done. Heaven forbid Lady Milton suspect me of evil intentions."

"I do not believe Lady Milton would ever consider *your* intentions untoward."

"You flatter me, Miss West."

Another thin smile escaped. "So you'll permit Lily to enter my employ?"

"I was rather under the impression you already believed she was."

She had the grace to blush. "I apologize if I have overstepped."

"Careful, Miss West, lest we find ourselves in agreement again."

She snorted, amusement flashing in her eyes before her face softened. "Such cursed timing for illness."

"Illness is never convenient, ma'am."

"Indeed it is not."

A knock prefaced Giles's entry. "The doctor is here, m'lord, Miss West."

"Thank you, Giles." Miss West turned, her eyes widening. "Oh. I'm sorry."

"Far be it from me to disagree with a lady."

She shot him a wry smile and moved to the door, leaving him to wonder: was allowing Lavinia's aunt such free rein mere hospitality, or would it result in turning his life upside down—and be the biggest mistake of his life?

🌾 Chapter Sixteen

Shadows pooled across the bedroom floor. She glanced at the windows, fringed with ivy, the golden leaves a promise of cool nights, apples, the fall harvest. Views of the parkland were made impossible by the bed position so she shifted her attention to the other side of the room. Every gold-etched panel, every piece of handsome mahogany furniture, every silken fold draped from the canopy above, right down to the ornate lotus blossoms carved in the bed frame, she could sketch in her sleep. Such a beautiful room. Such a lovely prison.

She coughed quietly, unwilling to disturb Lily, asleep on a cot in the adjoining chamber.

Lying in bed, her mind vacillated between former rational assurance and a dizzying kind of fog that refused the most basic thought. She longed to scratch at her scabs but every time she tried, Lily would say, "Miss, I beg ye wouldn't do so!" And she'd refrain—until her protectress left the room and she was free to scratch again.

Sometimes when she slept, the earl visited her dreams—surely a sign she was still unwell. For the things he said and did were nothing like his cold lordship's self. She could almost see him holding her hand, murmuring sweet words in her ear, looking upon her with soft kindness—such *ridiculous* things, she would die a thousand deaths before admitting to anyone! But still her mind played tricks, conjuring fantastical things, which could only mean more rest was necessary. Her nose wrinkled. More rest? Her spirit might protest, yet her flesh remained so weak.

Lavinia studied the fireplace, alive with crackling flames that suddenly blurred. Every so often the sadness would slip in, deep and unutterable, sur-prising her with its intensity. She'd lose her place in conversation or need to hide her face as she remembered the desperation in Bessie's eyes, the rasp-ing breath of her little babe, the fears of her children whose cup of sorrow had filled years ago. She would try to combat it with the long-ago lessons of choosing to think on good things, to remember the Thatchers were God-fearing people, that Bessie Thatcher would be in heaven now, her hard life behind, an eternity of worship before her. Reading her Bible helped, too, although her eyes grew easily tired and she couldn't read for long.

But for all her weariness and inability to hold a coherent thought, the hours of enforced rest had made some things clear. Pride had led her here. She who had always justified her actions as her Christian duty *had* known she was unwell. The earl had correctly challenged her pretensions, but she had ignored him—as usual. But his words of condemnation had wormed a hole in her heart. If he had not found her, she would have blithely gone home, most likely infecting her entire household, and with their recent illnesses, Papa and Aunt Patience might have easily died! Her heedless actions could have led to more deaths. No wonder the earl despised her. Tears burned her eyes.

His dislike had grown more pronounced of late. He'd not visited since Aunt Patience had arrived. Not that she blamed him. Why would he, when all he received from her were sanctimonious sermons about helping others, and constant reminders about his shortcomings. Hadn't he once decried her earnestness? How self-righteous *had* she appeared? No wonder the tension between them seemed thicker than the trunk of a three-hundred-year oak tree. What a bore she must seem! She groaned.

"Miss?" Lily's nutmeg hair shone in the candlelight. "Are you in pain?"

She forced her lips into a semblance of a smile. "No, thank you, Lily."

The pain she experienced wasn't physical. It could only be healed by an apology.

Hers.

TWO AFTERNOONS LATER she was reading when Aunt Patience appeared, along with the doctor, and, strangely, the earl. He remained glowering by the door as the doctor approached.

"And how are you feeling today?"

"Much better, Doctor, thank you, although my head still aches, and I feel as if my bones are made of water."

"It will take some time to recover your strength." He checked the last remaining spots on her palms and face. "It's good to see you have escaped the worst of the pox."

"Thank God."

He nodded gravely. "Thank God, indeed. Now, your cough? Does it still hurt?"

"Like fire in my chest."

He frowned. "I really would prefer to see more improvement before you go home."

"Oh." Disappointment speared her upper body. "When do you think I can go home?"

"A week? Two? It's hard to say."

She bit her lip. Aunt Patience wore a sympathetic smile; the earl's frown had deepened.

Of course. He would want her gone as soon as possible. He'd be disappointed she was forced to stay another week.

The doctor patted her shoulder. "I know you're anxious to go home, but if you wish to get better, you must rest." He turned to the earl. "I'm afraid I need to insist she stay awhile longer."

He inclined his head. "Of course."

"The good news is"—Dr. Hanbury smiled at her—"you're not infectious anymore, so if you feel strong enough, you have my permission to leave the room the day after tomorrow."

"Oh, but this room and I have become firm friends."

She glimpsed a wisp of a smile from the earl before it was swiftly replaced by his usual bored expression. Then he and Aunt Patience escorted the doctor away.

She picked up her Bible, flicking it open to where she had been reading this morning her mother's favorite verse from Second Timothy: "For God hath not given us the spirit of fear, but of power, and of love, and of a sound mind."

She bit her lip. Disappointment might exist, but God's spirit enabled self-control to push past the negatives to experience peace and love. She meditated on this and was feeling almost reconciled to her prolonged stay when her aunt returned. "I know you're disappointed."

"I *long* to see Papa. His letters are just not the same."

"Now that you both feel better perhaps he can come visit soon."

"I'm sure Lord Hawkesbury would love further interruptions." She sighed. "It feels like *years* since I was home."

"I'll see if another letter has arrived from your papa." Her aunt departed, replaced by Lily who settled into a chair by the fire with some mending. Lavinia offered her a watery smile and resumed her reading, but could only stare at the page blindly. She willed the tears away—such stupid tears that appeared unbidden so easily these days.

Floorboards creaked. She glanced at the doorway, framing the earl. Something leapt within. Her stupid imagination! She hid conflicting emotions with a smile.

"Come to frighten me, my lord?"

His eyes were cool. "Do you really see me that way, or is that just another of your aggravating remarks?"

Her cheeks heated. She lowered her gaze to her Bible, wishing she could hide under the bedcovers as she had as a child. What kind of Christian example was she? "I'm sorry."

"Miss Ellison?"

She glanced at Lily, still studiously mending, then looked up at the earl again.

His brow furrowed. "Are you in pain?"

"No, my lord."

He seemed to hesitate. "May I come in?"

"Yes."

He moved to stand at the foot of the bed, his focus on the coverlet. "I'm sorry you find your stay here so distasteful."

She swallowed, steadied her voice. "I apologize if I gave that impression. I'm only impatient to see Papa. And I do not wish to be an encumbrance upon you and your household." She met his somber expression. "I do appreciate all you have done. Everyone has been very kind."

"Present company excluded."

"No! I mean yes. Oh, I'm not sure quite what you mean." She rubbed her forehead. When would she think clearly again?

His eyes softened. "You are unwell. I will leave—"

"Was there something you wanted, sir?"

"Only to assure you that your presence here is not inconvenient, and my staff are desirous of making your stay as comfortable as possible."

Tears pricked again at his kindness. She blinked them away.

He stepped closer. "Miss Ellison, have I upset you?"

"No, sir." She studied her Bible, the words blurry.

Awkward silence filled the room as she waited for him to speak. Her nerves tingled, her heart felt raw and exposed.

"You are Lily's sole responsibility while you remain here. If you have any particular needs, please don't hesitate to ask."

"Thank you."

He glanced out the window, his gaze restless, not alighting anywhere, much less on her.

Her chest cramped. Her self-righteous behavior had caused this unpleasantness. She should make amends. But how to apologize for a lifetime of principle? She licked her bottom lip. He still refused to look her way. "My lord—"

"Miss Ellison"—his attention returned to her face—"I must apologize for how I spoke to you on that last occasion. I was wrong, and spoke hastily—"

Emotions clashed within, pushing out a hysteria-laden giggle.

His frown deepened. "I suppose you will now say I am often wrong."

"No!" The laughter died. "I'm sorry you would think that of me."

"I did not mean—"

"You have had every reason to believe that. I've always been your most severe critic."

He murmured, "Hardly my most severe."

"You are kind, my lord, when I have often been anything but, and for that"—she waited until the hazel eyes met hers—"I am truly sorry."

He swallowed. Shook his head.

He didn't believe her?

"Hawkesbury?" Aunt Patience appeared behind him, frowning. "What are you doing?"

He shot Lavinia a quick glance, turned to her aunt, and bowed. "Leaving." And with a nod to Lavinia, he departed.

Leaving her feeling emotionally depleted, feeling even worse than before. And increasingly determined to show him she condemned him no more.

⚜

The next morning, having changed from mud-spattered riding dress, Nicholas strode into the hall. Lily stood, wringing her hands.

"Excuse me, me lord?"

Nicholas dismissed Edwin. "Yes, Lily. What is it?"

"It's Miss Ellison, sir. She's gone missing."

"Missing?"

"I can't find her anywhere. And she's not supposed to leave her room yet."

"Where is Miss West?"

"She had to check something back at the parsonage. Meanwhile Miss Ellison—"

"Remains ever elusive." Nicholas sighed and went into the bedchamber. "Miss Ellison?"

No answer.

He frowned as Lily checked under the heavy bed skirts. Glanced around. The room held few secrets: the bed had been remade, and hiding places were limited to the wardrobe and the chimney. He bit back a grin at the thought of Miss Ellison hiding there. No, not even her most hoydenish ways would support such a thing.

He studied the heavy cream drapes that obscured the room's two full-length windows. As a child he'd often found the deep alcoves a suitable place to repair from the torments of his brother. Perhaps . . .

He strode quickly to the first set of curtains and drew them open. Nothing—save that glorious view of the park that used to offer such peace. He fumbled a prayer under his breath, "Lord, I need some peace."

He kept the drapes open, the weak sunlight filling the room with hope. He shifted to the other alcove, flung the curtains wide. And there, on the window seat, dressed in a flimsy cream dressing gown, curled Miss Ellison, fast asleep.

The morning light highlighted the violet shadows under her eyes, her sharpened cheekbones. She was so pale, her skin almost translucent, a mark above her left brow the faintest remnant of her smallpox encounter. His heart softened. "Miss Ellison, time to wake up."

She did not stir. He glanced at the open Bible on her lap. Psalms. Drops of water had mottled the page. Had she been crying?

"You found her!" Lily came to his side. "I swear I looked, me lord, but didn't see her."

"No matter." Nicholas bent closer, and lightly grasped Lavinia's upper arm. "Miss Ellison, wake up."

Stirring, she blinked up at him. The gray eyes had lost all luster, but still held the power to mesmerize. Her lips curved. "Hello."

"Hello." His chest tightened. One day she would waken to smile like that at another man. He frowned to banish the emotion *that* thought ignited. "You gave Lily a scare. She didn't know where you were."

"I'm sorry, Lily. I keep causing you trouble, don't I?" She smiled at the maid. "But if it's any consolation, I've had this habit for years. My father and aunt are now quite reconciled to the fact that I must disappear at times."

"Yes, miss." Lily bobbed a curtsey and glanced up at him.

Nicholas nodded to dismiss her then turned to Lavinia. "You *must* disappear?" He raised an eyebrow. "Hardly the act of a dutiful daughter, disappearing to leave your family to worry."

"I *am* sorry. I certainly did not intend to disrupt your morning responsibilities."

"No matter." He gazed out the window. Rose gardens stretched in formal lines, tended by several gardeners. "I remember when I stayed here as a boy the attraction of these windows. It was nice to escape a houseful of guests." And to escape the arguments of his parents, both between themselves and with Uncle Robert.

"I find that hard to imagine from such a sociable creature as yourself."

His lips twitched. "You must be feeling better, to make such impertinent remarks."

"I fear you will hardly know how to console yourself with my absence."

Her words struck deep. For all the inconvenience she provided, he would miss these regular interactions. He thrust his hands into his coat pockets.

She turned to look outside. "Look at the view! Is it not lovely?" She glanced back, a mischievous smile on her face. "Surely you cannot begrudge me preferring that to the familiarity of these surrounds?"

"I agree that the view is . . ." He paused at the sight of her uplifted face, the wide, gray eyes now shining with amusement, the lips quirked in a fashion that suggested suppressed laughter. His heartbeat quickened.

"My lord?"

He blinked. "The view can be quite enchanting."

"Enchanting." She nodded as if in approval. "It surprises me to hear you use such a poetic term, my lord."

"I fear you give me too little credit, Miss Ellison."

She studied him, all traces of amusement now gone. "Yes, that is true. You've been most generous and patient when I have disrupted your household." She lifted her hand. "Please forgive me."

"Of course." He gently squeezed her hand. "And I hope you will forgive me for"—he swallowed—"for the pain I and my family have caused in the past."

She stared at him a long time before inclining her head. "You are forgiven, my lord."

The tightness encasing his heart eased. "Thank you. I hope you'll also overlook my abrupt manner."

"Abrupt manner? Why Lord Hawkesbury, whatever do you mean?"

Her smile filled his chest with such warmth it was all he could do to offer his apologies that he must away.

Later, as he sat at his desk, thoughts of his houseguest continued to tease, pulling at the strands of his concentration until he gave up any semblance of work. He stared out the study window, allowing his thoughts to freely wander while his foolish heart dreamed.

🥀 Chapter Seventeen

Lavinia glanced out the large window atop the stairs. This, the first day she was permitted by the doctor to leave the room, was wild and wet. The park held none of its usual serenity, instead offering a rather barren, bleak prospect. Aunt Patience said a loud gale had blown in from the southwest last night, bringing squalls and storms. Wind shrieked around eaves, shutters clattered, ivy scraped against the windows, enough to give chills—deservedly so, Aunt Patience said, if she devoured Gothic novels.

"Ready to continue?"

"Yes." She pushed up from the landing's seat, her legs stronger after a little rest. Clutching her aunt's arm, she descended the stairs to the breakfast room, their passage accompanied by bows, curtsies, and smiling nods as the maids and footmen acknowledged her progress.

"Miss Ellison"—Giles bowed—"may I offer my felicitations on your recovery."

"Thank you for your many kindnesses these past weeks."

"We merely serve his lordship."

Her aunt's arm was supporting most of her weight by the time they entered the breakfast room. The room was painted a pretty sage and held a long oak table surrounded by at least a dozen chairs. Along one wall, a heavily carved sideboard was laden with covered dishes. Another wall held a bank of windows looking out onto gray skies and wildly tossing trees. A footman pulled out a chair. She sank down gratefully, drinking in the garden scene.

"I assure you that view is generally more pleasant than what you see today."

She glanced at the door. Lord Hawkesbury's smile held a degree of warmth she'd never noticed before. Or else prolonged illness had disturbed every rational thought.

Aunt Patience placed a teacup on the saucer. "I did not expect even an earl to have command of the weather."

"True. But one cannot help but wish the weather to cooperate as we rejoice over Miss Ellison's recovery." He nodded to the sideboard. "It seems Cook is in a celebratory mood."

"I fear I will not be able to do justice to such a bountiful repast."

"Ah, yes, that is a burden I, too, must bear on a daily basis."

She smiled and glanced down at her place setting, surrounded by a half-dozen little posies and gifts. "What are these?"

"My staff have been receiving offerings from well-wishers for a number of days now. I was even informed, by Mrs. Foster no less, that this calf's-foot jelly is the *very thing* to help you recover, Miss Ellison."

"She is too generous. I don't deserve—"

"It seems nothing is too much for the most popular invalid in England."

She lifted a posy of lavender, inhaling its sweet aroma, hiding her tears at his kind tone.

"Will you join us for breakfast?" Aunt Patience asked.

"Thank you, no. I have already eaten and wish to visit the village with Banning. I am sure Miss Ellison would like to see the Thatchers' roof restored as soon as possible."

"Really?"

He nodded. "By the end of this week."

"That's wonderful!"

The lines around his eyes softened, his lips pulling up into a pensive smile. He opened his mouth as if to say something.

"Lavinia?" Aunt Patience nudged her arm. "Would you care for some toast?"

"Oh!" She dragged her gaze from the earl. "Yes, please."

"Enjoy your meal." The earl offered a small bow and disappeared, leaving her once again to collect her scattered wits.

Following breakfast, she was shown into the morning room, an elegant, yellow-painted room that overlooked the parkland. From her position on the couch, she could see the lake beyond the ha-ha, the heavy clouds merging green vistas into gray as trees bent and swayed like dancers at a ball.

She glanced at the marble fireplace, whose flames crackled, offering cozy warmth. Lily sat nearby, mending, while Aunt Patience visited the parsonage, keeping Papa informed of her progress. Papa. How she longed to see him. But his health, although improving, still prevented his visit, and a cold carriage ride through such woolly weather would not help either of them. She pulled her shawl closer and tried to resume reading Psalms, but her thoughts kept straying.

Perhaps this house fitted the earl more than she had thought. Both held prepossessing exteriors, formal grandeur that could intimidate, yet they also owned inner reserves of warmth and charm. He was such a strange man, sometimes so cold and arrogant, yet also capable of such kindness. And wit!

She smiled ruefully. Of course, she had hardly shown herself consistent in character either—which was far worse, because she at least was supposed to represent Christ, whose character remained wholly consistent. It was strange how she could demonstrate grace and consideration to others but showed Lord Hawkesbury very little. Did she really set such stock in Aunt Patience's decrees that she forgot what the Bible said?

She frowned and flicked over to the second chapter of James. The rich weren't to be shown favoritism—just as Aunt Patience always said—but neither were they to be despised. In not wanting to insult the poor, had she discriminated against the rich, in some perverse form of snobbery? She rubbed her forehead. *Lord, I am sorry for presuming to know so much. Please forgive me, and help me to treat people as You would.*

She applied herself to studying Psalms once again, soon becoming lost in their poetry and promises.

"Miss Ellison?"

She glanced at the doorway. "Lord Hawkesbury! I trust your meeting with Mr. Banning was successful."

"Thank you, yes. Provided the weather cooperates, we endeavor to have the Thatchers' roof on tomorrow."

"I'm so pleased!"

"I am glad." His voice was low, soft as a caress.

Her heartbeat quickened; her smile faltered. Recently, the mocking glitter of his eyes was often replaced by this look of tenderness mixed with something like hope. While their mutual apologies seemed to have leveled the slippery slope of their acquaintance into something more stable, almost like friendship, he still possessed the power to disconcert.

"May I be so bold as to enquire as to what you are reading?"

"The Bible."

His eyes danced. "Yes, I gathered that. More particularly, what section do you read?"

"Psalms." She smiled. "More particularly, Psalm Ten."

He nodded. "Psalms are songs, are they not?"

"Yes."

He moved to the window, staring out across the parkland, hands clasped behind his back. "It does not surprise me you would like to read the musical part."

What was she to say? Why was he discussing the *Bible*? He who had made it very plain he thought believers foolish. An ember of the old indignation sparked within. She glanced at the page. Should she? The likelihood he would say yes was infinitesimally small. "Would you like me to read a portion aloud?"

"I believe I would."

Her mouth sagged in surprise. She glanced at the page. Did she dare?

"Whatever you were reading before." He remained staring out the window.

She swallowed. Very well, then. "Psalm Ten. 'Why standest thou afar off, O Lord? why hidest thou thyself in times of trouble? The wicked in his pride doth persecute the poor: let them be taken in the devices that they have imagined. For the wicked boasteth of his heart's desire, and blesseth the covetous, whom the Lord abhorreth. The wicked, through the pride of his countenance, will not seek after God: God is not in all his thoughts.'"

She slid a glance at the earl. He stood still, his posture tense. She resumed at verse five and finished reading the psalm.

"Is that what you think of me?"

"I beg your pardon?"

"A wicked, arrogant man who hunts down the weak?" He turned to face her. His eyes held no coldness or condemnation but something rather like a silent plea.

145

Remorse washed over her. Perhaps he genuinely sought God. She swallowed. "I do not think you wicked, nor someone who actively seeks the destruction of the poor."

His features twisted in a smile. "Merely arrogant, and someone who passively allows the poor to suffer."

"I did not say that!"

"You did not have to." He shifted to gaze out the window again. "It may interest you to know, Miss Ellison, that these past weeks have provided much food for thought. I . . . I do not consider all of my past behavior to be as it ought."

She blinked. Was she truly awake? She pinched her arm.

"I would be very much interested to know what parts of the Bible you would recommend for a man such as myself to read."

"Oh! You surprise me. I had not thought of this at all."

"For shame, Miss Ellison." He turned, his mouth curved up on one side. "I would have thought a reverend's daughter would know the exact place a sinner such as myself should read."

She pushed herself higher in the couch. Thank goodness Lily remained in the room. This entire encounter felt very . . . strange.

His hazel stare continued, entreatingly, kindly, disquietingly.

"As it so happens, I know exactly where you should read."

Both corners of his mouth now lifted. "I rather thought you might."

Her chin rose. "You should read about Jesus Christ in the gospels. The books of Matthew and John are good for helping understand who Jesus is and how He lived His life. Then, you could read through Romans. Your uncle often shared from it. It is an exposition concerning God's plan of salvation for all mankind. As you grasp the truths outlined there, you will see how generous God's love is for you and understand His righteousness is for you also."

He inclined his head. "Thank you. I am in your debt." He moved to leave.

"Lord Hawkesbury?"

He paused.

"It is I who am in your debt. I do appreciate your generosity. You are kind, my lord."

"Perhaps I am not quite the ogre some people seem to think I am."

She fought the smile. "Perhaps."

She was rewarded with a smothered laugh. "Please take care not to advertise the fact, madam, else I'll be forced to endure all types of people who count me as a soft touch."

"Sir, you can be sure I will never credit you unduly."

His smile lit up the green depths of his eyes before he nodded. "Of that, madam, I am certain." And with a small bow he exited.

A Bible was not too hard to come by. Uncle Robert's piety ensured he had several at hand. The one Nicholas had discovered in the chest of drawers in his bedchamber seemed most useful, as Uncle Robert had scrawled innumerable notes in the margins. He moved to sit by the fire, flicked to the Psalms, and reread Psalm Ten. Grimaced at the picture of the man he no longer wanted to be.

He read through the next few psalms. Far from being mere odes of praise, they indicated the believer too had struggles, but reliance in God continually gave courage. He read the start of Psalm Fourteen and smiled ruefully. He appreciated Lavinia's impertinence not stretching quite so far as to call him a fool, although she would have been right. Fools might deny God's existence, but they needed Him just the same.

Cautious of whatever confronting truths these songs might contain, he flipped through until he found the last book she recommended. Romans. Uncle Robert's favorite apparently, if all the notes were any indication. He started reading the underlined passages.

"For the invisible things of Him from the creation of the world are clearly seen, being understood by the things that are made, even His eternal power and Godhead; so that they are without excuse."

Memories flickered. Uncle Robert encouraging James and Nicholas to appreciate nature on country walks and to see the design in plants that suggested a Creator, provoking them to think beyond the immediate, quelling their wriggling impatience at services with a look.

He turned a page.

"All have sinned, and come short of the glory of God."

He frowned. That sounded hopeless. He thumbed over another page.

"For the wages of sin is death; but the gift of God is eternal life through Jesus Christ our Lord."

God's gift was eternal life?

His pulse picked up. Hadn't Mr. Ellison once preached something about God having gifts for him? Was eternal life one of these gifts? Nicholas swallowed. Hadn't he promised to do whatever God wanted, if He let Lavinia live?

Feeling like he stood on a precipice, he cleared his throat. "Lord, I know I deserve death, but You say eternal life is a gift. How do I get it?"

His voice echoed in the empty room. His gaze fell back to the Bible. Perhaps Uncle Robert had found the answers. He turned a couple more pages to the next underlined passage, almost halfway through chapter ten.

"If thou shalt confess with thy mouth the Lord Jesus, and shalt believe in thine heart that God hath raised him from the dead, thou shalt be saved."

His brows rose. That was all? Mere confession and belief? Didn't one have to prove something to God? Surely salvation couldn't be so simple.

He frowned. What had Lavinia said? Read through Romans? He turned back to chapter one, and read through to the end. When he finished, he sat motionless, staring unseeingly at the page, as the author's challenge continued to resonate in his soul.

Believe. Confess. Be saved.

Weight pressed on him, in him, as a litany of sins flashed before his eyes. How could he ever be good enough? How could forever feeling like he fell short be one of God's gifts?

He turned back to a passage that had caught his attention.

"There is therefore now no condemnation to them which are in Christ Jesus, who walk not after the flesh, but after the Spirit. For the law of the Spirit of life in Christ Jesus hath made me free from the law of sin and death."

No condemnation? No guilt? It couldn't be so simple. He moved to close the book, yet something about the phrase called to him, tugged at him, begged further reflection.

He glanced back. Studied the page again. All were sinners. All deserved death. But Jesus Christ came to set people free from the death and condemnation they deserved. His sacrifice a gift, freely given. People only needed to believe and confess, and they would experience salvation.

Believe and confess.

Confess and believe.

His heart thumped. His eyes burned. Throat thickened. He glanced at the bedchamber's door, still fastened shut. Glanced out the window at the heavens. Breathed past the whirling thoughts until one certainty settled feather-soft in his soul.

He had a very important visit to make.

The day after her first foray downstairs, the earl took Lavinia and Aunt Patience on a short tour. Hampton Hall was familiar from visits to his uncle long ago, but it was nice to be reacquainted with some of its lovely rooms. She spent a delightful hour pottering around the library before weariness claimed her and she returned to the golden morning room she'd found so comfortable yesterday.

It was here that Dr. Hanbury found her and, after his examination of her face and hands, made his recommendation that she stay another week.

"Another week?" She glanced at the earl who had just entered the room. "I'm sorry, my lord. I don't mean to sound ungrateful, but—"

"You are keen to be with your father," he finished smoothly. "Perfectly understandable."

She offered him a grateful smile before turning to the doctor. "I miss Papa, and Hettie, and—"

"Of course you do, lass. But your body is still so weak, and I fear that if you return home too quickly you will resume your responsibilities and end up so fatigued you become ill again."

"Dr. Hanbury, I will not do anything foolish."

"I know you, Lavinia, and I know you find it very hard to say no when someone asks for help. Here you are protected from a great deal of unnecessary obligation and exertion."

"But Lord Hawkesbury—"

"Is very happy for you to remain as long as necessary," the earl interrupted. "Under the watchful eye of Miss West and Lily, of course."

Aunt Patience sent him a sharp look before she, too, agreed.

The doctor's features eased into a gruff smile. "Good. I'm sure you both can moderate Miss Ellison's activity."

Treating her as a child! Lavinia clamped her lips together to avoid an unladylike protest.

The earl glanced at her and his mouth twitched before he escorted the doctor from the room.

Aunt Patience sighed. "Lavinia, this will only prove beneficial."

"I don't wish to complain, but— "

"I know you are not best pleased."

"I don't believe any of this has offered Miss Ellison much in the way of pleasure," Lord Hawkesbury offered from the door. "Illness has very little to recommend it."

"You sound as though you speak from experience."

Lord Hawkesbury nodded to Aunt Patience. "My time in France afforded many occasions to tend men in their sickbeds. I soon recognized boredom was one of the chief curses of illness."

Lavinia drew the shawl around her more tightly. "Will you tell me more about your soldiering life?"

He glanced at her as if surprised, and then lowered himself into the couch across from her. He shared about life on the Peninsular and in France, general details at first, before her questions probed him to share some of the more personal, such as his visits to the widows of his men. She studied him thoughtfully. His stories revealed courage, leadership, tenacity, compassion—qualities she'd longed for him to display. So why had he hidden these in his new role as earl? Were there other elements at work that had made the earldom so distasteful? Sympathy mingled with a newfound respect. "I imagine life as an earl can't be as exciting as being a soldier, but don't you find some aspects of your role similar?"

"You mean apart from chasing down errant knaves?" His crooked eyebrow lifted.

"Apart from that."

"I admit, there is something good about being in a position to help alleviate the suffering of others."

"I agree! I think that is what is meant by we being more blessed to give than to receive. People appreciate our assistance, but we feel so privileged to be the conduit of God's blessings."

"You must feel very privileged indeed."

Her cheeks heated. Was he mocking her? But the soft light in his eyes, his gentle tone, suggested otherwise.

"While blessing others benefits the giver, I think the receiving of help can be very hard sometimes. Don't you agree, Miss Ellison?"

"Why . . . yes. I believe you're right. One's pride doesn't always allow one to appreciate the gifts being offered."

"Or the advice so well-intentioned."

She glanced down. "I didn't realize until recently how presumptuous my pride made me."

"Which must be why our Lord was so deliberate in showing us a different way to live."

Our Lord? Her gaze met his. Was that *faith* shining in the green recesses of his eyes? Her heart thudded.

"So, Miss Ellison, will you accept the gift being offered?"

"The gift?"

"The gift of another week of quiet, so you can moderate your activity in order to attain full health?" His eyes twinkled.

"Far be it for my pride to stand in the way of such solicitude."

He smiled. "I promise we will do what we can to make your stay here as pleasurable as can be." He rose and held out a hand. "Come, see the music room."

❧ Chapter Eighteen

Nicholas frowned as he read over Banning's latest accounts. The estate seemed to be slowly picking up revenue, although the improvements in housing would eat into the profits substantially. But at least Banning was proactive, and careful, and willing to see the big picture to make decisions for long-term gain.

He leaned back in his chair, thinking about his recent decision, the decision that gave "long-term gain" quite another meaning. For the first time in a long time his heart held a measure of peace. His recent ride through the rain to see the reverend had resulted in a confidence for the future. He smiled, recalling the light in the older man's eyes during their conversation, light shining as it had in his guest's when he told her about the Thatchers' roof. A joy both for what his actions had earned for the Thatcher family and, it seemed, joy for him.

His invalid continued to confound him. During yesterday's conversation in the morning room, she had listened, asking intelligent questions about his time in France, her warmth and interest cocooning him in compassion. He had found himself wanting to share about the men, his responsibilities, the challenges, the deprivations. She hadn't flinched as he described some of the horror, but that wasn't surprising. She might be innocent, but she wasn't naive about harsh truths. Instead, she'd gently probed his experiences and then neatly challenged him to turn past exploits into a pattern for the future. Like she believed he could be that man again.

Which was impossible.

Yet so tantalizing.

He threw off his regrets and forced his attention to his accounts, making notes of things to discuss with Banning. A knock came at the door.

He shifted irritably in his chair. "Yes, Giles?"

"Excuse me, m'lord, it's Miss Ellison."

"What about Miss Ellison?" Nicholas raised his eyebrows in the old way, before remembering he was supposed to be living differently. He schooled his features. "Can't Miss West or Lily do something?"

"It is Lily's day off, and Miss West is visiting the parsonage."

"Very well. Where is she?"

"Halfway up the stairs, m'lord."

He exited the study, and ascended the stairs to the wide landing, whereupon he found his guest, asleep on the chaise. He hid the smile. No wonder Giles and the other servants were at a loss. Lavinia was in that strange category of being someone they knew well, and yet a guest. To shake an earl's guest awake was simply not the done thing.

He bent down. "Miss Ellison?"

She didn't move.

His pulse quickened. Was she unwell? He grasped her arm and shook gently. "Miss Ellison? Wake up, please."

She stirred, slowly blinking sleepy gray eyes at him. "Oh." She peered past him at the hovering Giles and Martins. "Oh! I'm so sorry. I was visiting with Mrs. Florrick in her parlor . . ."

Visiting the servant's quarters? He fought a frown as she yawned again.

"I found the stairs excessively tiring and needed a rest. But I did not mean to fall asleep. I certainly did not mean to cause so much trouble."

He dismissed the servants and turned back to her. "Were you attempting to go upstairs on your own?"

"I . . . I am used to being more independent. And I did not want to disturb anyone from their duties."

"No. Instead they are so perturbed they come and disturb me from mine."

Her gaze dropped along with his heart. Why was it easier to speak harsh words rather than kindness? He gentled his tone. "Do you feel well enough to continue?"

She nodded, grasped the proffered hand, and then rose, quickly dropping his hand as if his touch burned. "Thank you, but I will manage. I don't wish you to be disturbed any longer."

She slowly moved to the banister, grasped the newel post, and dragged herself up the first step, swaying, white-faced, like she was about to faint.

"Excuse me, Miss Ellison." He swept her up, ignoring her faint protest, wishing he could as easily ignore how good it felt to hold her close once again. But this time there was no dripping clothes, no wild icy wind propelling them homeward, no sense of urgency. He was conscious instead of the apple blossom scent of her hair, the softness of her gown, the way she so comfortably fit in his arms.

He forced the thoughts away and carried her carefully to her bed, uneasily aware of the impropriety, but unwilling for her to fall or possibly faint.

"Thank you. I felt so lightheaded."

"It's nothing." He moved to the door, away from temptation, away from her.

She sighed. "I have always despised such weakness."

"Not very charitable of you."

"I don't mean those who are truly sick. No, those ladies who always have fainting fits."

"Perhaps they deserve your compassion and not your censure," he drawled.

"Not if they are trying to attract attention from a man."

"And is that what you were doing?"

"Of course not!" Her face stained pink.

"I can assure you that I do not find that kind of lady in the least way attractive."

"And I can assure you that I am not in the *least* way that kind of lady."

He hid a smile. "Miss Ellison, I am very aware of what kind of lady you are."

As her eyes widened, he bowed and exited the room, his heart hammering.

What kind of lady? Only the most challenging, most intriguing, most dangerous lady he had ever had the good fortune to meet.

The Hall was quiet. The music room, painted in cool green and white, was situated toward the back of the house, with large windows looking out to the birch grove beyond. Aunt Patience and the earl were at services, and most of the staff attended also, leaving her undisturbed and free to worship God with the magnificent pianoforte—although after one scratchy attempt, God would perhaps be better honored *without* her voice.

She completed the second movement with an arpeggio and smiled. Looked up. Jumped. "Lord Hawkesbury! I had not anticipated an audience."

He moved from the open doorway into the room. "I had not anticipated coming back from church to hear music."

"I hope you don't mind. When your uncle was alive, I would often come and play here."

"Did I not invite you to do so the other day? Pianos are designed for making music, are they not? And we must do what we are created to do. And in your case—and the piano's—that would be to create lovely music."

Pleasure fluttered at his unlooked-for compliment. "How was the service today?"

"I found it surprisingly useful."

"You were surprised?"

"I confess to surprise whenever that Raymond fellow says something rational, but today I found quite a lot of what he had to say made quite a lot of sense."

"Such wonders!"

His amused expression grew soft. "That green becomes you, Miss Ellison. I am glad you are looking well."

"Why is that?"

"Because you have a visitor."

"Who?"

"For that, you must come with me."

He offered his arm, which she accepted, and he led the way to the yellow drawing room she often claimed for her own. He paused as Martins opened the door, then gestured her inside. "After you."

She took a few steps then— "Papa!" She rushed to clasp him in a hug.

"Ah, my dearest Lavinia." His voice rumbling in her ear, his familiar scent, his arms held such assurance. "I've missed you so."

She eased back, studying the new grooves in his wan face. "You are better?"

"Better for seeing you, my dear girl."

"As I am, you." She kissed his cheek and hugged him again. "I'm so glad you could come."

Her father's attention shifted beyond her shoulder. "His lordship was insistent."

Lavinia turned and gave the earl her brightest smile. "Thank you so *much*, my lord."

He gave her a wistful-looking smile, bowed, and retreated, leaving her filled with gratitude and free to enjoy the warm affection and sweet reunion with her earthly father.

Lavinia's beaming smile continued throughout luncheon, inducing great levels of satisfaction. Nicholas found himself catching every note of her laughter, wondering how many months it had been since he'd heard it so full. He smiled along with her, for no other reason than her joy was contagious. Her father might be the cause of her delight, but Nicholas was content to bask in her appreciation. The afternoon passed, the Hall filling with unprecedented levels of warmth and cheer, Lavinia's smile only dimming when her father needed to return home.

He stood at the front door as she kissed her father goodbye and gave him one last hug. His heart caught. What would it be like to be the recipient of such warm, open affection?

She waved until his carriage could no longer be seen. "Oh, Lord Hawkesbury, thank you so much."

"You're most welcome."

"It has been over a month. I don't remember him looking so frail."

"He is gaining in years."

Nicholas glanced at her profile as they walked through the hall toward the grand staircase. Her head drooped, as if the revelation that her father was growing old carried new weight.

As he searched for some encouraging comment, she said, "He seemed smaller somehow."

"I've never heard of pneumonia shrinking a body."

A smile flickered across her face. "Perhaps he hasn't shrunk, after all, and it is merely the effect of having to look up to you this past month."

"You've only looked up to me this past month? I am disappointed."

She gurgled with laughter. "You, sir, are incorrigible."

"Incorrigible perhaps, but not irredeemable."

She gave him that look of puzzled disbelief, as if not sure what his words signified.

He smiled. The sound drifting into the hall of the pianoforte being mercilessly played suggested her aunt would be engaged for some time.

"Miss Ellison? I was hoping you would do me two favors. Three favors, really."

"Why certainly, if I can."

"Seeing as we are to spend more time together, I was hoping you might deign to call me Nicholas. I confess I find the constant Lord Hawkesbury address rather tedious."

"How equalitarian! But I believe others would find that rather forward."

"What? There's nothing terribly forward about my name. In fact, I believe it dates back to Grecian times."

She made a sound suspiciously like a giggle.

Heartened, he asked the question that had bothered him for a fortnight. "I was also wondering if you might favor me regarding something else."

"Yes?"

"Who is Timothy?"

"Timothy?" Her brow wrinkled. "I don't know anyone by that name."

"When I found you that night, you were murmuring something about a man and being afraid. I only wanted to assure you that if someone is making you fearful, I—"

"Oh, Timothy!" Her expression cleared and she laughed. "My lord, I thank you for your solicitude, but there is nothing to be concerned about."

His cheeks warmed. "Really?"

"Timothy is a book of the Bible my mother often quoted from. One of her favorite verses concerns God not giving us a spirit of fear. I rather think that is what I might have been murmuring."

"Ah. You may need to show me that verse."

"Gladly." She tilted her head and smiled up at him, causing his chest to throb painfully. "You mentioned another favor?"

"Only if you are not too tired?"

"I am not."

"Would you please accompany me to the long gallery?"

"Of course."

He led the way to the long hall. A bank of large windows spilled light onto the wall containing dozens of ancestral portraits. She examined the paintings intently, a small smile on her face, before she sank onto a small settee, positioned to view the pictures in all their glory.

"We have a great many more paintings in the gallery at Hawkesbury House. But Uncle Robert never liked to throw away his ancestors."

"Casting off one's family members must count as the height of incivility."

"Indeed."

She glanced around. "I remember coming here as a girl. Your uncle knew I liked looking at the pictures. I've never known my grandparents, and my family is small, so it gave me such a sense of comfort to see the years of family so honored."

What a different perspective to his mother's. She had banished these particular portraits, labeling them old-fashioned and unsuitable for Hawkesbury House.

"Did you discover the special family emblem?"

"The badger?" She smiled. "I'm surprised you don't consider that my personal emblem."

"Far be it from me to ever point that out to a lady."

"No, not when you're such a gentleman."

They shared smiles.

He dragged his gaze away and focused on a painting of his great-grandfather posing astride his horse, Jupiter. Uncle Robert had always said Nicholas was the spitting image, from the dark hair and mismatched eyebrows to his love for horses.

She rose, and peered at it more closely. "That house in the background?"

"Hawkesbury House."

"It looks very grand."

"It is. Which is why my mother prefers living there when not in London."

"I have always thought the Hall here very convivial."

"I agree. I think it more pleasantly situated, too. Hawkesbury House is much too dark and has too many ill-conceived additions. The Hall is much nicer, more fitting as a family home."

He hoped she didn't misinterpret that last comment. But there was no knowing smile or flirtatious comment such as would trip from the tongue of so many young ladies his mother deemed suitable. Instead she was frowning.

"What is it, Miss Ellison? You seem displeased. Surely it's not the color of the draperies? I assure you they are very fine. Although my mother is demanding an overhaul."

The smile was fleeting. "The color of your draperies holds little interest for me."

"What an unusual female you are! Every other female of my acquaintance seems to hold very decided opinions about the colors and the furnishings of my houses. Why not you?"

She glanced about abstractly. "I should not like to be so rich."

"No? And how rich should you like to be?"

Her eyes were serious. "How many houses do you have, sir?"

"Three. Or is it four? My solicitor assures me the hunting lodge in Scotland is mine and not my cousin's, yet my cousin does not seem quite convinced."

"And how many of them do you actually live in?"

"Only ever one at a time."

She shook her head. "It seems quite wrong for one person to have vacant houses when others have such poor housing or indeed none."

The lightheartedness disappeared. "Are you moralizing again?"

Her cheeks pinked.

"What would you have me do, Miss Ellison? Move all the poor into my homes? I assure you, there may prove some difficulties with such a scheme."

She studied the floor, her lips pressed together. "I'm sorry, I . . . I believe I am rather tired after all, Lord Hawkesbury. Please excuse me."

And before he knew what had happened, she'd dropped a small curtsey and hurried away to the music room, where the abrupt halt of the pianoforte and low voices suggested she had found her aunt once again.

Leaving him feeling bereft, adrift, and calling himself every kind of fool.

꺄 CHAPTER NINETEEN

AFTER DINNER CONSUMED in her room, followed by a fitful night during which Lavinia worried what she'd say to the earl when she saw him again, her courage at finally descending the stairs for breakfast was rewarded with the news that the earl had gone for a long ride earlier.

She ate with her aunt and discussed the weather, now considerably clearer than the inclement conditions of the past few days, and then repaired to the music room while Aunt Patience visited the village. The music helped calm her frayed emotions. She was midway through the second movement when the door opened.

"Miss Ellison, I am sorry to disturb you, but you have visitors." Giles inclined his head. "In the blue saloon."

Anticipation hurried her steps to the hallway. "My father?"

"Alas, no."

"Is the earl returned?"

"Not as yet." He cleared his throat. "Would you be requiring tea?"

She blinked. "I could not wish to presume . . ."

He waited.

She drew in a deep breath. "If the visitors are still here after a quarter hour, or if the earl returns, then yes, tea would be lovely. Thank you, Giles."

"As you wish." He smiled.

She checked her appearance in the large hall mirror, smoothed her hair into something acceptable, glad her effort to cheer herself meant she'd chosen to wear her nicer morning gown.

Martins opened the door. She smiled her thanks then stopped in surprise.

"Livvie!" Pink satin and blond curls flew at her. "We were so worried!"

Lavinia drew back from the satin-encased arms almost smothering her in a hug, and laughed. "I am much improved now, Sophy."

"I am so glad!"

"We are all very thankful." Lady Milton offered a tight smile.

"Indeed, we are!"

The squire's genial expression put her at ease to be seated and ask him about the harvest and other village matters. His recounts and Sophy's bright chatter proved quite diverting, although Lady Milton's frown and continued silence were somewhat disconcerting.

"Would you like tea, Lady Milton?"

"I beg your pardon?" The frown intensified, and she glanced at the door again.

"Mama, Livvie asked if we would like tea."

"Tea? Oh, yes, thank you, tea would be nice. It's rather cool out."

After giving instructions to a footman, Lavinia returned her attention to her guests. "It feels an age since I was outside."

"Of course, my dear." The squire smiled. "You should be protected from the elements—"

"Where is your aunt?"

"I beg your pardon?"

Lady Milton leaned forward, her dark eyes snapping. "Perhaps Miss West did not explain matters clearly, or your recent illness has made it difficult to remember how a young lady should behave, but there are some people who would be scandalized by a young woman staying in the house of a single gentleman!"

Her breath caught. Could a slapped face sting any harder?

"Mama!"

"I'm sorry, Lavinia, but I think your behavior *most* improper. I know you don't have a mother to advise you, but I would have thought a reverend's daughter would be more aware of what the gossips will say!"

Her eyes burned. She pressed her lips, desperate to prevent an angry retort—or tears.

"Lady Milton," a deep voice drawled from behind her, "perhaps *you* can tell us what the gossips intend to say?"

One quick glance around the room had been enough to gain everyone's measure. The squire and his daughter sat stupefied, Lady Milton looked furious, while Lavinia's pink cheeks and downcast bearing spoke volumes.

"My lord! We did not expect you—"

"Evidently." He shot the squire's wife a look that had quelled lesser mortals.

"I am sorry, I did not mean to suggest—"

"Suggest what, ma'am?" His gaze narrowed. "That Miss Ellison had ulterior motives in becoming sick? That she *intended* to become unconscious, and somehow in her unconscious state manipulated the situation so as to end up here? Or are you suggesting that she deceived Dr. Hanbury, my entire staff, Miss West, and myself by merely pretending to have smallpox and such severe influenza that her survival is indeed miraculous?"

He paused for breath. Lady Milton's foolish mouth had fallen open.

"I am sure, ma'am, that you could not possibly conceive such ill-natured things. Why, the very thought is repugnant!"

"Repugnant!" Sir Anthony echoed, glaring at his wife.

"And anyone who even dared to impugn my character and contemplate that *I* would be so dishonorable as to take advantage of such a calamity must know they need never darken the doors of my house again."

"My lord, I did not mean to cast aspersions on your character at all!"

"Merely Miss Ellison's?" He lifted a brow. "Surely you must realize Miss Ellison is a most superior female, without conceit, without a devious bone in her body. Anyone who presumes to think otherwise is a fool!" He offered his blandest smile. "And I am persuaded you are no fool."

The door opened to admit a servant carrying the tea tray, his entrance swiftly followed by Miss West, whose quick survey of the room seemed to readily surmise the situation.

"I am terribly sorry. I was detained at the apothecary. Dr. Hanbury reminded me to ensure Lavinia does not travel until he determines she is strong enough." She moved to Lavinia's side and frowned. "Are you quite well? You seem a trifle flushed."

"I am a little tired," she replied in a low voice.

"Perhaps a rest will be necessary after tea." Miss West's dark eyes glittered as she glanced around the room. "I must confess, I certainly had not anticipated such a party."

Lady Milton half rose from her position on the settee. "We can leave now, if you prefer."

"Nonsense." Nicholas shot Miss West a glance. "Miss Milton has barely had a chance to talk with Miss Ellison. Let us not interrupt their time together."

He assisted Miss West by handing around the cups and saucers, noting Lavinia's studied avoidance of him and refusal to meet anyone's gaze, although Miss Milton's chatter did manage to coax a small smile from her.

He glanced at the squire. "I was inspecting the recent improvements to some of the estate housing, to see how it holds up under the recent weather. I am pleased to report the new roof does exactly as it ought."

Lavinia peeped at him, a small smile peeking out before her attention returned to Sophia. Satisfied, he allowed Miss West to carry the conversation as he sought to hear the girls' words.

"It feels an age since we saw you." Sophia sighed. "Mama did not want me to visit earlier, in case I came down with something."

"She was wise."

"I don't know why you had to visit the Thatchers, Livvie."

Lavinia's eyes shadowed, before she offered a gentle, "How are the children coping?"

"I haven't spoken to them, of course, but from all accounts, they are coping well." Sophia flicked a plump curl over her shoulder. "It must be hard to lose your mother like that."

He glanced sharply at Lavinia's pressed lips and rapid blinking. "I imagine, Miss Milton, it's very difficult to lose your mother regardless of circumstance."

Silence filled the room.

The remainder of tea was consumed in an awkward hush.

Not long after, the Miltons rose and made their departure, which was swiftly followed by the removal upstairs of Miss Ellison and Miss West. The tea things were cleared away, and Nicholas sat alone, ruing the years of habitual sarcasm that now proved so difficult to contain, and wondering what repercussions would eventuate, for himself and for poor Lavinia.

"I cannot believe she thinks that of me!"

"*I* cannot believe she had the nerve to say such a thing." Aunt Patience wore a scowl the likes of which Lavinia had never seen. "It is a credit to you that you held your tongue."

"I doubt she would have believed my denials, anyway."

And that was the hard truth. Her innocence was impossible to prove. Humiliation covered her indignation like thick goose grease did a burn.

"Perhaps she'll believe the earl. He looked thunderous, didn't he?"

Lavinia nodded. But had the earl appeared too anxious to deny any wrongdoing? Would his assiduous attention not provide further speculation that he may indeed hold something akin to affection for her in his heart? Or was this complete and utter fantasy, fueled by her stupid imagination and exacerbated by illness? She groaned.

Aunt Patience looked at her sharply and then pulled back the bedcovers. "Come, I think it's best for you to rest."

She agreed meekly, removing her shoes and lying under the blankets. But although she prayed and tried to believe things would somehow work out for good, the mortification continued to ebb and flow, the questions whirled, and heaviness of heart made sleep impossible.

CHAPTER TWENTY

NICHOLAS SPURRED MIDNIGHT through the increasing rain showers in a futile attempt to forget the stupidity of yesterday. He was a fool, a complete and utter fool, to have allowed himself to be so easily goaded by that woman. Despite the title, Lady Milton was no lady.

He *should* have resisted and held his tongue as Lavinia did, but something about how she looked so defenseless, like a baby bird faced with a snarling Brindle Terrier, had wrung his heart—and wrung sense from his brain.

Midnight cantered up the slope toward the Hall, his hooves thundering across parkland that had yet to turn to mud.

"Come on, boy. Nearly there." Icy chips of rain slithered down his neck. The Hall suddenly loomed in front of him, its lighted windows the promise of comfort.

Midnight veered toward the stables, his breath misting in the cool air. Nicholas ducked his head as he entered. Stable hands appeared from dim recesses.

"The weather's blowing in." McHendricks reached for the reins. "Getting nasty out."

"I hope conditions have improved around here."

"They must have if you can now make such remarks."

Nicholas nodded, appreciative of the head groom's willingness to overlook his foul temper of before. He strode to the house, walked inside, stripped off his gloves, and halted at the sound of laughter. Laughter? How long since he'd returned to a house of laughter? His childhood had consisted of cold propriety and continual competition with James. He took a step toward the sound and hesitated. He hadn't seen Lavinia since yesterday morning. Was she still avoiding him?

"Welcome back, sir." Giles hurried forward and took his cloak, hat, and gloves, before handing him a small towel to dry his face. "Miss West and Miss Ellison are in the library."

"Thank you, Giles."

He strode to the library and opened the door. Two heads lifted, one eyed him warily.

"Good afternoon, Miss West." He nodded. "Miss Ellison."

"Hello." Her eyes seemed lit with genuine gladness, her warm smile eliciting his.

His pulse danced. What would it be like to have a wife waiting for him with a welcome warmer than any paid servant's? He stepped nearer. "I am glad to see you look more refreshed."

"I was a little tired yesterday."

"Tired of her visitors," Miss West offered drily.

"It was kind for them to come. I did enjoy talking with Sophy. I have missed her."

Nicholas smiled. So his hint to the Miltons at church hadn't been entirely in vain. "I thought I heard the sound of laughter as I came in."

She lifted the book in her hands. "I'm reading *Twelfth Night*. I was in the mood for something comical, and this has always been my favorite Shakespearean play."

"Now why does that not surprise me? I might have supposed you to be a fan of Viola's proclivity for action."

Her eyes rounded. "You know the play?"

"'When mine eyes did see Olivia first, methought she purged the air of pestilence.'"

"*Olivia*, did you say?" Miss West raised her brows.

"Of course, ma'am." Ignoring her speculative look, he sat on the sofa opposite Lavinia and stretched out his legs. "I studied it at school. I hated it at the time, but then I was a callow youth."

"Caring more for your horse than your studies?"

"Perhaps."

Lavinia smiled, and he couldn't help but respond in kind. There was something so right about the way she looked, seated in front of the crackling fireplace as rain pattered the windows. The tension of the previous morning seemed forgotten, replaced by a sense of camaraderie that gave an ease to things now.

"I always thought Olivia quite an insipid character."

He glanced at Miss West. "I agree. Apart from beauty, she has little to recommend her."

She nodded, as if satisfied, and perused her slim volume of poetry.

"I have always felt quite sorry for Malvolio. He is treated extremely poor."

"You surprise me, Miss Ellison. Sympathy for one so proud? I would think you would enjoy his set down."

"I do not enjoy seeing anyone in pain, sir."

"Your compassion does you credit. But Malvolio's pretensions merely blind him to reality. 'Pride goeth before destruction, and an haughty spirit before a fall.'"

Her eyes widened.

"You seem surprised I know something of the Bible."

"Pleased, sir, rather than surprised."

"I must confess, I did not recognize its truth until, like Malvolio, my pride was assailed."

Her expression shifted into something akin to regret. "But sometimes the method of destruction can be overly harsh."

"Yet necessary, for the most stubborn of fools. And until it is destroyed, we cannot see clearly." He lowered his voice, "I am thankful for the lessons given me."

The color rose in her cheeks. "Now you are being nonsensical."

"And you do not like nonsense, I recall. I must think of something profound to say."

Her smile flashed. "Please do not strain yourself for my sake."

"Ah." He grinned. "Alas, like Orsino, I can only say, 'Still so cruel?'"

She laughed. "'Still so constant,' Lord Hawkesbury."

"Nicholas," he pressed.

"Nicholas," she murmured, her eyes luminous, before her gaze returned to her book.

He leaned back against the upholstery, watching her a moment longer. Her lips flickered into smiles, the shadows dancing across her face lengthening her lashes. Firelight caught the gold in her hair, making him wonder about the softness of those curls . . .

He blinked and slowly stood. He really must see about changing these clothes.

Over the next few days life settled into a new, strange routine. Mornings saw a steady parade of visitors, as everyone from Catherine Winthrop to Eliza Hardy felt free to visit, after the earl murmured something at church about Lavinia's need for company, or so Mrs. Foster said. Nothing would be seen of him until later in the afternoons, when visitors were not expected, and he would find her in the music room or here, in the library, and the subsequent conversation between Aunt Patience, herself, and the earl—no, *Nicholas*—would flow with convivial ease.

Her spirits had improved, due in no small part to her decision to forgive Lady Milton and not allow offence into her heart. Papa's daily visits helped also, his faith in her unmitigated—although she doubted he would even notice the innuendo should someone have the temerity to say something to him. Thinking about how wronged she was would not solve anything. God knew she was innocent, so she determined to think on better things.

Better things, like appreciating the many who wished her well. Appreciating time spent in a beautiful house, where a multitude of servants cared for her as she regained strength. Lily was yet another blessing. Aunt Patience, whose dry wit and insightful conversation engaged Lavinia's sense of humor and her mind. And Nicholas . . .

"Miss Ellison?"

She glanced up from her book, her cheeks heating. He seemed to appear at the oddest moments, almost like he knew she had been thinking of him. "Yes, my lord?"

"You appear to be wool gathering. I asked you a question, which you ignored, yet I am determined not to take offence."

"I am glad for your sake, my lord. To take offence at such a thing would display a stingy soul, indeed."

His lips curved. "Your wit indicates you are well on the road to recovery."

"Something you will no doubt miss when I am no longer here to plague you with it."

"I am scarcely plagued, Miss Ellison."

The humorous glint in his eyes, touched by something that looked remarkably like tenderness, made her heart flutter and her face warm further. "Was there a question, my lord?"

"Miss West has given you a remarkably well-rounded education. I wonder, has she ever taught you to play chess?"

Lavinia exchanged glances with her aunt, sitting away from the fire in the room's corner. "She has not."

"Really? I'm surprised. A pity. I was prepared to challenge you to a match, but . . ." He shrugged.

"I'm sure Lavinia would be able to play. She is a quick study."

"True, Miss West." The earl turned to Lavinia. "Would you like to play?"

She put her bookmark in place and smiled sweetly. "I believe I would."

Half an hour later, they were engrossed in a battle of wits, as her knight evaded capture from his bishop. He'd glance up every so often, catching her swiftly averted gaze, or the smoothing of a smile. Lavinia's playing ability proved her to be a *very* quick study indeed, but he didn't mind her subterfuge. Chess was merely a ploy to achieve his goal—more time with his houseguest.

He shifted his rook from danger and spent the next minute watching her. Lilac smudges under her eyes still testified to her illness; the pockmarks near her hairline were fading, yet continued to bear witness to her compassion. He was relieved. Her face seemed to hold even more character now, her outward appearance increasingly appealing the more time he spent with her.

Not classically beautiful, Lavinia possessed a luminous charm far more alluring. Her eyes sparkled with intelligence, her dimples hinted of her wit, her lips promised romance, her skin a canvas for her emotions . . . She could hide nothing. Like the fact she now enjoyed his company.

Which was just as well, because he enjoyed hers. She was interesting, well-read, able to converse on all matters of life. How refreshing to speak to a young woman whose topics of conversation were not limited to the latest fashions or gossip about others. And her quiet absorption in his conversation had led him to open his heart as he never had before. Yet he sensed that if he pressed his advantage, she'd simply retreat.

"Lord Hawkesbury?"

"Nicholas."

"Nicholas," she repeated softly, stirring his heart to sweetness. "I believe it is your turn."

He refocused his attention on the chessboard. She had countered his move. He frowned, studying the pieces, before a path revealed itself. He shifted his queen in a long diagonal move across the board. "Check."

He glanced up. Lavinia held his smile as their gazes connected. Her eyes were like the moonlit Bay of Biscay: beautiful, clear, sparkling with warmth. Something hot rushed through his chest, lending wings to his spirits, his heart, his soul, before she dropped her gaze to resume her perusal of the chessboard. He exhaled silently, watching candlelight flicker mysteries across her features as he waited. She shifted her king from danger so he swiftly moved his bishop, but in doing so, brushed her hand. Heat trembled up his arm, and it took a moment before he could drawl, "I believe that is checkmate, my dear Miss Ellison."

She studied the chessboard with puckered brow, before she moved her piece once again. "On the contrary, my dear sir, I believe *that* is checkmate." Her triumphant smile shone. "My queen takes your king."

He studied the board, saw that it was so, and shook his head. "You are quite a formidable opponent, Miss Ellison." He leaned forward until his face was quite close to hers. "Especially for someone who has never played."

She bowed her head, the glimmer of a smile still on her lips. "As always, I hesitate to contradict . . ."

"As always."

She laughed, low and husky. "But Nicholas, you must allow, I did not say I had never played. Just that my aunt had not taught me."

"Your tactics astonish!"

"So my father often tells me."

"He is your usual opponent?"

She nodded. "Papa taught me when I was a girl."

"You are a remarkable young lady. I congratulate you." He picked up her hand and pressed it gently. "Perhaps I should speak to your father about a match?"

She smiled. That warm, sweet sensation squeezed his heart once more.

"A match?" A new, unlooked-for voice cried shrilly. "What match could you possibly mean?"

ℜ Chapter Twenty-One

Lavinia looked at the door and froze. A most elegant woman, whose face wore an expression colder than the bleakest depths of winter, stood glaring at them both.

"Mother!" The earl's face drained of all animation. He dropped Lavinia's hand like a hot coal. "What are you doing here?"

"When I am informed that my only surviving child is at risk of smallpox, I immediately set out to see how he fares." She squinted. "This, I presume, is the chit who put my son in mortal danger?"

Nicholas rose. "Mother, this is Miss Lavinia Ellison. Miss Ellison, this is my mother, the Countess of Hawkesbury."

Her ladyship's eyes remained frosty as she ignored Lavinia's small curtsey.

"It is an honor to meet you, ma'am. And I assure you, I had no intention of endangering your son's life."

"Pah! You've insinuated your way into his graces and into his home. No doubt the entire county is gossiping about your conduct!"

"Mother!"

Lavinia swallowed, the heat in her cheeks rapidly spreading. "You're mistaken, your ladyship. I had no intention of coming here, but the fact that Nich—I mean, your son—found me when he did no doubt saved my life."

"Such liberties!" Pale blue eyes snapped at the earl. "You let this mere schoolgirl address you so familiarly?"

"She is *not* a schoolgirl. And Miss Ellison is correct: I gave her no choice but to come here. If she had not, Dr. Hanbury said she would most likely have died."

172

"Hmph!"

"You are correct about the county gossips." Aunt Patience rose from her corner of the room.

The Countess scowled. "Who is this person?"

The stiff silk of her aunt's skirts rustled as she moved to Lavinia's side. "They no doubt gossip about the wonderful generosity your son has shown to such an insignificant person as my niece."

A tiny smile hovered over the earl's lips, disappearing as he turned to his parent. "This is Miss Ellison's aunt, Miss West. Miss West, my mother."

His mother's eyes narrowed further. "You, you seem familiar. Have we met?"

"I have met many people in my life. I do not recall them all."

Lavinia stared at the faint pink staining her aunt's cheeks. Aunt Patience never blushed. *Had* she met the countess? How could she? Hadn't she always lived a quiet life of books and music? The earl's voice drove further conjecture away.

"As Miss Ellison's maid, and lately her aunt, have been in residence the entire time she has been here, there has been no hint of impropriety. Miss Ellison's sterling reputation, and that of her father, means no decent person would even contemplate entertaining such wicked notions." The earl's folded arms and stern glare brooked no opposition. "Let me not hear any more silly speculation."

His mother's lips thinned as she moved to sit on the settee, divesting herself of her gloves and silken wrapper, which she handed to a thin, elegantly dressed lady of indeterminable age. "Take this upstairs, Pierce. This room is rather warm." Pierce disappeared.

As the earl sent for tea, Lavinia glanced at her aunt, wondering if they should leave also, but Aunt Patience merely shook her head. She swallowed a sigh.

"Miss Ellison and Miss West have been a tremendous help in helping me understand some of the concerns of the local community, Mother."

The countess sniffed.

"Miss Ellison holds a real desire to help the poorer tenants attain better housing."

"The poor? Why should anyone care about the poor? Dirty wretches."

"Mother!"

Lavinia could keep quiet no more. "The poor are just like you and me. They deserve our sympathy, not our censure! How can we stand idly by and watch their suffering when we have it in our power to help?"

A footman appeared with the tea. She breathed past the quivering indignation, her hand shaking as she accepted a teacup from the earl.

The countess sipped her tea. "You are frightfully forward in your opinions, Miss Ellison, I must say."

Must you? Lavinia pressed her lips together.

The countess settled back in her chair. "Most well-bred young ladies of my acquaintance do not think of such things. Men don't admire such independent thinking."

"Then it's a good thing my niece is not looking to be admired by a man."

Lavinia fought to control her words, fought not to look at the earl. "I have been brought up to believe that my life is to be useful in the service of others. I understand that many young ladies of your acquaintance might be content to talk about clothing or draperies, but that is something that will never interest me. So it is most fortunate I will never be in London or some other fashionable place to appear so frightfully forward."

"Indeed!" Icy blue eyes bore into her.

The duel of wits had left her exhausted. Lavinia placed her teacup on the side table and rose. "Please excuse me. I am feeling rather tired."

"Of course you are." Aunt Patience offered her arm, as if determined to show Lavinia was an invalid. "Please excuse us both."

The earl rose, his lips upturned in seeming appreciation of her aunt's performance, before turning to his mother with a resigned look.

After escaping the drawing room, Lavinia gave a huge sigh of relief. She glanced to where Giles hovered in the hall, a twinkle in his eye, which disappeared with the reemergence of Pierce.

As Aunt Patience muttered something, Lavinia grasped the banister, half dragging her way upstairs, the sudden exertion causing no small loss of breath. When she reached her room, her weariness was great, but she forced herself to the wardrobe and began removing gowns.

Lily moved to her side, arms outstretched. "Miss, what are you doing?"

"Yes, Lavinia, what *are* you doing?"

"Packing."

"Whatever for?"

"We must go. I have more than outstayed my welcome."

"Lavinia, you are simply not up to traveling."

"It's not far."

"I know, but I would feel more comfortable to have the doctor come and give his consent." Her aunt nodded to Lily. "That will be all."

Lavinia met the maid's worried glance and managed a smile. "Thank you, Lily."

Aunt Patience waited until the girl had exited before speaking again. "If you leave as soon as her ladyship arrives, it may appear you have something to hide. Far better to stay for a few more days, giving the impression of her approval, than to go scurrying off like a fox set to hounds."

"Approval? She looked like she wanted me dead!"

"And why should that matter? Her opinion is simply that, an opinion. And you do not care what any Hawkesbury thinks of you, do you?" Her aunt stared hard at her.

She swallowed. No, she cared not for the opinion of the countess. But the earl . . .

"Remember, you have *nothing* of which to be ashamed. It is not as if Hawkesbury has any thought of you."

Her heart clenched. Of course he hadn't. This illness had made her such a fool.

Her aunt returned the dresses to the wardrobe, muttering, "I believe Margaret Hawkesbury has practiced that sneer for years."

"You *do* remember her."

Her aunt turned away, tugging down the cuff of her dress. "Some circumstances require a little dissembling. Now, I think you should rest while I summon the doctor. Today's exertions seemed to have wearied you considerably."

But as Lavinia lay on the bed, sleep refused to come. Her aunt's justification of pretense warred against years of her instructions in honesty. Questions continued, spinning cobwebs of confusion, obscuring all she thought she'd known, until exhaustion claimed her and dragged her down into oblivion.

Nicholas leaned back in his dining chair, watching the interplay between the three women from under hooded eyes. Since his father's death, his mother's forcefulness had escalated along with her coldness, to the point that most people bent to her will rather than face her icy ire. She had never coped well with other dynamic personalities, especially those she believed socially inferior. But apparently Miss West had not received *that* particular memorandum, as she continued in her disconcerting, abrupt ways and refusal to use formal address for her social betters. It was no surprise Mother detested her, or that in the past three days the two ladies had barely exchanged a civil word. Their sparring amused him, as it seemed to amuse Lavinia, when she wasn't trying to placate his mother regarding Miss West's more outrageous remarks.

He glanced at the reverend's daughter. Since his mother's arrival, she had avoided his gaze. Indeed, she'd barely spoken to him. He missed their repartee, missed the open sharing and the ease. He'd love to know why her brow puckered as she watched her aunt now.

The formidable Miss West. He played with his wine glass, thinking back three days to when she stood before him in the study, determination in her eyes and in the tilt of her chin.

"Hawkesbury, my niece is determined to leave, to rid your mother of any unwarranted concern. *I*, however, am concerned that may be precipitate. I wish to summon the doctor to ascertain whether such a trip should continue."

He'd ignored the flutter of unease the thought of Lavinia's departure provoked and acquiesced to her aunt's wishes.

Dr. Hanbury's diagnosis necessitated a further week's stay before he was satisfied she would be well enough to return home, much to his mother's displeasure—and Nicholas's private relief.

As the older women continued trading opinions and thinly veiled insults over the rights of the poor, he glanced across the luncheon table. "Miss Ellison, how do you feel today?"

The other conversation ceased as she replied, "Better than yesterday, my lord."

"Do you feel like venturing out of doors briefly? There's something I think you might like to see."

"What is it, Nicholas?" His mother frowned at him.

"Nothing that would interest you in the slightest, ma'am, I assure you."

Lavinia's glance moved from his mother to the dining-room window spilling sunshine onto the dark-stained wooden floors. "I have not been outside in *weeks*."

"Some fresh air will do you good." It was Miss West's turn to frown his direction. "As long as she doesn't catch cold."

He inclined his head. "It won't take long."

Lily retrieved a wrap and followed them at a discreet distance. The wind had mercifully died down, and the tall trees stood stiffly, as if at attention.

Lavinia breathed deeply. "I had forgotten how good this feels. It's wonderful to be out."

"Away from the hot air?" He cocked a brow.

"They *are* both strongly opinionated."

"Heaven forbid anyone hold a strong opinion."

She smiled.

"It surprises me you do not become more involved."

"I am trying not to air my opinions so much."

"Why?"

She glanced up. "Because I'm now aware how often pride has carried me into argument."

He almost stumbled. He offered his arm to hide his misstep.

"Besides, I do not want to be accused of being a bore."

"Miss Ellison, I do not think you could ever be a bore."

The roses in her cheeks bloomed. "Where is this thing you would like me to see?"

"The stables." Her hand clenched on his arm. "Do not fret. It's not a horse."

He led the way to the stables' back corner where McHendricks sat on a bale of hay. His groomsman nodded and then glanced at the reverend's daughter, his face softening. "Miss Livvie."

"Hello, Mr. McHendricks."

Nicholas guided her forward until the beagle bitch and four puppies came into view. "Surprise."

"Oh! They're adorable!" She bent to give the nearest bundle of fur a gentle rub. "How old are they?"

McHendricks cleared his throat. "Five weeks. She dropped a week before you got sick."

"They look so much like—"

"Aye. This is Dora, one of Mickey's little sisters."

The stable's dim light could not hide the sheen of tears or the rapid blinking as she held a squirming body to her face.

Nicholas moved closer. "They are still too young to leave their mother, but we wondered if you might like one when it comes time."

"Oh." She hugged the pup. "That's very kind of you."

"Not at all." He bent down to gently touch a rolling ball of tan and white with two fingers. "Just be sure this magnanimous gesture goes unmentioned."

"I'll be sure to do that." She smiled up at him. "There's just one thing."

"What's that?"

"I have a tradition of naming my dogs after my benefactors, and I couldn't have another Mickey."

"Of course not."

"And Early would not work. Perhaps it will have to be Nicky?"

McHendricks gave a dry laugh that quickly turned into a cough at Nicholas's frown. "I'm sure you can do much better than that."

She laughed and picked up—unsurprisingly—the runt of the litter and ran her hands over his wiggling body, crooning to him tenderly.

And the frustration of past days dissipated as his heart glowed with satisfaction.

CHAPTER TWENTY-TWO

LAVINIA WALKED INTO the stables' dim interior and smiled a greeting at McHendricks. "Good morning! How are you today?"

"Well, thank you, lass."

"I'm glad. And how are they?"

"Keeping well, though the young 'un seems a trifle out of sorts."

She hurried to the corner where the scamper of paws met her arrival. "Hello, Dora. May I play with your babies?" Dora's deep brown eyes gazed unwaveringly as Lavinia gently rubbed her head. "I promise to be careful."

She sank onto the seat of hay, waiting for the pups to draw closer. When the smallest nudged her slipper with his nose she rubbed his ears. "Hello."

He licked her hand and butted her arm with his head. She laughed as the puppies continued their antics. The past two days of stable visits had lifted her spirits immeasurably. The earl's thoughtfulness in keeping her amused—and out of his mother's way—helped her feel more relaxed, more herself, his offer of the pup tantalizing with the prospect of freedom again.

The puppy rolled over, flashing his tan-and-white belly and growling softly. She scooped him up and called over her shoulder to McHendricks, "Nicky seems quite happy!" She hugged him close, drinking in his delightful puppy smell. "You're such a darling, aren't you, Nicky?"

Someone coughed behind her. "It appears all manner of creatures delight in the receipt of Miss Ellison's endearments."

At the well-known drawl she turned and smiled.

"But when you address me, I'd much rather you use my full name, or at a pinch, Nick."

"I'll keep that in mind."

He grinned. "Please do. Although"—he leaned close—"I'd prefer my mother not hear."

Her heart scampered at his nearness. She pulled back, and thrust the puppy toward him. "Does he seem healthy to you? McHendricks thought he seemed a little off-color, but I believe he is well."

A smile glinted before he shook his head. "I have never laid claim to animal expertise."

"Except when it comes to horses?"

"Except that." His gaze grew tender. He stepped closer. "Miss Ellison, I was hoping—"

"Excuse me, my lord. Your horse is ready."

A rueful expression filled his face, and then he nodded to the stable hand. "Thank you." He offered Lavinia a small bow. "I will see you later, Miss Ellison."

As he mounted the big black horse and rode away, she returned her attention to the puppies, wondering why his words made her heart flutter, and what exactly he hoped for.

Nicholas shuffled the papers on his desk, fresh from his London solicitor. The Welsh investments seemed to be improving, and that little issue regarding the Scotland estate had been resolved, leading to more revenue this year than the previous. But while this was good news, his mind refused to settle as thoughts of his guest continued to intrude.

How long would she stay? Was she truly well? What would he do when she returned home? What would he do when parliamentary duties necessitated his return to London?

"Nicholas."

He glanced up, looked at the door. "Yes, Mother?"

"Tell me you are *not* serious about her."

"About whom?"

She snorted. "Don't play games with me. I refuse to allow an opinionated nobody from the country to hold influence over my son."

"And what makes you think *I* allow any such person to influence me so?"

"Why, you have changed!"

"You say that like it is a bad thing, Mother."

"It is! You seem to have forgotten your status and what your title represents."

"My title demands a duty of care to those for whom I am responsible."

"But your status! You cannot socialize with those not from our rank."

"Do you really believe we are superior to those born with lesser means? That my life holds more value than that of one of my tenants?"

She stared at him, as if he uttered Portuguese. "Nicholas, that is the way of the world. One cannot treat the poor as one's equals."

"Mother, one *can*."

He held her gaze until she blinked and turned to examine two small pictures. He exhaled.

A knock heralded Lavinia's arrival. She looked fresh, rose-cheeked. "My lord—" She stopped, glanced at his mother's stiff back. "Oh, I'm sorry. I didn't know you were busy."

"What can I do for you, Miss Ellison?"

She opened her mouth to speak when his mother interrupted. "These watercolors of the Hall, Nicholas. Do you know who painted them?"

"A local artist I believe." He glanced at the door. "Miss Ell—"

"I suppose Robert commissioned them. Just the sort of thing he would do."

He met Lavinia's amused eyes. She shook her head slightly at him and lowered her gaze, sunlight from the window glinting golden in her hair as his mother kept talking.

His heart skipped a beat. Lavinia's particular brand of loveliness well suited his study's simplicity. She required few adornments, her open countenance a respite from London hauteur, her modest, uncomplicated ways soothing his spirit in a manner unlike any other young lady he had met.

"Nicholas?"

At his mother's querulous tone he hauled his gaze away to meet his mother's hard stare, forcing him to grope for something innocuous to say. "I believe they were of Uncle Robert's choosing."

"Robert was never known for his taste."

"I find them quite charming, so I've never changed them."

She moved to examine them more closely. "Very pretty, if a little amateurish."

He restrained a sigh. His mother's critical nature couldn't help but assert itself.

He glanced at the door.

Lavinia had gone.

TWO DAYS LATER, familiar restlessness continued to make it impossible for him to focus on the figures Banning had presented that morning. He tried, but knowledge of the coming event continued to steal his concentration. The past weeks had proved a revelation—of himself, of God, and of his hopes for the future. Miss Ellison's presence lit his world with faith and assurance. How would he fare when she was no longer here?

He glanced out the window, lip curled in disgust. Depending on a woman? "You're a fool, Stamford." And the seventh Earl of Hawkesbury bent his will to the accounts again.

A half hour later, after laborious strain finally produced a result, he escaped the room. Giles emerged from the servants' quarters, to which Nicholas had never ventured, although he knew Miss Ellison had—and would bet his last guinea that she had learned every servant's name.

"Good morning, m'lord. The carriage has been sent for. Miss West waits in the library."

"And Miss Ellison?"

"I believe she is in the stables. Shall I send for—?"

"No, I'll go."

Ignoring Giles's small smile, Nicholas hurried outside. Fresh air tingled, the tang of crushed leaves further reminder of autumn's approach. He strode to the stables and nodded hellos in response to the greetings of the stable hands as he moved through to the rear of the building. As expected, Miss Ellison sat on the floor playing with the tumbling tan-and-white balls of energy.

He stood in the shadows, watching her face as she patted and murmured to her favorite. The dog's wriggles became less pronounced, his ears flattened, and his head drooped as she continued her ministrations. Envy rode hot and high. Lucky dog, to be the object of her affection.

McHendricks sat on a bale of straw nearby, hands in his coat pockets, his expression tender as always in Lavinia's company. "I be thinkin' he'll be right in two or three days."

"Oh, that's wonderful!" She hugged the dog to her chest. "Did you hear that, Nicky?"

The pup uttered a soft bark.

"Miss Ellison."

She jumped. "Lord Hawkesbury!"

"I believe your carriage is ready."

"Oh." She gave the runt a final hug and then carefully placed him on the floor. She stood, shook off the bits of straw clinging to her skirts, and turned to McHendricks. "Thank you for finding Dora. I still cannot believe it."

"Aye, 'tis the master ye should be thanking, lass."

"The master?" Lavinia stared at Nicholas. "Surely you did not find Dora."

McHendricks's grizzled countenance creased into a rare smile. "He commissioned me to."

Her expression grew soft. She opened her mouth as if to say something before closing it again and turning back to the old man. "Well, thank you. Thank you so very much."

She hugged him, taking the groom by surprise as much as Nicholas, judging from the apologetic look he sent Nicholas over the slight shoulder.

Nicholas frowned. One simply did not hug the servants. "Miss Ellison, it is time to go."

Her brows knit, as if surprised by his—unintended—harsh tone, before she turned, offered McHendricks a final small smile, and hurried from the room.

He caught up to her as she crunched across the gravel. "Miss Ellison—"

"Thank you, Lord Hawkesbury, for your exceeding kindness." Her relaxed manner had dropped away, replaced by poker-straight shoulders and a cool expression.

"Miss Ellison, your manner appeared to have embarrassed McHendricks."

"I have known him since I was a girl; he is like a grandfather to me. *He* was not the one embarrassed."

"But he is a servant! Surely you are not in the habit of hugging your servants."

She smiled sweetly.

He sighed. "You are, aren't you?"

"Mr. McHendricks is my friend. Perhaps one does not hug friends when one is an earl, but I am not so bound by any such strictures of society."

He stayed her with a gentle hand, kept his voice low. "Am *I* your friend, Miss Ellison?"

Her gaze faltered, her cheeks pinked. "That is something only you can answer, sir."

She eased her elbow from his grasp and hurried to join her aunt, who spoke with Giles and Mrs. Florrick near the front steps. Ivy in the urns drooped sadly, as if in agreement with the general mood.

His mother appeared beside him. "Why are the servants lined up like that, Nicholas? It's not as if you or I were departing."

"Apparently Miss Ellison has made quite an impression."

"Most unfortunate."

The horses nickered, flicking their tails, jostling the reins as they awaited the coachman's signal.

"Surely you do not allow them use of the best carriage?"

"Would you prefer our guests depart in a pony trap?"

"Well . . ."

He restrained a sigh just in time and moved closer to his guests.

"Thank you, Giles, Edwin." Lavinia gave them both a sunny smile before turning to the housekeeper. "Mrs. Florrick, you have been kindness itself. Thank you so much." She lightly clasped the older woman, Lavinia's head angled so she met Nicholas's gaze. Her smile widened.

"Oh, my dear girl." His housekeeper drew back and dabbed at her eyes with a handkerchief. "Now stay warm, Miss Livvie. No sense letting that nasty wind carry you off."

"I'll be sure to keep my feet firmly on the ground." Lavinia turned and curtsied to his mother. "Lady Hawkesbury."

"Miss Ellison. Miss West."

Lavinia glanced at him and curtsied. "Thank you again, Lord Hawkesbury. I hope I haven't been too much of a burden for you."

"Not at all."

"I'm sure you will appreciate some peace and quiet."

His heart tugged. Peace and quiet? Loneliness, rather.

"Thank you, Hawkesbury." Miss West stepped into the carriage, followed by Lily. "Come, Lavinia."

Nicholas assisted her inside. "Miss Ellison, I trust you'll be sensible and refrain from any visits to the poor and needy until such time as you are fully recovered."

"I appreciate your trust in me, my lord." Dancing eyes belied her meek words.

He smothered a laugh by clearing his throat. "I'll check on your progress tomorrow."

She settled into her seat and smiled down at him. "Until tomorrow."

"Until then, *friend*." He closed the door and with a word to the coachman, stepped back and watched them drive away, schooling his features to something appropriate for the countenance of the seventh Earl of Hawkesbury—and to cover his dismay.

🦋 Chapter Twenty-Three

THE MEMORY OF the earl's farewell smile lingered, a pocket of sunshine in her heart, even as she received a welcome home that was everything a beloved daughter could wish for. Papa's hug felt so much stronger. Hettie's happy squeal could have been heard two counties over. Even Albert had a tear in his eye as he expressed thanks for her safe return. And throughout, that special light in her father's eyes continued to glow.

Lavinia traced the textures of the wallpaper, reacquainted herself with her mother's paintings, the objects collected over the years, everything strange yet familiar. Here, love saturated every inch—unlike the Hall's grandeur which made it most definitely a Hall, not yet a comfortable home. She touched the pianoforte keys, marveling that such a simple instrument could hold as good a tone as the earl's. She gazed out at a vista of gardens and hills. The scenes she had known all her life now seemed freshly painted. She said hello to chickens, roses, fruit trees. Everywhere seemed to sing a welcome.

Hettie's welcome-home dinner seemed to outdo even the meal served to the bishop last year, with its number of courses and delicacies on offer. When Lavinia protested, Hettie said it was mostly donations from the village: the squire had sent a pork, there were sweetmeats from the Winthrops, a berry pie from Eliza, on and on it went.

"Everyone has been so kind already. I'll be writing thank-you notes for a week!"

"No doubt you will be called upon to give account for each food item as well." Aunt Patience lifted her brow.

"Then I shall attempt to do them justice, even if it seems enough will be left over for the next week."

And throughout the chatter and laughter ran a frisson of anticipation induced by the happy knowledge the Earl of Hawkesbury was coming to visit her on the morrow.

AFTER A GOOD night's sleep, Lavinia spent the morning in a state of nervous expectation. She attempted to read. Attempted to play the pianoforte. Attempted to draw. She even picked up the embroidery of long ago but that—unsurprisingly—could not hold her attention either.

Papa looked up as she entered the drawing room—again—on the pretext of searching for a book. She felt his gaze as she stroked the leather bindings and as her thoughts refused to settle.

"What is wrong, my child?'

"Nothing, Papa."

"You seem anxious." His brow furrowed. "Are you happy to be home?"

"Of course!" She moved to kiss his cheek. "I am *extremely* happy to be back."

"Surely your time at the Hall was not unpleasant?"

"No, not at all. The earl was kindness itself."

He nodded, his gray eyes watchful. "He has been most solicitous toward you."

The warmth in the earl's gaze, in his smile, his insistence on being called Nicholas, that he was her friend . . . She swallowed, striving to hide the heat in her cheeks by pretending to look for a piece of music through the pile atop the pianoforte. "I'm sure he is like that with most people."

"Hmm. No doubt you are right."

His words, no doubt designed to soothe, filled her eyes instead. She knelt at the piano stool, fingering through the music sheets until the moisture was sufficiently blinked away. The earl's attentions had tickled her vanity: that was all. That was all!

She glanced up to find she remained the subject of her father's scrutiny. She forced a smile. "I am nothing special."

"Ah, my precious girl. That is where you are wrong."

Her heart warmed at his look of tender regard. "You are biased, Papa."

"Perhaps."

But his enigmatic look lent wings to fancies already stirred, and words and looks she could not forget, try as she would.

The clatter of hooves brought her to the window. Pleasure mingled with disappointment upon recognition of Sophia's arrival. She pushed the negative emotion to one side.

"Sophia! How kind of you to come."

She did her best to focus on her friend who had come rather than the one who had not.

But when he did not appear that afternoon, she began to question her memory. Had he said he would visit, or had he only meant he'd find out how she fared? Had she misread his interest after all? He *was* difficult to read, and her experience with understanding men of his ilk nonexistent. But surely the light that filled his eyes when he saw her during those last few days must be more than mere relief that she was feeling better.

The questions continued the following day, when morning squalls prevented her attendance in church. As she played the piano and worshipped God with a sadly scratchy voice, she tried to ignore the anticipation underlying her song. Surely he would visit today.

But throughout the long afternoon, she began to feel a disappointing certainty that the earl, after a promising beginning, had once again lost the ability to keep his word. She felt further chagrined at the levels of self-delusion that made her think he cared, evidence of yet more of her overweening pride! And when dusk fell, the disappointment redoubled upon recognition of just how much she had counted on seeing him, and that, far from possessing a level head, she was just as foolishly susceptible to ridiculous sensibility as girls like Sophia, after all.

"I declare, Lord Hawkesbury, the Hall is everything it should be."

Nicholas looked with disfavor at the young lady ambling beside him. The Honorable Clara DeLancey, she of overbearing parents, a sizeable fortune, proper manners, that *his* overbearing parent had invited to stay, along with Clara's parents, the Viscount and Viscountess Winpoole, at *his* house. Politeness had prevented him packing them off immediately, but after two days of nonstop chatter from the Winpooles and Winchesters—another family with rank and money his mother evidently deemed suitable for a house party—those good manners were now worn to a thread.

He motioned to the windows. "Tell me, what do you think of my drapes?" She smiled prettily up at him. "They are wonderfully fine, sir!"

He soon regretted his mean-spirited test as she spent the next ten minutes expounding upon draperies. He stifled a yawn, stifled impatient replies, stifled the impulse to saddle Midnight and head to the parsonage to see the young lady whose conversation held as much interest for him as her eyes.

He missed Lavinia. Missed her smile, her laughter, and how her presence warmed his house in a way a dozen extra bodies could not. The visit he had promised last Friday had been postponed with his unexpected guests' arrival. Certain she would be present at church, he had routed the entire house party to attend services this morning, only to discover she had stayed at home. Disgruntled guests had demanded his attentions ever since, which was why he stood in the picture gallery with Miss DeLancey, who now fluttered attention at the paintings.

"That is a wonderfully fine building!"

Nicholas dragged his gaze from the twilight shadows lengthening across the park to see Miss DeLancey staring at the picture of his great-grandfather. "That is Hawkesbury House."

"It looks very grand. Lady Hawkesbury mentioned it is your principal seat, and that we should come for a visit soon."

"Did she now?"

"Oh, yes. She said you have spent a great deal of time in Gloucestershire recently, though."

"I find the Hall wonderfully fine," he replied gravely.

But she merely dimpled up at him. He restrained a sigh.

"Nicholas?"

He turned to see his mother smiling from the door. "I hate to disturb you and your charming guest, but when you have a moment?"

"Of course, ma'am." He escorted the young brunette back to the yellow drawing room, took his leave, and followed his mother to the study.

As soon as the door shut she said, "I've had a marvelous idea!"

"Have you invited someone else to one of my estates? Perhaps got up a Scottish hunting party?"

She sniffed. "There's no need for sarcasm, Nicholas. I've said you're welcome to invite your own guests."

"Most magnanimous of you."

"We shall have a ball." At his raised eyebrow, she hurried on. "Well, more of an evening party, with some dancing. A proper ball will prove a trifle difficult to arrange quickly here, what with finding suitable flowers, and musicians, and refreshments."

"You seem to have proceedings well in hand. I'm surprised you require my input."

"Well, it is your house. I thought our guests would enjoy an elegant evening, and it provides the perfect reason to open the ballroom."

"For the non-ball?"

She carried on as if he hadn't spoken. "Clara is quite a pretty dancer, and I'm sure Harriet Winchester likes to dance. We could invite some of the more select families from the district."

For the first time since hearing his mother's suggestion, he felt a flicker of enthusiasm. Perhaps this might provide opportunity to see Lavinia at last.

"Now Nicholas, if you agree, I will take care of all the arrangements. I know you are busy."

"Thank you, Mother. That is kind of you."

She returned his smile and departed, no doubt to inform Giles, Mrs. Florrick, and Cook what joys awaited them.

But the excitement kindled. Yes, this evening idea of Mother's could be just the thing.

THE FOLLOWING MORNING he was surprised by the early arrival of Captain Thornton. "Thornton! Please join me." He waved to the breakfast table, thankfully devoid of others. "I did not expect you so soon."

Thornton helped himself to toast and coffee. "Ah, but your missive sounded like you were in trouble. One must do one's best to help a friend in his hour of need." He grinned. "And the fact it involves distracting pretty young ladies is a small price to pay for the joy of knowing I am rescuing Nicholas Stamford from dire straits."

"If you can distract their mamas I would be even more grateful."

"You can demonstrate that gratitude by telling me how goes Miss Ellison. I trust she is feeling more the thing, poor girl. Since your letter I have kept her in my prayers."

"She has been in mine, too."

"Prayers, Stamford?" Thornton's brows rose. "Does this mean that you now . . . ?"

"Believe? Yes." Weight fell from his shoulders as he shared about his new faith to Thornton's backslapped encouragement. "You're the first soul I have told, apart from the reverend, of course."

"So Miss Ellison does not know?"

"She may suspect, but I am trying to show her through my actions. Apparently my words carry little weight. But I must confess, it is dreadfully easy to revert to former ways."

"Putting off the old man is a challenge, but possible with Christ's strength," Thornton said. "I'd like to see her, and Miss Milton, too. Can you manage time this morning?"

But it proved to be rather later in the day before they both were able to escape the clutches of the young female houseguests. He had spoken privately to his mother after luncheon, when the other ladies had retired to their rooms.

"And the Ellisons received an invitation? I will be seeing them today."

"But Nicholas, you cannot desert your guests!"

He remained patient, calling to mind the verses he'd read this morning, until she calmed. "And the invitation?"

She sniffed. "They were delivered this morning."

"Thank you."

Upon entering the stables, their plans were further delayed as McHendricks asked him if they wished to take the pup to Miss Livvie. Thornton's immediate assent meant a carriage needed to be prepared rather than horses, so the sun was much lower in the sky by the time they finally arrived at the parsonage. He couldn't help but notice the marked difference between her warm reception of both Thornton and the pup, and the cool gray eyes she turned to him.

"Good afternoon, Lord Hawkesbury."

"Miss Ellison, I am pleased to finally see you." He lowered his voice as Thornton spoke with the reverend. "I am sorry my visit has been delayed until now. I have had guests."

"Miss Milton said as much when she visited earlier today. She was most illuminating about current activity at the Hall."

Her voice held an edge, but perhaps she was just tired. He offered a smile. "I had hoped to see you yesterday at services."

"So Papa told me." She gently stroked the puppy, her expression guarded, as though she waited for him to say something more, but what, he did not know.

He glanced at Miss West, but she, too, held an expression akin to wariness. His heart sank. Perhaps ladies with bluestocking tendencies did not attend balls.

Thornton smiled his easy smile. "For someone so recently in the wars, you look remarkably well, Miss Ellison."

Lavinia dimpled. "Thank you, sir. I feel better by the day."

Nicholas frowned.

The reverend drew his attention to recent events in France, and together with Miss West, they were able to converse more easily for the remainder of the visit until it was time to leave.

Lavinia, having deposited the sleeping pup in a basket, took Thornton's proffered hand and smiled. "I am so pleased to see you, Captain. Please come again soon."

But when she turned to him, though her lips spoke appreciation for the pup, her eyes told something more akin to disappointment. And her averted gaze at his farewell made his heart sore, his temper short, and caused Thornton to murmur something about the old man.

Four evenings later, the anticipation fizzing round the Hall the past days had escalated into excitement worthy of a youth's first visit to Vauxhall Gardens. Mother had certainly been industrious, or rather she had provoked his staff to levels of industry, resulting in lavishly decorated rooms and a mountain of food.

The dinner preceding events was for his house party, so it wasn't until later, after the Miltons, Winthrops, and several other guests had arrived—including his cousin, Maria Pettigrew, finally making her entrance after journeying from Bath—that he realized the Ellisons had not.

"Nicholas, why are you frowning?" His mother snapped her fan at him in a corner of the room. "This is a lovely evening, is it not? And you know the dancing cannot begin until the host stands up. You must do your duty."

"Where are the Ellisons, Mother?"

"How would I know?" And before he could question her further she had slipped away to talk to Lady Winpoole.

He gritted his teeth. Excused himself. Scrawled a note and gave it to Martins and then entered the ballroom once more. Tried to dance as though his thigh did not ache, as though he didn't mind the young ladies' wearying conversations, as though he wasn't watching the door. When Martins reappeared, it was all he could do to not gnash his teeth as Lady Milton tried to engage him in further inane chatter. He finally escaped into the hall, where Martins handed him a small cream envelope. He ripped it open and read the neat cursive:

> *Thank you for your kind invitation. I regret I am otherwise engaged and must decline.*
> *Yours sincerely,*
> *Lavinia Ellison*

Dismay flooded his heart. He nodded to Martins and maintained a calm demeanor, but the evening seemed to have lost all sense of purpose. He reentered the ballroom and found his mother, carefully maneuvered her into a corner of the room where they would not be overheard. "You did not invite Miss Ellison, did you?"

She shrugged. "I tried to include the upper echelons of whatever society exists around here. Proper daughters of country ministers do not attend balls."

His lips quirked, despite his annoyance. Lavinia's sense of propriety would never meet his mother's criteria.

"Besides, why would you miss a little church mouse with so many glorious young ladies here?"

He leaned closer. "I fail to understand why one little church mouse would bother you so much. Why is that, Mother?"

Her eyes flashed. "You cannot throw yourself away on one such as she. Understand?"

"Oh, I understand perfectly."

But recent lessons in forbearance were swallowed by resentment at his mother's many interferences in his life over the years. He smiled grimly. Tonight he would endure, but he would make amends with Miss Ellison soon, as well as somehow let his mother know her meddling was unwelcome and must cease.

🎋 Chapter Twenty-Four

Lavinia arose late on Saturday morning, her eyes reddened with weariness and a few tears she'd been unable to prevent escaping onto her pillow last night. She dressed, patted her face with cool water, breakfasted, and diverted herself from last night's humiliation by writing a long letter to the *Morning Chronicle* espousing the benefits of free education. The sound of hooves drew her attention to the drive.

The earl was here to apologize? Well, perhaps she would forgive him for the insult of a last-minute invitation, after all. She peered past the curtains and saw a chestnut horse, not black. Disappointment was swiftly overtaken by fresh indignation, but she managed a polite smile for the captain as he entered the drawing room with her aunt. After exchanging greetings, and her aunt excusing herself to write letters, he seated himself opposite her in the morning room.

"You were missed last night." He smiled. "By certain people, anyway."

"Really? I gather the countess was not one of those."

His lips twitched. "She is a very ambitious woman, with ambitious plans for Nicholas. It may comfort you to know she is not particularly enamored with me, either."

"No?"

He studied her for a moment. "You must pardon my plain speaking, Miss Ellison . . ."

"Plain speaking need never be apologized away, Captain Thornton."

His smile faded. "I fear being the second son of a viscount is not quite who she envisaged as Nicholas's best friend." He sighed. "I believe the loss

195

of her husband and James has made her cling to Nicholas and try to control his destiny as she couldn't the others."

Her heart writhed. Of *course* Lady Hawkesbury would feel that way. Of course Nicholas would try to please her. The resentment dimmed a notch.

"I also believe those who have encouraged him to think differently, to have faith, she finds something of a threat."

She blinked. "He is a believer?"

"Yes. It seems your sickness finally propelled him into faith."

Her eyes filled with tears and she glanced away. Perhaps she had mistaken everything, and God *had* used all that had occurred simply so Nicholas could find salvation. Salvation, how truly wonderful! Even if it meant nothing else. She swallowed the pain, concentrated on the good. "That's marvelous news."

"He's only a babe, though, so allowances must be made."

She nodded. "None of us are perfect."

"Very true. So we must be patient, even though he might sneer."

"Or yell."

"That's curious. He was always so levelheaded on the battlefield. Nicholas's clear thinking and courage are why so many of us made it out alive. Did you know he got shot in the leg for shielding a group of men whose horses fell? And not once did I hear him raise his voice, even when he was hit." He shook his head. "He really is a good fellow. It's a shame his mother holds such pretensions, surrounding him with silly chits she wants him to marry."

She could say nothing. Her smile felt glued on.

"I'd never seen him so impatient as he was to get here the other day. He told me a little about how much he enjoyed your stay, how you make him laugh, which is more than any other young lady has managed to do."

She bit her lip to stop the tremble. Mama's watercolor on the wall grew blurry.

"Miss Ellison, a thousand apologies."

She blinked, shook her head, and steadied her voice. "I am glad, sir, that you do not stand on ceremony in regards to truth telling. I despise deception."

"You share that with Nicholas, too." He grinned.

She fought to keep the smile on her face. "And how long have we the pleasure of your company, Captain Thornton?"

And as he continued to visit, she strove to appreciate his attentions, all the while aware of underlying conflicting emotions that tomorrow at church she would have to face the earl—and the countess.

The relief Nicholas felt when he saw Miss Ellison in church made listening to the sermon something of a challenge. He forced his attention to the front, hiding his anticipation from his guests, who again attended services at his request. He'd been unable to disguise his eagerness from Edwin earlier that day, however, when he'd discarded coat after coat, thus lending weight to Lavinia's long-ago charge of dandyism.

Edwin had smiled. "I expect Miss Ellison will attend services."

"Yes." He frowned, fighting to tie his neckcloth more stylishly than the look his usual carelessness produced.

"You have missed the young lady, my lord."

"Edwin, I do not pay you to offer unsolicited comments."

"They come free, sir."

"You seem to have adopted the incurable impertinence of—" His lips clamped together.

His valet grinned. "Exactly, my lord."

"Don't you have a coat to press or something?" he snapped.

"I'm sure I do. Excuse me, my lord."

"Gladly!"

He touched his neckcloth—the seventh after six failed attempts—and fixed his attention on the stained-glass windows, to prevent glancing across the aisle and thus betraying himself. But after the final hymn, he could wait no more, and looked over.

Lavinia had disappeared.

His heart tripped. But no, she'd merely exited early. He went outside.

She was surrounded by people.

He forced himself to wait, to make conversation with Mrs. Foster, his tenants, the squire, Thornton, and Miss Milton, until finally she was freed. "Good morning, Miss Ellison."

"Good morning, Lord Hawkesbury." Her gaze was wary, her voice flat.

"I wish to convey my apologies for the mix-up concerning the ball."

"Was it a mix-up?" Her smile flashed before she glanced away again.

"My mother appears to have overlooked your invitation. I am very sorry."

"It does not matter. It is of little consequence to me, my lord."

He frowned. "I am hosting another evening this Tuesday. I was hoping you and your father and aunt would come to dinner, and then afterward, grace us with some music."

She gave another quick smile to someone nearby, obviously not attentive.

"Miss Ellison? Am I boring you?"

"Pardon?" She turned clear gray eyes to him again. "I'm sorry. It is wonderful to see so many whose company I've foregone over the past month. Now, sir, what were you saying?"

His conscience stabbed. He gentled his tone. "I was hoping we would have the pleasure of your company this Tuesday evening. I've been telling my guests of your wonderful singing and your skills with the pianoforte and have arranged an evening so they can hear your talents."

"But I have not yet fully regained my voice! I would not have you embarrassed by my poor ability."

He'd heard this modesty before. He smiled. "I hope you'll still condescend to attend."

"Are you sure my presence won't be problematic?"

"Problematic? I don't know what you mean." He leaned closer. "I never pictured you as someone who backed away from a challenge."

She stared at him, uncertainty filling her features, as his pulse thundered faster than Midnight's fastest gallop, willing her to accept.

"Please, Miss Ellison, will you come?"

"I—I'd be honored."

Her eyes shone shyly, yet she smiled with such sweetness that his heart began to sing.

Surely, this musical evening would allow others to see Miss Ellison at her finest.

The blue drawing room had not felt quite so formidable during her previous stay. The wall hangings and pictures were unchanged, the tall glass vases filled with fresh flowers, but the company—save for her aunt, Sophy, and Catherine— was decidedly cold, the other ladies conversing among themselves as they waited for the men to join them after their post-dinner port.

The door opened, and all languid female activity ceased. Lavinia glanced at the earl, who surveyed the room before giving her a glimmer of a smile, the first from him since she'd arrived hours ago. He spoke briefly to various others before wending his way through scattered couches to where she sat near Sophy and Catherine.

He bowed. "Ladies, I wonder if you would care to attend a picnic on Friday. We had planned to visit a scenic location near Dursley yesterday, but the inclement weather forced its postponement."

Sophy and Catherine's squeals meant she did not need to guess their feelings—nor that of the other ladies, judging from the disappointment lining *their* faces.

"Miss Milton, Miss Winthrop, as you both ride you could perhaps join Captain Thornton and me, if your mothers agree."

"Of course, my lord," chimed Lady Milton and Lady Winthrop.

"Miss Ellison, if you would prefer to travel with the other ladies in the carriage, that can be arranged."

She glanced at their startled faces. This invitation she judged to be entirely his doing, and as such, did not meet with their approval. "Thank you for the kind invitation, but I believe I have a previous engagement."

She caught her aunt's frown.

He smiled. "Let me hazard a guess. Something to do with a visit to the poor?"

Her cheeks heated.

"*I* have duties to attend, but Lavinia has nothing that cannot be altered for another day," Aunt Patience said. "Thank you. My niece will accept."

Lavinia studied her aunt, now wearing a small, tight smile. How could she stoop so low?

"We look forward to your performance tonight, Miss Ellison. And you, Miss West."

199

Lavinia finally found her voice. "I hope we do not disappoint."

The earl bowed and turned. She would be hard-pressed to perform well tonight. Her voice was still a little husky from the aftereffects of her illness.

It did not take long before the gentlemen began to press the ladies to perform. Miss Winchester went first, her turn at the pianoforte hesitant and uncertain as her personality seemed to be. After a typically ambitious performance from Sophia, the earl asked Aunt Patience to play. She executed a difficult piece, resulting in copious applause.

Then the earl looked in her direction. "Miss Ellison, would you please grace us?"

She rose, wincing as Sir Anthony loudly exclaimed, "Now we are in for a treat," and settled at the piano stool. She glanced up once, glimpsed the earl's faint smile—and the angry look of his mother as she noticed.

Her performance of *Rondo alla Turca* was mechanical rather than expressive, but it flowed without a hitch. She dipped her head at the applause and moved to go when the earl stood. "Thank you, Miss Ellison. Now, would you be so kind as to sing for us?"

"My lord—"

"Please?"

She bit her lip, but reseated herself. The Handel melody she chose was well within her normal range, but she soon noticed her voice straining, growing ever more raspy, and right at the end, she missed the note entirely, ending in a squeak.

Hot shame slithered across her heart. She bowed at the polite applause and resumed her seat, unable to look at anyone, as her aunt squeezed her hand in sympathy.

Miss DeLancey stood and moved forward to take her place at the pianoforte. Her performance of a Beethoven concerto was competent, indeed elegant, and her voice was very pretty. She finished with a flourish to rousing applause.

The countess exclaimed, "Now that is *real* musicianship."

Lavinia's cheeks grew hot. She ducked her head as the earl rose to his feet. "Thank you ladies, that was lovely." And the evening continued with tea.

Captain Thornton handed her a cup. "Miss Ellison, that was charming." She managed a small smile. "Not as charming as I would have liked."

She glanced across as the earl moved into view, his face wearing a frown, almost like he was concerned about her talking with the captain. Which was silly. Captain Thornton was kind and thoughtful, but after an initial misjudgment, she now knew he regarded her as a sister, just as she saw him as the brother she never had. She refocused her attention.

"I will be sorry to leave," the captain was saying. "I've enjoyed my time very much."

"When do you leave, sir?"

"On Monday next week."

"Oh. Well, I can imagine you will enjoy seeing your family again."

"Yes," he replied absently, turning to study Sophia.

Tiredness mixed with disillusionment. She turned to her aunt. "Shall we depart soon? I think it's getting rather late for Papa."

Aunt Patience gazed at her shrewdly. "Yes, I believe it is time." She caught the eye of the earl, who had been busy talking to Miss DeLancey for most of the evening.

He finished the conversation and moved forward. "Your servant, ma'am."

"Thank you for a delightful evening, Hawkesbury. I fear tonight has been rather a strain on my niece, and we must depart."

"Of course. I will send for the coach at once." His brow knit. "I hope tonight has not hindered your health, Miss Ellison. I would not wish you to miss the picnic." His voice dropped, his hazel eyes holding warmth she'd not seen since his mother's arrival. "I would be very disappointed."

Her mid-section fluttered. She dropped her gaze. "Thank you for tonight, my lord."

"Come, Lavinia. It is time for us to go."

After a flurry of farewells, they were soon ensconced in the carriage the earl had arranged for their use. Lavinia listened to her aunt's diatribe about the rudeness of the *ton*, their shallow ways, their manipulations.

"So why did you insist on my attendance at the picnic if these people are to be despised?"

"Did you see their faces when Hawkesbury asked you? Filled with consternation!" Her aunt gave her brittle laugh. "I may not enjoy their airs and graces, but I do enjoy the polite fiction they must maintain. It will be good for them to realize their money and titles don't mean a thing."

Don't mean a thing? Lavinia sank against the cushions and closed her eyes. What did Aunt Patience mean?

🏵 Chapter Twenty-Five

The day of the picnic, not a cloud filled the sky. Resigned to its occurrence, Lavinia determined to look for things to enjoy. The weather was pleasant, she would have friends in attendance, and the countryside, with its rolling hills of olive and umber, was always very pretty.

The earl rode up mid morning. He descended, smiling as she and her aunt went to greet him. "I suspected Miss Ellison would not require as much prompting as other ladies."

Was he implying she was too eager? She lifted her chin. "I have always held it as impolite to keep people waiting."

"Such a superior young lady." His eyes twinkled. "Would that more followed your lead."

A slow-moving carriage rumbled into view. "Thornton and Miss De-Lancey are riding with some of the other ladies. I expect we'll be in North Nibley in an hour's time."

"North Nibley? Where William Tyndale was born?"

He smiled. "The very same. I thought you might enjoy that."

The warmth in his eyes echoed the heat in her cheeks. She glanced down. Surely he hadn't arranged today's destination with her in mind?

The carriage pulled up, and the earl stepped closer to hand her inside. The countess sat with Lady Winpoole, opposite the earl's cousin, Miss Maria Pettigrew. She couldn't help but note the ladies' looks of dismay and the way their skirts drew back, as if such a lesser mortal might contaminate them. She swallowed her misgivings, thanked the earl, bid farewell to her aunt, and determined to be pleasant. "Good morning."

Their nodded greetings were quickly superseded by a low conversation between the two matrons as the carriage began to move. Lavinia exchanged small smiles with Miss Pettigrew before the older woman's gaze fixed on the views outside. Lavinia sighed internally.

"My daughter rides very well, does she not, Lady Hawkesbury?"

Lavinia glanced out the window to see a laughing Clara riding next to the earl, her attire and deportment everything attractive to secure a man's attention.

"My son needs to marry someone who shares his interests, and everyone knows he is a champion on horseback."

"So true," Lady Winpoole nodded.

The countess shot her a look. "Do you not agree, Miss Ellison?"

Perverseness made her say, "I'm sure many people know he is an excellent horseman."

The countess surveyed her with a frown before turning back to her seat companion and resuming their exclusive conversation.

When the carriage finally pulled next to a field in North Nibley, Lavinia felt almost ready to scream. Well might her aunt enjoy mocking these people's false niceties, but *she* had to endure it. Constant reminders of God's grace had been necessary in order to curb her tongue as the countess disparaged everything from the state of village greens to the marked rusticity of the locals. This last had been said with a glance at Lavinia, which had forced her to call upon every ounce of self-control. At least Miss Pettigrew had been agreeable as Lavinia had pointed out elements of Cotswold beauty, but then, the other ladies had ignored Miss Pettigrew as well. The trip had almost been bad enough for her to consider that perhaps she should learn to ride after all!

A tap on the door brought the earl's smiling face into sight. It seemed he had enjoyed his ride—or his companions—very much. "Ladies, I trust your trip was pleasant."

"Nicholas, why are we here? A farm is *not* what I envisaged for today."

"Mother, we have but a short walk to a most pleasant picnic site the servants have readied for us."

A few minutes later found them in a lovely wooded area, with trees swathed in vines and autumn foliage. The picnic food was abundant, the

crystal and silver-edged crockery lending an elegance unlike any other picnic Lavinia had attended. She ate with Catherine and Sophy—on whom
the captain danced attendance—while the other ladies and gentlemen were
seated a little way away.

The meal was reaching its conclusion when a shifting of seats saw Clara
draw close. "How did you enjoy the trip with the mamas?" She smiled sym-
pathetically, as if assigning Lavinia to her dotage. "I declare I had the most
delightful ride. Lord Hawkesbury has the most wonderfully fine seat on a
horse." She turned to Sophy and Catherine. "Did you notice his many compliments to me on my riding? I was *quite* overcome by his attentions."

Lavinia swallowed a sour taste as her friends murmured their agreement.

"Your dress is quite charming, Miss Ellison."

"Thank you, Miss DeLancey."

"In fact, I'm sure I had one similar several years ago."

Lavinia smiled sweetly. "Who would imagine we could share such similar taste?"

Clara's eyes narrowed. "I said to Mama I'd not seen a bonnet like that
for simply ages!" Her laughter drew the attention of the gentlemen, who
enquired what was so funny.

Lavinia rose and managed a stiff smile. "Miss DeLancey finds certain
elements of the countryside rather amusing. Please excuse me."

She moved away, closer to where the horses patiently nuzzled grass,
blinking away the burn in her eyes. This picnic was everything she had
feared. Why was she here? Her time would have been much better spent
with Eliza or Mrs. Foster. Why had the earl insisted she attend? He'd barely
looked at or spoken to her all day. And why did that matter? She unclenched
her hands. One deep breath, two deep breaths, three—

"I did not think you cared for horses, Miss Ellison."

The kindness in the captain's voice threatened more tears. She forced a
smile instead. "No, but there are times when four-legged creatures are preferable to the two-legged kind."

"Livvie, are you well?" Concern filled Catherine's eyes as she and Sophia
drew close. "I cannot believe how rude she is."

The Captain pursed his lips. "If you refer to the Honorable Miss De-
Lancey, it is well known that she does not take competition lightly."

"Competition?" Sophia's blond curls quivered. "What do you mean?"

The captain smiled. "I fear I have said too much."

"Said too much about what?"

Lavinia held her breath at the smooth, deep drawl of the earl, refusing to spin around like her friends did, let alone look up adoringly at him.

"Has something upset you, Miss Ellison?"

She turned to see he wore his habitual frown. She caught her friends' gazes and shook her head. "I am quite well, thank you." A quick glance revealed the picnickers' interest. She stepped away to study the view through the trees, willing him to leave. If his previous attentions had wrought such spite, what would this now do?

"I suspect Miss Ellison is not so impervious to mean-spiritedness as she purports to be."

The earl's low-voiced concern filled her eyes again.

"Miss Ellison, you do not seem well," said the captain. "Do you wish to go home?"

"I do not wish to put anyone to any trouble." She turned. "Thank you for your concern, Captain Thornton, but I believe I shall stay." She found a smile. "Fresh air is good for clearing away headaches."

The captain inclined his head and turned to Sophy and Catherine. "Miss Milton, Miss Winthrop, did you see the bell flowers? They are exceedingly pretty . . ."

Sophia clutched his arm and moved away, Catherine a step behind. Lavinia watched them for a moment, unwilling to turn to fully face the earl. Why did he remain? She sighed.

"Come now, Miss Ellison. Surely you are not that disappointed to lose your champion?" He stepped closer. "You know he must find a well-heeled young lady to be his bride."

She glanced up. "I fail to understand, my lord, why you think I must be in need of this information, but I can assure you that it does not pertain to me in the slightest."

His hazel eyes widened fractionally. "You do not care for Thornton?"

"I care for him—as I would a brother."

A slow smile curved his lips. She turned away, her heart thumping . . . ridiculously!

"Nicholas!"

"Excuse me, Miss Ellison." Uttering a faint groan he moved slowly away. "Yes, Mother?"

⁂

"Nicholas!"

He pressed his lips together and bowed to his mother. "Your servant, ma'am."

Her blue eyes narrowed. "You are neglecting your guests."

"I was of the impression they were *your* guests, Mother. I have been trying to be considerate of the people I invited."

"What you have been trying to do is to harm the consideration the Winpooles have toward you." Her voice trembled. "I will not tolerate it, Nicholas."

"And *I* will not tolerate innocent country misses being abused whilst on an excursion with my mother. Do you understand me?"

Her eyes glittered. "I comprehend perfectly. But you need to realize that Miss Ellison will never be good enough for you! You are playing a very foolish game, my boy."

He tucked her hand over his arm and led her back to the picnickers. "But it is *my* game, Mother. How I treat Miss Ellison is my concern, not anyone else's."

A twig cracked. He turned to see Miss Milton's furrowed brow as she stood nearby, next to Thornton. "Ah, Miss Milton, Thornton. Do you wish to see if the view at the hilltop is as glorious as the guidebooks suggest?"

At their assent, a small climbing party was formed, consisting of all of the younger ladies and gentlemen, while the older ladies, save for Cousin Maria, declared themselves too tired to attempt such a steep ascent.

With Thornton and Miss Milton at the lead, Nicholas was kept busy assuring the other young ladies that their efforts would be well rewarded. The wooded copse provided shade, and their excitement was palpable, although it quickly descended into complaint as the path led higher.

During one of these sunnier sections, he heard a voice behind him say, "Thank you, Miss Ellison. I've heard it is a marvelous sight."

He turned. Lavinia and his cousin were trailing the others by several lengths, Maria leaning heavily on Lavinia's arm, who only smiled encouragement.

"Come now, Miss Pettigrew. It's not that far to the top. And then you may see that wonderful view you said you've wanted to see for so long."

"No, my dear." His cousin stopped to fan herself. "I think I'll walk back."

"Ladies? Do you require assistance?"

"Oh!" Maria fluttered. "I'm so sorry, Nicholas. I did not mean to interrupt—"

"Nonsense. We had grown worried about you." He offered an arm to each. "Allow me."

Maria took his arm eagerly, but Lavinia hesitated. "Please assist Miss Pettigrew, my lord. The path is not wide enough for three. I can walk alone."

"I would not have you walk alone, Miss Ellison."

Her cheeks pinked, and after a moment, she rested a small gloved hand on his arm.

Warmth glowed through his heart to have her so near. She uttered no complaint, even as Maria exclaimed about the heat, the height, the buzzing insects. Instead she diverted the older woman, pointing out a tiny robin perched on the sprawling roots of an ancient fig, the glimpsed vistas of the River Severn, and sharing snippets of history about the Battle of Nibley Green.

"Miss Ellison is a veritable guidebook, is she not, cousin Maria?"

Lavinia stiffened as Maria offered a soft affirmative.

"She is one of the most fascinating ladies I've ever had the good fortune to meet. I'm very glad she agreed to come today." Nicholas met Lavinia's gaze and smiled. "Thank you."

She offered a small smile, and they proceeded up the last section to the peak. Despite his cousin's flagging spirits, he couldn't be sorry, because her slowing steps allowed him more time to enjoy Lavinia's musical voice, her sunny smile, the way her bonnet revealed two delectable curls upon her neck.

"Livvie!" Miss Milton hurried toward them. "We'd become convinced you had turned back, even though you are the one most used to tramping around."

"It may take a while before I can match my previous exploits."

Of course. Her illness. He was a fool to suggest such an excursion. "Do you wish to rest?"

"Thank you, my lord, I am happy here."

Miss Milton shot him a troubled look and led Maria to a slight incline where the others were exclaiming at the patchwork of fields and villages far below.

Lavinia walked closer to the edge. "It is spectacular, is it not?"

Sunlight caught the wisps of hair playing around her face, her upturned face proof of her pleasure. He studied her beautiful, soft pink lips. What would her kiss be like? His heartbeat quickened. "I find it delightful."

She glanced across and saw his attention still firmly fixed on her. Her cheeks suffused with color. "Is this more of your nonsense, my lord?"

He smiled. Perhaps one day she might believe him.

She faced the wide swath of natural wonder and sighed. "I cannot help but think of God's magnificence when I see such beauty."

"'For the invisible things of Him from the creation of the world are clearly seen . . .'"

Her eyes widened.

"I don't know if I ever thanked you for pointing out such verses to me, Miss Ellison."

"The captain told me you now . . . believe."

"It will take me dozens of years to attain a smidgeon of the faith Thornton has, and I can never aspire to your great goodness, but I hope you will be patient with me."

Her eyes kindled, yet she did not drop her gaze, her smile more beautiful than the view before them.

For a moment, perfect ease flowed between them, contentment highlighted further by sunny skies, birdsong, and the hush of breeze in the trees.

A cough lifted his focus. Thornton stood with Miss Milton, and both wore frowns. Just beyond them stood a glowering Miss DeLancey.

His stomach tensed.

❦ Chapter Twenty-Six

The following day, Lavinia was surprised by a visit from Sophy. After exchanging reminiscences from the picnic, Sophy paused, and said, "Livvie, there's something you should know."

Lavinia looked up from her embroidery and smiled. "That I am to wish you happy?"

"No, no," Sophy giggled. "Captain Thornton is all that is amiable, but he has not, that is, he would not—"

"Be enamored of the prettiest girl in Gloucestershire? No, why would he? If he were not that would make him a very foolish man indeed, and I am certain the captain is no fool." She smiled as Sophia colored. "How feels your mama?"

"Oh, she likes him enormously. Papa, too. But"—her smile faded—"that is not what I needed to tell you."

"What troubles you, Sophy?" She glanced at her last uneven row, sighed inwardly, and bent to unpick her stitching.

"It . . . it's something I overheard yesterday."

"Come, Sophy. You know eavesdropping on others' conversations never ends well."

"I didn't mean to. But when the earl said—" She bit her lip.

Lavinia fought the flicker of interest. She attempted to rethread her needle, but it suddenly proved difficult indeed. She would not ask. She would *not*—

"It was about you, Livvie!"

Sophy's insistent voice drew her gaze to her face.

"It's all a game! That's what he said to his mother. That you are only a game to him."

Something cold stole over her soul. Surely his looks, his words, his kindnesses, his profession of faith could not be designed. She slowly placed the needle down as Sophy continued.

"I didn't think you would care too much, you've always railed about his type and about how he doesn't fulfill his duties. But I had wondered if perhaps, after your illness, you seemed a little tender toward him. And I would *hate* for you to be hurt by him." Sophy's bottom lip trembled.

Hurt by him? How many times had that occurred already? A chuckle of disbelief escaped, sounding more like a groan. At Sophy's widened eyes, she forced iron into her words. "Thank you, Sophy, for your concern. But I cannot be hurt by mere words."

But his actions . . .

"So you are unhurt?"

She lifted her chin. "I am quite well."

"I am so glad! Of course, Mama says anyone can see he must marry someone of his rank, like Miss DeLancey, and that if anyone from around here was to think he'd condescend to their level, they must be a trifle touched in the attic." She giggled. "He is tremendously handsome, though. So I don't blame you for looking."

Mortification scorched her cheeks. What had she done to give such an impression? How blatant must it have been for *Sophy* to notice, of all people? Why, why, *why* hadn't she listened to her aunt's lessons in propriety?

"Can you imagine having the countess as your mother-in-law?" Sophy's eyes widened. "She always looks like a gargoyle!"

She had no words. No rejoinders. Shame at how meekly she'd been taken in rippled across her insides. What stupid pride for her to have dared think—

No. She would dare no longer.

"I'm glad I told you. Captain Thornton wasn't sure I should."

"I beg your pardon?"

"Are you sure you feel well, Livvie? Your voice sounds funny. Anyway, I was so worried, and I couldn't just ask anyone, and the captain is *so* kind and knows the earl so well, I thought I'd ask his opinion. And he agreed that the earl would marry only someone of his social standing and said Lord Hawkesbury's actions were reprehensible."

For some reason, this assertion from Nicholas's closest friend filled her eyes in a way none of the other comments had. But hadn't the captain warned her previously? She bit the inside of her bottom lip to stop the tremble, shifted the talk to Sophy's anticipations, and was not at all sorry when her guest soon departed.

THE FOLLOWING MORNING Lavinia was thankful the Sunday school demanded her full attention. The earl and his party—save the Winpooles—had arrived in good time, and she had managed to keep away, her embarrassment too raw to encounter any knowing gaze. Spending time with the children, while exhausting, proved sufficient diversion from self-recrimination, until the congregation was released and she could linger in the small room no longer. She moved outside and chatted to a number of congregants, all the while keeping an eye out to avoid Lord Hawkesbury. Now that she was in possession of his true intentions, what could she say to him? A restless night had refused to proffer any answers. She glanced past Eliza chatting quietly with the blacksmith's family but couldn't see the dark head and broad shoulders anywhere. Where—?

"Ah, Miss Ellison." She turned to meet the earl's warm eyes. "I had begun to wonder where you were hiding. Out with your children again?"

"Yes." She stepped back. No one would have reason to question her motives today.

"Miss Ellison? Are you well?"

She dropped her gaze. "Quite well, my lord."

"I fear this may be the last service I attend for a while. We travel to London tomorrow."

"So soon?" She winced at her breathlessness.

"Yes." He sighed. "I received word yesterday of some business I must attend to immediately. And my parliamentary duties mean I will not be back this way for many months."

Many months? Her chest grew tight. Proof that Sophy's assertions were correct. How much of a fool was she to have thought otherwise. "I trust you will have safe travels, my lord."

She looked away to see his mother watching avidly. Lavinia pressed her lips together.

"Is this all you have to say?" He grasped her hand.

"Unhand me, sir." She pulled it free. "You may need have no care for your reputation, but I must."

"So the reverend's daughter has finally decided to take heed of herself." His silky voice dropped as he leaned closer. "I shall make my farewells to your father and aunt this afternoon."

"Nicholas!" hailed the countess.

He grimaced. "Until then." He bowed and went to speak with his mother, leaving Lavinia is a whirl of conflicting emotions—and more determined than ever to avoid him.

After luncheon, Lavinia removed to her sanctuary, holding the pup in her arms as she carried the basket. It was foolish, perhaps, to think she might get any painting done, but the puppy's antics guaranteed she would not be morose. And she would not waste this beautiful afternoon waiting inside to be further insulted by a man such as the Earl of Hawkesbury.

The light was growing dim when she finally returned. The puppy's quivering exploration of his surrounds had meant she'd spent more time chasing him than painting, with the result that her hair was in disarray and her clothes were rather dirty. Definitely not fit company for anyone—not that she need mind. The hour for visiting had well and truly gone.

She hurried past the small stone barn, rounded the corner, and crashed into a large form. "Oh, my goodness!" Her basket clattered to the ground, her wooden paint case falling open as Nicky scampered away. "Oh no!"

She fell to her knees, picking up the dirt-encrusted cakes of pigment, flicking at the specks uselessly until a large folded handkerchief was handed to her, but the embroidered NS was such fine handiwork that could not be soiled. "Thank you, my lord, but—"

"Just use it, please." As she bent to clean the ground he snapped, "For yourself! Get a servant to do that!"

Her eyes filled. She pressed her lips together and dabbed at her dress while the earl disappeared inside. A moment later he reappeared, closely followed by her aunt and Lily.

"Lavinia! What—"

"It appears Miss Ellison is determined to remain as elusive as ever." The earl's hazel eyes glittered dangerously. "Did you forget we were coming to see you?"

She tossed her head, hating the fact that her traitorous cheeks heated. "I am sorry, Lord Hawkesbury. I was of the impression it was Papa and my aunt you were coming to see."

His eyes narrowed, his lips lifted to one side.

"Lavinia, go upstairs and get changed."

"But Nicky—"

"Forget him. His lordship was about to go searching for you. He and the captain have been waiting for over an hour!"

Shame hurried her movements so it was only minutes later when she appeared in the drawing room. The captain and earl rose at her approach.

"Miss Ellison! At last. We had begun to despair of seeing you." Captain Thornton smiled.

"My apologies, sir."

"Note the singular," the earl drawled. He flicked the captain a wry look before coolness settled on his features again, his gaze hard and watchful.

She focused on the captain. "I do hope you have enjoyed yourself these past weeks."

"Nothing could be more delightful. I have enjoyed renewing friendships."

"I know you will be missed very much in these parts." She smiled at his flushed cheeks.

"Again, the singular."

She glanced at the earl. "I beg your pardon?"

"Nothing, Miss Ellison." He waved a hand. "Pray continue."

She conversed awkwardly with Captain Thornton a few minutes more before he rose and took her hand. "I hope to see you again soon, my dear Miss Ellison."

She smiled back warmly. "I hope for that, too."

After pressing her hand he retreated to converse with her aunt and Papa by the door. She turned uncertainly to the earl.

He possessed her hand in both of his, his eyes darkly glittering. "My friend has spoken my sentiments exactly."

"How unfortunate then that I am never in London." She pulled away but his grip was like iron.

"Is this all the farewell you give me?" His voice was low. "Am I to be left so unsatisfied?"

She gasped. "What satisfaction could you wish to have?"

He shook his head, gave a grim smile and a mocking bow, and muttered, "What a fool."

She felt hot. Cold. Hot again. He thought she was a fool?

As Papa and Aunt Patience escorted the men outside, she sank onto her seat, pressing her lips together tightly, willing herself not to cry while disillusionment chased anger faster than any hooves outside. Only after a lengthy period did she become aware of the loud howls from her pup, now trapped inside the laundry, whose cries echoed her mournful spirits.

He was a fool. A complete and utter fool. To have thought that chit might actually hold some regard for him? A fool!

Midnight's sides were heaving by the time they arrived at the stables. He felt a moment's remorse for his horse before Thornton dragged him away to a corner, out of the groom's hearing.

"What is wrong with you? You raced from there like we did from Burgos!"

"I need to get inside. Everyone is waiting—"

"And they will be waiting a lot longer until you pull yourself together! Stamford, you cannot go in like this. You look like thunder!"

He heaved out a breath. Another. The red spots dancing before his eyes gradually faded.

"Stamford, I'm your friend. You know that. But you're starting to concern me."

"A thousand apologies."

"You cannot treat people in such a high-handed manner and expect them to like it."

Remorse bit. "I am sorry, Thornton."

"I don't mean me! Miss Ellison. You've treated her abominably."

"I beg your pardon?"

"You should beg hers! Can you deny you've been toying with her affections?"

"Toying! I do not answer to you."

"No, of course not. To whom do you ever answer?"

"You are being most unfair."

"Unfair? Your treatment of Miss Ellison is unfair. It is just as well we leave tomorrow to put an end to this. These past weeks you've singled her out with smiles and attention, but for what? What possible reason? To be leg-shackled? Is that your game?"

"I do not play games."

"Miss Milton heard you say so! To your mother, no less! Do you dare deny it?" He threw a hand through his fair hair. "Your intentions are what, then? She is your prey, your sport, is that it?"

"No!"

"So your intentions are honorable. You do wish to marry her."

Heat filled his cheeks. He replied stiffly, "I have no desire to become betrothed—"

Thornton snorted. "For shame! You may lie to yourself, Stamford, but you can't deceive me. What did you think? That you, an earl, could marry a commoner?"

"Miss Ellison is not common."

"Of course not. But your rank demands you choose someone of similar status."

"Careful, Thornton. You begin to sound as snobbish as my mother."

"Pshaw! For years I've heard you go on about family duty and responsibility. And now your rank demands you choose a wife from among your peers."

"But I don't want any of them!" He winced. He sounded like a whining brat.

"You may have many things in this world, but you can't have Lavinia."

Jealousy rushed hot through his veins. How dare Thornton speak her name? He strove for his most sarcastic tone. "Oh. Am I to wish you happy?"

"Not with Miss Ellison."

"So why concern yourself in her affairs?"

"Because she is a good, pure-hearted girl who has suffered from your family's carelessness much too often." He shook his head. "I will not allow my friend to hurt her."

"I will not hurt her!"

"Because you will not have her. You *must* see that."

"But—"

"Stamford, if you claim faith, you must trust God with this." He turned and walked away.

Trust God?

How could God help him with these feelings? How could God save him from the fate society dictated? A heavy, helpless despair flooded him, blacker than the autumn sky.

Nicholas trailed Thornton through the darkness, crunching over gravel to the lighted Hall, its windows filled with the eager faces of his mother, the Viscountess, and Miss DeLancey.

Duty. Rank. Responsibility.

He gritted out a smile.

❧ Chapter Twenty-Seven

October drifted into November. Nights were longer, the darkness colder. Lavinia continued her visits, her church duties, her responsibilities, thankful her health had improved enough to do so. Her painting and music had improved also—would that Clara DeLancey could hear her sing now—but she derived little joy from such activities. A crimson leaf or well-sung aria might lift her spirits momentarily, but then flatness would resume.

Melancholy was her friend, singing her to sleep each night, murmuring on the outer edges of her soul each day. Hope had flitted away, leaving this strange sense of numbness. She, who had always thought herself clever, had been duped by a few soft words and her own imagination. The earl was right: she was a fool, a rabbit-like fool who had nearly succumbed to the hunter's charm. Which could only prove a fatal mistake.

She swallowed the rawness in her throat and rubbed her pup's head as he snored on her lap. The drawing room's curtains were closed against the early onset of wintry winds, and a fire snapped warmth through the chill. She tried to read Miss Burney's novel while her aunt stitched and Papa worked in his study.

"Lavinia?"

She looked up. Concern lined her aunt's dark eyes.

"Are you feeling unwell?"

Lavinia forced a smile. "I'm a little tired, is all."

"I'm not surprised, spending hours at the Thatchers today."

"I was happy to help. Mr. Thatcher needs as much assistance as possible these days."

"Be that as it may, you must be careful of your health. Perhaps we should reemploy Lily. She would prevent unnecessary endeavor."

"Lily is very happy back at the Hall."

"So Mrs. Florrick said last week. But it's more than that." Her aunt frowned. "Do you miss the earl?"

She blinked. "Aunt Patience!"

"What? Did you expect me *not* to notice you had developed a *tendre* for that man? You realize you will never suit the countess."

Lavinia nodded stiffly. "I am well aware of that, ma'am."

Her aunt's eyes narrowed. "You do not need to rely upon a man, Livvie. I have managed a perfectly satisfactory life, without requiring marriage."

Because she depended on Lavinia's father. Lavinia swallowed the words.

"I am content," her aunt said forcefully. "You can be, too."

"But I am not you. This, this"—she waved a hand—"I don't know if I can be satisfied with this anymore."

"What do you mean?"

"I have tried, but I no longer feel content. I love St. Hampton Heath, but sometimes I wish I could see more of the world. I don't want to molder away here forever."

Aunt Patience's eyes flashed. "Is that what you think I've done? Wasted my life here?"

"No!" She moved to kneel at her aunt's seat. "I am *immensely* thankful for you, and the sacrifices you made after Mama—" Her eyes pricked; she blinked hard. "I don't know what Papa and I would have done if you hadn't come." She swiped away an errant tear.

"There, there, child. Let's have none of that." She patted Lavinia's head. "It's been no sacrifice. You have filled my life with meaning these past years."

Lavinia swallowed. "But I will have no niece to care for or family who needs my help. What am I to do with the rest of my life? Other people get married, have children, but I cannot see that happening—unless I'm so fortunate that Mr. Raymond makes me an offer."

Her aunt smiled thinly. "He does care for God and for the church, I suppose."

"He may care for God, but I fear I cannot care for him."

Lavinia shuddered. Would she ever care for someone? Would anyone truly care for her? Sophia's girlish chatter and confidences almost filled her with dread these days. How could she assume an interest in something that constantly reinforced her own singleness?

She stared at the window, trying to picture her mythical husband. Definitely not someone like Mr. Raymond. Apart from possessing little in the way of wit, he wouldn't be able to carry her to safety on a mild day in June, let alone through a storm . . .

She blinked and turned back to meet her aunt's thoughtful gaze.

Aunt Patience sighed. "I suppose it had to come to this one day. You are your mother's daughter, after all." She rose and exited the room, leaving Lavinia to stare.

Several minutes later she reappeared, along with Papa.

"My dear girl," he said, holding her hands, "is it true what Patience says? That you desire to leave?"

"Oh, no, Papa! I don't wish to leave you or my aunt. I'm just . . ." She shrugged.

"Sad? Lonely?" he said gently. "I have suspected something of that nature."

Her eyes filled. "I don't know what is wrong with me, but I cannot seem to shake it."

"Have you asked God?"

She nodded. "He reminds me His plans are good."

"That they are." His eyes, so wise and clear, grew tender. "I will miss you."

"Miss me?"

He smiled. "Patience wants to take you on a little journey."

"Where to?"

Her aunt slid a look at Papa before returning her attention to Lavinia, her expression resigned. "To my sister's."

"But . . . you no longer have a sister!"

"I do. In London."

"What?" Lavinia sank onto a lounge, her mind spinning faster than a weaver's loom. "Why have you never told me?"

"My mother said some terrible things when Grace died. My younger sister, too. I was not—"

"Wait! I have a grandmother, too?"

Her aunt nodded, refusing to meet her gaze. "In Salisbury."

"But why do I not know them?" Lavinia glanced at her father. "Papa?"

"Grace knew what her family would do when she married me." His eyes held regret. "I loved her too much to say no."

"You saved her from a life of manipulation is what you did, David. Here she was loved for who she was, not just what she was."

What else didn't she know? Lavinia forced herself to speak through the fog. "What do you mean by 'what she was'?"

Aunt Patience turned to her. "My parents were hard people with strong ideas on what was right and proper. When Grace met your father, my parents' ideals were challenged to the core. She was of age, but her refusal to bend to their will meant they cut her off entirely." She shook her head. "Constance and I were too young and weak-minded to do anything until we were informed of Grace's death and that you were here and needed me."

"Mama was banished? But why?" She turned to Papa. "Why would they object to you?"

"Because I was not rich enough or titled enough to suit." He offered a plaintive smile. "I had a nice living, and this property, but that did not satisfy them."

"I cannot believe this! Do you mean to say you eloped, Papa? Did you go to Gretna Green?"

He smiled. "Nothing as romantical as that. My father was the minister here and married us. We lived here with them until they died just after you were born."

She stared at them, rubbing her forehead. "I do not understand. I really have family I've never met?"

"My poor girl, I am so sorry." Her father's eyes sheened. "Our only intention was to protect you. We hoped to avoid scandal and gossip by hinting your mother's family had died."

"But Aunt Patience—"

"Was traveling on the Continent at the time." Aunt Patience seemed to have aged ten years. "And when I learned of Grace's death, I came as quickly as I could, regardless of my mother's displeasure. After that, I too was struck from the family. I am sorry if you feel misled, but at the time, it did not seem necessary to tell you otherwise."

"But why tell me now?"

"Because I'm persuaded Constance will be amenable to a visit from her long-lost niece." Her aunt smiled. "You would like to go to London, would you not?"

Hope stirred her heart. "To visit the museums? And library? And see concerts?"

"And perhaps some of London's other attractions?" Her aunt's eyebrows rose.

The earl! Her foolish heart kicked. She shoved that stupidity aside and fought to remain composed. "I would love to! But Papa, what about you?"

He shook his head. "My presence will be needed here, especially if you two are away."

"Oh, but—"

"But nothing, my child. Fulfilling our Christian duty does not mean denying all enjoyment. Even our Lord had to withdraw to restore His weary spirit." He held her hands. "This year has proved most trying. You deserve some pleasure." His eyes sparkled. "And I believe London will be the very place."

A WEEK LATER, after a rush of planning, preparations, and farewells, Lavinia sat with her aunt in the mail coach to London, along with an elderly couple who had already nodded off and a sober-faced man who looked to be in his forties and sat in the far corner, reading a newspaper.

"A post and chaise is far more comfortable"—Aunt Patience winced as they drove over another large bump—"but this is the quickest way."

Lavinia glanced at the man, who continued to studiously ignore them, and kept her voice low. "But how can you be sure Aunt Constance will even be home? She surely would not have received your letter."

"My sister has never liked to stir too far from the nest. If she is not home, we will stay in a hotel."

Lavinia's brow knitted. Aunt Patience seemed to have assumed a new persona, her ease at travel and insight into potential London treats at odds with the woman who had raised her in country domesticity.

"My dear girl, stop that frown. We have hours ahead of us. You must enjoy the sights and sounds of experiences unfamiliar."

And so for the next fourteen hours, that's exactly what she did.

THE COACH ROLLED into the Seven Horses Inn early Thursday morning. Lavinia blinked grit from her eyes, grit that had filled the air since they'd reached the outskirts of London. The air was filled with a heavy sourness that made it difficult to breathe—or perhaps that was the effect of the rather portly gentleman who had entered at Reading and taken more than his share of seat.

But the time had proved interesting: snatching bites to eat at inns as they stopped to change horses and listening to all manner of people—from solicitor (as the newspaper reader proved to be) to the overly chatty widow who had gotten on in Bath. The varying landscape had also helped while away the time—and distract from the cramped conditions. But the most interesting moments had been spent listening to her aunt share girlhood memories of her sisters, disclosed in whispers when the others were asleep. Mama came alive to Lavinia again. She could almost see the confident young beauty who had chosen love over pecuniary security. Lavinia only hoped her newly discovered aunt would hold her in affection as Aunt Patience did.

After their bags were transferred to a hackney, they traveled a few more miles to a much more genteel part of London. Through the gray light of dawn, Lavinia could see that here the houses were very grand, with at least four stories and banks of windows looking onto the wide street surrounding a pretty central park. As it was so early, few people were about, which filled her with trepidation in case they should be refused entry, but Aunt Patience only shushed her fears.

"Grosvenor Square may refuse entry to many, but not to me."

Her aunt's claims were soon put to the test as the hackney pulled up outside a large residence. Lavinia remained in the carriage as her aunt trod up the steps. A knock on the door soon produced a butler, whose heavy eyebrows rose as her aunt spoke, before he bowed her inside. A liveried footman appeared, opened the carriage door, and assisted Lavinia indoors.

She glanced around. Hampton Hall had always been the epitome of elegance; this residence made the Hall look humble. Stained glass pooled dim swaths of color on the black-and-white tiled floor; liveried footmen stood at attention, their handsome faces expressionless; the reception room she followed her aunt into held gold-striped settees and a thick cream carpet. The footman opened the curtains, spilling weak daylight across the furnishings. Aunt Patience wandered around the room, a tiny smile on her face as she touched ornaments and studied paintings, her tiredness at her long journey seemingly gone.

"I've never seen so much elegance," Lavinia said in hushed tones.

Her aunt paused her perusal, her smile a little fixed. "My sister may hold different values than Grace and I, but she has never lacked style—or the means to fulfill her taste."

The nerves that had steadily built all morning clamored to a crescendo. Did she mean—?

Speculation was cut off as a murmur of voices preceded the opening door.

A lady wearing a pale pink robe and mobcap over dark blond curls walked in, her tired features sharpening as she beheld her sister. "Patience! So it is true. I thought it a dream when Parsons informed me. What are you doing here?"

Lavinia's breath caught.

"So you did not receive my letter. A pity, but it cannot be helped now. Constance, I want you to meet someone." She turned and gestured for Lavinia to come forward.

The lady paled, placed a hand over her mouth. "Grace?"

"No, Constance. Don't be so foolish. This is Lavinia, Grace's daughter."

"You look so much like her." The woman continued to stare, wide-eyed. "It's like seeing a ghost, to see Grace twenty-five years ago."

"Yes, well, this little ghost has traveled a long way to see you." Aunt Patience smothered a yawn. "We're both tired, and hungry."

"Oh! Of course." Aunt Constance rang a bell and quietly issued orders to the maid. She turned, her disconcerting stare rippling nerves through Lavinia's insides. "Lavinia, I am very pleased to meet you."

"And I, you, Aunt Constance." She offered a small curtsey.

"Aunt Constance." She smiled softly. "I never thought I would hear those words."

"And I never thought I'd say them." She smiled.

"Oh, but you're like Grace."

A warm glow filled Lavinia's heart. To have family? To be compared to beautiful Mama?

"Lavinia has just learned some of the family secrets."

"Some?" Aunt Constance raised delicate brows.

"There will be time for more."

"How much time, Patience? Or am I to be completely at your leisure?"

"I rather hoped you would be. Lavinia needs to meet some relatives and see something of London."

"Society is rather thin on the ground at the moment."

"But never too thin where you're concerned. Besides, I believe we'll be rather more interested in seeing sights than seeing society."

Aunt Constance's eyes closed briefly before she looked at Lavinia once more. "You are most welcome to stay, my dear." Her gaze trickled over her clothes. "But before any sights are seen I must insist on proper attire."

"Oh, but Aunt Constance—"

"No buts." A stern look so much like Aunt Patience's flashed. "No guest of mine will leave these premises in anything of which I would be ashamed."

Lavinia nodded, swallowing the protest as embarrassment coiled inside. Aunt Patience had warned of her sister's differing values, but such vanity . . .

The maid reappeared in the doorway. "Your ladyship, the rooms are ready."

Your ladyship?

Aunt Patience smiled thinly. "Yes, Lavinia. Your Aunt Constance is married to the Marquess of Exeter."

🦋 Chapter Twenty-Eight

The next few days passed in a whirl of introductions, to Uncle George and her younger cousins, Henry and Charlotte, as well as to a host of Aunt Constance's afternoon visitors. In between innumerable dress fittings and outings to places such as Westminster Abbey and the museum, Aunt Patience escorted Lavinia to places such as Forty-Eight Grosvenor Square for an evening amongst artists and poets listening to Sir George Beaumont espouse the value of the Picturesque. Aunt Patience's lessons on genteel behavior held Lavinia in good stead, and she was as surprised by the level of deference shown her—due, no doubt, to the fact her uncle was a marquess— as she was by the welcome her aunt received.

That night, safely ensconced at home, Aunt Patience commented, "You enjoyed tonight."

"Oh yes! It was most interesting. Sir Beaumont's painting collection sounds magnificent."

"He is friends with Wordsworth, you know. Often lends his farm to him." A small smile tilted. "I noticed you spent some time talking with Mr. Chetwynd."

"Oh. Mr. Chetwynd was very kind. I think he could see I felt a little out of my depth."

"He comes from a good family, too, even if he does hold poetical aspirations."

Her cheeks warmed. "He was very amiable, but I think his only interest in me was the fact we were the two youngest in attendance."

"Nonsense. I overheard him tell Lord Danver you were as intelligent as you were pretty, and Lord Danver agreed."

"Oh. Lord Danver seems very nice. He asked about Gloucestershire and what we did there."

"Yes, I saw the two of you having a nice coze. Danver has always had a soft spot for the common man, but then, he is a Whig."

"How *do* you know these people, Aunt Patience?"

A soft light filled her aunt's eyes, but she waved a dismissive hand. "I've known them for years. You will find there are *some* people in London who care more about a person's mind than their family name. Now tomorrow night, I plan to take you to another evening where you will meet others who value conversation over cards."

"That is, if I survive tomorrow morning."

Aunt Patience patted her shoulder. "You will do more than survive; you shall overcome."

Her aunt bid her good night, and Lavinia snuggled under the thick blankets, her mind still whirring with all she had seen and heard in the past days. So many fascinating people, so many wonderful sights. Only two things served to mar her enjoyment: concern that Papa was well and not lonely, and Aunt Constance's insistence Lavinia learn to ride. This second concern had eventuated the day of the mantua-maker's visit. Aunt Constance's gift of clothes—for the years she had done nothing for poor Grace's child, so she said—had become such an extravagance, Lavinia had finally worked up courage to protest: "But I am only here for a few weeks. Surely I will not need ball gowns."

"A few weeks! Nonsense, my dear. We cannot lose you when we are just making your acquaintance."

"But I must return for Christmas. Papa needs me."

Aunt Constance's face tightened before she smiled. "Well, we shall make do with only three ball gowns, then." Her gaze grew sharp. "You do dance, don't you, Lavinia?"

"Not very well."

"Dancing lessons with Charlotte tomorrow, then."

"I had hoped to visit the library tomorrow, Aunt Constance."

She waved a dismissive hand. "The library will still be there the next day; Mr. Finetti may not." One glance at cousin Charlotte's face suggested Aunt Constance would not be easily swayed.

But when Aunt Constance murmured something to the dressmaker about riding clothes, she simply *had* to assert herself. "Aunt, truly I am thankful, but I do not require riding clothes."

"Why ever not?"

"I do not ride, ma'am."

Her aunt and cousin gaped at her in astonishment. "You live in the country and don't ride?"

She swallowed. "I do not like horses."

Her aunt's frown gave way to sympathy. "Grace's accident. You were there, weren't you?"

She nodded. "Aunt Patience never insisted I learn."

"Well, she always preferred her books and music. And I suppose your father would not be able to afford to keep stables, so learning to ride may have been a little precipitate."

Her chest heated at her aunt's condescension.

"No matter. Charlotte has a placid pony that will do. You may have riding lessons on Thursday morning before breakfast."

Torn between horror and amusement at her aunt's autocratic "permission," Lavinia had kept her mouth closed—and decided to pray for Thursday morning rain.

She rolled onto her other side and pulled the sheet up to her chin as unease about tomorrow's activity intensified with recognition of a third cause for disquiet. The lingering concern that she might see the earl—a very real possibility given Parliament was in session, as her uncle's presence here in London attested—and that if she did, he might suspect she harbored feelings for him. Which was most *definitely* not true.

At all.

❧

Nicholas glanced across the half-empty chambers as the Home Secretary rambled on and on. He stifled a yawn and caught the amused gaze of the honorable member seated directly opposite. He offered a half smile and tried to concentrate on the bill being proposed, but the words only swam as the elderly statesman droned on.

He rubbed the bruise he'd gained at Jackson's Saloon this morning, certain to well into gray loveliness and earn the ire of Miss DeLancey when he saw her next. His chest grew tight. Perhaps the only benefit of such lengthy, life-sapping debates was the fact it cut short the time he must spend with the Winpooles. *Brave* man he was, needing excuses to avoid them. But lately, Clara's company felt almost smothering, the smugness her family showed at his and Clara's eventual union like a noose around his neck.

He clenched his hands. Unclenched. His mother was right; he had to marry someone suitable from his station in life. He supposed Clara would do, even if fulfilling his duty to his rank felt like he was condemning himself to something rather less than what he'd dared imagine.

Early morning rides lifted his spirits only a little. He would much prefer to be away, but Parliament demanded attendance until Christmas, which meant staying, listening, learning. Fulfilling his duties.

Banning's letter this morning informed that the final tenant house had been completed, just in time for the first early snowfall. That was something. Perhaps his time in St. Hampton Heath hadn't been a complete waste.

If only . . .

Queasiness rippled across his stomach, just as it did every time he thought about that last day. He was such a fool. Thornton had been right to reprimand him—he saw that now. If he ever did see Lavinia again, he'd be at a loss as to what to say. He'd apologized too many times. She wouldn't believe any more.

He rubbed his forehead. Perhaps the bump sustained this morning had conjured the ridiculous vision he'd had this afternoon on the way to the House of Lords. Coming along the Strand, he'd spied a slight figure outside the circulating library. For a moment, he was *sure* it was Miss Ellison, her profile and hair color so similar. He'd jerked his phaeton to a stop, but her modish dress and the unfamiliar young man escorting her laid evidence to the contrary.

He breathed slowly, forced his heightened heartbeat to slow. He was a fool.

There was no other word for it. Wanting the impossible, knowing dreams were but illusions.

The session continued for another half hour before finally closing for the evening, unresolved—hardly surprising as so many were absent. He stumbled to his feet and blinked against the brighter light outside chambers. He nodded to the other peers rushing to the exit.

"Lord Hawkesbury."

Nicholas turned to the older man. "Lord Danver."

"Well, that was a waste of an evening."

"It was a little dry."

"Dry is a trifle generous." Danver gave a genial smile. "Going to White's? Care to travel with me?"

"I thought you were a member of Brook's."

"Ah, yes, that is so, but I am one of the Whigs you Tories are prepared to tolerate in your hallowed halls."

A short time later they were seated in the private dining room, eating grouse and smoked eel, as a parade of notables passed around them. Conversation touched on London, laws, France.

"I must say I have been rather impressed to see a man of action endure such tedious debate for so many days."

Nicholas offered a half shrug. "It's our duty, is it not?"

"Duty doesn't seem to motivate many others to attend. Nor, if I may be so bold, did it seem to inspire your father or brother."

"I have learned many things this past year about the obligations my position demands."

"Interesting you should say that. I heard something quite similar just the other day at Beaumont's. A most eloquent speaker, with a remarkably well-informed mind." His gaze sharpened. "You have a place in Gloucestershire, haven't you?"

"Yes."

"I found her quite enchanting. One of the Westerbrookes, you know. If I were a younger man . . ."

Nicholas blinked. Danver must be fifty if he was a day.

"You must come with me, Hawkesbury. There is a little evening at

Holland's tomorrow night. Should be very interesting." He smiled slyly. "I promise it won't be too Whiggish for you."

The Duke of Argyll stopped to chat with Danver, leaving Nicholas to concentrate on his meal. He had just finished the last morsel when the duke nodded farewell. He looked up to see the Honorable Richard DeLancey enter the room. His stomach clenched.

"There!" Lord Danver's dark eyes flashed. "I've seen you wear that face many a day now, sitting opposite in the chamber. If I may be so bold, you seem somewhat troubled, Hawkesbury."

"Thank you for your concern, but it is nothing."

DeLancey laughed loudly. Nicholas fought a contemptuous curl of the lip.

Danver twisted in his seat. "I gather that young man is the brother of your young lady."

"She's not my young lady."

"No? Whispers have reached even my ancient ears about a possible alliance."

Nicholas grimaced and toyed with his water glass.

"Duty need not extend *that* far, Hawkesbury."

Cold despair pushed truth out. "I have an obligation to my family name."

"And a responsibility to your heavenly Father. Have you sought His will?"

He blinked. "How did—?"

"People change when God touches their hearts. I have seen you at services these past weeks. Your attentiveness and worship do not appear mere outward show." Danver smiled gently. "Might I suggest prayer is preferable to worry? Our Father has good plans for you, not plans you will despise."

For a moment, hope glimmered like a faraway star. Everything within Nicholas wanted to believe, but how could God disentangle this mess? Swift's Gulliver could not possibly feel more bound.

Lord, would You give me some direction?

"Hawkesbury!" Candlelight glinted off Richard DeLancey's ostentatious ruby ring as he drew closer, his too-quick smile ingratiating as always. "Will you be coming to Mama's evening tomorrow?"

Nicholas glanced at Danver. Surely an evening at Dr. Holland's had to be more interesting than another insipid affair with the Winpooles. He turned to the younger man and forced a smile. "I regret I have other plans."

Richard's stare grew hard. "Clara will not be best pleased."

He refused to catch Danver's gaze as he said, "I will visit the following afternoon."

And the noose tightened a little more.

𝕽 Chapter Twenty-Nine

Lavinia gripped the reins so tightly her fingers ached. Perched precariously, her legs to one side, she felt frighteningly inept and much, *much* too high. She inhaled deeply, but her new riding dress was not designed for such things. Modish she might appear, but her bodice was too tight, the stays digging into her, unlike the loose, practical dresses Aunt Patience had always insisted she wear.

"Miss Ellison! Keep up, please."

She sighed, swallowed the fear, and gently nudged Charlotte's pony, which seemed ecstatic at such encouragement and immediately began to trot.

"Stop, Shadow!" She tugged the reins to no avail. Panic rushed up her throat. "Stop!"

The gray pony ignored her pleas, maintaining the pace that made her bobble wildly on its back. What were her instructions? How was she to hold the pommel? *Why* must she do this? "Please, Shadow!"

"Lavinia, calm down." Charlotte moved alongside on her dappled mare. "Horses can sense our fear."

"I gather ponies do, too?" Shadow slowed, much to her relief—and the riding instructor's disgust.

"Miss Ellison, how many times must I remind you that horses are designed for speed? If you want to learn to ride, you must be prepared to go faster than a walk!"

"But I do not want to learn," she murmured.

Mr. Horrocks rolled his eyes heavenward.

Charlotte giggled. "Do not let Mama hear you say such things. She will have a fit."

"You may be sure I will not."

It was certainly pointless to argue with a woman who either acquired deafness or threatened a spasm whenever her decrees were questioned.

They stopped near a large elm as a rider on a large dark horse raced some distance away, along Rotten Row. The gentleman leaned forward, coat flying, devil-may-care attitude evident as he propelled toward a thick hedge. Her breath caught. Would he make it? The horse jumped, sailing high, strong, over the hedge to safety, before the rider patted its neck and they continued their breakneck speed. She exhaled. Despite her aversion to horses, that was beautiful to see.

"Now *that* is fine riding," Charlotte said.

Lavinia nodded. Given its head, the horse rode like black wind.

Mr. Horrocks muttered, "Fools like that should be locked up!"

"There is hardly anyone about at this time. The only danger is to himself."

"Miss Ellison, that does not provide license for any silly individual to recklessly race around the park on an out-of-control animal."

"He looked like he had his horse under control and knew exactly what he was doing."

Merely trying to escape the rigid strictures and straits of polite society through excess, though futile, speed. And for that, the man had her full sympathy.

A half hour later, they had returned to the park gates. There was a little more traffic now, grooms exercising horses, an occasional curricle trundling along the carriageway, a few other young ladies with their riding instructors.

Her stomach grumbled in an unladylike fashion. She smiled at Charlotte's giggle as they waited for a hackney to pass. The time outside among trees and grass provided respite from the usual foul, smoky air, but her body ached, her legs were tired, and her fingers felt numb from holding the reins. The sooner they were home—and had breakfast—the better.

"I believe—yes, I am sure it's her."

"Who do you mean, Charlotte?" She followed her cousin's gaze to where two smartly dressed riders trotted toward them.

Charlotte whispered, "It's Miss DeLancey and her brother. They are ever so elegant, are they not?"

Her chest tightened. She resisted the impulse to check that her clothing and hair were still presentable as the riders drew alongside.

Clara DeLancey's haughty expression neatly matched her brother's as they managed cool nods before her eyes widened and she stopped. "Miss Ellison?"

"Good morning, Miss DeLancey."

"I did not expect to see *you* here." Her gaze traveled over Lavinia's riding attire. A small frown appeared. "I did not think you rode."

Lavinia summoned a smile and motioned to her cousin, whose excitement was palpable. "Miss DeLancey, may I present my cousin, Lady Charlotte Featherington."

Clara's eyes narrowed as Charlotte murmured a greeting. She tilted her head to the man beside her. "My brother, Richard."

His blue stare bored into Lavinia, making her feel most uncomfortable. She nodded and then turned to Clara. "I trust you will enjoy your ride."

"Oh, I always do." She glanced around before her attention settled back on Lavinia, her smile not reflected in her eyes. "I don't suppose you've seen Hawkesbury anywhere?"

Her breath caught. He was here?

"He arranged to meet us here this morning." An affected laugh escaped even as the green eyes hardened. "You are not here still trying to chase him, are you, Miss Ellison?"

Lavinia's chin lifted. "I can assure you, Miss DeLancey, that *I* have never chased him, nor am I the one trying to do so now. Good day."

She ignored Clara's gasp and turned Shadow away—and desperately tried to recall how to not bounce as usual. Charlotte's mount soon caught up.

"I feel sorry for him," Charlotte muttered.

"For whom? The brother whose sneer prevented him from uttering a word?"

Charlotte laughed. "No, Lord Hawkesbury, of course! They say he's as good as engaged to her."

Engaged?

Charlotte chattered on, but Lavinia paid no heed. The ice in her fingers was spreading rapidly through her soul. She was a fool. An exceedingly *stupid* fool. As they turned into the mews, she tried to recall Nicholas's many faults and crimes, but they suddenly seemed insignificant, replaced by memories of his kindness, his warm wit, his great fortitude at her capricious ways. How could he marry *Clara*?

Her vision blurred, and she stumbled from the stables, not to breakfast, but to hide her woe in her room.

The coach wheels clattered over cobblestones as they drove to Holland's evening party. Danver leaned forward from his seat opposite. "There is no need to look so worried. As I promised, tonight shall not be too Whiggish."

"I am sure tonight will be unexceptionable."

"Ah, now *that* I cannot guarantee."

Nicholas mustered a laugh before glancing outside at the streets, whose darkness matched his mood. He'd been sorely tempted to cancel tonight, before realizing a night of wit and ideas might be the best diversion from wallowing in the realization he was nearly affianced to a woman with none.

After a hard ride early this morning, his good spirits had come crashing down upon discovery of Clara and her brother. He supposed Richard must have informed his sister of Nicholas's whereabouts—he certainly had no desire to share the high point of his day with her and had never publicized his morning activities.

After her initial delight, Clara had grown oddly quiet. When he had finally succumbed and asked her what was the matter, she'd refused to answer. Why she insisted on playing silly games and not answering in a forthright manner was beyond him, but apparently some ladies had not the benefit of a Miss West in their education.

His fingers clenched. What had that fool Richard said? He wracked his brains, trying to remember. Nicholas had expressed surprise at seeing them both, Clara had gone beet red, and Richard had said something along the lines that his sister need not chase men—unlike some. The significant look that passed between the two had filled him with unease.

"I'm afraid I do not take your meaning, DeLancey."

"Some young ladies are not what they seem, sir, acting like an innocent country miss when really they have designs on a gentleman."

His chest grew hot just thinking about it. Was it some veiled reference to Lavinia? He had merely eyed the man who would call him brother and drawled, "In my experience, some young gentlemen are not as they claim, either."

That comment had flushed the young man's cheeks to accord with his sister's, and Nicholas had left them soon after, but the entire episode had left him troubled. Could he really align himself with people who cast such aspersions?

"Here we are, Hawkesbury." Danver's eyes seemed lit with excitement as the carriage rolled to a stop. "I trust tonight proves diverting for you."

"I hope so, too."

Nicholas ascended the steps into the town house, nodding to people he recognized, including several lords from Parliament and people whose faces he recalled seeing at church.

"See that lady over there?" Danver nudged him. "That is Miss Farren, the former actress, now the wife of the Earl of Derby. Edward certainly did not marry to suit societal expectations."

Well good for him. Nicholas forced a polite smile. How long must he stay?

The conversations grew louder, the chatter eating into his frayed nerves. He accepted a glass of wine as Danver introduced him to countless people whose faces soon blurred into non-importance. Someone commenced talking about the proposed Corn Laws and their impact upon the working man, which soon escalated into an argument he wanted nothing to do with. He glanced around the room at the press of dark-clothed men of varying ages, interspersed with more vividly dressed ladies. Somewhere music was being played well, a harmonious backdrop to the cacophony of shrill laughter, high-pitched voices, and loud exchanges.

"Come. This is a veritable crush."

He followed Danver through a door into another, less populated reception room, the gilt-laden walls echoing gently with the pianoforte being played in the corner.

Danver's face softened. "There she is."

Nicholas followed his gaze to see a dark-haired, well-dressed lady talking animatedly to an older couple. Danver moved to her side, spoke quietly, and she turned.

"Miss West!"

Danver frowned. "This is Lady Patience Westerbrooke."

He stared. The stylish woman before him seemed a world away from her no-nonsense Gloucestershire self. While still somewhat unadorned—especially in contrast to the peacock-feather-wearing woman beside her—her dress and poise suggested experience at such events.

She came forward. "Hawkesbury. We certainly did not expect to see *you* here."

"It is a day for surprises, *Lady Westerbrooke*." He raised a brow.

Her cheeks pinked. "Yes, well, that is rather a long story."

"One I'm sure I'd find fascinating."

A smile flitted across her face, but she held her peace as Danver smiled warmly at her. "I was telling Hawkesbury about your niece."

"Which one? I have two, you know."

Nicholas's jaw sagged. "I beg your pardon? I thought Miss Ellison an only child."

"She is."

"But she never mentioned—"

"She did not know." She shifted as if to walk away.

"Please, Miss West—I mean, Lady Westerbrooke, is Lavinia in London?"

"Lavinia, is it?" Her brows rose as she subjected him to a hard stare. "Are you not affianced to Miss DeLancey?"

"Yes! That is—no."

"Which is it, Hawkesbury? You do not sound like you know your mind, and until you do, I'm afraid I will not be able to recall where either niece may be."

Her challenge blazed truth across his soul, burning away the shrouding uncertainty of weeks. Regardless of his fortunes, regardless of his mother, he would not—he *could* not in all good conscience—connect himself with someone he might learn to like but could never esteem, could never love. Faith demanded courage; his future required hope. "I am not engaged to Miss DeLancey, nor," he added firmly, "do I have plans to be so."

Weight dropped from his shoulders. He exhaled. Truth freed, indeed.

"It appears your mother does not share your plans. Remember, plans can . . . change." Her gaze flickered to Danver. For a second, he glimpsed regret mingled with anguished yearning before her eyes shuttered again.

Startled by this revelation, his voice was softer than it might have been. "My mother's plans are not mine. Miss DeLancey is amiable, but she can never compare to Lavinia."

She nodded. "I'm glad to see you possess some degree of common sense."

He glanced around, his heart thumping with hope. "Is she here?"

"Miss DeLancey? I think not. Discussions about anything beyond her looks seem sadly beyond that young lady."

He chuckled despite himself. "Your wit, ma'am, will soon prove my undoing. Is Miss Ellison here?"

She smiled and glanced at the corner. Bodies shuffled, and suddenly he saw tonight's pianist—smiling up into the eyes of a gentle-faced young man.

His heart burned. Who was he? Why did he stand so close to her? Why did she let him? But he could not blame him. Lavinia looked lovelier than he ever recalled, her hair glowing gold under candlelight, her pale green gown simple yet graceful. She laughed at something the man said, before shifting, her gray eyes sifting the crowd to alight on him.

Her eyes widened, the smile faded, the music ceased. Something like sorrow crossed her features, and she turned a soft white shoulder to him, angling away so he could not read her face.

The ache in his heart grew. He took a step toward her, pausing as the man beside her murmured something in her ear. She shook her head and remained seated, her face lowered as Nicholas made his slow approach.

"Miss Ellison."

She glanced up, her gray eyes tinged with caution. "Lord Hawkesbury."

The space between them felt vast, strained, awkward. He cleared his throat. "This is an unexpected pleasure. I did not think to see you in London."

"London *is* rather a large place. I could be easily missed."

"You have been," he answered in a low voice.

Pink stained her cheeks, and he smiled as some of the wariness in her eyes melted away.

She gestured to the man standing beside her. "Lord Hawkesbury, this is Mr. Chetwynd, who has poetical aspirations. Mr. Chetwynd, this is Lord Hawkesbury, who holds none."

Nicholas ignored the edge in her voice and nodded as the man murmured a greeting. "I claim no poetical aspirations, it's true, but as for aspirations, I am not completely without hope."

She glanced quickly at him before moving her attention past his shoulder.

He followed her gaze to where Danver continued chatting with Lavinia's aunt, whose face was softer than he'd ever seen.

He cleared his throat. "Are you enjoying London?"

"It has been"—she eyed him—"tolerable, I suppose."

Chagrin filled him at remembrance of his ill-natured comment that first evening in St. Hampton Heath. "I trust, like others, your first impressions may be permitted to improve?"

"I have found that decided opinions made upon a fleeting acquaintance rarely stand the passage of time."

"I, too." He glanced at Mr. Chetwynd, mouth agape at the conversation. "No doubt a poet can find beauty in regret, but I am a simple man and not so fortunate." He faced Lavinia. "I can only offer remorse for past failings and claim a faith that offers hope to imperfect men such as myself."

Her eyes shimmered. She glanced down, her eyelashes fanning her cheeks.

Mr. Chetwynd mumbled something and moved away. Around them the hubbub of conversation continued, but Nicholas's focus remained solely on her. "Miss Ellison?"

She glanced up.

"May I call on you tomorrow?"

Her eyes shadowed. "Wouldn't your betrothed mind?"

What a fool he'd been to become snared by the ambitions of others. He fumbled a silent prayer that nothing be misread or detract from the hardwon concord wavering between them. "Miss DeLancey is not my betrothed, nor will she ever be."

Emotion played across her face. His heart paced faster than during Midnight's run this morning as he silently begged her, willed her, to say yes.

"Please, Miss Ellison? I cannot dare to hope that you have missed me, but I confess I have missed you immeasurably."

She bit her lip. Time stretched between them.

"Then," her luminous eyes lifted, "I would enjoy your visit."

And her smile filled his heart with hope and sent his spirits soaring.

🌂 Chapter Thirty

"And its dedication to Saint Paul the apostle dates back to the first church on this site, which was founded over a thousand years ago."

"AD 604." Lavinia murmured. Papa's historical professor friend had been most adamant.

"Ah"—the elderly guide consulted his notes—"it appears the young lady is correct."

"But of course." The earl smiled. "I am only surprised the young lady does not feel qualified to act as our guide."

"That, sir, would be most presumptuous indeed, and as you well know, I am *never* presumptuous." His chuckle reverberated around the high stone arches as she continued. "Mr. Hollins is doing a marvelous job, and I am learning so much." She smiled at the aged man, who appeared somewhat gratified.

He led their small party down the aisle, pointing out other features that Lavinia found fascinating and Charlotte and Henry did not yawn about. Lord Hawkesbury's interest she had yet to ascertain.

"And this is the Great Dome."

Lavinia joined the others in staring up. A bank of windows, interspersed with statues, spilled light to highlight eight scenes from the life of Saint Paul. "It is wonderful, is it not?"

"It's enormous!" Charlotte said. "I shouldn't like to be up so high."

"How else will we get to the Whispering Gallery, Lottie?" Henry said with a boyish eagerness somewhat at odds with his usual inclination for more worldly pursuits. "Surely you want to see if it's true about the whispers."

"I assure you it is true," their guide said to Henry, walking with him and Charlotte to the side. "Even the softest murmur can be heard on the other side . . ."

"I have felt like Saint Paul sometimes."

Lavinia glanced at the earl. "Shipwrecked in Malta, fending off snakes?"

He smiled. "The snakes I've survived were not from Malta and tended to be more of the two-legged variety. No." He studied the pictures overhead. "Like Paul, I was blinded by my arrogance and could not see."

"We are all guilty of pride, my lord." She added, softly, "Especially those of us who claim to see." His gaze caught hers, and they shared rueful smiles.

"Come"—he offered his arm—"we best not keep Henry waiting. He may never forgive us."

She accepted his arm as they followed their tour guide around the cathedral. This side of the earl—this thoughtfulness, this valuing of others she'd seen hints of during her illness—had been on full display in the past days. Since the evening party at Holland's last week, the earl had visited every afternoon, much to Aunt Constance's dismay.

"My dear girl," she had said, "you cannot expect our family to welcome anyone of his. Think of your poor mother!"

"But I do. Mama was always full of grace to others."

"Oh." Her brow had knit. "But he is promised, is he not? To that DeLancey chit? Though really, I don't blame him for seeking *you* out over her. You might say outlandish things, but at least you're not stupid! No"— she shook her head—"I simply cannot have him here. If he insists on coming, I will end up having another of my spasms!"

So his visits had become excursions, often accompanied by Henry and Charlotte, and had consisted of expeditions to Richmond Park, an outing to Astley's Amphitheatre to see the horse riding—which had led the earl to laughingly allude to Swift's Houyhnhnms—as well as to a performance at Drury Lane, together with Aunt Patience and Lord Danver. The earl's solicitude was evident throughout, just as now.

He leaned down to murmur, "Thank you, Miss Ellison, for consenting to my driving today. I have enjoyed this immensely."

"Oh, I'm glad! I don't think Henry and Charlotte have very much, although perhaps the crypts *were* a little dark for Charlotte. But how *could* one possibly miss seeing memorials to so many notables? To ignore Lord Nelson's tomb would be a crime!"

"I cannot believe how quickly some choose to pass that of Sir John Donne. Indeed, to not appreciate such poetical elegance marks one as a fool."

The word made her stiffen as memories surged of his last visit in St. Hampton Heath. She moved to withdraw her fingers from his sleeve, but he stayed her with a gloved hand. "Miss Ellison?" His brow knit. "You seem troubled."

How to explain the bruise his word had left on her soul? She couldn't. Perhaps it was best to just forgive, and try to forget, like Mama surely would. "I . . . I did not think you cared for poets, sir."

"Like Mr. Chetwynd, you mean? I confess I've always had little inclination for the overly romanticized nonsense of so many of today's poets, but these past few months I've come to see how a man can fall into folly."

She caught her bottom lip between her teeth. Did he refer to his association with Miss DeLancey, or something—someone—else? She lifted her gaze, searching his face for the truth.

"Ah, those eyes. I can never hide long from such silvery perception." The amusement in his eyes drained away, replaced by something akin to regret. "You know I called myself a fool a thousand times that day we parted. I'm so terribly sorry. I treated you abominably, to my eternal shame."

It was like a tapestry, whose tawdry tangled picture she'd only seen from the reverse, had suddenly turned to reveal its glorious front. "You said that about *yourself*?"

"Of course. Why, you did not possibly think I could call *you* a fool?"

Her cheeks heated.

"Ah, my dear Miss Ellison, whose 'pure and eloquent blood Spoke in her cheeks'—"

"You know Donne's works?"

"I might never aspire to write poetry, but I can appreciate the gifts of others." He smiled. "You may be many things, but a fool you never will be, my *dear* Miss Ellison."

His words wrapped tenderness around her heart. Why, one might almost suppose the earl held feelings for—

"Lavinia, did you want to see the Whispering Gallery?" Henry called. "I have an engagement at Manton's in an hour that I'd rather not miss."

The earl sighed. "Lord Featherington has a most unfortunate sense of timing, has he not? I suppose we must follow." He brightened. "Perhaps Donne may be able to lend me other words, and we can see if they travel to you on the other side of the wall." He leaned closer, his gaze warm. "'Dear love, for nothing less than thee would I have—'"

"Hawkesbury!" The shrill voice echoed through the nave.

The earl's eyes closed briefly before he offered Lavinia a tight smile and turned. "Miss DeLancey, Mr. DeLancey, what a surprise. I did not think you liked to frequent churches."

"We saw your carriage outside." Clara's eyes scanned Lavinia from top to toe. "What are you doing here with *her*?"

"Do you possibly refer to Miss Ellison? Miss DeLancey, I would have thought it obvious what we are doing." His affected drawl contained a whip-like touch.

Clara's face reddened. "We missed you last night."

"As I explained in my reply to your mother's note, I had a previous commitment and could not—"

"With her?"

Lavinia stiffened under the siblings' angry gazes.

"Mr. DeLancey, no doubt you heard me say the young lady's name is Miss Ellison." The earl's eyes glittered dangerously. "And why you concern yourself in my affairs, I do not know. Now, if you'll excuse us, we must not keep Lord Featherington waiting any longer."

Lavinia offered a quick nod in farewell as the earl drew her away.

"Do not worry, Miss Ellison," he murmured as they walked to where Mr. Hollins waited with her cousins, their faces alive with curiosity. "The DeLanceys play an imprudent game."

Memories flickered. She pulled her hand away. "I've heard that *you* play games with people also."

He sighed. "Your Miss Milton, I suppose?"

She blinked. "You know?"

"Thornton told me, amidst the biggest dressing down of my adult life."

He grimaced. "What she heard was merely my attempt to avoid my mother's machinations. You can see how well *that* turned out."

She answered softly, "But I do not want to be the subject of *your* manipulations, sir."

"I assure you"—his eyes darkened as a sweet smile crossed his lips—"your happiness is my only wish. Now tell me, do you plan to attend the Bathurst ball Thursday week?"

But throughout the remainder of the visit, even as the earl sought to regain the lightheartedness prior to the DeLancey interruption, she could see his troubled frown, which only fueled her unease. If Clara could see the earl's affections had altered, did that point to his lack of fixed character? And if so, how long until his affections changed again?

Nicholas stifled a yawn as the Winpoole dinner party droned on and on. He glanced down the table to see his mother chatting excitedly with Lady Winpoole.

"Lord Hawkesbury," Clara's voice cooed, "we are wonderfully grateful you have chosen to dine with us this evening. After the unpleasantness yesterday . . ." She pouted.

His lip curled with scorn. "I am prepared to overlook the unpleasantness if you promise it will not happen again."

Her eyes widened. "Sir! I did not mean—"

"I know exactly what you mean, Miss DeLancey, and I find it hard to believe that anyone as sweet natured as you would expect me to turn my back on my neighbor. Tell me that could not be true!"

Her brow furrowed. "I would not have you think so ill of me."

"I knew you would not. Now, please tell me about your music."

As Clara prattled on, he finished his roasted capon. This dinner party had been orchestrated between his mother and Lady Winpoole, whose in-person invitation this morning caught him unawares and unable to manufacture an excuse. From the concerned looks and questions he'd fielded all evening, it was obvious they were worried he was no longer a surety. His mother had been more direct this morning when her crony had departed. "When will you make her an offer, Nicholas?"

Sorely tempted to use his quizzing glass for the first time since that initial evening in St. Hampton Heath, he had settled for obtuseness. "Make whom an offer?"

"Why, Miss DeLancey, of course!" She frowned. "You are not thinking of making an offer to anyone else, are you, Nicholas?"

"Surely, ma'am, my plans to make a lady an offer are simply that—mine."

"You must marry Clara!"

"*Must*, ma'am?" He raised a brow. "Because she stands to inherit fifteen thousand?"

"It will make managing the estate far easier," she snapped.

"I'm sure it would. But allowing myself to become leg-shackled simply to make our finances a little easier is rather a hefty price to pay. Do you know, Mother, sometimes I think I would much prefer for you to learn to manage your finances a little better, so such a drastic step as my getting married need not be the only solution."

"You . . . you are impossible!"

He smiled. "So I've been told."

To calm his irate parent, he had agreed to attend tonight, but his regrets renewed as Miss DeLancey continued to talk but with nothing to say.

He cleared his throat. "I wonder if you could help me."

"Anything, my lord!"

"Mother tells me the pinnacle of musical soirees are held at Lady Asquith's."

"She is my godmother, you know."

"Yes. You have played at one of Lady Asquith's musicales, have you not?"

"Sir! Don't you remember? You were there a fortnight ago! A wonderfully fine evening, so you said."

"Oh, of course." He hurried on. "I was wondering if, as a tribute to your generous nature, you might find it in your heart to encourage your godmother to extend an invitation to poor Miss Ellison to perform."

Her eyes narrowed. "Why?"

"I'm afraid some young ladies are forever looking for excuses to share their gifts. Of course Miss Ellison isn't one to boast . . ." His words might malign Lavinia, but he wanted these arrogant people to realize how ridiculous their pretensions were in the light of true talent.

Clara's frown evidenced her struggle to accede to his request. Clearly she believed her talent superior to Lavinia's, but could she run the risk of inviting a rival? On the other hand, did her credit remain so strong that she could afford to disappoint him?

Eventually she sighed. "Some young ladies would do well to develop their gifts before feeling the need to parade them, but I will see what I can do."

He smiled. "Your generous nature does you credit, Miss DeLancey."

And her starry-eyed, voluble response made him wish for the thousandth time he was anywhere else.

Chapter Thirty-One

"This is an honor, Lavinia. I did not think you were acquainted with Lady Asquith."

Lavinia pulled down the half sleeves of her cream gown as she stared critically in the mirror. "I do not recall meeting her."

"Yes, well, she would hardly be the type to grace those types of meetings you and Patience seem so fond of attending." Aunt Constance frowned. "It is most peculiar."

"I am pleased to have been invited. An evening of good musicianship will be most interesting."

"Hmm." Her aunt picked up the letter on Lavinia's dressing table, looked at it, and then carelessly tossed it back. "Patience has kept busy, hasn't she? I've barely seen her."

Lavinia smiled. "Lord Danver *has* been attentive."

"Yes. I remember . . ." Her aunt glanced out the window, abstractedly.

"Remember what, ma'am?"

Aunt Constance shook her head. "Enough of the past. I came in here to say I found something you might like." She handed Lavinia a small velvet box.

Lavinia opened it and stared. A small cross, fashioned from tiny pearls, looped at the end of a fine gold chain. "It is beautiful!"

"It belonged to Grace."

Lavinia lifted the chain and traced the delicate workmanship. Mama had worn this?

"After Grace left so hurriedly, Mother gave us leave to look through her things. Of course Patience never had any use for jewelry, and although it is pretty, I never could abide crosses—they always make me think of death hanging around one's neck."

"Oh, but an empty cross symbolizes life!"

"Life?" Aunt Constance frowned.

"Yes. Although Christ died on a cross, He then rose from the dead. A cross represents life and gives hope for all who believe in Him."

Her aunt's face grew tight. "I see you've been well and truly indoctrinated by that father of yours."

"Influenced, not indoctrinated. The truth is plainly found in the Bible, ma'am."

"Hmph. I don't require a sermon from a young lady."

"I'm sorry if my words are unpalatable." She smiled. "But I cannot be sorry as to their truth."

Aunt Constance stared hard at her before stepping back. "Well, enough of that. Now you look presentable enough. That shot silk does wonders for your complexion, I must say."

"It is a very pretty dress." Tiny apricot rosebuds sewn along the scooped neckline together with the gauze overdress embroidered with more flowers made her feel as pretty as Sophy might in her finest hour. With her hair pinned up with tiny rosebuds and the cross now safely fastened around her neck, she felt confident to face any societal dame's high expectations.

A sound downstairs drew her aunt to the door. "Here is Patience now. I trust you will enjoy tonight. I am sorry my engagement at the Seftons' prevents my attendance."

Lavinia moved to give her a hug. "Thank you for the pendant. It is truly beautiful. And knowing it was Mama's makes it even more special."

"Yes, well . . . ah, good."

Lavinia smiled and resumed her seat at the dressing table. Before pulling on her gloves, she picked up Papa's letter and reread it. Papa was getting on well, the curate displaying worthy attempts at playing the organ, although the children did not mind him during Sunday school. Papa was to conduct the wedding of Captain Thornton and Sophy, their banns having been published—she smiled at the excitement *that* news meant for the Miltons. He had included other news of the village: the apothecary's wife was in the family way; Eliza Hardy sent her best wishes and had requested Lavinia be told the blacksmith's son had come calling; the Thatchers' health and fortunes had improved considerably thanks to Banning's assiduous improvements.

Her eyes filled with happiness. Tonight might hold its challenges, but at least she might see the earl and thank him for his good work.

"Lavinia?"

She turned to see Aunt Patience at the door. These days she held a light in her eyes that made her glow. Or maybe that was the effect of the simple yet elegant clothes she now wore.

"You're wearing Grace's pendant." The angular lines of her face softened. "I didn't know Constance kept it."

"It is lovely."

"Father gave that to her when she turned eighteen. He was a man of faith, with certain Puritanical tendencies"—she spoke drily—"like the names he gave his daughters."

"But he died?"

"A few months after Grace's marriage. If he lived, perhaps things might have been different."

She nodded. Pensiveness was a new emotion for her to see her aunt wear. "Do you think Grandmother would ever want to see me?"

Aunt Patience sighed. "Mother does not do anything that demands a whit of self-sacrifice. I'm afraid your resemblance to Grace would only result in a door shut in your face."

"But—"

"I don't know how many times I have sent letters that were returned, or paid calls that went unacknowledged. Grace's banishment, and my own, seem as fixed as they were decades ago. Now, don't look like that. We have music to perform, have we not?"

"Oh, I don't think I will be asked to play."

"Nonsense. Apparently someone in this town can recognize true talent. Get your music. I don't want to keep Lord Danver waiting."

Lavinia asked slyly, "Has he been kept waiting long?"

Her aunt smiled. "Long enough, I believe."

"Mother, are you ready?" Nicholas leaned against the oak doorframe of his mother's suite. "You won't want to miss the Asquith's musicale this evening."

Pierce finished dressing his mother's hair and curtsied as she exited.

"I fail to understand why tonight is so important. Unless . . ." Mother arched a well-practiced brow. "Will Miss DeLancey be in attendance?"

"I believe so." He had avoided her the past few days, not wanting to fuel any further speculation about his intentions. When not in Parliament or out with Lavinia, he'd spent time with old army cronies at his club instead.

"Clara did play well, I recall. Unlike that other one, what was her name? Bold as brass."

"I'm sure I don't know who you mean, ma'am."

"Yes, you do. You know, the one who *claimed* to be sick."

"Do you mean the reverend's daughter, Miss Ellison?"

"Yes." She frowned as she fiddled with a curl. "Do you know Amelia Pennicooke had the nerve to ask me at cards the other day about *that* young miss." She eyed him in the mirror. "Apparently you have been seen driving with her. Here. In London!"

"I did not know that was a crime, ma'am."

"Well it is when you should be driving Miss DeLancey, and when I have people of the likes of Amelia Pennicooke asking about you! I do hope she will not be there tonight. That chit and her aunt hold pretensions."

Stung, he murmured, "I have never known either lady to claim to be more than what they are."

"Then she has sadly deluded you, Nicholas."

He flicked an imaginary speck of dust from his coat but said nothing.

"I am surprised that you're escorting me and not Miss DeLancey."

He smiled and offered his hand to help her rise. "But, Mother, who could want to attend a candle when they can enjoy the sun?"

She uttered a rare creaking laugh that was quickly repressed. "That's enough of your nonsense. Take me downstairs. We will see if tonight holds any true talent."

With an uneasy sense of foreboding, Nicholas accompanied his mother outside to the waiting carriage.

An hour later, having battled a horrendous crush of vehicles, suffered his mother's usual lament concerning the lack of sedan chairs, and survived

Lady Asquith's mild inquisition about his sudden interest in musicales, Nicholas hastened them to seats toward the back.

"Why must we sit here, Nicholas?" She motioned to the lady in front whose ridiculous concoction of a hat, complete with madly waving ostrich feathers, screened her view. "I cannot see a thing!"

He leaned close. "Musical appreciation mostly demands the ability to hear, I understand."

"Hmph."

He settled back, wondering exactly where in the program the remarkable Miss Ellison was to perform. After several unexciting performances his mother only sniffed at, the short, stout master of ceremonies stood up to introduce the next performer.

"Now we are pleased to invite Miss DeLancey to share her talent with us."

His mother sat up as the Winpooles led the applause from the front row. Nicholas's height meant he could see above the heads to catch Clara's anxious glance across the crowd before she found him. Her smug expression caused more than one face to turn a speculative eye to him—enough to make him long to retrieve his quizzing glass once more.

Her performance *was* pretty and received demands for an encore from Lord Asquith, but his mother's forehead only creased.

"Mother? Are you quite well? Would you like to move closer to the fire?"

"No, no." She waved a hand.

"Did you not enjoy Miss DeLancey's performance?"

"It was prettily done . . ."

"But?"

"That woman is here."

"I must beg your pardon for my obtuseness. Which one?"

"That woman." She pointed several rows in front. "The one with the ridiculous looking turban on her head, like she's the Queen of Sheba."

He followed her gaze to see Miss West—Lady Westerbrooke—seated next to Lord Danver.

"The aunt of that girl we talked of earlier. What is *she* doing here?"

"I imagine she is here to enjoy the music, too."

"Hmph."

The master of ceremonies stood again. "Ladies and gentlemen, we are privileged tonight to witness the return, after many years' absence, of one of our most accomplished pianists. Lady Westerbrooke, please join us."

"Westerbrooke?" Mother's eyes snapped. "*Westerbrooke* did he say?"

Lavinia's aunt moved to the pianoforte and commenced a recital that was a lesson to all who had gone before. Although he had often found her musicality to be commanding rather than emotive, tonight he heard a gentle strain that pleased far more than technical excellence.

Amidst the applause that greeted her three pieces—she'd received demands for two encores—he noticed his mother's face had paled.

"Mother? Are you quite well?"

She waved him away, her expression grim.

The short man stood once more and nodded to the golden head Danver's girth had hidden before.

Nicholas's heart leapt. She *was* here. She *would* perform. As the master of ceremonies finally introduced her, Nicholas coughed loudly enough to drown out Lavinia's name—and to draw Danver's amused glance.

"Who is this?"

Nicholas shushed his mother, unable to drag his eyes from Lavinia. Her coppery golden curls were twisted into a small knot, her poise evident as she smiled briefly at the crowd before lifting her chin in that characteristic way, as if aware of the critics in the crowd.

The music began soft and sweet. He didn't recognize the melody, but it was evident by nods and finger taps that others did. Then she began to sing: clear, pure, true. Contentment swelled within him at the harmonious pairing of voice and piano, unmarred by the strain of sickness as it had been before.

He glanced at his mother, who wore a rare, pleased expression. She nodded at intervals as Lavinia's voice soared, matching the exquisite playing. Nicholas smiled in true pleasure, glad that Lavinia was performing so well, but thankful also his mother finally could appreciate something about this unique young lady.

"Now *that* is true musicianship. Who is that girl?" She tried to peer around the violently shaking ostrich feathers of the woman in front who clapped vigorously. "She must be Italian or someone from the Continent. I haven't heard such true pitch in years."

Once the encores had been played, and the applause had finally ceased, a break in proceedings was announced. Nicholas grasped his mother's elbow. "Let's go meet the prodigy."

"Splendid idea." She looked up at him. "Thank you for bringing me tonight, Nicholas. It was a very kind idea. I'm quite looking forward to meeting her."

He smiled, wondering if she'd still think so in a few moments.

"Ah, excuse me, Lord Hawkesbury, Lady Hawkesbury." Miss DeLancey wore a broad smile. "I'm *so* glad you could come. Have you enjoyed this evening?" She batted her eyelashes in a sad attempt at coquetry.

He bowed. "I continue to find it immensely entertaining."

Her brow puckered.

As Lady Winpoole rushed to speak to his mother he murmured, "I must thank you for your kindness in encouraging Lady Asquith to extend Miss Ellison an invitation."

"Oh." Miss DeLancey's frown became more pronounced. "I did not know she could play so well."

"I thought you did not. Wonderfully fine, do you not agree?"

"Nicholas." His mother gestured. "Come, let's meet tonight's *true* sensation."

He bowed and escorted her to the front, where a crowd of admirers continued to flock around Miss Ellison. He nodded to Lavinia's aunt, whose glance at his mother widened her smile.

Eventually the crush of bodies moved to reveal Lavinia, her smile as sweet and modest as her cream-and-apricot-beribboned gown.

His mother's shocked gasp was reflected in Lavinia's widened eyes as she saw them.

"Lord Hawkesbury! And Lady Hawkesbury." She curtsied.

"You!" His mother looked at him. "Tell me *she* is not the prodigy."

"Mother"—his eyes narrowed warningly—"I cannot tell you that, because that would be untrue."

With one hand, he stayed his mother and with the other caught Lavinia's hand. She had not yet had the chance to restore her gloves, and her skin felt smooth and warm. He pressed her fingers gently. "You delighted everyone tonight, Miss Ellison. Indeed, my mother said how much she enjoyed your music." He smiled, enjoying the soft expression that filled her eyes at his honest compliment.

"Thank you. You are very kind, my lord."

"Not at all." He reluctantly released her hand and turned to his mother. "Isn't that what you were saying, Mother? You think Lavinia possesses *true* musicianship."

She nodded stiffly.

Lavinia offered his mother a small curtsey and smile. "Thank you, Lady Hawkesbury. That means a great deal coming from you."

He caught his mother's slightly mollified expression at Lavinia's words before she inclined her head and moved away to speak with Lady Asquith. His attention returned to Lavinia.

Her face was aglow. "Lord Hawkesbury, I'm *so* pleased to have the chance to talk with you."

His heart rippled with gladness.

"I simply must thank you for the wonderful news about the Thatchers."

"Ah, yes. The Thatchers." He fought the trickle of disappointment as she shared news from home. God bless Banning's faithfulness, but he didn't want his steward the object of Lavinia's thoughts and affection.

"Miss Ellison?" The master of ceremonies interrupted. "Some people want to meet you."

"Excuse me." She smiled and bowed her head.

He extracted his mother from Lady Asquith and led her back to their seats for the remainder of the concert. As soon as they were heading home in the privacy of the carriage, the steam evident in her face since Lady Westerbrooke's performance was finally vented.

"You tricked me!" she hissed. "You knew she would be there, didn't you?"

"Mother, Miss Ellison has many excellent qualities. I hope you can come to appreciate her as much as I do."

Her eyes narrowed. "What are you saying? You aren't thinking of doing anything rash!"

"Rash would be aligning myself with a family whose values I find abhorrent."

"You cannot mean the Winpoole—"

"Of course I mean the Winpooles! They are shallow and self-seeking, without a care for anyone but themselves! I cannot—I *will* not marry Miss DeLancey. She is the last woman in the world with whom I could ever find happiness."

"And Miss Ellison is the first?" Her voice sounded old.

"She is the *only*."

"Oh, Nicholas . . ."

"I want you to know that I will not tolerate any more of your shenanigans concerning a lady I respect and admire so much as I do Miss Ellison."

"But—"

"No, Mother, that's enough! I don't want to hear another word against her."

Silence filled the carriage for a few minutes before his mother finally spoke. "Do you know who her grandmother is?"

He breathed in irritably. "Who?"

She told him. And his heart—and hopes—dropped like a stone.

ℛ Chapter Thirty-Two

LAVINIA LOOKED AT the mirror in horror. "I cannot! It is simply scandalous!"

Aunt Constance's brows rose. "It is a perfectly elegant dress made by London's finest mantua-maker! Are you criticizing her taste or mine?"

But there was so much skin! She continued to look miserably in the mirror. If only Aunt Patience was here instead of visiting in Wiltshire! "The neckline seems very low."

"Nonsense. Necklines are lower this season." Her aunt frowned. "You don't believe I would ever have you dress in anything less than modest?"

"No, ma'am."

But despite her silk dress containing layers of petticoats, delicate puffed sleeves, and rows of cream silk flowers adorning the low squared neckline, she could not help but feel almost naked. What would her father think if he could see her? "Papa—"

"I do *not* want to hear another word about your father, Lavinia."

"Perhaps a fichu—"

"No!" Aunt Constance's eyes snapped. "You have a lovely figure. Why must you insist on hiding it away?"

"I would rather be admired for my mind and character than for my appearance."

"Hmph! I will never understand you. You're just like your mother."

Lavinia smiled for the first time that day. "Thank you."

Aunt Constance sniffed and withdrew. As Charlotte chattered from her position seated on the bed, and the maid fussed with her hair, pinning it up into curls with pearl-encrusted combs, she resigned herself to the inevitable.

Tonight she would endure to the best of her ability—and wear a shawl as long as possible.

Her aunt returned with a small flat box. "Perhaps this might meet with your approval. This too was given to your mama." She slid open the lid.

Charlotte softly echoed Lavinia's gasp. "It's beautiful, Mama!"

Lavinia tentatively touched the exquisite necklace of pearls and diamonds. Far more substantial than her pearl cross, more like a collar, the gold filigree and swirling strands of tiny diamonds kept it from appearing too heavy. "Is it real?"

"Of course it's real. Grace was given it by our grandfather. It was always passed to the eldest child, and so now it is for you." She attached it around Lavinia's neck. "I know it's not the usual thing for a young lady to wear, but it's not as though you're just out of the schoolroom."

She looked at herself in the mirror. The twinkling rows of diamonds and glossy pearls did much to hide her décolletage—but would also draw the eye. She bit back a sigh.

"Livvie, you look positively beautiful!" Charlotte's face filled with admiration. "I cannot wait until next year when I can attend balls."

"I hope you'll be more grateful than your cousin here."

"Aunt Constance, I am ever so grateful for all your kindness. I do not wish to seem rude."

"Yes, well"—her aunt appeared somewhat mollified—"you do look very well, which is only as you ought, as the lace and silk of your gown alone cost nearly one hundred guineas."

Lavinia's jaw dropped. "One hundred guineas? For one dress? Why, there would hardly be a man in St. Hampton Heath who could earn that much in a year! I am sorry, Aunt Constance, but I simply cannot—"

"Do you really want to besmirch the family name by being dressed inappropriately?"

"Of course not." She swallowed. "But I also have no designs to impress people who need others to wear expensive clothes in order to be impressed. I cannot—"

"Enough! Let me not hear another word!"

Her aunt whirled from the room, Charlotte trailing in her wake, leaving Lavinia to remain under the mute ministrations of Aunt Constance's maid.

Her hair was patted a final time, a curl was tweaked, and she was handed her long white gloves.

"Thank you, Ellen."

The maid dropped a curtsey and left the room.

With a deep sense of apprehension, she rose, refusing to look at the mirror, wrapped her shawl around her, and went to await her relatives as they finished their own preparations for the ball.

"Ah! Lord Hawkesbury. I am so pleased you decided to attend our little evening."

Nicholas bowed. "I could not miss tonight."

He glanced around the crowded room, trying not to let his boredom at his hostess's vapidity be too obvious. As plain Jane Saville, whose father's estates bordered Hawkesbury House, she had always seemed a flighty girl, her conversation asinine. Now Lady Bathurst, she was never known for understatement save in her approximations of the numbers who attended soirees such as these.

His gaze alighted on a group of bucks surrounding a young lady who wore an extremely modish low-cut gown. He frowned. She stood with her profile to him, but the graceful lines of her neck, the curve of her cheek, that particular hue of golden curls so artfully arranged . . . surely not.

"I see you are entranced also." His hostess's dry voice made him conscious he'd lost all semblance of interest in her story. "She is rather a fetching thing. But surely you would know that. She is from your way, I believe. A Miss Ellison?"

He strove for a neutral expression and inclined his head. "I am somewhat acquainted with her."

The rosy lips widened. "I understood it to be far more than mere acquaintance." Lady Bathurst waved an ivory-feathered fan. "In fact, I heard something rather scandalous about Miss Ellison."

He forced his jaw to unclench. "Miss Ellison is a *most* proper young lady."

"So proper that she spends great swaths of time in your house, unaccompanied?" Her brows arched. "Most proper, indeed."

He gritted his teeth.

She tapped his arm with her fan. "Come, come, Nicholas. We have been friends long enough for you to know I don't disapprove of your dalliances. But, really, a reverend's daughter?"

"She was sick, with the smallpox."

Lady Bathurst's breath hissed inward and she inched away, as if the dreaded pox lurked in the very air.

"As her maid was there the entire time, I fail to see what the problem could be." Thank God for Patience's foresight in claiming Lily's services.

"Hmm. Are you sure she had the pox? I fail to detect any mark at all."

He could tell her precisely where Lavinia's face bore the faintest trace of the ravages of her illness: an indent, halfway between the peak of her left eyebrow and her hairline.

"But then, with all those diamonds, who would pay attention to her face!"

He frowned. It was apparent the men standing near Lavinia were less interested in any necklace than in the contents of her gown which she so helpfully displayed.

"I grant you she is pretty, but a hero from the Peninsular could have his pick of any number of eligible young ladies. So thus you replace Miss DeLancey?"

"Miss DeLancey was never in any position to be replaced."

Her head tilted, like a cunning bird about to extract a tasty morsel. "Did she know that?"

Guilt made his answer stiff. "Miss DeLancey and I would never suit."

Her smile grew sly. "Well, tonight I can see why Miss Ellison might suit better."

"Miss Ellison holds to the highest principles."

"How dull."

"I hold to them also."

"Oh. Well, that is a bore." Her expression grew thoughtful. "I understand she holds musical aspirations?"

"Not just aspirations. She *is* very gifted."

"But really, Nicholas, a reverend's daughter?"

"Jane, your interest in a country miss is most fascinating. If you will excuse me?"

She laughed. "Yes go, get reacquainted—if you can. Miss Ellison has caught many an eye, it appears!"

He bowed and departed, smiling grimly at that truth. Lavinia was surrounded by admirers, no doubt being flattered about everything from the color of her eyes to the style of her gown. As he made his way around the room he thought back to those times in his drawing room and library when they'd shared many an in-depth conversation about the vapidity of the social set. But looking at her now, that innocent sparkle drawing people like bees to nectar, he wondered if she'd forgotten.

He angled between the Marquess of Abbotsbury and an elegant young Corinthian and bowed. "Good evening, Miss Ellison."

She turned, and he caught the full splendor of the jewels, serving as a dazzling signpost to the low neckline of her gown. Why didn't she cover up? His eyes lifted to meet hers.

"Good evening, Lord Hawkesbury." The gray eyes were soft, tinged with something like relief. "I'm so glad to see an old friend among so many new ones."

Hurt twisted his heart. He was but an old friend? He held out a hand. "Miss Ellison, would you do me the honor of a dance?" At least if she were with him he might be able to protect her from the ogling of lascivious rakes such as these.

"Oh. I regret nearly all my dances are promised."

Disappointment cut keen as a saber.

She offered an apologetic smile. "Perhaps we may talk later. I have left the waltz free, because I knew Papa would not want me to dance that."

The words rushed out. "And do you always consider your father's sensibilities?" His gaze flicked to her neckline.

Hurt filled her eyes as she flushed and inched away. "Excuse me."

And before he could apologize, the very rich and eligible Marquess of Abbotsbury whisked her away.

The nauseous feeling in his stomach intensified as the night progressed.

Unwilling to dance with anyone else, he wandered to the cardroom, but card playing lent itself to gossip he could ill afford to hear, and besides, he could barely afford to throw away money, especially when the stakes played for were so high. He moved to the ballroom and forced himself to ask some acquaintances to dance, but those diamonds kept drawing his attention to Lavinia again and again. She whirled around the dance floor, as light as a feather drifting in the wind, more beautiful, more alive than any other lady present, the animation only pausing partway through a quadrille when she caught him watching. Her hurt expression sent shards of ice to his heart.

Shame prevented him from approaching her during the first waltz she sat out. Instead, he endured conversation with fellow officers from Peninsular days, all the while wishing he had the courage to talk to her, so she'd grace him with smiles instead of the homely young lady she conversed with.

"Stamford! Stop staring at the pretty miss and attend to us."

He dragged his gaze away to frown at the major and several lieutenants.

"Is it true she's the daughter of a reverend?"

"Yes."

"I wish to God all reverends had such daughters! Y'know, she rather puts me in mind of a young actress I had the pleasure of spending a considerable amount of time with when we first returned. Same hair color, similar form." The captain's smile turned sly. "Quite enchanting."

"That DeLancey miss is staring daggers at you again, Stamford."

Which was another reason he preferred to skirt the perimeter. Evasion was the best form of prevention as far as she was concerned.

"So it is true you threw Miss DeLancey over for the other. Can't blame you, though. Did you see those jewels?" The major uttered a mild oath. "She must be worth a tidy fortune!"

"And a tidy armful I wager, eh, Stamford?" There was a round of sniggers.

His jaw clenched. "Miss Ellison is lovely, it is true. It is also true she is innocent, and anyone who questions her virtue will have to answer to me!"

He stalked away to their muttered apologies, finding a quiet place near the Palladian window where he could pull himself together. He was a fool, a jealous fool. He should leave. He could not stand to see Lavinia smile at another man, let alone dance with him. His hands clenched.

He glanced across the crowded room and encountered the Marchioness of Exeter's scathing stare. He inclined his head to Lavinia's aunt and moved outside to the terrace. He himself was proof that what his mother said was right: the Hawkesbury family would always be as dung to all those associated with the Duchess of Salisbury. He dragged in fresh air, but it helped only a little.

Because regret, always regret, weighed his soul down again.

❧

Lavinia watched the earl's departure with pain. He looked so sternly handsome in his black tailcoat and snowy starched neckcloth, but his disappointment in her made her want to weep. Pride had held her head high so far, but if she did not escape soon, she would crack.

She turned to the girl beside her. "Please excuse me, Miss Windsor. I must have my skirt attended to. It has been lovely chatting. I do hope you enjoy the rest of the evening."

"Thank you, Miss Ellison." Her plain face wreathed in a smile. "I feel much better now."

Lavinia's smile became brittle as she walked across the room. People kept watching her, women whispering, men staring at her chest, their eyes sliding all over her body, their glances dirty, hot, and soiling. Once she'd glimpsed Clara's white face before the crush hid her from view. The air felt stifling, sticky with gossip and speculation. Her head ached from finding polite ways to fend off men who wanted introductions so they could dance. One foolish fellow had even proposed!

She stumbled to a small withdrawing room where a maid was prompt in sewing the small tear in her train that Lord Asquith, whose dancing possessed more enthusiasm than skill, had torn. The maid finished but Lavinia retained her seat in the corner and closed her eyes.

A group of ladies entered, their murmurs echoing around the salon. ". . . pretty young thing, but fast. Terribly fast, I believe."

Lavinia rose. She should go. Tucked away here she could not be seen—

"I understand Constance was shocked by her arrival."

"Out of the blue, after being hidden in the country for so many years."

Her breath caught. These ladies referred to her?

"Well, apparently she had a most unusual upbringing. Not at *all* what you'd expect from the Westerbrookes. I imagine Her Grace would *not* be amused."

Her Grace? Aunt Constance was a marchioness, not a duchess. Who—?

"I understand she has her claws into young Hawkesbury. Frederica Winpoole was telling me how her girl was all but promised to him when this chit waltzes in and snatches him away."

"Scandalous, I call it!"

"He is a man, though. You saw her in that dress tonight."

"And he does need to marry money. And judging from the size of *her* gems he'll have plenty of that, I dare say."

"That is, if her highness ever agrees!"

There was a cackle of laughter, the sounds of a door closing, then silence.

Lavinia pressed her lips together. Her eyes burned. Mortification seared her cheeks. How much of what those women said was true? She *had* felt uncomfortable in the gown since first donning it. She *had* known the Winpooles would not take competition lightly. But Nicholas wanting her for her money? She shook her head. She had none. Aunt Constance had money. Her mother's jewels would be worth something, but Nicholas had begun to pay her attention long before she had ever worn a pearl. Had he known something earlier? Were all his attentions a ploy to persuade her of his care?

"Excuse me, miss?" The maid reappeared, worry knotting her brow. "I was concerned when you did not come."

"Thank you." She rose unsteadily and placed a hand upon the wall for balance.

"Are you unwell? Is there someone I can fetch?"

"Thank you, no. I shall be quite well directly."

She staggered to the ballroom where the whirling figures and noise only exacerbated her lightheadedness. People called to her but she did not hear; touched her but she shrugged them away. Her senses swam. She would *never* dress like this again. Never!

"Miss Ellison?"

She turned, bumped into a tall figure dressed in black. She stared at the snowy neckcloth unseeingly.

"It is a lovely neckcloth, is it not?"

She glanced up. Richard DeLancey smiled, his eyes fixed on hers, not dipping to her necklace—or neckline. Relief made her smile warmer than it might otherwise have been. "Good evening."

"It is a veritable crush tonight, don't you agree, Miss Ellison?"

"These rooms are rather stuffy."

"You seem tired. Would you care to walk on the terrace?"

She nodded. He led her outside to where the cool night air gave welcome relief. Lights spilled from the open windows, gently illuminating the sculptured hedges of the garden beyond. Shrubs in white pots loomed in the terrace's darkened sections.

"Are you enjoying yourself this evening, Miss Ellison?"

His unexpected solicitude caused her to admit, "Not as much as I thought I would."

"That's a shame." He offered an arm and drew her away from the noise, down to a dimly lit section.

Here she could breathe, and she took in great quaffs of fresh air. Slowly the giddiness passed. "Thank you, sir. I feel better."

"Do you enjoy London?" He leaned closer, his breath caressing her cheek.

She backed away, farther into the shadows. "It is the antithesis of St. Hampton Heath."

"I imagine it is." He studied her neckline.

Her skin crawled.

"Clara told me you were considered its most virtuous do-gooder." Dim light from upper windows showed his thick, sensual lips. "You seem to have become more like London than you wish to admit." He moved closer, forcing her to step deeper into the darkness.

"I wish to go inside now, sir."

She moved to go but he snatched her close, pinning her arms to her sides. "I don't. I'm quite enjoying this."

"Let go of me!" She struggled but he was too strong. Tried to scream but her voice had frozen.

"Scream if you want. All the old biddies inside will have a field day." His hand touched her chin, slid down her throat—

"Don't! Please don't!" She tried to claw, scratch, kick, anything to keep his slithery hands away. "Lord, help me!"

"You know you want this." He bent his lips to her neck and murmured, "That dress tells me so."

Twisting away, she froze.

She caught a glimpse of wild glittering eyes, heard a snarl, before being yanked free and pushed away near the wall. She huddled, gasping, shivering as the two men scuffled. A potted plant crashed to the ground. She heard a crack, a wheeze, muttered oaths, an exchange of blows. The two figures wrestled wildly, before the earl's superior height and strength gained him the upper hand. Like a dog with a rat he shook Mr. DeLancey and then, with a loud smack to the jaw, felled him.

He stood over the prone figure, breathing hard. "You are a cur and a scoundrel!"

Lavinia drew back. Never had she seen him look so terrifying.

"If you were in my regiment, I'd see you thrashed!" His voice was low, taut as a whip. "How dare you treat any woman so? How *dare* you touch Miss Ellison?"

Mr. DeLancey groaned as he shifted into a sitting position. "Name your secon—"

"Do not insult me! Would you have your sister know her brother is a villain of the lowest order?" The earl glanced at her, his expression softening a touch, before he scowled at the younger man. "I doubt Miss Ellison ever wants to hear your voice again, but I insist you apologize!"

When no answer came immediately, he bent and shook the man.

She barely heard the muttered regret, as her attention remained fixed on the earl. The dim light revealed his broad-shouldered strength, his soldierly authority, his care for her. Her eyes filled.

"Do not dare to even *think* about seeing Miss Ellison again, else you will wish yourself in Hades. Do I make myself clear?"

Clara's brother spat something vile and slunk away, leaving them alone on the terrace.

"Miss Ellison"—the earl drew close, his voice soft—"are you hurt?"

Hot tears spilled. "No, my lord."

"You're trembling." He stripped off his bloodied gloves and gathered her close.

Her cheek pressed against his coat, the steady thump of his heart as reassuring as the strength in his arms. Here she was safe, protected, cherished. She closed her eyes, drew in a deep breath, her senses tingling at the tantalizing scent of fresh linen, bergamot, and another, indefinable masculine essence. As if by their own accord her arms stole around his back. His clasp tightened, his lips grazed her forehead. They stood still for a long, long moment, his breath ruffling her hair, ease wrapping around them like a cocoon.

Too soon he sighed, lowered his arms.

She drew in a shaky breath. "Th–thank you, my lord."

"My dear Miss Ellison . . ." He thumbed away the dampness on her cheeks before smoothing her hair and moving into the light. "We had best get inside."

"But you are bleeding." She tugged off her glove, touched the small cut on his cheek. "His ridiculous ring, no doubt."

"No doubt." He gently clasped her hand to his cheek, the heat in his eyes flushing her warm all over. He shifted, pressed his lips to her palm. Fire danced at the site of his tender caress. "Your solicitude gives hope that you are not completely indifferent to me."

Time stretched as his gaze held hers. The lights and music and chatter were inconsequential as certainty arrested her soul. *Here* was a man she could trust. Twice now, he had come to her rescue and would doubtless do so any time she required his assistance. "How can I be indifferent, my lord? When you have . . . when you are . . ."

A sweet expression crossed his face. He kissed her palm again. "Straighten your dress and pin on a smile. At least one of us should look presentable when we return. We cannot have the dowagers making a fuss."

"Heaven forbid there be a scene." Doing as he bade, she smoothed her gloves and adjusted her sleeves as he worked on the intricate folds of his neckcloth. She glanced up, smiled shyly. "Do I look acceptable now?"

Despite the dim light she could see his eyes darken and intensify. He took a step nearer then paused, opened his lips as if to speak and then closed them, his focus on her so compelling she could feel her body sway toward him.

He cleared his throat. "You are"—he lifted a hand, caressed a curl behind her ear—"you are lovely as always, Lavinia." The searching look in his eyes deepened as his fingers trailed fire down her cheek.

Her breath caught. The air seemed to crackle with promise, with hope, with longing.

CAROLYN MILLER

The sound of high-pitched laughter spilled from the open doors, break-ing the spell. He blinked, offered a rueful smile, dropping his hand to offer his arm. He covered her fingers with his and walked her slowly toward the lit door. "I wonder, Miss Ellison, if you would be so kind as to grant me two favors?"

"Of course."

"Would you please find it in your heart to forgive my carelessness ear-lier this evening? I behaved abominably and should not have insulted you. I humbly beg your pardon."

Her steps ceased, her gaze fell. "You said nothing I did not already know," she murmured.

"I was a jealous fool. Seeing you surrounded by those I knew could never appreciate you like I could, wishing I had the right to claim every dance with you. Please forgive me."

His words were as honeyed balm to her earlier shame. "Of course, my lord."

"And I hope you will overlook the fact that I neglected to say you are, without doubt, the most beautiful lady here tonight."

"I am prepared to overlook it. This once."

He chuckled. "You are generous."

"Thank you."

"And despite the fact this exceeds the two favors originally requested, I cannot but hope your tremendous generosity will also permit me the honor of a dance?"

"I find myself quite unable to refuse."

They reentered the ballroom, and she followed his lead, lifting her chin, her smile firmly fixed as if unconcerned by the upraised brows and whis-pers behind fans. The earl led her onto the floor to join a set, his smile and the press of his fingers reassuring when she encountered the scorch-ing glares of the Winpooles and her aunt. She forced herself to dance and laugh and exchange banter. Yet although her feet moved through the steps, underneath the assumed gaiety something whispered—had the earl truly changed or did underlying intentions mean he would continue to lead her on a merry dance?

🌿 Chapter Thirty-Three

THE TOWN HOUSE smelled of lilies, roses, and lilacs, the hothouse arrangements filling the hall and the parlor. Despite last night's challenges, and its subsequent uncertainty, today's visits and flowers from her dancing partners had boosted Lavinia's spirits. The afternoon proved a respite from activity, Aunt Constance happy to spend time stitching as Lavinia read. But the words passed her by without meaning, as her mind toyed with fragments of conversations from the ball.

"Terribly fast . . ."

No. How could people judge her so? Perhaps her dress had seemed a trifle risqué, but her behavior had never given anyone reason to doubt her character.

"He must marry money."

Surely the Hawkesbury estates were not in such dire circumstances that Nicholas must be forced to find a wealthy bride. But if so, perhaps that explained his mother's preference for Clara.

The look in his eye when the earl said she was "the most beautiful lady here tonight."

Her heart beat faster. He couldn't be serious. Why, the idea was utterly nonsensical! But oh, how she wished he were . . .

A footman entered, holding a salver. "Excuse me, m'lady. The letters have just arrived."

Aunt Constance stretched out a hand. "Oh, there's one for you, Lavinia."

Lavinia pried open the envelope, read the few sentences, and gasped. "I cannot believe it!" She glanced at her aunt who had paled. "Is yours from Aunt Patience, too?"

"Of all the things to do! I knew they were fond of each other, but a special license? Mother will be beside herself!"

"Lord Danver is such a kind man. Surely she cannot object."

"You'd be surprised." Aunt Constance placed a hand over her eyes. "Oh, I think I might be having a spasm."

Lavinia rose. "Should I get someone? Ellen? Parsons?"

"No, no. I will be better momentarily."

She reseated herself, working to curb the bubbling disappointment at missing her aunt's secret wedding. She reread the letter:

> Dear Lavinia,
>
> Your words the other day gave me pause. Edmund has been kept waiting too long, and it is time that was remedied. I hope you will forgive the abruptness of this decision, but understand that opportunities for such happiness rarely come twice. I have every confidence that you shan't let fears shape your life, especially as you remember God's gifts of love, power, and a sound mind. I am trying to also, so now my husband and I go to face the duchess.
>
> Much love always,
> Patience Danver

Despite everything, laughter burbled up and escaped. "I cannot believe it."

"It is hardly a laughing matter, Lavinia! Typical Patience—doing her own thing before anyone can talk reason to her."

Lavinia smiled, studying the neat copperplate. "Aunt Constance, who is the duchess?"

Her aunt peered over the small eyeglasses she never wore beyond family. "Do you mean Patience never told you?"

"Told me, ma'am?"

Aunt Constance's brows pushed together. "Your grandmother, my mother, is the Duchess of Salisbury."

What?

"Oh, do close your mouth, Lavinia. It is most unbecoming."

"A duchess?" Her mind whirled. "But why didn't they tell me?"

Aunt Constance sniffed. "Grace and Patience never valued rank appropriately. I suppose they never told you because they did not think it important. And Mother did make it very clear when they left she wanted nothing to do with them."

"But why? Aunt Patience tried to explain, but I cannot believe anyone to be so cruel."

Her aunt put down her needlework, removed her eyeglasses, and settled back on the gold-and-white-striped settee. "You need to understand Mother's devastation when Grace left. She had always been very proud of Grace. She was the most beautiful debutante of the season. Her looks, her pedigree, her charm, everything about her said she was a diamond of the first water."

Her gaze settled on the portraits above the fireplace, her face soft in lost reminiscence. "Mother always said that Grace's success would open the way for Patience and myself to make splendid matches."

Aunt Constance fiddled with the pleat of her russet gown. "I suppose that as the only child of the Duke of Grantham, Mother had been used to getting her own way, which probably explains why she fell madly in love with my father. See his portrait there, next to Mother's? He was very handsome, wasn't he?"

Lavinia nodded, moving to study the faces more closely. She recognized traces of her grandfather in both Mama and Aunt Constance—the fairness, something about the shape of the eyes—though Aunt Constance's features were more tightly drawn than the softness she remembered of Mama.

"He was the second son of the impoverished Duke of Salisbury, not the heir, so her parents made such a fuss, yet she paid them no heed. I remember Mother once saying after Grace went away that she, too, had married for love and experienced lean years, until the older son died and Father attained the title."

She waved a hand. "Of course, *then* my grandfather forgave her, bestowing her with all his wealth that was not entailed away, including the Grantham jewels, but she never forgot those hard years. Although Mother loved Papa very much, she determined that none of us would throw themselves away for matches based on mere love. So when Grace did almost the same thing, falling in love with your father the way she did after that first season, my mother determined to cut her off penniless if she didn't repent and marry someone of Mother's choosing. It turned out that Grace, despite her gentleness, had also inherited a will of iron and refused to succumb to Mother's wishes. And so they departed."

"And were married, with only Papa's family in attendance," Lavinia said softly.

Her aunt looked down at her hands. "I'm sorry to say I was too easily persuaded. I . . . I have regretted that ever since." She glanced at Lavinia again. "I've always wished I could be more like Patience. She's never cared what Mother thinks, which has meant she's made her own choices. No doubt at times that has been challenging, but at least she is free."

Lavinia gazed around the ornate room, suddenly understanding all of the hidden meanings and intrigues concerning the state of affairs at Twenty Grosvenor Square. Aunt Constance obviously lived in the pockets of this infamous grandmother.

She resumed perusing her grandmother's portrait. Pride suffused every line, from her haughty stare to the aquiline nose both Lavinia's aunts had inherited.

"When Grace died, my mother decided that all would be forgiven if only your father would release you to come live with her. But your father refused, saying how important you were to him."

Lavinia remembered back to those first hard weeks of mourning. Papa had seemed so lost, which had been the catalyst for Lord Robert's kindness in distracting her with music and puppies. But now she suddenly recalled the nights when Papa had come in and hugged her hard. "Oh my dear girl, how could I lose you, too?"

Her eyes filled. How *hard* life must have been for her father. Grieving his wife, fearing his daughter might be taken away. Other memories flooded in. The curate who had led the services for a month until Papa felt well enough again. The hampers of food from the villagers and the Hall—too much food it had seemed at the time. The way the servants were too distraught to do their jobs properly, until Aunt Patience made her home with them, after seeing the shambles things had been when she'd visited for the funeral. The servants quickly improved, and Patience started investing in Lavinia's education. She'd approved of the visits to the Hall, saying Lord Robert was one of the few peers she had met with any intelligence. It all made so much more sense now.

"Mother washed her hands of Patience when she left to care for you. I know Patience has written to her, even tried to visit, but Mother remained adamant that defiance must be defied."

"But she's her daughter!"

Aunt Constance nodded tiredly. "I don't necessarily agree."

Or did she not disagree unnecessarily? Keeping in her mother's good graces seemed to have served Aunt Constance quite well.

"It is my understanding that the portion of inheritance due your mother has been preserved. I think Mother always hoped your father might relent and let you live with her, and as time went on her will never changed. So I believe you really are something of an heiress." She adjusted the folds of her gown. "To the tune of forty thousand pounds."

Lavinia gasped. "But . . . but that is absurd!"

"Not absurd, just unexpected." Aunt Constance shrugged.

"Why did no one ever tell me?"

"Because, my dear, the very rich are not the only ones whose sin is pride."

The flowers' scent grew overpowering, nauseating. Is that why she had received so much attention in London? People were kind because they knew of her family connections? Knew she had money? Were the gossips correct, after all? Had Nicholas sought her out because of the wealth?

Suddenly all the warnings her Aunt Patience had ever given her raced through her mind. The *ton* were shallowly fixated on either titles or money. Character and talent might be applauded, but rarely were they considered to be factors for marriage.

She bit her lip as her aunt's face grew suddenly blurry.

What did this mean about Nicholas?

As the horses began another circuit of the park, Nicholas shot Lavinia a glance. She wore a pretty carriage dress and a pelisse the same blue as that worn by the Hussars, which made her hair glow and her eyes appear more jewel-like than ever. The chilly afternoon air saw her hold a fur muff, the likes of which even his mother would envy, but it was the pensiveness she wore that ate into his content. Despite his best efforts to point out Hyde Park's pretty features, such as the Serpentine, and a pair of frivolous squir-rels, Lavinia, save for some inconsequential remarks about the beauty of the plane trees, had said little.

"Miss Ellison, is something the matter?"

"Oh! I'm sorry for not attending. I beg your pardon."

"Are you concerned about the beggar woman from earlier? I am sure she will be well looked after at the mission."

"I hope so. Thank you so much for agreeing to take her there. I know it wasn't what you expected today."

He smiled. Driving an elderly woman to the Brent Street Women's Home certainly had not been on his agenda, but Lavinia's pleading look had made his answer easy. "It was my pleasure."

"Your pleasure? Why sir, I *am* surprised at what you find pleasurable."

"Someone once told me how blessed it is to give rather than receive." He glanced across. "I don't know if I ever thanked you."

"For badgering you to help today?"

"You didn't badger. She needed help, and we could assist."

We. He smiled. How good it felt to say aloud.

"I am thankful you cared enough to help."

"And I am thankful you have taught me to care."

Her cheeks tinged pink. She looked down.

"Miss Ellison? You seem troubled. You are not anxious about DeLancey? I assure you, if he sets a foot within one hundred yards of you, I will deal with him. I will protect you."

"That's very kind of you, but how exactly do you propose to protect me?"

Hopes and dreams stirred within. He opened his mouth to share his heart—

"Oh, look! There is Mr. Chetwynd."

He slowed the horses at the implied request, taking courage at her smile of appreciation, even as he wished the young poet a thousand miles away. He managed to say all that was polite, to offer trivial remarks about the weather, even as he watched Lavinia, animated for the first time that day. She bent down to murmur in the younger man's ear.

His stomach twisted. Was he mistaken? Did she prefer the poet after all?

Soon Mr. Chetwynd made his excuses, freeing Nicholas to snap the reins. *Now* Lavinia would attend to him.

"Oh, I fear I have something of a headache." She rubbed her forehead.

He swallowed his disappointment. "I can take you back, if you like."

She shook her head. "I cannot go back just yet."

"Cannot?" He frowned. "Is there a problem?"

"No." She studied her muff.

"Miss Ellison"—he dropped his voice—"Lavinia, you can trust me."

She nodded stiffly.

"Have you committed your worries to God?"

"You are good to remind me." She bit her lip.

"You are in my prayers." He heard the catch of breath, saw a shimmer of tears blinked away. "And it would be my honor to assist in alleviating any trouble."

"Alleviating?" She laughed suddenly. "We don't need to *alleviate* a marriage."

A marriage? Jealousy surged across his chest. "If you refer to Thornton and Miss Milton—"

"No, I am very happy for them. No, I refer to my aunt and Lord Danver."

"What?" His grip loosened on the reins so the horses began to bolt. Amidst a scramble to steady them, he heard her smothered giggle and murmured "the great Hawkesbury."

He fought a smile, snapped the reins, and soon the horses were behaving again. "Your aunt and Danver? You cannot be serious."

"I am."

Oaks blurred past as his thoughts whirled, settled. "But that is good news, is it not? They have known each other an age, and share faith and similar interests. Surely friendship must be integral for a marriage to succeed."

"I suppose." She turned to face the barren trees. "If one intends to marry."

He almost lost his grip on the reins again. Did Lavinia's bluestocking tendencies extend so far as to avoid marriage? He swallowed the fear thickening his throat. "Do you not intend to marry?"

She pulled her muff higher. "One cannot simply intend it to happen. There must be suitors, not just dance partners carried away in the rush of emotion who desire money or a title more than a good mind. And I hardly have a long line of genuine suitors before me."

His voice was low. "You only need one."

The color on her cheeks rose. He longed to take her in his arms again, to hold her, to learn if her lips were as soft as they appeared. He had barely been able to sleep remembering the other night: her sweet scent, the way her form nestled into his sparked heat inside, the vulnerability in her eyes that ignited protection deep within. Everything seemed to cry: *She is mine. Mine!* Possessiveness made him fierce, made him foolish, made his heart fragile. If she didn't share his feelings . . .

She sighed. "It is just so difficult to see things clearly in London. There is so much artificiality here. One never knows who is being honest and true."

"I will always be honest with you."

"Yes, I suppose you are." Her expression grew thoughtful. "Even when you're cross with me, I know you're being honest."

"And when I say I think you're beautiful, you can trust I'm being honest, too."

Her smile flashed. "Yes, well, you might be nonsensical and prone to fits of exaggeration, but I don't think you've ever lied." The light in her face faded. "You would be one of the few."

He frowned.

"No, things are never as simple as they are in the country." She appeared to tremble.

"Are you cold? Do you wish to go home?"

"Home?" she replied absently. "Yes, I suppose Papa will need to know."

A small groove appeared in her brow.

And worry furrowed his heart.

THE NEXT AFTERNOON Nicholas arrived at Twenty Grosvenor Square to discover the house in an uproar. His request to speak with Miss Ellison was met by the butler's wringing hands.

"Oh, Lord Hawkesbury! I'm so sorry, but the young lady seems to have disappeared!"

"Disappeared? Surely you are mistaken—"

"No, sir, there's no mistake. She hasn't been seen since this morning. Not since that fellow's visit."

Fear trampled his heart; he tamped it down. "What fellow?" Surely DeLancey would not dare—

"The poet fellow."

"Chetwynd?" No. The doubts surged again. "Where is Lady Exeter? I must speak with her immediately!"

He was escorted to an upstairs parlor where Lavinia's aunt was sprawled on a settee. Charlotte sat near her, holding a small vinaigrette and a worried expression.

"Hawkesbury! Where is my niece?"

"I beg your pardon, ma'am, but—"

"You mean you don't know?" The marchioness sat hurriedly, her eyes wide. "You've spent so much time together, and she seems to like you more than anyone. I thought she had run off with you!"

Dread filled his stomach. "She has run off?"

"Yes! Charlotte says some of her clothes are missing, although"—she frowned—"none of the ones *I* bought her. Oh, the ingratitude!"

"Your butler thinks Chetwynd—"

"That milksop?"

"She did not leave with him," Charlotte murmured.

Relief coursed through him, chased by concern. "How do you know?"

"My bedchamber overlooks the street. I was surprised to hear an early morning visitor, but he left after only ten minutes or so. Alone," she added, with a decided nod.

"But what was he doing here so early? He must know something!" Lady Exeter lifted a delicate hand to her head. "Oh, to have had such an ingrate living under my roof. The scandal! Just imagine the scandal when this comes out!"

"Let's not," Nicholas muttered. "What has been done to find her? Lord Exeter—?"

"He left early this morning to go to Parliament—but wait, you are not. Oh, I don't know where he could be, either! Oh, everyone is running away!"

Nicholas smiled grimly. The marquess likely was in the private gaming lounge at White's.

"Sir," Charlotte said softly, "Henry has asked all the staff. Nobody recalls seeing her. He has gone to check the circulating library."

"She did not leave a note?"

"A note?" Lady Exeter blinked. "Charlotte, Hawkesbury, run and see." She collapsed again on the settee. "Oh, my poor nerves. Why did she do this to me?"

He restrained a sigh of disgust and followed Charlotte to the bedchamber. The room was neat, a small wooden box on the dresser the only item gaining attention. He slid the lid open and stared at the pearl and diamond necklace.

"I think Mother doesn't know whether to be upset or relieved Livvie didn't take that."

"She said nothing to you?"

She shook her head. "She did seem rather quiet after the ball. I even thought she might be unhappy perhaps."

After Lavinia's experiences, he imagined she had much to concern her. He paced the carpet. She would know to avoid DeLancey, but what if he had threatened her? But then, how would she have managed to collect her clothes? She must have planned this to some degree. Hurt burned his heart. Why had she turned to Chetwynd? Why hadn't she trusted him?

"Now I think about it, she was rather pensive last night. She gave me and Mama rather big hugs, almost like—"

"She was saying goodbye." His heart thudded as memories arose of the girl who hugged her friends, coupled with sweet desire. If only she thought of him so . . .

A scream brought them running back to the parlor.

"That girl!" Lady Exeter held a note. "That stupid, *stupid* girl!"

"Mother!"

"Betsy has just cleaned the downstairs parlor and found this on the mantelpiece!"

He snatched it, ignoring her protest, and read it hurriedly. "She says she must leave London and is going to see family." He frowned. "You think she's returned to Gloucestershire?"

"I expect so." She moaned. "Oh, this is perfectly dreadful! I should never have told her!"

"Told her what? She was concerned about something yesterday. What did you say?"

"I told her about her inheritance."

"What inheritance?"

She stared at him hard. "Oh, I suppose it does not matter anymore. We kept it quiet, just in the family, but I do not recall if I told her that. She is to receive her mother's share of the Westerbrooke estate. She is worth forty thousand pounds."

"What?"

"She will be surrounded by fortune hunters, and with such limited experience with men, I'm afraid she will be taken in by the first who professes his admiration."

Nausea slid through his stomach. Is that what Lavinia thought of him? That he wanted her for her inheritance?

Lady Exeter prattled on. "Of course, she is rather more like Patience than we expected. Independent to a fault! Perhaps with such wealth she may decide never to marry."

His throat grew thick. The carriage ride yesterday, her melancholy. "Did she say that?"

"Oh, words to that effect." She wrung her hands. "Sir, I know we have not always agreed, but I know she has counted you something of a friend."

Only something of a friend? Despair swam beneath anxiety as the marchioness continued.

"She said that it was nice to know someone who wasn't trying to dazzle her with elegance or frippery, who knew her before all this." She waved a hand. "Heaven knows she'll need all the friends she can find when this comes out!"

"You *cannot* say anything to anyone. I will find her, and bring her to safety, but there will be no need for scandal."

"No need—? But girls do not simply disappear. She will be ruined!"

"Not if she agrees to marry me."

"Marry you! But the duchess—"

"Has nothing to do with anything, I assure you."

After gaining her wide-eyed assurance that she would keep Lavinia's hasty departure a secret as long as possible, and positive he would get nothing more from the inhabitants, he made his exit, only to encounter Henry's return from the library, with the news Lavinia was not there, either.

He rode away, thoughts churning about all he would need to do before traveling to St. Hampton Heath, even as his heart twisted between hope he would soon find the elusive Lavinia and beg her to become his, and gnawing despair that bade him to crawl away and hide, and lick his wounds like a dog.

✺ Chapter Thirty-Four

Lavinia stood alone on the stone steps. A cool breeze shivered from the oak grove and rippled across the large lake, dampening her courage. Two gray gargoyles scowled from lichen-smudged plinths atop the stairs. She beat the heavy brass knocker again. Surely someone had to be home?

Movement inside, a scrabbling of keys and locks led to the door being opened by a liveried servant. "Yes?"

"I have need to speak with Her Grace."

The footman looked down his nose. "Her Grace is not to be disturbed."

She lifted her chin. "I believe she will want to speak with me."

"And whom shall I say has come to call?"

"Her granddaughter."

His eyes enlarged ever so slightly. After a moment, he pulled the door wider and gestured to a room on the right. As he brought in her bags, she caught a glimpse of an ornate hall with high chandeliers and a huge staircase that put even Aunt Constance's London house in the shade.

She entered a small reception room whose neat elegance was marred by enormous paintings of ancestors, frowning down in an intimidating manner. Lavinia settled herself on a small couch, removed her bonnet, and smoothed her tan traveling gloves. She might have spent all her pin money traveling many hours by mail coach to Salisbury and then hiring a gig to get here, but the grandeur of Salisbury House suggested she not look that way.

As the minutes dragged by, her bravado began to falter. Yes, she was now inside, but she couldn't very well go running through the house searching for her grandmother; her willingness to break with propriety had *some* limits. Regret twisted her heart. Perhaps she should have accepted Mr. Chetwynd's escort, after all. He'd been horrified by her request, insisting it would be most improper for him to assist her in procuring a seat on such transport, but she'd overborne him with her declarations that she'd travelled via such means before and that she would leave anyway, regardless of whether he helped or not. So after their brief discussion yesterday in her aunt's drawing room, she'd placed her note, collected her bags, and snuck out the back through the mews, something like shame hurrying her steps to where he'd been waiting.

She lifted her chin, pushing down her remorse. Yes, she should have said goodbye properly, but her aunt would have created such a fuss, and she had to get out of London. *Had* to. The snobbery and pretension stifled one so. And as for the ever-whirling questions over the earl and his intentions . . .

Her heart panged. She forced her attention back to her present challenges. What would she do if the duchess refused to see her? How would she get home to Papa?

A neat middle-aged woman appeared. "Miss, Her Grace is not receiving visitors."

Lavinia rose. "But I am her granddaughter. I have come a long way to see her!"

"Her Grace does not see anyone without prior arrangement."

"But—"

"If you'll be pleased to leave." She gestured to the door.

"I'm sorry, but that does not please me at all." Lavinia reseated herself. "You may tell Her Grace that Grace's daughter has come to see her and will not leave until she does."

Her eyes widened. "Grace's daughter?"

"Yes." She smiled. "So if you'll please inform her."

A few minutes later she returned and gestured for Lavinia to follow her. Lavinia moved back into the hall, caught more than one footman's look of shock as she passed, then followed the woman into a great reception room papered in carmine and crowded with dark furniture.

Anticipation drummed through her as she moved toward the fireplace. An elderly lady dressed in a pale violet gown frowned at her approach.

Doubts assailed her as she stood. Was she right in coming? Would this woman listen?

The Duchess of Salisbury shifted back on the brocade seat and lifted her glass to stare.

Lavinia stared back, catching the glimpse of surprise before her eyes were hooded again.

"Are you the person claiming to be my granddaughter?"

"I am Lavinia Ellison, Grace's daughter."

"Grace . . ." The name was whispered almost reverently, before she blinked, reverting to her previous impervious manner. "You hold a passing resemblance, I admit, but many claim to be what they are not."

Lavinia's spirits sank. How sad this woman held no trust. "You are correct, Your Grace. Many claim, but some of us are who we say." She pulled the cross from the folds of a lacy scarf.

"Grace's cross!" The eyes sparked before coolness settled again. "And what do you wish with me?"

Lavinia swallowed, sinking into the seat to which her grandmother pointed. Apparently there would be no happy reunions here. "Until quite recently, I was unaware of the existence of any relations on my mother's side other than Aunt Patience."

"Patience?" Her grandmother's frown deepened. "Such a foolish girl! Coming here, expecting me to bless her union with that Danver fellow? Pah!"

"She was here?"

"Not for long, I assure you."

Lavinia bit her tongue to prevent her reply.

"You say Patience did not tell you? I don't suppose that scoundrel, your *father*"—she almost spat the word—"did, either?"

"They did not. They were of the impression you wanted nothing to do with them or me."

"So how . . . ?"

"Aunt Constance."

"Of course. She was always one to prattle on." Her grandmother sighed. "What is it you want? I suppose you want me to apologize for cutting off your mother."

Lavinia tilted her head. "Do you feel like you need to apologize?"

"Such impertinence! I never apologize."

Now there was a surprise. She suppressed a smile.

"I imagine you want your share of the inheritance. I assure you, I have no intention—"

"Oh, no." She shook her head. "I want nothing, except the chance to know you."

Her grandmother sent her a hard look, peering through her quizzing glass until Lavinia wanted to squirm like a child. But she had nothing of which to be ashamed. She only spoke the truth.

"I do believe you mean it." She snorted. "If you're anything like your mother, I suppose you will not be tempted by riches."

"I place value in people, not things."

Her grandmother gasped.

"Grandmama?" Lavinia leaned forward as a footman moved to her side.

Her grandmother waved off the footman, her gaze pinning Lavinia to her seat. "That is what *he* said."

"I beg your pardon. Who?"

"Your father." Blackness crossed her face. "When he came and took my Grace away!" She lifted her chin. "He cared for nothing save my Grace. And she cared only for him. Not her own family, her reputation, or her inheritance. The day she left, he stood there, proud as sin, and spoke those very same words to me."

Her heart panged at the pain she saw in the older lady's eyes. "I am sorry this still grieves you."

"I don't want your pity, child!"

"I am not giving it." *Lord, give me patience and wisdom.* "I know how many years it has taken me to forgive those responsible for my mother's death."

"Some things are unforgivable!" Her grandmother's blue eyes flashed.

"All things are forgivable, when we realize how much we've been forgiven."

"Pah! You're talking just like *him* now."

That thought gave her no small amount of pleasure. She smiled and slowly stood. "Grandmama, I thank you for taking the time to see me. I don't wish to intrude any further on your time."

"What? You're not leaving."

She hesitated. Was that a question or a command?

Her grandmother turned to the footman. "Go, tell Simpkins to make up the Rose Room. My granddaughter will be staying for a while."

"Yes, Your Grace."

Her grandmother turned back to Lavinia. "You will stay. I need to know this granddaughter of mine who speaks so freely." She nodded. "You put me in mind of someone."

"My mother?"

Her grandmother allowed herself a thin smile. "Myself."

THE NEXT FEW days passed in a blur of wonder. Her grandmother was by turns difficult, impervious, sharp-tongued, but capable of astonishing generosity. The Rose Room had been her mother's, left untouched since her elopement twenty-five years prior, but in it Lavinia found treasure upon treasure: Mama's old ball dresses, their giant hoops now ridiculously out of style, but made of the prettiest silks. Drawings Mama had executed of her family, various animals, a sketch of the Salisbury estate—even as a young girl Grace had shown much promise in her ability to capture a likeness, revealing something of the character of the person or object, rather than mere superficialities. An ornately carved box contained a selection of jewelry—no fabulous jewels as Aunt Constance had once hinted—but pretty trinkets that revealed Grace's elegant taste.

But the best treasure was the journal, hidden in the folds of an exquisitely rendered quilt, carefully packed in the large wooden chest at the end of the four-poster bed. Lavinia spent hours reading her mother's thoughts and girlish dreams, gaining more insight into this family of which she knew so little, yet knew so needed God's love. That prayer was constantly in her heart.

On the third night, after dinner, her grandmother presented her with a large flat box.

"I know you most probably have no use for such a thing, but by all rights, it is yours."

Lavinia slowly opened the lid and gasped. The diamond and pearl tiara—a perfect complement for the necklace she had left in London—almost took her breath away. She lifted her head and faced her grandmother. "I don't know what to say."

Her grandmother lifted a shoulder. "I was thinking about what you said before. I am not unwilling to let you have what is rightfully yours. Your mother's things are of no use to me. They are yours."

"That is kind of you." Lavinia slowly placed the headpiece back in its velvet casing, thinking furiously. Was this some kind of test? Was this a chance to show God's love? "Grandmama, how much are you willing to let go?"

"What do you mean?"

"Will you forgive my father?"

Her grandmother's eyes narrowed. "After what he stole from me?"

Lavinia pressed her lips together. *God, give me wisdom* . . . She said slowly, "Grace chose to go. My father did not steal her."

"He did! With all his promises and dreams!"

"Promises of what? Papa only ever dreamed of helping others, of being a godly influence in this world. He is a man of honor who keeps his word, not a scoundrel. He has never made rash promises."

Her heart wrenched as an image of the earl flickered into her mind. He too was trustworthy, someone willing to help the unfortunate. She swallowed.

"But I don't understand." Her grandmother's eyes sheened. "Why would she want to leave all this?" She waved a hand at the ornately furnished room.

Lavinia reached to hold her grandmother's thin, bony hand. "Because she loved someone more than all this."

Her grandmother glanced down at her lap.

"I think it's a family tradition, is it not?" Lavinia murmured.

"What? What do you mean?"

"Did your parents approve of your choice?"

The older lady's jaw slackened. "You are a most impertinent young miss."

"Who loves you." As she spoke, warmth cascaded from her heart to her grandparent.

The duchess stared at her a long moment before her face finally creased into a smile. "Oh, but you're like Grace. She could charm her way out of anything with a smile."

Almost anything.

"Oh, but I miss her." Her grandmother's eyes filled once more.

Lavinia's throat clogged with emotion. "I miss her, too." And she gently wrapped her grandmother in a hug.

ℋ Chapter Thirty-Five

The next afternoon Lavinia and her grandmother were enjoying tea in the sitting room, a necessary interlude, as Lavinia's earlier prowess with the piano had once again set her grandmother to reminiscing, verging on tears. But now, after all emotion had been sufficiently blinked away, conversation had moved to the more inconsequential, until the duchess placed her teacup firmly down and eyed Lavinia.

"So, my dear, is there a young man in your life?"

Lavinia hedged for time, sipping her tea, whilst desperately stifling thoughts of the earl. "I am not the kind of woman to which young men pay attention."

Her grandmother gave an unladylike snort. "You may not act like the typical miss, but I warrant young men don't mind your appearance."

"But I have neither title nor dowry of any significance."

"Is this a hint?"

"No, Grandmama, not at all. It is but the truth."

"I will give you your mother's inheritance."

Lavinia shook her head. "That will not be necessary."

"What do you mean?"

"I do not want a man to marry me for money."

"Spoken just like your mother." Grandmama snorted again. "You have no use for money?"

Lavinia swallowed. Money would help a multitude of people: the establishment of a proper village school, assistance for war widows, the London women's refuge. Should she really ignore its power for good? "There is always need, but . . ."

"I gather that *you* are not the one in need."

"No."

"Well, your mother's inheritance should go to someone who lacks greed, I suppose." The faded blue eyes examined her shrewdly. "I can't help thinking that you *have* found someone you admire."

Lavinia stilled.

"So that is the way of it." Her grandmother laughed, low, throaty. "What is the problem? He's too poor?"

"No."

"Untitled?"

"You know those things are not important to me."

"His family objects to you?"

Her lips tightened.

Grandmama's eyes flashed. "How dare anyone object to my own grand-daughter?"

She swallowed a smile. Her grandmother had ignored her very existence for how many years?

"What family? Give me a name. I want to know who dares object to you!"

"I do not need you or anyone else interfering, Grandmama. Besides, he has not made his intentions clear."

"But he has secured your affections. He must have done something to show his regard."

She stared at the rich russets and golds in the Axminster carpet. Nicholas had shown his regard in many ways, but he'd never spoken of the future. "His mother despises me."

"Who is she?"

She kept her voice low. "Lady Hawkesbury."

Her grandmother gasped. "You cannot be serious!"

"She has taken me in dislike."

"The brother of the man who killed my Grace?" Her face was pale. "It cannot be. It *will* not be. You *cannot* marry that man."

"Lord Hawkesbury cannot be held responsible for his brother's mistakes or his mother's incivilities any more than any person is responsible for their relations' less-than-agreeable qualities."

"Mistakes?" Her grandmother gasped. "You forget yourself, young lady. No, I will not have it. You will *not* have anything more to do with that man. I forbid it."

She lifted her chin. "I do not wish to be told whom I may or may not marry."

"You will lose your inheritance!"

"How long must you play this game, Grandmama?" She sighed. "You may control some purse strings, but you cannot control me."

"Such insolence!"

Lavinia kept her eyes steady on the older woman. "Grandmama, I am sorry you think me insolent. It is not my intention." She rose. "I thank you for your hospitality and for Mama's things, but I must beg your leave. Papa surely pines for me now, and I must be home before Christmas."

"If you leave you must never darken the doors of this house again!"

Her heart softened with compassion. "Is that truly what you wish?"

Her grandmother's gaze remained unflinching.

Lavinia made a small curtsey. "Grandmama, thank you. I am very glad to have met you." She bent forward and gave the surprised woman a kiss on the cheek. "Goodbye."

And with a heavy heart she went upstairs to pack her things.

Nicholas pounded on the heavy oak door with his fist. During the last few miles of travel, an icy wind had begun, threatening to cut through his coat and tear despair through his soul.

The door opened to a supercilious footman, whose sneer became less pronounced when he saw his manner of dress and the coat of arms on the travelling coach. "Yes?"

"I am here to seek an audience with Miss Ellison."

"I am afraid that is impossible, sir."

"I believe she is here."

"Thomas?" A thin voice came from within. "Who is there?"

"A gentleman, Mrs. Simpkins."

The door creaked open wider. A small woman dressed neatly in somber black surveyed him. "What is it you want?

"Miss Ellison. Is she within?"

"Who might you be?"

He fought the irritation at her tone and gritted out, "I am someone who wishes to speak with her. Can you help me or not?"

She blinked, nodded at Thomas, and gestured to a small room. "Please wait here."

After rushing for days on fruitless missions from London to St. Hampton Heath and now here to Salisbury, it seemed like hours before she finally returned and beckoned him to follow.

His heart danced in anticipation. Lavinia was here! He would speak, he would share, he would convince, he would beg if necessary, but he would not rest until she knew his heart, and—

"Please enter." The woman gestured him forward.

He entered a room that was dark and overstuffed with old furniture. He maneuvered around a nest of tables toward the fireplace, whose hearth was alight with welcome heat. An elderly woman with steely blue eyes and an air of discontent scowled at him. He doffed his hat and bowed, and she acknowledged the courtesy with the slightest inclination of her head.

"And who might you be?"

"I am Nicholas, Lord Hawkesbury."

"You!" Her eyes widened then grew icy. "What business have you with my granddaughter?"

"Begging your pardon, Your Grace, but it does not concern you."

Her eyebrows rose. "You and your family have done enough damage to mine! You must leave Lavinia alone. I will not tolerate insubordination."

"Insubordination is a crime dealt with most harshly in the army, but ma'am, I am not under your authority. I see no reason why I should reveal my purposes to you when I have yet to speak to the lady." He forced his voice to calm. "Now, may I speak to Miss Ellison?"

"No, you may not."

He tensed. He would beat down any servants who might get in his way!

"I know what you want. You think you will force her to marry you!"

"How did—"

"Constance!" She waved a letter. "She might have the sense of a pea-hen, but she understands what must be made known to me! How dare you presume?"

He gazed at her evenly. "I love Lavinia."

"Love?" She gave a reedy cackle. "Your family doesn't know the meaning of the word!"

"But I am trying."

"Pah!" She motioned to the footman, as if to ensure his swift removal.

He breathed past his anger. *Lord, help me!* "Your Grace, please let me speak with her."

"No."

His eyes closed as ribbons of despair wound tightly around him.

"I cannot."

He opened his eyes. "Cannot?"

"Miss Ellison has lately quitted the premises."

"She's not here?"

"No!"

Frustration snapped his hat through the air. "Thank you." He bowed stiffly and moved through the cluttered fine furniture of a bygone era, which he was tempted to kick on his way to the door.

"It will be of no use, you know. She will have nothing to do with you."

He turned. "I beg your pardon?"

"She will have no inheritance. I will cut her out of my will if she continues to hold you in regard."

Hope thumped his heart. "She holds me in regard?"

The duchess's face appeared pained. "Your family, your mother, your relations have hurt mine excruciatingly. I will not tolerate any alliance between these two households."

He dipped his head slightly. "For your pain, I am sorry. For the sins of my family, I beg your forgiveness. But for my feelings toward Lavinia, I can plead no such thing. I love her, I care about her tremendously, and I will do everything in my power to make her happy." He quirked an eyebrow. "With or without your approval."

She gasped. "You are as insolent as she!"

Trust Lavinia to speak so boldly. "She is a remarkable creature, isn't she?"

And with a smile on his lips and in his heart, he made his exit. He now knew exactly where she would be.

❧ Chapter Thirty-Six

The hills were dark, mottled with brown. Leaden clouds told of winter's arrival, but no snow had fallen this week. Lavinia sat in the seat Papa had carved all those years ago, stroking a pup whose snores sounded more feline than canine. Smoke from a dozen chimneys drifted up from St. Hampton Heath, curling tendrils of white in the cold air. The pungent scent of crushed leaves tugged at her senses, reminding her of her duties, but she ignored them.

She wrapped the heavy shawl close, enjoying the chance to rest. The past few days had proved punishing. Traveling home from Salisbury was made a little easier by Grandmama's insistence she use her coach, but stopping to rest the horses every ten miles had made the journey seem interminable.

But she was home. Papa's joy had been almost eclipsed by that shown by Aunt Patience—Lady Danver now—when the coach trundled up the drive.

"Lavinia! We've been so worried!"

Wrapped in her aunt's hug, she could only reply, "I have been to see Grandmama."

Once inside, divested of wraps, and after the coachman and maid were fed and commenced their return journey, she described her past week— though her experiences at the ball were somewhat censored—and heard her aunt's tale. Aunt Patience and Danver expressed regret at the secretive nature of their wedding, but waiting months until they saw each other again seemed wasteful, especially when they had yearned for each other for years. They would make their home up north in Durham, as his estates demanded immediate attention. This news had pooled loneliness in Lavinia's heart, but how could she argue with the happiness shining in her aunt's eyes?

"But I am sorry if my disappearance upset you, Lavinia."

"It did not."

"But you are perturbed. I see it in your forehead's wrinkle. Was it Mother? Was she very dreadful?"

"Not as dreadful as it appears she was to you."

Aunt Patience sighed. "She is a hard woman."

"And lonely."

"I often thought her manner was driven by fear." Papa had nodded. "God does not want us to be motivated by fear, but love."

Love.

She studied the small village snuggled in the valley as the thought nestled close. Long hours in the carriage traveling home were spent thinking, feeling, understanding. She realized now that Grandmama's actions, as manipulative as they seemed, were motivated by fear. And while she might never possess warmth, Grandmama did love her, as evidenced by her generosity in allowing Lavinia to keep Mama's possessions, which had filled the carriage on the way home.

Grandmama's ultimatum had helped her realize something else. Lavinia loved the earl. *Loved* him. All the qualities she'd ever thought necessary in a man he possessed. Faith. Intelligence. Wit. Compassion. How torturous to think he remained in London surrounded by so much worldly decadence. He was strong and courageous, but would his mother's machinations result in producing another young lady—one more suitable than Clara? One more acceptable than herself?

Her breath hitched. She could only wait and hope and trust God that the earl might share her feelings. Surely he could not marry anyone else. He could *not*. It was unthinkable!

She chuckled self-mockingly, her breath wisping white in the cold air. How much like Grandmama *was* she?

Moodiness broken, she tickled Nicky awake. "Come on, lazy boy. Back to work."

Cold air nipped her face as she resumed the clearing begun months ago. Albert had been ill, the chilly air no good for his cough, and she'd been happy to exert herself physically after the confines of the past month. Weeks of neglect had allowed weeds to proliferate, but recent rain made them easy to remove. The fresh air and exercise invigorated, as did her prayers, wherein she asked for blessings on her family, Eliza, Mrs. Foster, Sophy's nuptials, Charlotte, even Clara. The shadows of her heart were soon overthrown, as she concentrated on making this patch of garden as it ought. Perhaps she had no ability to determine other outcomes, but this, *this* she could.

Nicky growled and then trotted off to chase a moth—his preference for flying insects, just like his uncle Mickey. She smiled, wiped hair from her eyes, and rose from her kneeling position. Mud clung to her skirts, but that did not matter; only the bravest of souls ventured a visit on days like these. As soon as she removed the pile of rose cuttings that *still* remained from months ago, she would go inside and clean up.

Nicky's barking grew more agitated. She turned. Dropped the dead branches. "Lord Hawkesbury!"

"I'm sorry, Miss Ellison. I did not mean to startle you."

Why was he here? What did she look like? What must he think of her? She covered her confusion with a smile. "Have you come to scold me for gardening?"

"Of course not. I know your father's man—Albert, is it not?—is unwell and should stay out of the cold. I imagine Hettie is quite busy caring for him." He added softly, as if to himself, "Mrs. Florrick can send over meals and the like until he is better."

"How do you know that? Have you been here?"

He nodded. "Several days ago. I met Danver and his new bride—who both seem happier than I ever recall having seen them. Lady Danver finally explained the reasoning behind her appellation as Miss West." His expression grew wry. "I do not blame her in the slightest."

"They left this morning."

"And no doubt you miss her already."

She nodded, heart keening at his understanding. She drew in a deep breath. Blinked. He continued to stand before her: tall, handsome, kindness in his lips and eyes. No figment of imagination.

He gestured to the rose cuttings. "Is this all that remains to be done? Where should they go?"

"But your coat!"

"Can be cleaned." He smiled. "And I have others."

She watched in amazement as the tall, once-proud man collected the branches and followed her to place them on the pile to be burned. When he had disposed of his burden, he brushed off the dirt, stripped off his gloves with a rueful smile, and returned with her to the garden. She slipped her muddied gardening gloves into a pocket, wrapped her shawl tight, and looked up.

He smiled, stepped close, and gently wiped her cheek. "There. You had some mud."

"Oh. Thank you, my lord."

He sighed. "Nicholas. What will it take for you to call me Nicholas?"

"You are being nonsensical, my lord. I cannot—"

"You can. It's not nonsense—it *is* my name, after all."

He seemed lighthearted, playful even. Why was he here? Would that she could ask! "Will you come inside? Papa will enjoy seeing you again."

His brow knit. "Do you wish to be rid of my company?"

"No! Not at all."

The contours of his face softened as he continued to gaze at her, a small smile on his face. Wind rushed over grass. Dead leaves shivered in the trees. Somewhere a crow cawed. Coolness pinched her cheeks as his intent perusal continued. "My lord?"

His look grew rueful. "How I wish that were true."

"Pardon?"

"I wish that you truly regarded me as yours, because, dear Lavinia, I would truly like you to be mine."

Her breath caught. Did he mean—? No. He could not. Now *she* was being nonsensical!

She spoke quickly, "So, are you here for the wedding?" He looked startled, so she reminded him. "Sophy and Thornton? The banns have been posted for three weeks. They are terribly excited. Papa is inside working on his address for Sunday."

"Banns. I forgot . . ." He shook his head.

He was acting most peculiarly. "Do you want to go inside?"

"No, not yet." His brow furrowed. "Unless you are cold."

She shook her head. For some reason, his presence made her warm.

He took possession of her hand. Heat stole up her arm as he led her to the carved seat and lowered himself beside her. The late afternoon light revealed gold glints in the depths of his eyes as his gaze remained fixed on her.

"I . . . I am sorry I did not get the chance to say goodbye before I left London."

"Lady Exeter *was* a little concerned about your hasty departure."

She sighed. "I thought I'd explained things, but I could not stay. I had to visit my grandmother."

"The duchess. Yes, I know."

Her brows rose.

"I visited her, too."

She blinked. Why? Surely it wasn't—No. She strove to keep her voice light. "That must have been a highly pleasant experience for you."

"Pleasant, no. Instructive, yes."

"Oh." Her spirits plunged. "You know I'm supposed to have money, do you?"

"I learned that your inheritance is dependent on whether you marry according to your grandmother's wishes. I also learned that your grandmother does not approve of your choice." He shifted closer. "Now, I know I've allowed pride to govern much of my thinking over the years, but I couldn't help hope this meant you might not be entirely impartial to me."

Fire scorched her face.

"Ah, Miss Ellison remains so eloquent even without words." Sweetness lit his features as he smiled.

She studied his eyes, full of tender clear light, the quirked eyebrow, the lips so full of humor and wit, the jaw slightly shadowed yet firm and sure. A thousand butterflies seemed to have taken residence within her. She swallowed. Swallowed again. "You still have not explained what you are doing here."

"I need to speak to your father."

Disappointment crashed against her chest. She glanced down.

He gently cupped her face, lifting her chin until her eyes met his. "It is customary, is it not, when a man seeks to pay his addresses to the lady he loves?"

"He loves?"

"He loves."

The butterflies rose, fluttering as one. A delicious warmth stole across her heart. He loved her! He loved—

"But your mother!"

"Will behave."

"And my grandmother—"

"Need not concern us." He smiled. "Us. I like the sound of that, don't you?"

He brushed his fingers down her cheeks, tracing heat along her skin, his expression one of wonder. "How could he not love someone so pure, so lovely, who charms with her words, her voice, her deeds?" His fingers reached her lips, his eyes darkened. "No man should dare touch these lips, unless he is prepared to love and cherish their owner until his dying day." His thumb gently touched her mouth.

Her breath caught.

"Now, I know I have been accused of holding few poetical aspirations, but I did find something most apt in Uncle Robert's Shakespeare: 'She is a woman, therefore may be wooed; she is a woman, therefore may be won; she is Lavinia, therefore must be loved.'" He captured her other hand.

Her heartbeat quickened. This was not a dream!

His smile grew pensive, his voice hoarse. "Tell me you can be won."

"I can," she whispered.

"Tell me you can love me."

"I do love you, Nicholas."

His eyes filled with softness. "You speak my name like music." He pressed his lips to her hands. "Lavinia, tell me, will you marry me?"

Joy saturated her soul, preventing utterance. She could only offer a small nod.

He wrapped her in his arms, bent his face, and claimed her lips with his own.

Heat streaked through her, curling her toes, stealing her breath. The butterflies escaped, dancing in wild delight. Joy quivered in and around her as he kissed her tenderly, possessively, fiercely, reverently. Her hands stole around his neck, her senses melting as he kissed her lips, her cheeks, her forehead's scar.

Just when every part of her was set tingling, he drew back, an expression of wonder on his face. "I can hardly believe the elusive Miss Ellison deigns to be held by one like me."

"One like you?" She smiled. "Only you, dear Nicholas." She offered her lips again, thus diverting his chuckle as he accepted her invitation for another long, delightful moment.

"Come, my dearest, most lovely Lavinia. Let's find your papa and tell him his daughter shall soon be his neighbor."

And together they walked from the cooling shadows into the warmth and light.

ℛ Acknowledgments

A NOVEL CAN be but a dream, written on a heart, locked in a computer, destined to forever remain unread, unless others believe the dream is worth bringing to reality. I'm so thankful to the following for making this dream of mine come true.

Thank You, God, for Jesus, the Ultimate Gift, for giving this gift of creativity, and for the amazing opportunity to express it.

Thank you, Joshua, for your love and encouragement. You are so much better than Mr. Darcy—because you're real.

Thank you to my four wonderful children—I'm so proud of each of you, and the creativity God has blessed you with. I'm blessed to be the mum of such smart, witty, *nice* children.

To my family and friends, whose support I've needed when I felt like giving up—thank you. Big thanks to my sister, Roslyn, who first shared her love of Georgette Heyer, and my mother, Kay, and sister in Christ Jacqueline, for being patient in reading through so many of my manuscripts.

Thank you, Tamela Hancock Murray, my agent, for helping this little Australian negotiate the big wide American market.

To my editors and the fabulous team at Kregel, thank you for making *Miss Ellison* look so pretty and read so much better.

Finally, thank you to my readers. A novel is merely words on a page until someone reads them. I hope you enjoyed reading mine.

God bless you.

Visit carolynmiller.org for a book club discussion guide and more about upcoming titles.

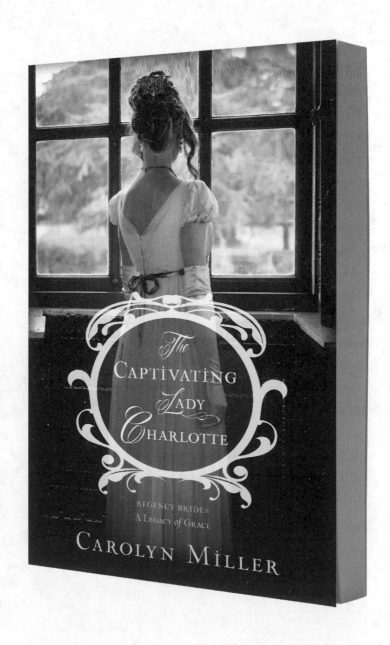